STATE OF RESU

Brian Morrison was born, the son of a docker, in
London's East End in 1944. After a perfunctory
education at Plaistow Grammar, he embarked
on a career as a sales manager and commercial
agent for various companies, and travelled
extensively in Latin America, the Middle East
and Europe. He now owns a trading company
and lives in Paris, in a converted bath-house in
the 11th arrondissement, with his wife and
daughter. *State of Resurrection* is his first novel.

BRIAN MORRISON

# State of Resurrection

FONTANA/Collins

First published in Great Britain by
Fontana Paperbacks 1988

Copyright © Brian Morrison 1988

ISBN 0 00 617513-9

The events described in this book are fictitious, and
the characters are imaginary with the exception of
persons of note referred to by their true names.

Made and printed in Great Britain by
William Collins Sons & Co. Ltd, Glasgow

To Helen and Laura,
and to Chris for being so kind
about the very first chapter of all.

# I

NOVEMBER IN EL SALVADOR was a terrible month. The air hung still and heavy, in expectation of rains that would not come. The naked children playing in the filth of the dirt alley glistened with sweat. Suddenly, they turned from their game and ran squealing to the bulky figure that appeared at the end of the alley, walking slowly under the polished lead of the sky. The man's sombre expression exploded into a delighted grin. Laughing, he took up a small brown body in each arm and continued walking through the dust, talking animatedly to the children. Others ran alongside him, clutching at the cloth of his creased cotton trousers and calling for his attention.

The man halted in front of a low building of wood and corrugated iron sheet. With a quick gesture, he deposited the two protesting children back among the group at his feet and ducked through the low entrance.

The heat inside was appalling. The man plucked in distaste at the shirt plastered to his chest. Reaching both hands behind his neck, he unfastened the clerical collar he wore and pulled it, with a low sigh, away from his throat. He stripped off the soaked shirt and screwed it into a ball. Rubbing absently at his chest with the shirt, he walked from the dim lobby into a sparsely furnished bedroom.

He kicked off the worn sandals and stripped off the rest of his clothes. The pattern of the sandals gleamed white on his tanned feet. Pushing aside a curtain he stepped into a rudimentary shower cubicle and tugged sharply at a length of thick cord. He held it down. Water spluttered from an aperture above his head. Taking a sliver of soap from a tobacco tin nailed to the wall of the cubicle he released the

7

cord and soaped himself vigorously, singing cheerfully and inaccurately as he did so. Thoroughly lathered from head to foot he groped for the cord again, his eyes squeezed shut against the soap, and let the tepid water sluice the lather from him. Still singing, he pressed water from his hair with his palms, shook himself, and stepped from the cubicle.

He was naked, towelling the expanse of his chest with a piece of threadbare linen cloth when a small man dressed as the other had been, in light slacks and shirt with a clerical collar hurried into the room. He stopped short at the sight of the naked man in front of him. His broad Indian features worked, as agitation and embarrassment struggled in them. He looked down at the bare wooden floor.

The other man went on unconcernedly drying himself, his back arching as he groped with the towel between his thighs. His deeply tanned face broke into a grin. He knew that the Indian was not embarrassed at his nakedness. It was the matted dark hair covering his shoulders and chest that troubled him. Being themselves smooth and hairless, the hairiness of Caucasian men never failed to unsettle the Indians.

'What is it, Juan?' the big man asked. His tone was kind but his eyes were fixed hard on the newcomer, trying to interpret his excitement.

'Father Gregory! It's the soldiers, Father! They've returned! They're out at the edge of the village. Searching houses!' His breath came in short gasps. 'They're approaching the clinic!'

With a curse which the Indian did not understand but which made him move an involuntary step backwards, the big man hurled the towel from him and snatched the crumpled trousers from where they lay. He was running for the door before he had fastened his belt.

'Vamos, Juanito!' he called to the little priest. 'Show me!' Mason woke up with a start and cracked his elbow on the metal frame of the sofa-bed.

'Ouch!' He rubbed the spot with exaggerated self-pity. Across the room, the girl looked at him over her shoulder, smiling ironically.

'*Dzien dobre*, Peter. Good morning. Did you sleep well?'

'Too well.' He picked speculatively at the deposits of grit in the corners of his eyes. 'I feel awful.'

'Maybe that had something to do with it.' Still smiling, she nodded to where two empty vodka bottles stood beneath the sink. He shuddered in half-real horror and pushed himself off the bed. Groaning softly, he walked to the window. In the distance he could see the tip of the Palace of Culture. It was Warsaw's ugliest building, in a city where the competition was fierce. A thick winter overcast clung low over the city and a scattering of people trudged cheerlessly through the streets. Incongruously, several of them carried flowers. It cheered him. Flowers were important in Poland. On name-days, more important than birthdays, they were customary. Today must be an important one, Andrzej, maybe, or Sofia.

'Coffee.' At the call he turned from the window. The girl poured coffee into two glasses and placed them into two tarnished metal holders. She set them down on the chipped formica table and sat down. He sat opposite her, peered into the dirty brown liquid and looked up at her mournfully.

'Barbara,' he asked, his voice already tinged with defeat. 'Do you have any milk?'

She held his eyes for a moment. '*Nie ma.*'

They both laughed. Since 1980 it had become a sour joke. *Nie ma.* There is none. The commonest words in the Polish language.

She gnawed at her lip. 'There is no milk, Peter. Unless you have children.'

He raised an eyebrow. 'Since when? Has another packing plant collapsed?' His voice was serious. It had happened before. A brand new plant had simply fallen down two years earlier.

'No, not this time.' Her tone was very bitter. 'This time

9

it's worse. It's ever since Chernobyl. No one's admitting it, of course, but it's common knowledge. There's a whole chunk of the country where they don't dare let cattle graze.'

'Still?'

'Of course, still. We got some of the worst of it here. As usual. Naturally, nobody tells us, but plenty of people have friends or family over there. We know.'

'Yeah. Well, if it's any consolation, when it comes to lying about leaks from nuclear plants, our government is second to none.'

She laughed: 'Anyway, I don't drink milk.' Her voice became sombre again. 'But, Peter, you know it's not just milk. Not just food. It's, it's…things. Everything.' With a sudden gesture she rose from the table and disappeared into the tiny bathroom.

He sat for a moment. Then he rose, refilled his glass and stood, leaning one shoulder against the frame of the bathroom door. He watched silently as she washed and began putting on her make-up. Drying tights and underwear hung in dense festoons all around the cramped room, almost concealing the scaling yellow of the walls.

'Barbara,' he said softly. 'Why do you do this?'

'What?' She flicked mascara at an eyelash.

'This. Going out to work every morning. It doesn't make sense.'

'Yes, it does.' She looked at him in the mirror, gravely. 'You know it does. I have to do it. Or I have to explain to the authorities why I don't. Explain to them that you, and others –' she lowered her eyes quickly – 'mean I don't need a job. Anyway,' she went on, more vivaciously, 'I happen to like my job.'

He shook his head. There was no point in arguing any more. He patted her buttock. 'Get a move on. I need a shave.'

She finished her preparations and made way for him at the cracked sink. He took his razor from the crowded cabinet and began shaving carefully. Squinting at his own reflection, he found himself wondering if anybody else's razor was concealed in the impossible clutter of the room. Recently, he had been thinking about the others more and more. The thought depressed him. He shook his head to banish it and nicked himself. He cursed emphatically.

Surprised by the vehemence of the curse, Barbara spun to face him. 'What's wrong?'

He pointed sheepishly at his chin. A minute globule of blood swelled from it.

'That?' She pointed, incredulous, at the minute cut. 'All that fuss for that?'

Reaching out a hand behind him, he found her hand and squeezed it gently. 'No,' he said softly. He held her gaze for an instant longer, then dropped her hand and, with a faint shrug, continued shaving.

He rinsed his face and walked back into the bed-sitting-room where his clothes lay scattered. As he finished dressing he reached into his hip pocket and peeled off, by touch, two fifty-dollar bills from the wad in his pocket. In a swift, discreet movement, he pushed them under a corner of the crushed pillow. Barbara, emerging from the bathroom, caught the movement. She blushed. Neither of them spoke.

Abruptly, he stooped and retrieved his shoes from beneath the bed. He pulled them on and straightened quickly.

'I have to go.' She nodded and looked at the floor. Her teeth bit into her lower lip, whitening it. 'Is there anything you need, Barbara? Next time. Anything I can bring you?' He asked out of habit, already knowing the answer.

She shook her head. 'No, Peter. Thanks.' She jerked her chin at the pillow. 'That helps. It helps a lot,' she said, very quietly.

'I know.' He bent his head quickly and kissed her.

Turning abruptly, he lifted his coat from a hook behind the door. Beneath it, pinned with two thumb-tacks, was a picture cut from a magazine, a face he recognized. He half-turned to mention it and saw her dab the knuckle of her first finger at her eye. The knuckle was damp. He dropped his coat and took her gently by the shoulders.

'Barbara,' he asked softly. 'Are you okay?' The next moment she was clinging to him, sobbing silently and uncontrollably. He held her, not speaking, waiting for the first force of her crying to be spent. After a while, he leaned back and looked into her eyes.

'Barbara?' he said tentatively.

She twisted her head and wiped the tears on his shoulder. 'I'm sorry, Peter.'

He smiled, still holding her to him. 'It's okay.'

'It's just...Oh, Peter, it's just that everything's so awful. So much worse. You can't imagine how tired it makes us.'

'Maybe I can. Partly, anyway.'

She tried to grin at him. 'Yes, perhaps you can. Partly. At least you try. More than the others do. But you don't live here. Every night those lunatics come on television and tell us everything's getting better, and every day in the streets everyone can see it's getting worse.' She laughed. The laugh held a faintly hysterical note. 'Apart from when you bring them, do you know when I last had an orange?' He looked at her. 'Over eighteen months ago. Can you imagine that? More than a year and a half.'

He felt a kind of embarrassment rising in him. It was a familiar feeling, a form of guilt at living in a land where such problems had been unknown for two generations. As usual, he sought for something encouraging to say. He knew he was going to feel foolish.

'But I thought you could get oranges now. Recently.' He did feel foolish.

'Ha! Yes, of course, if you know where to look, have half a day free to queue, and want to spend a week's salary for a kilo.' She sobbed again. 'It's not just for me. Of course I could get them, and most other things, if I really wanted. But why should it have to be that way? Why can't normal people go out and buy normal things? Where's the sense of it?'

They were all good questions. He shrugged. 'It's not

perfect with us, either, Barbara. We have a few problems too, you know. There are plenty of lunatics trying for a chance of power in the West.'

She had heard his attempts to minimize the differences before. She patted his cheek and spoke with gentle sarcasm. 'You have to go. You don't want to miss your plane. You'll be home by five. In time to scour your neighbourhood for the last remaining lemon.'

He swallowed. 'Goodbye, Barbara,' he said hoarsely.

Two minutes later he emerged into the raw chill of the morning. He shuddered and drew his coat closer around his throat. Hesitating for a moment, he weighed his chances of finding a taxi. They were small. He began walking.

In the car park of the building opposite a well-dressed man, uncomfortable in the cramped driving seat of an anonymous green Polski car, watched Mason emerge from the building and grinned with relief. He jabbed an elbow into the bicep of the man who dozed beside him. The other man's chin jerked up from his chest.

'There,' said the driver, glancing to where Mason stood. 'That's him.'

The other man groaned and tried to stretch his legs. Laboriously, hindered by his heavy overcoat, he reached behind him and pulled from the back seat a heavy camera, made awkward and ungainly by a protruding telephoto lens.

The children fell silent and watched gravely as the two men burst from the house and began running down the alley. The big man's long stride carried him ahead of Juan, who struggled in a bow-legged scamper in his wake. He called over his shoulder to the panting Indian.

'Where are they, Juanito? How many?'

Gulping for breath, Juan answered, 'At the house of Tomas, Father. Maybe by now at the clinic. They are not many. One jeep. Six soldiers, maybe.'

The bigger man shortened his stride and sprinted,

13

leaving the younger man struggling behind him. As he passed, people ran quickly from the shacks that lined the street, snatched up their children and disappeared again into the spurious protection of the flimsy buildings. Frightened eyes watched him from the dark, unglazed windows.

At the end of the street stood a more substantial building of corrugated iron on a stout timber frame. An attempt had been made to paint it white, but it had failed when the paint ran out. Above the front of the building a rough wooden cross stood out against the sky. Beneath the cross a bell hung from a metal bracket.

'Quickly, Juan, sound the warning.' As he spoke he turned and raced along the side of the church.

Behind the church he emerged into a maze of alleys lined with shacks poorer even than those on the street. Only cats moved among the rubbish that lay in the dust. He ran on, knowing that inside the shacks people cowered, holding their children to them, forcing even the babies to be quiet.

The uncanny silence was pierced by the sudden sound of the bell. It rang three times, and then after three seconds, twice more. A short pause and then it was repeated. It was the warning peal. He ran on, angry in the knowledge of its futility. As the bell tolled again, he came to another building, roughly the same size and structure as the church but lower, and with more windows. It was painted white all over, except for a red cross as tall as a man, on each side. The close mesh of fly-screens covered each window. Behind them faces followed the running figure.

Gregory emerged into a square of hard-packed, swept earth in front of the clinic. Two spindly trees struggled to provide shade to a pair of rough wooden benches. The door of the clinic was closed. In front of it, his back to the door, stood another Indian. Like Juan, he wore a clerical collar. Sweat coursed down his face, and he was trembling.

Gregory ran to the man and laid a hand on his shoulder.

14

He gulped air and spoke in a low, urgent voice. 'Where are they, my son? Have they been here?'

The man shook his head so violently that drops of sweat flew in an arc from his forehead. Dumbly, he looked past Gregory.

Gregory turned to follow the man's gaze. On the far side of the next square a jeep emerged from a narrow entrance between two buildings. In front of the dusty, camouflage-painted vehicle two soldiers stalked, scanning the street with angry eyes. Four men sat in the jeep, three wearing the same steel helmets as the foot soldiers. The man beside the driver wore a soft red beret. The studied casualness with which they wore their uniforms, chinstraps dangling and tunics open to the third button, contrasted chillingly with the immaculate shine of their weapons and helmets.

From a distance of fifty yards they looked like boys playing at soldiers. As they advanced across the square, the stupid animosity in their faces drove out any such impression.

Gregory reached behind him and opened the door of the white building. 'Quickly, my son. Inside.' Without a word, the trembling priest disappeared into the building. Gregory closed the door and moved a step so that he stood with his back against the rough wooden planks. The jeep stopped three yards from him. The two foot soldiers trained the sinister muzzles of their automatic rifles on his naked chest. For what seemed like several seconds, the only sound that broke the utter silence was the plaintive pealing of the bell.

'Step aside, Father.' The man in the red beret spoke softly.

Gregory stood motionless.

The muscles of the officer's jaw tightened. 'Father,' he said in a taut voice, 'move aside. We just want Hernandez. Nobody else. We won't hurt anybody else.'

Gregory's ferocious blue eyes met the officer's deep-set brown ones. 'No, Captain,' he said firmly. His voice was resonant in the stillness. 'This is a hospital. You have no business here. Leave us.'

The officer drew a long breath. His nostrils widened. 'We have come for Hernandez, Father. He is not sick. Give him to us, Father, or we shall take him.' He let his glance fall on the foot soldiers. 'You cannot stop us, Father. Let us have him.'

Gregory settled his weight more firmly against the door. 'No, Captain,' he said levelly.

A flash of anger lit the officer's eyes. He sprang down from the jeep and swaggered across to where Gregory stood. One hand rested on the revolver which dangled, cowboy fashion, from an open holster at his hip. Eighteen inches away he stopped, his eyes on a level with Gregory's chin. He looked up at the serene face of the tall priest.

'Move aside, Father. I have been sent to take Hernandez. You must know he is a dangerous man. A communist. A terrorist. We know all about him.' His right hand clenched around the butt of his revolver. Behind him the two soldiers advanced half a pace. The bell had stopped. The metallic sound of their weapons being cocked sounded extraordinarily distinct in the heavy air.

For a further second there was no sound at all as the officer struggled to master his fury and humiliation. 'I have orders,' he said, distinctly. Beneath the air of authority there was a note of something plaintive in the officer's voice.

'Obey them, if you wish,' Gregory answered. 'You will have to kill me first, however. Do your orders include that, Captain?' he added, so softly that only the officer could hear. 'Is that what your leaders have told you to do? Kill Father Gregory Kozka?'

Anger and frustration jostled in the man's face. He glanced quickly behind him at the other soldiers who sat silently watching the confrontation. Without warning, the officer swivelled and strode to the jeep. Calling a sharp command, he swung himself up beside the driver. The two foot soldiers turned, and ran to spring onto the back of the jeep as the driver gunned the engine. The officer looked across at Gregory. He spat into the dirt. '*Communista.*' In a spume of dust, the vehicle raced across the square and away down the narrow street. In its progress it upended one of the two rough benches.

It was a fast forty-minute walk back to the hotel. Mason's mind was on Barbara. She was still a mystery to him, even after all this time. Before meeting her he had been friendly with a lot of girls who worked the hotel bars and lobbies. They spent their money as fast as they earned it. Their cramped flats were filled with the latest output of the Japanese electronics industry, their wardrobes with this year's Western fashions, imported from France and Germany. They drove Volkswagen Golfs with smoked glass windows. Barbara owned four pairs of shoes, a six-year-old car – the smallest model made in Poland – and a hand-operated coffee grinder.

As she had done this morning, she took the money he gave her, thanked him shyly, and talked of other things. It was as though she had a purpose. One which needed money and no other encumbrances. Like leaving the country.

At the traffic light ahead of him the green Polski waited for the light to change.

'Did you get him?' the driver asked, conversationally.

'Uh-huh. Full-length, half-length. Portrait.' He glanced down at the camera in his lap. 'Wonderful things, these. From two hundred metres you can see the expression on his face.'

'And how was it?'

'Miserable.'

'Well, this is Warsaw. Perhaps he's just trying to be inconspicuous.' They both laughed. The light turned green. 'Do you need any more?'

'No. What we've got is fine.'

'All right.' The driver pressed hard on the accelerator. 'Let's go and get some breakfast.'

# 2

The light was against Mason. A bus, its windows opaque with the winter's grime, raced past, sending an arc of filthy black slush slashing at the legs of the half-dozen pedestrians who stood in front of him. Their brief protests were almost lost in the roar of the motor. As the bus receded, pursued by a choking cloud of diesel fumes, he watched the anger in their faces subside leaving a film of bitterness around their mouths.

A man of about fifty-five, heavy-set, in soiled working clothes, flicked at the spots of damp mud that flecked his cheap coat. 'Bastards,' he said distinctly. Mason looked at him in surprise. The man grinned, without any trace of humour. 'They'll learn. Someday, soon, they'll all get a surprise.'

The rest of the crowd moved off as the light changed, but Mason hung back. The man straightened, looking at him. 'All the bastards, friend. We'll send them all back where they belong.'

Mason raised his eyebrows. Not since the late seventies had people spoken openly on the street of their hostility.

The man leant closer. 'Jaruszelski, Olchowski. All the shits. Back to Russia. They'll be among friends.' He laughed coarsely. Mason recoiled. The man's breath was rank with alcohol, but he was not too drunk to catch the movement of Mason's head. He reached out a hand like a spade and gripped the other man's arm.

'Think I'm drunk?' he asked, in a disappointed tone. 'Well, perhaps I am.' He shrugged. 'It makes no difference, though. Pissed or sober, I hate the bastards.'

His face was three inches from Mason's. Curious to hear the man, Mason stood his ground. The breath wasn't so bad, once you got used to it, like cigarette smoke in a room.

'Look! Look here!' The man dropped his arm and began rummaging in a pocket of his coat. He pulled out a loose packet of greasy brown paper. With the drunk's laborious care, he unwrapped the parcel. A small piece of sausage lay among the folds together with a couple of chunks of bread. The man thrust it indignantly towards Mason. 'See that?' He fixed him with an accusing gaze. Mason nodded, unable to help smiling. 'Think it's funny, do you?' the man asked with sudden aggression.

The smile disappeared. 'No,' he said, 'it isn't funny. What's the matter with it, though?'

The man looked at him warily. 'You a foreigner?'

Mason let his shoulders rise and fall. His smile returned. 'My accent? It gives me away every time. I'm British.'

'Oh.' The man paused as though studying the implications of Mason's nationality.

'I'll tell you what's wrong with it,' he went on after a while. 'It's all the meat I've got till next Monday. It's what's left of my ration. This and a bit of pork I've got at home.' Abruptly, he thrust the parcel back in his pocket and turned to walk away. 'You tell 'em that when you get back home,' he called fractiously over his shoulder. 'Tell your friends what a working man gets to eat in Poland!'

Mason watched him go. He was not smiling any more. He could understand the drunk's anger, and Barbara's. Nothing in the country worked. And yet whenever he invited factory engineers to the West for study trips to learn about the machines he sold them, the invitations were appropriated by so-called 'directors' of the factories. Usually party hacks who expected to be provided with food, drink and, invariably, women, before returning to Poland with nothing more to show for it than a further deterioration in their livers. The factories went on breaking down.

And he was set that morning to sign a contract that would bring him a fortune. A contract to re-equip three of the big furniture factories in the West of Poland. The factories where they made the excellent furniture that was exported in huge quantities, not the shoddy chipboard and plastic monstrosities offered for sale to the Polish public.

He shook his head. He should be feeling jubilant. Instead, the conversation with Barbara and the encounter with the drunk had revived a lot of the doubts he had always felt about dealing with the system. He sighed and pushed open the door of the hotel.

The knots of people waiting around in the lobby were mostly men and mostly loud. The Western businessmen wore expensive fur hats. The Poles they thought they were impersonating wore lumpy peaked caps or under-sized brown trilbies that might have been bought in a KGB garage sale.

The reception clerk gave him his key, a telex message and the faintly pitying look hotel desk clerks reserve for guests who stay out all night.

In the lift he realized the walk had dispelled his hangover. The realization made him smile appreciatively at his fellow passenger, a broad-hipped chambermaid with hair sprouting exuberantly from a large mole on her cheek. He stepped from the lift, leaving her giggling girlishly.

In his room he stripped and climbed under the shower. He could have showered at Barbara's but in the hotel the water was less likely to turn to a mysterious brown colour, or stop altogether in mid-shower.

He turned off the shower and began towelling himself vigorously. The condensation on the mirror-tiled wall cleared to show his reflection. Leaning closer, he checked the progress of the flecks of grey infiltrating his short, unruly hair. At 39 he had long ago stopped caring if he was handsome. He knew he looked intelligent and humorous, and women seemed to like him better as he got older. Maybe they could no longer be so choosy.

He put on a fresh shirt, underwear and socks and the

same tweed jacket and woollen trousers. They were the only ones he carried. He pushed his few dirty clothes and minimal toilet gear into the bottom of the leather flight-bag that doubled as luggage and briefcase. Years of arriving in ill-lit small towns two hours after the last taxi driver had given up and gone home had taught him the virtues of travelling light.

He closed the bag and checked his pockets. Money, passport, air ticket. He glanced at his watch and grinned. His meeting was not for another hour and a half. Time for a decent breakfast and some more coffee. This time with milk.

'Is he going to die?'

The doctor was a woman. She ran a hand through her untidy grey hair and chewed at the shaft of her spectacles. She put the glasses back on and looked hard at the man opposite her. He dropped his own gaze under the weight of her stare.

'Well?' he urged, irritably.

'Probably,' she answered, without taking her eyes from his face. 'The stroke was massive. People have recovered, more or less, from such strokes. Sometimes.'

'But will *he*?' The man shifted in his chair. His voice was tinged with petulance. He had been sent to get facts and for half an hour this woman had been equivocating.

She shook her head slowly. 'I don't think so. He seems to have been very fit for his age. Even so, there appears to be brain damage. I think he is very unlikely to recover. Not with the treatment we can give him.' Her voice rose slightly. 'We don't have the equipment we should have, or the drugs.'

'Perhaps we can be of service, there,' the man suggested, his tone suddenly suave. 'If there's anything you need just tell me. I'm sure I can help. Anything we can do to save a life, you know.'

The doctor looked at him sourly. 'Would you like to see him?'

'Yes, yes. I would.' The man rose fussily to his feet, looking determinedly helpful. 'Lead the way.'

The doctor strode from the room and along a bleak grey-painted corridor. The man followed at her shoulder. His stride was shorter than hers, forcing him into an ungainly scuttle in the effort to keep up with her. He hated hospitals. They reminded him of all the things that might one day happen to him. Cancer. Leukaemia. This thing AIDS they had now in the West.

The doctor stopped in front of a door with a frosted glass pane. He collided with her and looked at her peevishly, as though she had tried to trap him. Holding a finger to her lips, she opened the door.

A gaunt figure lay motionless on the bed. Thin arms emerged from crumpled pyjamas. One hand twitched like a small, emaciated animal. The other, contorted into a claw, lay absolutely still. Tubes ran from the patient to plastic containers suspended from brackets over the bed. The man followed the doctor to the bed, staying behind her shoulder, as though afraid the prostrate figure might leap at him.

They peered down into the face. The mouth was frozen into a ghastly grimace. Bubbles oozed imperceptibly at one corner of the mouth, like the salivating of a crab on a fishmonger's stall. The man paled visibly and backed away a step.

'Good morning, Mr Kozka,' the doctor called cheerfully. She stooped and tugged at the rucked sleeve of his pyjamas. 'It's a beautiful day outside. It makes you want to be up and about in it, eh?'

The patient's eyes showed no flicker of understanding. The doctor went on talking for a couple of minutes, her tone never once betraying a suspicion that the patient might not be totally conscious of every word she spoke. She turned to the man, who was watching her in dumb astonishment.

'Okay?' she whispered. 'Seen enough?'

He nodded, closing his eyes as he did so, and they left

22

the room. The doctor closed the door with a cheerful goodbye.

'Does he understand?' the man asked, incredulously. 'Does he know what you're talking about. I mean, with the brain damage, and everything?'

The doctor shrugged and began walking back to her office. 'I don't know,' she said grimly. 'Maybe. You can never tell in these cases. But,' she fixed him again with her penetrating gaze, 'how would you like it if you were lying there like that and everybody addressed you as though you were a piece of broken masonry, awaiting disposal? Especially if you really were aware of what was going on.'

The man shuddered. He was silent for a moment. 'It's very good, the private room,' he said officiously, relieved to bring the conversation back to administrative matters. He was good at administrative matters. 'I'm very glad to see you were able to comply.' His voice was oily again.

'Me, too,' the doctor replied icily, and entered her office.

'So, then, Doctor,' he said, settling himself in the chair, 'you think he might live for a while.'

She pinched the bridge of her nose. 'With proper treatment. And proper care.'

He hitched himself closer to the desk. 'What would that involve, exactly?'

Ten minutes later the man had two pages of notes. Ignoring the doctor, he read them over. He nodded. 'H'mm, good.'

He looked across at the doctor who stared coldly back at him. 'I'm afraid I have to make a telephone call, Doctor.'

She waved a hand negligently at the telephone. 'Help yourself.'

He shook his head and smiled ingratiatingly. 'No, Doctor, you don't understand. It's a – er – confidential call. I'll have to ask you to let me use your office for a while. Alone.' Without a word, the doctor rose and left the room, slamming the door hard behind her.

Mason nodded to one of the taxi drivers lounging outside the hotel. He knew the man. He was one of the group that only worked the hotels, the tourists and businessmen. They disdained to take Polish passengers. Or Polish money.

The man sprang into his taxi, a newish Mercedes. He looked expectantly in the mirror.

'Rollimpex.'

The driver threw the car into gear with an enthusiasm that suggested it was the one place in the world he most wanted to go.

'Change money?' the driver asked, before they were off the hotel forecourt.

'No.'

'Good rate. Nine hundred to the dollar.'

'Forget it. I'm going home this afternoon. You want some zlotych? Very good rate.'

The driver laughed.

For a while they drove in silence. Ahead of them Mason saw a queue stretching fifty yards from the entrance to a shop. He looked at his watch. Nine-thirty. The shops did not open until 11.00.

'What are they queueing for?' he asked, indicating the queue to the driver.

The man glanced without interest at the queue. 'Oh, that. Meat,' he answered.

'At this hour?'

The driver shrugged. 'Some of them have been there since 7.00 probably.'

Mason frowned. 'But what for? I thought that was the idea of rationing.'

The driver looked pitying. 'It is. So what. Anyway, if they're too stupid to make other arrangements.' His tone implied that he was to be congratulated on not being one of them. Mason was meditating a deflating reply when he caught a sudden swirl of movement near the rear of the queue. Abruptly, a woman was catapulted from the crowd and stumbled to her knees. In an instant she was at the centre of a gesticulating mêlée. He craned forward in his seat. The crowd around the woman were shoving her and shouting. Across the wide boulevard a militiaman started running towards the scene, unslinging his baton from his belt as he went.

They drew away from the scene.

'What was all that?' Mason asked, turning to look out of the rear window.

'Queue-jumping, probably,' the driver answered indifferently. 'It's happening a lot lately.'

It was a couple of minutes before a quarter to ten when he entered the offices of Rollimpex, the state monopoly for imports of industrial machinery. He walked through the submarine twilight and stale cigarette smoke that characterized Polish public buildings to the reception desk.

Behind the glass a blonde woman with an awesome bosom sat trying to keep middle age at bay with a compact mirror and a run-down stub of lipstick.

'*Dzien dobre*, Mrs Pavlowska.'

'Mr Mason,' she exclaimed girlishly, '*dzien dobre*. How are you?' She stowed the lipstick and reached for the telephone. 'For Director Zulawski, I suppose?'

'Please.'

'He's sending someone down, Mr Mason. Would you like to take a seat while you wait?' She nodded at a group of uncomfortable-looking benches on which the stuffing oozed from slits in the black vinyl covering.

Giving her a brief salute, he walked over and sat down. He pulled a copy of *Time* from his bag. In Eastern Europe patience was a cardinal virtue. But it was difficult to concentrate. His mind kept straying back to the incident at the butcher's shop. He had never seen such violence in Poland before.

His musings were interrupted by the sound of quick footfalls on the marble floor. He looked up to see Dobruszka, Zulawski's secretary, walking rapidly towards him. She transferred her half-smoked cigarette to her left hand and shook hands warmly. Turning, she led him through the over-heated gloom to the lift. A 'no smoking' sign hung from one screw, acknowledging its own futility.

'How are you doing for supplies?' he asked cheerfully, taking two packets of Dunhill from his bag and handing them to her.

She blew smoke at the ceiling. 'Okay, so far.' She held out a thin yellowish stub for him to inspect. 'At least we can still get these. They're Bulgarian, but they're all right. It's almost impossible to get Marlboro though. There were some, from Yugoslavia, but they disappeared weeks ago.'

'Aren't they going to ration them, too?'

'Everybody says so. You know how it is, though. No one wants to admit there's a problem.'

He thought again of the scene he had just witnessed. 'I'm not even sure it helps,' he said, his voice distant.

'Neither am I. I don't know what else they can do about it, either.'

'You could give up smoking,' he said, his voice neutral.

She squinted at him through her smoke and decided he was probably joking.

Zulawski's office was spacious, with a long wooden desk and a conference table which could seat a dozen people. On the walls, several framed certificates attested to unspecified services to the state. The desk was absolutely bare except for a fresh blotter, an empty coffee cup and a silver frame holding a photograph of Zulawski's wife. Looped by a short silver chain from a corner of the frame hung a very small crucifix.

Zulawski, a squat man with a bull neck and huge hands rose from an impressively unholstered chair and charged around the desk towards Mason. He enveloped Mason's outstretched hand in a massive two-handed clasp.

'Good morning, Peter. How are you?' he asked, nodding to Dobruszka, who silently withdrew. Still grasping Zulawski's hand, Mason looped his other arm around the other man's shoulders and allowed himself to be half-led and half-towed to a chair.

'I'm great, Andrzej. Fine,' he said, grinning, as he was

pressed into the chair. 'How about you? And Elisabeth?'

The pause before Zulawski replied was almost imperceptible. 'We're fine, Peter, fine.' If Mason had known him less well he would not have noticed the slight veiling of the deep-set eyes as he spoke.

'And how are things generally?'

Zulawski pulled a couple of glasses and a bottle of Courvoisier from a drawer. He filled the glasses and pushed one at Mason. 'Generally,' he said, almost inaudibly, 'things are terrible. Cheers.' The Pole tossed off the cognac at a gulp.

'Help,' Mason muttered faintly, and then downed his own drink. He grimaced. All the years of practice had still not taught him to enjoy drinking in the morning. 'Cheers, Andrzej,' he said, standing the empty glass on the desk, '*Sto lat.*' A hundred years. The traditional Polish toast.

Zulawski was already refilling the glasses. Mason tried to cup a hand over his. He was too late.

'Christ, Andrzej. Go easy. I had a rough night.'

Zulawski took up his glass. 'Here's to our friendship, Peter.' He threw back his head and downed the drink. Mason hesitated an instant, puzzled by something, a strident note in his friend's behaviour. Then, with a shrug, he swallowed the cognac. His stomach burned. By the time he drew breath Zulawski was trying to fill his glass a third time.

Half-laughing, but at the edge of irritation, he pushed the bottle away. 'Later, Andrzej, please. Let's ask Dobruszka to bring in the contract. Then,' he rose to his feet and did a pirouette, arms out-stretched, 'we can celebrate.'

Zulawski was not smiling. His broad countryman's face had clouded.

Mason's arms dropped. 'Andrzej? What's up? What's wrong? Your people haven't changed anything, surely? Not at this stage?'

The Pole's eyes rose to meet his. 'I'm sorry, Peter,' He shrugged, letting his enormous hands fall onto the desk in

27

front of him. 'There's a problem.' He shifted uncomfortably. 'We won't be signing the contract today.'

Mason leant towards the slumped figure. 'When, then? What problem? Yesterday everything was settled, you told me.' Sudden anger welled in him. 'If this is a stunt, some sort of last-minute negotiating ploy...'

Zulawski cut him short. 'It isn't, Peter. The project's cancelled. For now. Maybe permanently. I don't know. I had a call from the Minister, half an hour ago.' He looked up at him desolately.

Mason did not move for a long time. After a while he sank slowly into the chair. Reaching for the bottle he filled the two glasses. Brandy ran over the edge of the glasses onto the unmarked blotter.

'*Sto lat*, Andrzej,' he said, with a lop-sided smile. 'A hundred years.'

'I hope not, Peter,' the Pole replied softly.

# 3

Gregory stood motionless and watched the jeep disappear. Slowly, a smile spread across his severe features. *Communista*! Him. He walked over and righted the fallen bench as villagers timidly emerged onto the deserted streets. It was all the officer knew. Anyone who did not side with them in their mad brutality had to be a Communist. It kept it simple. Something the soldiers could understand. He turned and entered the clinic.

All the beds in the spotless white interior were full. Three Indian nuns and the young priest were gathered at the door of a partitioned-off section which served as a dispensary. All of the faces were turned fearfully to him as he entered. He made a calming gesture, patting at the air with both palms turned down.

'We are safe,' he said, his voice deep and reassuring. 'They have gone. For now.'

The fear drained from the faces. Some, the sickest ones, went blank, others smiled. Gregory strode to the far end of the clinic and stopped by the farthest bed. The man in the bed had the cheekbones of an Indian and the light blue eyes of a European. He grinned at Gregory.

Gregory's own smile faded. 'Tomas,' he said, sitting on the edge of the man's bed, 'show me your arm.'

The man drew his arm from beneath the sheet. A dressing covered it from the elbow to just below the armpit. Gregory took his hand and raised the arm high. The man was still grinning. Gregory let the arm fall. 'It's nearly healed. You must leave. You cannot stay here.'

'If you think so, Father, I will go home.'

'No, Tomas. You must leave the village. You should go today, together with your family. They will be back for you. Next time they may not listen to me.'

The man's grin faded. 'But where can I go, Father? This is my home.'

'I know, Tomas. Have you no family that could help you?'

'My sister, Father. But she lives far away from here. In the mountains, in San Julio. I haven't money to go there.'

Gregory glanced at the Indian priest who stood at the other end of the room, watching alertly. 'Ask Father Miguel. He will give you what you need.'

He stood up and strode from the building.

Walking barefoot through the dust back to his house he thought again of the irony of the officer's reaction. Gregory Kozka, a Communist! As a young man in Poland he had known many of them. Most had been good men, men to whom Communism had seemed the answer to the Fascism of the thirties. In the post-war years it would have been easy to believe they were right. Often, in his early work as a priest he had found himself working with them, their shared patriotism and eagerness to rebuild Poland more than overcoming their ideological differences. Stalin had changed that. The emergence of the power-seekers and the apparatchiks had left no room for the kind of Communists he had known.

Unable to stomach their perversion of the truth, their blind self-seeking adherence to a system that threatened to ruin all he had wanted to help build, he had manoeuvred to get himself moved to the Vatican. He had hoped that there he would have a voice, the opportunity to speak out against the oppression and tyranny he saw all around him. Within a short time he had discovered that the innate conservatism and internal politics of the Vatican gave him very little opportunity to do it.

A dozen years ago his frustration had finally boiled over. Quitting the comforts of life in Rome he had left for Central America, in an attempt to find a practical outlet for his views. It had not been difficult. There was all the poverty and oppression a missionary with a reputation to make could ask for.

Four years ago the Nobel prize had given him the voice to go with the satisfaction. He knew he was not a humble man. He wanted to tell the world his mind and the prize had given him the chance. He had taken it with both hands, speaking and writing and preaching as much as he could find time for. It had made him many enemies. In the Communist world he was seen as a dangerous subversive. Here he was a *Communista*! He was under no illusions. If it was the prize that had given him the voice he had wanted, it was also the prize that gave him protection against the consequences of using it. If the encounter of a few minutes before had occurred five years earlier, he would have been shot out of hand.

Dinner that night was a subdued affair. All their thoughts were on the events of the afternoon. The priest, Juan, broke the long silence.

'They could easily have killed you, Father. These soldiers are so young. They have no training. They like to hurt people.'

'Of course they could have, but they didn't. It would not

have been worth their while. Not for Tomas Hernandez.'

'But you can't be sure. Hernandez was responsible for the attack on the mine up at El Portel. The whole village knows it.'

Gregory pursed his lips. 'Was anybody hurt? They gave warning. I understand the mine was cleared before the explosion.'

'That's true. Nobody was injured. That time. But it will be many months before the mine can be reopened. And the owners are very close to the army.'

'But very far away from Tomas Hernandez, I hope.' Gregory looked at the other priest, Miguel. 'He did leave, I suppose?'

'Yes, Father. He set off this evening. He promised he would go to his sister.'

'Good. Up there in the hills it will be harder for him to get into trouble.' He smiled. 'I, too, have had enough trouble for today. Good night.' He bowed to the group around the table and went into the bedroom.

The next morning Gregory rose, as usual, at 5.00. He had not finished his prayers when he heard the sound of the approaching motor. He broke off, crossed himself hurriedly and got to his feet. He padded to the door and listened as the badly-tuned motor idled hesitantly in the street outside. An object struck the door with a soft thud.

A lumpy canvas sack lay in the dirt. He stooped and carried it into the simply-furnished room that served as living room and study. Taking a wooden-handled knife from the work table, he slit the cord binding the neck and up-ended the sack. Letters spilled onto the floor. Ever since the prize it had been the same. Twice a week the mail arrived from the capital. A sackful. Most of it was requests for help or advice, invitations to speak all over the world, or requests for articles.

He perched a pair of wire-framed glasses on his nose, lit the lamp, and began working methodically through it. As he finished reading each letter he put it into one of half a dozen piles, depending on the response it warranted. At the end of an hour he was no more than two-thirds of the way through it. He stretched and walked out of the house to the open lean-to area at the rear which served as a kitchen. He greeted the woman who sat cleaning vegetables and served himself a coffee. After a few words with the woman he strolled back to his desk.

The next letter he selected carried a Polish stamp. Sipping his coffee, he turned the letter over. There was no sender's address. Awkwardly, he opened the letter one-handed, reluctant to put down his coffee cup. He shook the single sheet of paper from the envelope and began reading the type-written sheet.

His knuckle whitened as his fist involuntarily clenched around the sheet. The coffee cup fell from his hand and rolled in a splash of coffee beneath the desk. Gregory sat motionless for a while and then sprang abruptly to his feet.

'Juan,' he called. 'Juan, come quickly. Prepare the truck. We must go to San Salvador.'

It had begun to rain. A steady, relentless rain that drove people close to the sides of buildings, many of them holding newspapers or cheap briefcases over their heads in futile attempts to protect themselves from the freezing downpour. Lines of people waited grimly in front of the vacant windows of shops. Some had umbrellas, the others stood stoically as the rain soaked through their clothes, unwilling to abandon the queue.

He looked at the pinched, mostly elderly faces. Many of them must have lived through the war. They had seen the obliteration of Warsaw, the destruction of their country. They were the ones who had toiled at the rubble with their bare hands. Toiled until they bled to rebuild their city. Whatever vision had motivated them then, it could not have been this. Not standing in the rain on a broken pavement, waiting for hours to buy the most basic of life's necessities. He wound up the window and leaned back in his seat. He had problems of his own.

The taxi drew up in front of the dilapidated airport building. He climbed out, groping in his pocket for cash. He peeled three single dollars from the crumpled wad and pushed them through the window to the driver. The man eyed them grudgingly, looked at Mason's face to see if it were worth a little swift blackmail, decided it definitely was not, and expressed his resentment by gunning the car away from the kerb in an assertive flurry of wheelspin.

Mason pushed his way through the sagging door into the departure hall. The standard half-light of Polish buildings engulfed him again.

Customs clearance on leaving was slow. In the last few months procedures had tightened a lot. For a foreigner the examination was still reasonably cursory, a question or two about the amount of currency he was carrying and a quick illegible stamp on the destination-tag of baggage. For Poles, though, it was different. Every bag was opened and thoroughly searched. Mason had to avert his eyes as people were put through the humiliation of exposing to the gaze of officials and other passengers their meagre possessions and the tragically insignificant gifts they were taking out to offer to friends abroad. He was relieved to be dealt with before the elderly lady next to him was obliged to spread out the contents of her toilet bag under the officious eye of a surly young officer.

The transit lounge stank of tobacco smoke. The gloom persisted. He felt lousy. There was an hour to kill and two ways of killing it. Either he could hang around the duty-free shop, pricing watches, or fight his way to the tiny bar for a drink. He already had a watch.

He shouldered his way through the crowd and ordered a Scotch. The barman gave him the drink, told him the price and stood waiting, like an actor awaiting his cue. Mason gave it to him.

'In dollars?'

It was the last joke the system played on you, when you thought they had none left. Seconds earlier, he had been asked whether he had Polish money. It was illegal to bring

33

it out. Now he was supposed to have some to pay for his drink.

The barman made a show of scrupulously calculating the rate. 'Three dollars, sir,' he announced, helpfully.

Mason handed over the notes and smiled as the barman slid them into his pocket. He would reimburse the till with the official price and sell the dollars on the street for four times more. It sometimes seemed as if the entire Bolshevik Revolution had been planned by catering staff.

He retreated a long way from the bar, away from the crowd that stood buying each other drinks in order to buy time to explain how important they were. The morning's events had left him in no mood for their transparent boasts.

Installed in the plane, Mason ordered another drink, watered it, sat back and took a long look at his situation. Not much different to the one he had been in before breakfast, except that he was about a quarter of a million pounds poorer than he had expected to be. He drank off half his drink and tried to see the funny side of it. He failed. He was surprised to realize how many plans he had been making on the expectation of a much improved bank balance. Most of all, it would have enabled him to cut down his travelling. Lately, he had been feeling the need of a family acutely. At his age there was not much time to waste. He had seen too many people try and fail to mix family life with the kind of travelling he did. It was probably a major part of the reason for his own divorce.

'Fuck it,' he said aloud, just to get it out of his system. He smiled a vivacious apology to the startled woman beside him and pressed the call button for the stewardess and another drink.

At Heathrow Mason strode through the green channel, ignored by a pair of languid customs men, and crossed to the car park. Automatically, he circled the dented Renault. Satisfied that all the wheels were still on it, he climbed in and started the motor. The car had developed a sound he had not noticed before. Penny used to reproach him often for not changing the car and getting something more up-market, a BMW or a Mercedes. He had resisted more than was reasonable. He just did not believe you could keep middle age at bay with ritual objects. He tuned in the radio and headed for the motorway, ignoring the new sound already.

In a room high in the building occupied by the Interior Ministry, three men waited for the call from the hospital. One stood gazing morosely over the rooftops of the city to where the Vistula river shone dully in the distance. The other two sat leafing through sheaves of blurred photocopies stapled at one corner. One of them tossed the dirty, dog-eared document onto the table in front of him with an exclamation. The other two men looked at him.

'This is terrible. It's dangerous stuff. It has to be stopped.' He looked aggressively at the other two.

The man at the window looked at him, a mixture of pity and exasperation in his face. 'We know, Deputy Minister,' he said distinctly.

'The man's dangerous, a traitor. How would it be if this stuff were freely available? We must act quickly.'

The man at the window spoke again, faintly weary. 'We may be a little late, Minister.'

The Deputy Minister struck his fist on the wide table. 'How is it possible? Why was I not kept informed? This can't be allowed to continue.'

The man at the window spoke again, his exasperation growing. 'Minister, how do you want to stop it? These are done on Xerox machines. Anybody with access to one can produce a thousand of these things in an hour.'

'Well then, access must be limited to authorized personnel. The machines will have to be registered.'

The man left the window and sat down opposite the Minister. 'They already are registered. In government offices access *is* limited to authorized people. It's still probably where half the stuff comes from.' The Minister looked injured. 'Anyway,' the man went on, 'these are only transcripts of cassettes. Even if you stop this you couldn't hope to stop people duplicating the cassettes. They're the real problem.' He looked into the Minister's eyes and saw a trace of panic. 'Have you ever heard him speak?'

The panic rose closer to the surface. 'I know what he's like. Very dangerous. Demagogic. That's why I think your idea is so, so...' Before he could finish the telephone rang.

All three men snatched at the phones that stood in front of them. The Deputy Minister spoke briefly into his.

Seated in the doctor's office the man at the other end began speaking. He spoke in a colourless drone, anxiously fingering the pages of his notebook. They let him continue, uninterrupted. When he had finished he coughed softly, hoping he had done well. He had. The Minister told him so.

'Good. Thank you, Major.' He glanced at the two other men who looked back at him expressionlessly. Giving the beginnings of a pout, he went on talking. 'They will get everything they need, Major. The necessary orders will be in hand this morning. I will attend to it personally.' He put down the telephone. The others did the same. 'Well, gentlemen,' he said grudgingly, 'so far it looks as though you have been right.' He bit his lip. 'Are you absolutely sure he has no one else? There's no other family? Nobody else here in Poland? You've checked with my people?'

The two other men looked at him with faintly hostile pity. 'Yes, well, of course, I'm sure you have,' the Minister continued uneasily. 'Well,' he pushed himself up from the table, suddenly expansive. 'I'll have the hospital director write to his son today.' He turned to the door. 'I'll – er – be downstairs, gentlemen, if you need me.'

He left the room. The nearer of the two men walked over to the door and checked it was closed before they began speaking in low, animated voices.

# 4

The Land Rover pick-up lurched and shuddered over the rutted dirt, obliging Juan to crouch forward, grasping the wheel so hard that his knuckles showed white even under the coppery sheen of his skin. Gregory sat beside him, keeping a firm hold on the grab handle. Had he been a driver himself, he might have had some misgivings about his helper's insouciant disregard for the dangers offered by the ruts and potholes. In fact, Gregory had left Poland long before private car ownership was common. It had never occurred to him to obtain a licence since. Having spent most of the last few years in the third world, Juan's hell-for-leather style actually struck him as rather conservative.

At present though, as he stared, frowning, through the dusty windscreen, he was indifferent to the dangers or discomforts of the road. His mind was on the letter in his pocket.

In the last fifteen years he had not been in Poland more than three times. The last time was six years ago when his mother had died. Since then his applications for permission to visit had been systematically rejected. The attempts he had made to contact directly the authorities in Warsaw had been fruitless. No explanation for the refusal to allow him to visit had ever been offered. He could furnish his own. The President of the United States might go on television at press conferences and brand him as a dangerous Communist agitator, the men in power in Warsaw and Moscow, despite their sloppier tailoring and hopeless haircuts, were much more sophisticated. They had always known his work represented something that was a bigger threat to their system than to any of El Salvador's northern neighbours. He had heard that his sermons and articles had lately begun to circulate in Poland, making him even less welcome.

He drew a deep breath. His father was dying. He had to return. He had to try one last time.

Without changing gear, Juan swung the pick-up abruptly from the dirt road onto a thin ribbon of pitted asphalt that wound across the plain between run-down plantations. If all went well, in another four hours they would be in the capital.

The Consul was a tall, spare man with an ill-fitting suit and inadequate air-conditioning. He ran a bony finger around his collar before speaking petulantly to the secretary, who stood just inside the closed door.

'Can't you get rid of him?' His voice held the beginnings of a whine. The secretary stood immobile, her lips pursed, as though she were holding back her contempt. 'Tell him I'm engaged. I can't see him. I'll be tied up all day. Tell him I've got a meeting.'

Silently, the secretary nodded. She turned and left the room.

The Consul blew hard as he saw the door close behind her. He rose and walked over to the window where the clattering air conditioner had been amateurishly fitted. He fiddled distractedly with the controls. Achieving nothing, he stretched his face up to the flaccid stream of cooler air.

The secretary returned. 'He says it doesn't matter. He'll wait.'

The Consul walked busily back to his desk and sat down. 'But tell him it's no use,' he said, irritably re-arranging the few objects on his bare desk. 'I'm busy. Didn't you make it clear to him? I'll be tied up all day.'

The secretary nodded. 'I told him,' she said express-ionlessly. 'He said he'll wait.'

In exasperation, the Consul picked up a marble paper-weight and made as though to slam the object onto the desk-top. At the last moment he pulled the blow, and let the marble slab settle soundlessly back onto the surface.

'But, Mrs Bujak,' he said, trying to smile indulgently,

38

'does he realize? I won't be free at all today. This is a consulate.' He gestured vaguely around at the room. 'There are things that have to be done!'

The secretary's expression remained utterly neutral. 'I'll tell him, sir.'

She went out of the room, leaving the Consul with his hand flapping impotently as his gesture died. He hauled a handful of folders from a drawer and laid them purposefully on the desk. From an inside pocket he drew a gold Waterman fountain pen, unscrewed the cap and laid the pen on the desk in perfect alignment with the top of the files. He began reading the first file. Occasionally, he wrote a short comment in a margin.

The Consul fidgeted with his pen. He wanted to go to the toilet. It would mean crossing the room where he knew his visitor sat waiting. Nervously, he got up and walked around. A few magazines lay on a table. He scanned them desultorily before returning to his desk. The heap of files appeared to offend him and he pushed them away with a brusque movement of his hand.

Gregory had finished the three-week-old Polish newspaper the secretary had offered him a half an hour ago. Now he sat motionless in the uncomfortable wicker chair, his arms resting on the arms of the chair, his dusty, sandal-clad feet set wide apart on the cool, ceramic-tiled floor. Waiting was easy for him. He had acquired the habit of repose many years before.

Mrs Bujak's voice came to him softly, almost apologetically. 'Could I get you anything, Father? Coffee? Some Tea? Something cold?'

Surprisingly, his smile made her blush. 'A coffee would be fine, please. And perhaps a glass of water.'

Still blushing, she disappeared into the kitchen. She returned a few minutes later, more composed, carrying a tray bearing a tiny cup of very black coffee and a tumbler of water.

'I'm sorry, Father,' she said, indicating the water glass,

'it's just tap water. We don't have any mineral water left. I hope it's all right.'

He grinned. 'The only thing that could upset my stomach is that it will have far fewer microbes than I'm used to. In the village you can almost see them.'

She smiled, gratefully. 'Father,' she said, her voice almost a whisper, 'I'm sorry,' she glanced at the door across the room, 'about the Consul.'

'What is there to be sorry for? He has things he must attend to, of course. It's just that I would rather not spend a night away from the village if I can avoid it. As you know, these are difficult times in the countryside.'

She looked again at the Consul's closed door, contemptuously. 'But, Father,' she said softly, 'he hasn't any visitors. He's alone. He's afraid, that's all. Afraid of you.'

'Of me?' Gregory guffawed. Lowering his voice to a more discreet pitch, he went on. 'Why on earth should he be afraid of me?'

'I don't know, Father. He's very nervous. I think he's been having nightmares about having to deal with you ever since he arrived here. It's his first posting. He's very worried about causing any fuss in Warsaw.' Disdain overcame discretion and she raised her voice. 'Whatever the reason, Father, I know he's lurking in there now, wasting time, hoping you'll go away.'

Gregory smiled quizzically, mildly surprised at her frankness. 'We'll see whose patience wears out first, then. What's your name?'

A minute later the two of them, under the influence of Gregory's authoritative charm, were in a lively conversation. She was fascinated by his work in the countryside, he was hungry to hear news of Poland from someone who had last been there only a few weeks previously. They were talking animatedly when the Consul emerged from his office and scuttled across the room to disappear into the bathroom.

The Consul bolted himself into the bathroom, unzipped his fly and with a long silent sigh that was almost a sob,

40

began to relieve himself. Damn the man. His preaching, his political writing, his meddling, had been driving everybody crazy in the last few years. And now he was here getting ready to make more trouble. He wrenched his fly closed and in his bitter distraction caught a fold of cloth in the zipper. He struggled briefly to free it feeling angry and foolish. Finally he straightened, patted the zip to reassure himself it was properly closed, slid back the bolt and strode from the bathroom. Gregory rose to meet him.

The Consul closed the door firmly behind Gregory, tossing a reproachful look at Mrs Bujak who sat studying the keys of her typewriter and trying to keep a smile off her face.

'Sit down, there,' he told the priest in a surly voice. Gregory sat down. The Consul circled the desk and settled in his own chair. He tried several postures before he found one satisfactory. 'Well,' he said, 'what can I do for you?'

Gregory placed the letter on the desk in front of the Consul. The man read it without picking it up. He looked up again at Gregory, his face a little less set.

'I'm sorry, Father,' he said quietly. Then, as though regretting his lapse, he continued in a gruffer voice. 'But what has it to do with me? What business is it of mine?'

Gregory looked at him steadily. 'I want to visit him. I would like you to contact Warsaw and tell them that. I want to spend some time with my father before he dies. He has nobody but me. Tell them I would like to return. I would be ready to discuss their conditions.'

Half an hour after Gregory left, the Consul emerged from his office, holding a piece of paper on which he had drafted an encoded message. He put it onto the desk in front of his secretary.

'A telex, Mrs Bujak, for Warsaw.'

She glanced at her watch. It was twenty past one. Normally she would have locked up and gone home twenty minutes ago. She smiled at the Consul. 'Certainly, sir, I'll send it immediately.'

*

Mason watched the few remaining leaves of the horse chestnut tree as they trembled under the driving rain. It seemed to have been raining constantly in the ten days since his return from Warsaw. He drained his coffee mug and turned from the window. Ignoring the heap of washing-up that lay in the sink, testimony to the previous night's dinner party, he refilled his own mug, plus a fresh one, tucked the paper under his arm and headed back up the stairs.

A tousled brunette smiled up from the pillow as he entered the bedroom. Her smile widened as she caught sight of the coffee. She struggled up onto one elbow and reached for a cup.

'Good morning,' she said faintly. 'Great party.'

'M'mm.' He handed her the coffee and clambered back into bed, tossing the paper down between them. The girl scuffled among the segments while he fitted himself into a cross-legged position. He reached for the papers.

'Shit!' he said in mock exasperation.

'What?'

'You! You've taken the business section! Don't you know women are supposed to start with the bit with the fashion pages?'

'Macho bastard,' she mumbled, sipping unconcernedly at her coffee. 'Read the fashion stuff yourself. You ought to. Your clothes are terrible!'

He laughed and grabbed at the news section, but was cut short by the insistent rasp of the doorbell.

'Shit!' he exclaimed, his exasperation real this time. He clambered off the bed and pulled a dressing gown from the bottom of the wardrobe. 'I'll be back,' he said softly.

He padded down the stairs pulling the towelling dressing gown closed around him. It was the first time he had used the thing in months. Most of the time he forgot he even owned it. He was not even sure he did own it. He had a vague feeling it belonged to Penny.

The bell rasped again. He had been meaning to change

the buzzer for a couple of years. Two shadows darkened the frosted glass pane of the front door. He wondered which they would be, insurance salesmen or Jehovah's Witnesses.

# 5

'Mr Mason? Peter Mason?'

Jehovah's witnesses would not have known his name.

'M'mm.' His tone left them room for doubt.

One of the men had none. 'Mr Mason,' he said, confidentially, 'we were wondering if we might speak to you for a few minutes.'

Still holding the door only half-open, he studied the speaker. The man wore a dark suit, a white shirt that was not fresh, a dark knitted tie and a crumpled raincoat which hung open, showing a detachable lining. His thinning dark hair was combed back in a pronounced widow's peak. Beneath the coat the man's shoulders were oddly out of alignment. Mason's eyes flicked again over the man's non-descript clothes. If he were selling insurance he was probably not doing it very well. He closed the door a defensive inch.

'What about?' he asked, in a voice that was only just cordial.

'Poland, Mr Mason.'

Mason's brows drew a fraction closer together. He looked more attentively at the dark man.

'What about Poland?'

'About conditions there. What we can do to help. What *you* can do to help.' The man was smiling ingratiatingly. He cast a quick look around at the empty street before turning back to Mason with a look of man to man complicity. 'Perhaps we could talk inside?'

As he finished speaking the man made as though to step into the house. Mason closed the door another quarter of an inch. With a faintly rueful smile the man fell back on his heels.

'What are you?' Mason asked curtly.' A charity?'

The other visitor spoke. He was three inches taller than his companion, and more heavily built. 'No, Mr Mason,' he said, laughing briefly, 'we're not a charity. Far from it. We're not asking for money. On the contrary. We're spending it.'

Mason looked the man over. His clothes were more casual but no better than the other man's. He wore a chain-store sports jacket and slacks, in colours that might have matched in the artificial light of the store, a woollen polo-neck sweater and no overcoat. His short, grey-blond hair grew low over his wide forehead. Nobody would have wanted the address of his barber.

'Good for you. What on?' Mason asked with impatient sarcasm.

'On you, perhaps,' the man answered, smiling. 'We hope so.'

He squinted at each of the men in turn. 'What exactly is this?' he asked at length, in a voice made low with subdued irritation.

'What it is, Mr Mason, is that we have a proposal to make to you.' It was the dark man who spoke. Mason eased the door closed another fraction. 'You know, you should listen to us, Mr Mason,' the man said hurriedly. 'What we have to offer could be worth a great deal of money to you.'

Mason looked sceptically back at the man. A great deal of money was a relative term. He wondered what a man who wore soiled shirts called a lot of money. 'How much?'

Before speaking, the dark man exchanged a quick glance with his companion. 'A hundred and fifty thousand pounds.' The voice, soft as velvet, was utterly distinct, utterly authoritative. Slowly, Mason looked from one to the other of the men. They gazed steadily back at him,

44

their faces impassive.

Another four seconds passed. He looked once over his shoulder at the stairs behind him. Then he gave a small shrug and jerked his head. 'Come in,' he said quietly.

With another glance up the stairs towards the room where the girl lay reading, he showed the two men into the living room, indicated the sofa and closed the door. He sat down opposite them.

'Why don't you tell me who you are?'

The two men exchanged glances. The smaller one spoke. 'It's a long story, Mr Mason. I'll summarize it for you as best I can. We work for a foundation, a private foundation with, one could say, charitable aims. Don't worry,' he added, smiling, 'we are not here to ask you to contribute.'

Mason ignored the joke. 'And what exactly are those aims?'

'Well, essentially the Foundation exists to gather information about conditions in the Communist world.'

'They're terrible,' Mason said drily. 'What do you do with the information once you've got it?'

'We make sure it's published. In newspapers, in books. We also work to ensure that information about life here reaches people over there.' He jabbed an emphatic finger at the bookcase, as though it concealed the Soviet Union.

Mason groaned inwardly. Communism was not his cup of tea, either. That did not mean he wanted to spend a Sunday morning hearing a lecture from a pair of envoys from the Moral Majority. He leaned towards the two men. 'Look, gentlemen,' he said, a rising note of impatience in his voice. 'I know Eastern Europe well. I *know* what's wrong with it without you coming here to tell me. As a matter of fact, one of the things most the matter is their press acting as stooges for the governments. So if you're looking for me to help you with planting articles over here, forget it.' His impatience was turning to anger. 'Keep on bribing the journalists on your own. You don't need me.'

The dark man leaned back, and made a reproving

clicking sound with his tongue. 'Bribery? Mr Mason,' he said suavely, 'I'm glad you mentioned the word, even if the context was regrettable.' He paused, still smiling his unpleasant smile. 'After all, it's a subject on which you might be regarded as something of an expert, h'mm?' He raised an eyebrow.

Mason sat without speaking, his face rigidly neutral, not responding to the man's insolent tone. Only an imperceptible tightening of the fist that was hidden in the pocket of his dressing gown would have betrayed the tenseness inside him. Somewhere at the back of his brain an alarm bell began sounding softly.

The man went on speaking. 'It's an unpleasant word, bribery. And yet what is it? When you invite a client to lunch? When you bring him a couple of films for his video? Perhaps even the video itself?' He shrugged. 'You have to do it, everyone does. Without it you would do no business.'

Still Mason sat silent, his eyes on the man's face. The alarm in his head had grown to a clamour.

The taller man broke in now, his voice more emphatic, more excitable than that of his companion. 'With us it's the same kind of thing. We take a journalist to lunch, make friends with him, or with her. Occasionally there might be a trip somewhere, at our expense, for study.'

Mason laughed curtly. 'Of course. Strictly for study. And on their return they print the rubbish you have provided as though it were their own.'

'No,' the dark man interjected sharply. 'They use the information we give them as a basis for a story. It's good information, Mr Mason. They know they can depend on us.'

'I'll bet they can,' he replied in a voice loaded with disgust.

'Don't scorn what we do. We didn't dream up the labour camps. We didn't dream up the exile of Sakharov to Gorki for all those years. But, by God, we do our best to ensure the public never forgets they were dreamed up!'

46

Mason looked at the man through narrowed eyes. 'Nice work,' he muttered carelessly. 'Where does the money come from?'

'As I told you, we are a foundation.' It was the smaller man again. 'We have income from investments. We receive donations.'

'Who from?'

'Individuals. Some companies. There's no need to go into detail.'

'Try some, anyway. The CIA? Some other bunch of the security services, even crazier than they are?'

The man smiled indulgently. 'No, not the CIA. Nobody like that. No government agencies, from anywhere. We are strictly a private foundation.'

'Not so private you won't tell me its name? Or yours?'

With a quick apology the dark man reached into his breast pocket and drew out a visiting card. At the same time the blond man pulled a slim black leather holder from his jacket and slid a similar card from it. They handed the cards to Mason. He held them out in front of him examining them. The beginning of a smile pulled at his mouth.

'The Freedom Foundation,' he murmured, looking ironically at the dark man.

The man caught the look and shrugged. 'The name is unimportant. The aims are all that count.'

'Of course, Mr Brooke, you're a man of principle.' He glanced at the other man. 'You too, Mr Carroll. A pair of idealists.'

Above their heads a floorboard creaked. Abruptly he tossed the cards onto a small table. 'All right,' he said brusquely, 'let's stop wasting time. You came in here talking about a proposal.'

The dark man had heard the sound from above them. 'Yes, indeed. Ah' he glanced up at the ceiling 'can I, er, talk? What we have to say is somewhat, shall I say, delicate.'

With a sour look at the man, Mason got up and crossed

47

to the door. He opened it and listened for a moment. He closed the door quietly, an expression of open distaste on his face.

'Okay. Go on.'

The dark man leant forward and began to speak. His voice was very low. 'Our proposition is simply this. There is a man in Southern Poland, a Pole, who spent many years in the Soviet Union. He is Jewish. When the Nazis invaded Poland he fled, along with many like him, to the East. He remained there after the war, for many years. Only in 1958 did he return to Poland, already very well known in his field. He was a man who had a lot to be grateful to the Soviet Union for. Nevertheless, as time went by he became more and more conscious of what the domination by Russia was doing to Poland. What it had always done, over centuries. That you are well aware of, of course?' It was a rhetorical question. Mason answered anyway.

'Very well aware. They hate the Russians.' He thought of a friend, Janusz, who had married a Russian girl while studying in Kiev and whose own family refused even to meet the girl. 'What makes his case special?'

'He was not content to complain quietly within his own family. He was an eminent man, a scientist, very well known in his field. He had friends in the Soviet hierarchy. He felt he had a voice, that his status obliged him to speak out and that people would listen. Well, they certainly did listen, but only long enough for them to decide how to stop him.'

'And then?'

'And then, of course, he disappeared. The early sixties were still a very bad time, even if Stalin were dead and gone. For many months his family were without news. Left to suppose he was dead. And then, after well over a year, his wife received word. A minute scrap of paper with a message in her husband's hand came through the mail. The envelope was posted in Poland by, as her daughter found out afterwards, a man who had been with her

48

husband. In a labour camp. That piece of paper was the only word, the only hopeful sign she had until the day she died, Mr Mason.'

The whole time Brooke was speaking Mason's gaze stayed on the man's face. He was intent on the story the man was telling, but at the same time alive to every nuance, every skilful attempt to manipulate his feelings.

'When did she die?'

'Three years ago. But let me continue. The daughter continued the campaign her mother had led, writing to everyone she could think of who could possibly have any influence on the case. From Kruschev, through Brezhnev and Andropov to Gorbachev, on down to their local mayor. None of it had achieved the least result. Until September of this year.'

Brooke paused dramatically. Mason admired his timing. 'What happened then?'

'Professor Kodec came home!' He looked triumphant. Mason felt less surprised than he was presumably supposed to. 'He was brought home to his daughter. A sick man. The camps are hard on young, fit men, Mr Mason. On a man in his sixties they can be intolerable. He was very frail indeed.'

'And where is the Professor now?'

'Still at home, being cared for by his daughter. He's really a very sick man.'

'What's wrong with him?'

'His heart, mostly. He's a broken man. That's why they released him. It's why they release most of the political prisoners, if they release them at all. Criminals serve their time and they're out. The politicals can stay there forever. About the only chance some of them have of leaving is if they become too sick to keep. It costs too much, in money and resources to keep them and they are too feeble to pose a threat, so they send them back to their families. If they still have families by then.'

Brooke paused. The room was utterly silent. Mason broke the silence.

49

'Look,' he said, his eyes on Brooke's, 'a few minutes ago you were talking about paying me to do something for you. Let's get to the point. Tell me what it is.'

'We want you to go to Poland and contact Professor Kodec.'

'And?'

'Obtain his testimony. Life in the Gulag. How a man of such eminence can be made to simply disappear for a generation. In short, Mr Mason, we want the Professor's story.'

'And all I have to do,' Mason said negligently, 'is walk out through Polish customs with enough stuff in my briefcase to send me to a labour camp for twenty years or so.' He shook his head. 'Sorry. You had better –'

Carroll cut him short. 'Of course, you would be provided with equipment, once you were there. You would photograph the documents and bring out just the film.'

'Just the film,' Mason mimicked, anger edging his voice. 'Is that supposed to make a difference?' He pushed himself to his feet. 'Come on, both of you.' He gestured brusquely at them to rise. 'You're leaving. If I'm looking for ways to go to gaol for twenty years I can stay here and find some. There's no need to go to the trouble of a trip to Poland!'

He was standing at the door now, holding it wide open. 'Come on, Out. Now!'

Neither of the men moved. Brooke looked at his companion and gave a small shrug. Then, slowly, as though it were causing him great pain, he reached into an inside pocket of his jacket and withdrew an envelope. He proffered the envelope to Mason.

'Sit down, Mr Mason, please. Before you say anything foolish. Look at these.'

Mason brushed the envelope aside. 'Forget it. I don't want to see anything from you.'

Brooke pursed his lips and shook his head as though dealing with a petulant child.

'Yes you do, Mr Mason. You want to see these. They concern people you know. Mr Sokolik, for example. And also Barbara Wisniewska.'

Mason's stomach muscles clenched, as though from a blow. He walked back to the sofa and sat down heavily. The alarm in his brain was clamouring furiously.

# 6

The decoding clerk gave a petulant pout when the message arrived on his desk. It was nine o'clock. Normally a quiet time on his shift. Pushing aside his half-completed crossword puzzle, he was disappointed to see the call sign at the head of the paper. El Salvador. Nothing interesting ever came in from there. His favourites were Washington or Western Europe. Irritably, a part of his mind still grappling with the last crossword clue, he began working on the message.

Forty minutes later his irritation had dissolved. In its place was a tremor of excitement. Gregory Kozka was coming home. His mother would never believe it. Father Gregory had been her hero for years: the flat was full of pictures of him. Reading the message through one last time, he thrust it into one of the steel pods that lay by his desk and carried it to where an arrangement of pneumatic tubes carried the pods around the immense building. He pulled a short switch and with a faint sigh the message was sucked away.

Less than fifteen minutes later the telephone rang in the beautifully restored house in the old town of Warsaw, where the Deputy Minister made his home. Turning from the big window over the River Vistula, the Minister picked up the phone and listened for a few minutes, letting a

51

complacent smile creep over his fleshy features.

'Thank you,' he said at length. 'That's excellent. We'll talk about it in the morning.' He hung up, and poured himself a large whisky from the bottle that stood on an ornate table near his desk. He tilted the glass in salute to his own satisfaction and drank off a long draught.

By the time news of Gregory's request had reached the Deputy Minister, Gregory's Land Rover was beyond the last roadblock and careering over the rutted surface of the road back to the village.

It began to rain. First a few slow drops plopped lazily onto the windscreen to make patterns in the thick dust. Then, without further warning, it began falling in great vertical rods, battering the parched dust of the road. Juan set the windscreen wipers to try to cope with the torrent and crouched closer over the wheel. He glanced at the glowering face next to him and spoke shyly, but loud enough to be heard over the ferocious drumming of the rain.

'How were they, Father?'

Gregory blinked and looked suddenly at Juan, as though surprised to see him there. He laughed suddenly. 'They were okay. Afraid, I think, more than anything. I seem to be an embarrassment. They would prefer me to stay away. I think they would prefer it if I were not Polish at all.'

'Afraid, Father. Of you? Who would be afraid of you? You would not hurt anybody.'

Gregory pressed the Indian's shoulder. 'Thank you, Juan. I hope you are right, though lately I'm not so sure. I see so much wrong. So many people hurting others.' He broke off, staring at the driving rain.

'But, Father,' Juan went on, a faint note of bewilderment in his voice, 'surely they want you to go back. You are famous. They must be very proud of you.'

'Too famous, perhaps,' Gregory answered wryly. 'Maybe it would have been better if I had never received the Prize at all.'

'You cannot speak so, Father. The Prize has helped so much with our work. In Europe they appreciate our work. In Europe the governments are not tyrants. Not like here.'

Gregory smiled, a tired smile, and placed a hand on the other man's shoulder once again. 'No, Juanito. Not like here.'

The first photograph Mason pulled from the envelope turned the tight knot in his stomach into ice. It was a picture, taken from maybe fifty yards away, of himself and a hawk-faced man about to enter the Hotel Beau Rivage on the shores of Lake Geneva. He recognized the man, Jerzy Sokolik, for long one of his most important contacts in Poland. The knot in his stomach grew tighter.

Across from Mason, Brooke and Carroll sat silently watching him. His head spinning, he slid the next photograph from the envelope. As he examined it he felt physically sick. It pictured himself and Sokolik in a room in the hotel. Mason himself sat hunched on the edge of an armchair, a briefcase open on his knees. Sokolik sat on the bed leaning towards him.

Mason ran a hand over his eyes. It had all taken place over two years ago. Sokolik had brought the matter up, casually at first, in his car in Warsaw. If Mason wanted to get the business then Sokolik expected to be 'looked after'. For a long while Mason had resisted and then the pressure had become too great, the stakes too high. The briefcase in the photograph had contained twelve thousand dollars, in low denomination bills.

And the two bastards opposite, maybe with Sokolik's connivance, had photographed it all. The implication of their earlier conversation, the talk of bribery, was clear now. If these pictures were to get into the wrong hands in Poland he would never get a visa again. The thought that Sokolik would certainly go to prison left him strangely unmoved. He had trouble enough of his own.

'You fuckers,' he said, with bitter emphasis.

Brooke ducked his head, as though acknowledging a

compliment. 'There's more, Mr Mason. Look at them. Go on.'

With a look of purest venom at the two visitors he pulled out two more pictures and let the envelope fall to the floor. He looked at them in stunned silence. Both were taken in a bar or a night-club and showed, from different angles, Barbara and an overweight blonde woman in thick make-up and thin clothes.

'What are these supposed to mean?' he asked, fighting to keep his voice level.

Brooke's lips formed a thin smile. 'Just this,' he said softly. 'The woman with Miss Wisniewska is what she looks, a prostitute. An excellent cover for her other work, as an organizer for one of the best of the escape organizations.' He paused. For a moment the room was quite silent as the two men watched understanding seep into Mason's face.

'Yes,' Brooke said, at length. 'This photograph was taken in the night-club in East Berlin that the woman uses as her headquarters. Your friend, Miss Wisniewska has organized and, incidently, paid for, her own escape.'

Still wearing the smile, Brooke got to his feet. Carroll did the same. Brooke looked down at Mason. 'We need your help, Mr Mason. We are willing to pay you well for it. If you are willing to cooperate in what we ask, all will be well with Miss Wisniewska. If not...' He shrugged and took a step towards the door. 'These pictures may fall into the wrong hands.'

Brooke allowed Carroll to precede him through the door. Turning, he looked back at Mason, who still sat blankly studying the photograph of the two women. 'You have until Wednesday, Mr Mason. If we don't have your agreement by then...' He shrugged again. 'Please don't bother to see us out.'

# 7

Mason was still sitting motionless when the door opened. Startled, he spun to see the girl standing in the open doorway, wearing one of his shirts.

'Whatever's the matter? What's up?' She took a step towards him, frowning.

'Nothing. Sorry, Sheila. They were just some visitors. It was about some business.'

'It took long enough. You were ages.' She took a further quick step towards him. 'Peter,' she said, reaching out a hand. 'Who were they? You look like a survivor of a plane crash.'

'I feel like one.'

He looked at her for a moment in silence. He had known her a long time. Since before he met Penny. They slept together sometimes, when it turned out that way. Mostly they were very good old friends. He grinned at her. 'Let's go and make some fresh coffee. I'll tell you about it.'

Seated at the kitchen table with fresh mugs of coffee in front of them, he told her everything. Sheila sat listening raptly. At the mention of Barbara a frown passed momentarily across her face, but her journalist's curiosity quickly got the better of any feeling of jealousy.

'But, Peter,' she asked, when he had finished, 'why *you*?'

He shrugged. 'I speak Polish. That's pretty unusual for a Brit. I go there often, so from that point of view I'm inconspicuous. I need the money.'

'Who doesn't?' she interjected.

He gave a sour laugh. 'M'mm, I know. Everyone. The only thing is, they have enough on me to wipe out my career. They must have been nursing those pictures, waiting till they needed me.'

'But are they genuine? The photographs I mean? Did you really bribe that man? Just like that? Handing over piles of money?'

By way of an answer, he made a wry face and spread his hands.

'Peter!' He was surprised by a rising note of admiration in her voice. 'How exciting.' She reached out and touched his arm. 'And the girl. Does she mean a lot to you?'

He nodded slowly, wondering how much to tell her. He had met Barbara nearly three years earlier. She had not been hard to meet. She had been seated at the hotel bar, examining the ice cubes melting in the bottom of her glass. Dressed more demurely than the other girls, she was the only one who did not flash him a garish smile. That was why he had chosen to talk to her. They had spent that night together. Then on subsequent visits, ten or fifteen times a year, they had spent increasing amounts of time together until...what? He tried to pin down the moment when the turning point had come and found he did not know.

'Yes, Sheila, she does.'

'Since when? You've never mentioned her.'

'A while now. I've never mentioned her to anyone. Nobody knows. Except,' he added harshly, 'those two bastards who were just here.'

'If you agreed to do what they're asking, would it be difficult?'

'It depends. Up to now, the most illicit thing I ever brought out was a jar of black market caviare. And even that made me sweat. Carrying the sort of stuff they are asking for, I'd probably crap myself. Customs officers are trained to notice things like that.'

Sheila laughed. 'I guess they are. Anyway how important is this man, Kodec? Do you know any background on him?'

He shook his head. 'No, not a thing. Nor on the organization those two characters work for. In fact I was wondering...'

'Uh-huh,' Sheila intervened, laughing. 'You were wondering if I could help you with a little research.'

56

He returned her laugh. 'Well, since you mention it...' He became abruptly serious again. 'Could you, Sheila, please? I'd like to see everything you could dig out on Kodec. And on the Foundation. Its backers, its aims, its history. Everything.'

'By 10.30 tomorrow, of course.'

He began to reply, not noticing the faint irony in her voice.

'Hold it a moment.' She held up a hand. 'I've got an article to finish by noon tomorrow. I'll do it, but by Tuesday. I'll have it for you Tuesday afternoon, okay?'

He smiled and patted her hand. 'Thanks, Sheila, Tuesday will do fine.'

'Good. Now, I have a favour to ask you.' Her face had become grave. She took his hand in hers.

'Sure', he said leaning earnestly across the table, 'what is it?'

'Take me to bed,' she whispered. 'Now.'

Mason looked at his watch and gave a soft grunt of satisfaction. He would just make the 8.15 flight. Pulling his coat and briefcase from the back seat, he locked the car and strode across the covered catwalk to the terminal.

The concourse was moderately busy, mostly with businessmen like himself. Mason bought a one-way ticket to Zurich. The soberly dressed man behind him smiled an apology at the girl behind the desk, turned away without buying a ticket, and sauntered upstairs to the departure lounge and across to a row of telephones.

Ninety minutes later, Mason alighted into the antiseptic hush of Zurich airport, walked unchallenged through customs and took the direct train to Zurich's main railway station. He buttoned his coat, breathed deeply, relishing the cold, crystal air, and set off briskly along the Bahnhofstrasse. Ten minutes later he was being ushered into the presence of Herr Frisch, the manager of the small, discreet bank he had been using for his business affairs for the past few years.

They exchanged a brief handshake and Frisch, a small, neat man, so clean-shaven his face shone, gestured Mason to a plain tubular steel and black canvas chair placed on one side of a wooden desk. Frisch sat opposite Mason and placed his forearms symmetrically on the desk, his fingertips grasping very lightly the two ends of his pencil.

'What is it I can do for you Mr Mason?' he enquired softly.

Mason drew from his briefcase a single handwritten sheet of paper and slid it across the empty desk.

In less than half an hour he emerged into the bright winter sunshine and began making his way back down the street. On the enclosed café terrace across from the bank, one of the several women with taut faces, discreet jewellery and the good fur coat that was practically camouflage on the Bahnhofstrasse in winter, dropped a few coins beside her half-empty coffee cup and followed, the click of her high heels drowned by the noise of the busy street.

Vienna airport had less of Zurich's church-like hush but was just as efficient. Mason took the bus into the city centre. From the terminal behind the Hilton he walked the few blocks into the heart of the old town to his favourite hotel, close to St Stephen's church.

Vienna is a quiet town. In no mood for the opera, he killed the evening with a meal in one of the restaurants that nestled in the labyrinth of narrow streets around the hotel. By 10.30 he was in bed.

Like the rest of the city he was up early the next morning. At eight o'clock he pushed through the frosted glass door of a bank. It was a non-descript building in an unremarkable street. Privately owned, they made no effort to attract a passing clientele, working almost exclusively with people who had received a personal introduction from an existing client. Among whom their discretion was legendary. In this they were helped by the Austrian banking laws which, if less well known than the Swiss, are equally draconian. He was the only client in the place.

He walked to a desk where a blonde young woman sat smiling with the wary politeness of somebody who thought he might be about to waste her time.

'Good morning. I should like to see Herr Eckard. My name is Mason. Peter Mason.'

The girl's expression did not change. 'Do you have an appointment, sir?'

'No. Please tell Herr Eckard that Herr Frisch recommended I speak to him. Herr Jochem Frisch, from Zurich.'

Looking unimpressed, the woman rose to her feet. 'Would you wait a moment, sir? I'll see if Herr Eckard is free.' She disappeared through an unmarked door. A short while later she returned. She smiled at him, committing herself this time.

'Would you like to come this way, Mr Mason?'

Half an hour later he pushed his way out through the glass door, possessor of two new, anonymous, and, as yet, empty, numbered Austrian bank accounts. He felt richer already.

He strode the short distance to the busy underground station and shopping complex close to the Opera. It was still the rush hour and he was obliged to wait for a few minutes before a telephone box was free. More from a habit of discretion than from any real idea that anybody cared he stood close to the phone as he dialled, concealing the number from any watching eyes. A familiar woman's voice came on the line.

'Herr Frisch, please.'

'Mr Mason?' He had never met the telephonist at the bank but she never failed to sound pleased to hear him.

'Yes. Good morning, Frau Stadtler.'

'Good morning. I'll connect you.'

After a few seconds silence he heard Frisch's voice.

'Herr Frisch? I have the numbers for you.' He drew a slip of paper from his breast pocket.

'Go ahead Mr Mason.'

He read two eleven-digit numbers from the paper.

Frisch repeated them back to him to ensure he had them correctly.

'Very well, Mr Mason. We shall do as you instruct. Good morning.'

Mason hung up, stood for half a second in deep thought and then turned and surrendered the booth cheerfully to a large lady with a fox-fur coat and a harrassed expression.

# 8

Mason was on his feet the moment the Austrian Airlines Boeing came to a final halt. Grabbing his briefcase, he pushed his way past passengers struggling into heavy coats and stepped out into the tunnel leading to the arrivals hall.

On the way to collect his car he stopped to call Sheila.

'Sheila? I'm back! Can I come over?'

She laughed. 'You mean have I got the stuff? Yes, I've got it. Not much, but something. It's interesting.'

'You're marvellous! See you in an hour or so.' He hung up.

Sheila opened the door so quickly when he rang that it was as though she had been standing behind it, waiting for him. They hugged and kissed each other quickly. He released her and walked ahead into the big cluttered double room that served as living room and study.

'Over here', Sheila said, indicating the trestle table that stood in the bay window, 'pull up a chair.'

He sat down beside her as she pushed aside the loose sheaves of paper to make a clear space on the desk.

'Here.'

He took the manilla envelope she proffered and shook

the contents onto the desk. Sheila pointed to two photocopies of newspaper clippings. One was annotated 8 June 1983, the other 4 September of the same year. Both were from the *Washington Post*. He read them. They were short articles, no more than fillers. They spoke of an organization being set up by a pair of American senators, Burley and Roach, to 'combat the spread of Socialistic propaganda by means of the obtaining and disseminating of truthful and neutral information on life within the Communist countries'. They claimed widespread support from committed Christians. Mason snorted softly. Senator Burley's name was known to him. He was a notorious nutcase from the Republican party's lunatic fringe with a long and laughable history of espousing right wing lost causes. He was currently eager to see the bombing of Nicaragua without further pussyfooting.

He read on. The second article shed light on the 'committed Christians' of the first. The main funding of the organization, now named the 'Freedom Foundation' came from the Church of the New Temple which existed in America, mainly on television, and was led by a television preacher, Reverend Tom Carswell. He was as crazy as Burley, but looked better on television. Lately there had been a lot of talk of his growing political ambition.

The rest of the material on the Foundation was essentially cuttings of speeches by one of the three leaders in which they referred to it. There was no reference to any specific achievement.

He turned to the material on Professor Kodec. There were several copies of papers he had given to various international symposia during the fifties. Some of them were in Russian which Mason read only very badly, some in Polish, and some in English. He looked them through. Even without his taking in the detail, his heart sank.

Pushing aside the scientific papers, he went on to newpaper cuttings. There were not many. Three, from Polish newspapers in the mid-fifties, eulogized about the work he was doing in Moscow, speaking in glowing terms of his increasing stature. One of them even praised, over a quarter-page, the Professor's gallant wartime record in the Polish army fighting alongside the Russians, and before that with the Ukrainian resistance. It was the record of a brave man, if it were true.

He finished the last newspaper article and turned to Sheila. She was watching him, her brows drawn together anxiously. Mason's face was sombre.

'Is it any use?'

He sighed, gathering the papers together and pushing them into the envelope. 'Yes, it is. Thanks.' He waved the envelope. 'Can I keep it?' he asked, standing up.

She got quickly to her feet. 'Of course. It's for you. Are you leaving?' She laid her hand on his arm, restraining him.

Surprised at the warmth of her manner, he stepped closer and looked down into her eyes. He shook his head. 'Sorry, Sheila.'

She nodded ruefully and dropped her hand. Briskly, she led him to the front door. 'Well,' she said, with an effort at irony, 'maybe you'll at least buy me dinner sometime, for my efforts.'

He turned to answer in the same bantering tone and saw that she was crying. Flinching, he held her gently to him. It took her only a few seconds to regain control.

'Sorry, Peter,' she said, with an attempt at a laugh. Then, her face quite earnest, 'Do you really care that much for her? Enough to do this?'

It was the same question he had been asking himself for the last three days.

'Thanks for everything, Sheila.' He kissed the top of her head and left the house.

The telephone was answered on the first ring.

'The Freedom Foundation.' It was the voice of a mature woman, harsh and faintly irritable, as though she thought answering the phone ought to be someone else's job.

'Mr Brooke, please.'

'Whom shall I say is speaking?'

'Peter Mason.' He was seated at the kitchen table. While he waited for Brooke to come on the line he sipped coffee. He grimaced. He had run out of coffee beans and reheated some left over from the previous night. It was lousy.

'Mr Mason.' Brooke's voice was friendly. 'I was waiting for your call. Have you thought over our proposition?'

'Yes. I have.'

There was a short pause, as though Brooke were expecting him to say more. 'Well?' he asked eventually. 'What's your answer?'

'No.'

Again there was a long silence. A soft click and a sudden ethereal quality on the line indicated that somebody had picked up an extension.

'Mr Mason,' Brooke said, weighing his words carefully, 'do you fully understand what you're saying? Is it possible that you think we are people that make idle threats? Have you fully realized what would happen to your business? More important, have you considered the future of the girl?' He paused. 'We are very serious people, you know.'

Mason pinched the flesh on the bridge of his nose. 'I know. If I didn't think so I wouldn't be phoning.'

'But are you refusing our proposal?' Brooke's voice was at once truculent and curious.

'Yes, I am.' He let the words lay for a fraction of a second. Then he added, 'As it stands.'

Brooke was guarded. 'What does that mean?'

'That we have to talk about it. I'll come and see you. This morning.' Mason spoke with matter-of-fact authority, sensing that he had Brooke off balance.

There was a silence on the line. It was a full five seconds before Brooke spoke again.

'Hello. Are you there? Good. Yes, Mr Mason, we think it would be a good idea if you could come in here.'

Mason glanced at his watch. 'I'll be there at eleven.' He put down the phone and allowed himself a grim smile.

63

The taxi wove through the snarled traffic of Marble Arch, made a couple of left turns, and stopped in front of a row of probably Georgian houses, set around the kind of railed-off garden to which the inhabitants would have the key. In the centre a deserted tennis court lay under a thin coating of old leaves from the big scaling plane trees that stood in the square.

Mason examined the small brass plates set by the door. Two were for doctors; the kind of doctors who have the latest *Country Life* on their waiting room tables. A very small plaque announced that the Freedom Foundation was on the third floor. A semi-circular table with spindly fluted legs stood against the wall of the hall, bearing a white vase filled with an enormous bouquet of fresh irises. Above the flowers hung a good print of a hunting scene.

He climbed through a thick undergrowth of carpet which ran out at the second floor. Reaching the third floor, he pushed open the door and entered a sparsely fitted-out waiting room. An overweight woman of around 30 sat at a desk that looked like the aftermath of an accident, typing on a typewriter that emerged like an iceberg from the surrounding sea of documents. She looked up.

'You must be Mr Mason, for Mr Brooke.' She sounded so authoritative he felt he might have been tempted to agree, even had he been the telephone repairman. She took up the phone and dialled a three-digit number as though she had just had an argument with the handset.

'Mr Mason is here, Mr Brooke.' She replaced the receiver. 'He's coming,' she said, her eyes already back on the sheet of paper in the typewriter. Mason smiled amiably and looked around for a seat. The only choice was deep in overspill from the desk. He drew a sharp breath, just to pass the time, and was aware of the sour aroma of body odour. Withdrawing to the far wall, he examined a calendar. As entertainment it would have to do. He had only got as far as checking the next four weeks for public holidays when Brooke entered through a door behind the receptionist. He stood holding the door open.

'Good morning, Mr Mason. Come in.'

Mason nodded and walked past Brooke. The office held an empty desk, two metal filing cabinets and four chairs covered in brown imitation leather. Mason tossed his raincoat onto one of the chairs and sat down. Brooke walked round and sat behind the desk. 'Mr Carroll will join us,' he said curtly.

Mason nodded agreement. 'Your receptionist is a treasure,' he said amiably. 'Where did you find her?'

'She serves our purpose,' Brooke replied flatly. 'We are not here to impress.'

'Of course not. You're here to bribe journalists. And, of course, to 'combat the spread of Socialist propaganda!'

'You've been doing your homework.'

The voice was Mr Carroll's. Mason looked around to see him entering through the door from the reception area. He jerked his head in greeting. 'Yes, I have,' he answered, looking back at Brooke who met his gaze levelly. 'You could have saved me some trouble if you had told me you were a bunch of neo-Fascist lunatics.'

Brooke's expression did not alter. 'Does it make any difference?' he asked with a cool sneer. 'After all, a man in your position seems ill-placed to assume any moral superiority, don't you think? Just what is it that gives you, a man who makes his living dealing with, for example, the Ceauşescu regime in Romania, a right to the moral high ground?'

It was a question that had been giving him trouble for a long time. He let it lie.

'You might not know it,' Carroll broke in, 'but the Reverend Carswell's church has over four million voluntary contributors. They do much good work.'

'And Hitler built terrific roads!' Mason retorted.

'He certainly did!'

He looked for a trace of humour in Brooke's face. None was there. Passing up the chance for a futile argument, he brought the conversation back to firmer ground. 'All right, Brooke. Let's agree that one set of madmen is much like another and it doesn't much matter who pays me. What do you know about Kodec?'

'We already told you his history on Sunday.'

Mason gave the two men a cold grin. 'Except that you left out an important detail.'

Brooke raised an eyebrow. 'What was that?'

'Kodec's field. Nuclear physics. You forgot to mention that he had worked in Sakharov's team, in the fifties. On the Soviet H-bomb.'

# 9

'Juanito!' Gregory bellowed, 'Come here! Quickly!'

Juan ran into the room, still pulling a shirt over his shoulders, his face anxious. 'What is it, Father?'

Gregory waved the paper he held in his hand. 'They have agreed! We must prepare to return to the city immediately.'

The Indian's face creased in a delighted laugh. 'That's wonderful! You see? It's just as I said. Poland is your country, after all. They are your own people. They couldn't refuse you.'

Gregory gave a soft snort of laughter. 'Perhaps, Juan. Perhaps not.' He shrugged. 'There will be a great deal to do here. They have allowed me a month. I may be gone for all of that time. Go and wake Miguel. There is much we must discuss before I leave.'

Juan ran to wake the other priest, Miguel, and the three of them sat at the work table to discuss the running of the mission during Gregory's absence. The two priests listened eagerly as Gregory detailed what needed to be done, firing questions every few seconds in their anxiety to have everything clear. Their enthusiasm contrasted with the tinge of sadness that had crept into Gregory's face.

Miguel looked across at him, his face clouded. 'What is it, Father? Have you more news of your father? Bad news?'

Gregory shook his head. 'No, Miguel. As far as I know my father is still the same.' His voice was melancholy. 'It is here, the mission, that I am thinking of now.'

'But, Father, you don't need to worry,' Juan broke in. 'Miguel and I can manage things. We always have, when you have been away.' He looked momentarily mortified. 'You have no reason to be displeased?'

Gregory snorted softly and touched Juan's arm. 'It isn't that.' He looked at each of the men in turn. 'No, what worries me now is what will happen here. The soldiers. Each time they become bolder. The war is going badly for them. It is making them more aggressive, more full of hate for everyone who they think is not on their side. Like us,' he added wearily. 'They hate us because they think we shelter their enemies.'

'But, Father, we do them no harm. We care for the sick, that is all.'

Gregory rubbed a hand across his face. 'I know, Miguel, I know. But for the soldiers it is not like that. You saw them last time they came, how they threatened?'

'But you resisted them, Father, and they went away.'

'Yes, Miguel, I resisted them. And I was afraid. For myself and for all our work here. You must have no delusions, we are protected only by the Prize and by the fame it brought us. I am afraid that when I am gone the soldiers may come again.'

'But, Father, you must go,' Juan said quietly. 'Your own father is dying. You cannot stay here.'

'No, Juan. I cannot stay.' Gregory stood up with a tired smile. 'Would you ask the sisters to gather in the clinic? I will speak to them before we leave.'

It was late afternoon by the time the Land Rover approached the shanty towns that signalled the outskirts of

San Salvador. The roads had been badly affected by the flooding that followed the torrential rains, and their passage through the roadblocks had been tedious.

A camouflage-painted jeep splashed at speed through the surface water to meet them. The officer seated next to the driver waved them down. He saluted formally.

'Good morning, Father,' he said with elaborate courtesy. 'Welcome to the city. We have the honour of escorting you to your destination.'

'Thank you, Captain, but we know the way,' Gregory answered. 'We are in no need of an escort.'

The Captain grinned ostentatiously. 'Ah, but you perhaps don't realize, Father, how dangerous the city has become. With terrorists everywhere, it's no longer safe to be on the streets, even here in San Salvador itself.' His tone became icy. 'We shall escort you to your destination.'

Gregory shrugged. 'As you like, Captain.' He turned to Juan. 'Let's go on.' Followed closely by the jeep, they drove to an elaborate mud-brick church with a neat wooden house beside it, the whole surrounded by a low fence, in a middle-class suburb of good adobe houses with tiled roofs.

A priest in early middle age came down the steps of the church to greet Gregory and Juan. Half an hour later Gregory was installed in a small room in the house and Juan in a somewhat bigger room at the rear of the church. The jeep with the soldiers lounging in it remained parked next to the Land Rover.

For some seconds after Mason had last spoken the only sound in Brooke's office was the muffled clacking of a typewriter from beyond the thick door.

'We told you he was a scientist,' Brooke said, at length.

Mason gave a short laugh. 'That's right. You just weren't specific,' he said, speaking very distinctly. 'The man worked on the Russian *bomb* programme. Have you considered what that means? Kodec may be a Polish citizen, but he's a Russian problem. Getting mixed up with a man like that could mean twenty years in the Gulag for me.'

Brooke nodded. He smoothed the dark hair back from a temple with the palm of his hand. 'About what it would mean for Miss Wisniewska if you refuse,' he said suavely.

Mason fought down an urge to hit the man. He had walked into the room with a plan. He could not allow their provocation to upset it.

'Look,' he said, leaning forward in his chair, 'you can forget about the girl. She's a nice girl, I like her a lot, but she's still a prostitute. I'd hate to see her go to gaol, but if she does...' He shrugged, leaving the sentence unfinished. 'What worries me is my own future. If I refuse, you've got enough on me to prevent me ever getting into Eastern Europe again. Or, worse still,' he grinned vivaciously, 'to prevent me getting out.'

The two men's eyes stayed unblinkingly on Mason's face. His palms began to sweat. 'On the other hand, if I accept, there's a fair chance I could end up in Siberia until well into the twenty-first century.'

'A remote chance, I should say,' Brooke interjected.

Mason smiled, 'If you like. But a chance all the same. I'm 39 years old. If I did get caught, I'd be an old man before I came back.'

'Mr Mason, what exactly are you driving at?'

'Money, Mr Brooke.'

Brooke's eyes flickered for an instant to Carroll's. 'What are we to understand by that?'

'Simply this,' Mason replied, leaning back in his chair and scanning the faces of the two men. 'I'll do what you want, but for double your figure. I want three hundred thousand.'

Brooke began to speak. 'You realize your situation. Your business career will be finished. The girl...'

Mason raised a restraining hand. 'Send the pictures to the Polish Embassy. Have the girl put away. As you like. I want three hundred thousand. Otherwise you find another candidate, and I'll find another career.' He looked from one to the other.

Brooke glanced at his colleague, who nodded imperceptibly. He stood up. 'Mr Mason, would you wait outside for a few moments, please?' He walked across to the door and opened it.

Mason got up briskly and left the room.

He had waited only four minutes before Brooke opened the door again.

'Come in, Mr Mason,' he said, forcing a smile.

Mason fought to keep the elation from his face. He knew he had them.

It took over an hour to hammer out the full details of their agreement. A third of the money would be paid to him before his departure, deposited into the Swiss bank whose address Mason gave them. The second part of the money would be paid over in the same way when he telexed to confirm that he had contacted Professor Kodec. They agreed on a phrase to be used in the telex to confirm this. At this time the negatives of the photographs of Barbara would be deposited at the bank. If for any reason he was unable to contact the Professor, or if he decided to abandon the project, Mason undertook to return the money. The last third would be paid on his return with the material.

In the event that he came out without documents bearing the Professor's signature, or film, or photocopies of them, he would also return the money, less five thousand pounds. He was to be the sole judge of success. He would bring what he could. If it were less than they were expecting, too bad. He would let Professor Kodec tell his story. If they did not like the story, it was their problem, not his.

'One last thing,' Mason said, looking at each of them in turn. 'What if I go to Poland, contact Kodec, send you the telex, and then disappear as soon as the negatives and second payment are at the bank?'

'You won't, Mr Mason, will you?' Brooke's tone was softly reasonable. 'You would have to return to London, or at least dispose of your house. The proceeds would be transmitted to you somewhere. You would contact your sister. We would employ people to look for you. They nearly always succeed, you know. It's very difficult to disappear completely. It wouldn't be worth it. Take the job if you want to, leave it if you don't. Fail, perhaps, but don't steal our money.'

He smiled at Mason. The smile would have stopped a nosebleed.

'Okay, Mr Brooke,' Mason responded laconically, 'we have a deal. When should I be ready to leave?'

Carroll answered. 'A week or ten days. By the way, would you like something like this to be made available over there?' As he spoke he drew from a drawer of the desk a bag of soft cloth, like a shoe-bag. He slid it across the desk.

With a quizzical look at Carroll, Mason loosened the draw string and tentatively pushed a hand into the bag. An instant later he snatched his hand away as though it contained a snake. With a shudder of anger, he thrust the bag away from him, sending it skidding heavily into Carroll's lap.

'You prick,' he said, contemptuously. 'You must be out of your mind. Do you have any idea of the penalties for carrying that in Poland?' Shaking his head, he turned to Brooke.

'Getting back to the Professor, how do I get in touch?'

Brooke took a manilla envelope from a drawer of his desk. 'You'll find it all in there. Look it over. Memorize it. On no account take any of it to Poland. Understand?'

Mason nodded. 'And the camera?'

'You'll be contacted when you arrive. It's all in there. Meanwhile get yourself a visa and relax for a few days.' Brooke rose and came round the desk. He put a thin white hand on Mason's shoulder and squeezed it in a gesture that was almost friendly. 'Call us if you've any questions.'

Mason looked at him sourly, as he too stood up. 'When can I expect the first payment?'

Brooke studied the tiny leaf of the aluminium calendar

folded around his watchstrap. 'The instruction will be telexed today. It should be on your account by Wednesday.'

He folded the envelope and pushed it into the pocket of his raincoat. To his mild surprise both men held out their hands. He briefly shook hands with them both, turned and walked quickly out of the room.

He said a cheerful goodbye to the receptionist. She kept her eyes determinedly on her typewriter, as though she thought he might be a flasher.

Back on the street he called a taxi. Only when he was out of sight of the building, did he allow himself a long, long sigh. It had worked. By Monday afternoon the first hundred thousand pounds would have arrived in Zurich. The same afternoon, through a series of unconnected transactions, it would have been transmitted to Vienna.

In Vienna it would have been transformed into German municipal interest bearing bonds. Half would be in the account in his name. Half would be in Barbara's.

# IO

It was precisely eight o'clock when Mrs Bujak ushered Gregory into the Consul's office. The Consul rose and greeted Gregory. His manner was an uneasy mixture of officiousness and deference. He indicated a heavy set man who sat next to him, perspiring slowly in a grey worsted suit. The man remained seated.

'This is Mr Kowalski,' the Consul began. His hands fluttered nervously in front of him. 'Mr Kowalski is from the Ministry of the Interior. He is here to talk to you about the, er, conditions, about the letter you received.' The Consul finished his last words in a rush, like a schoolboy finishing a recital, and made to sit down. Kowalski's voice froze him in an absurd half-seated posture.

'Perhaps you would leave us alone for a short while, Consul.'

Behind the civil words there was an authority that transfixed the Consul. In his ill-fitting clothes with his protruding wrists and nervous eyes he reminded Gregory of a frightened hare. After an instant of confusion he pushed himself upright and left the room, shepherding the quietly smiling Mrs Bujak busily in front of him.

Gregory was alone in front of the seated man. Kowalski's eyes travelled slowly from Gregory's tanned, sandal-clad feet up to the ferocious blue eyes. He silently returned his gaze.

'So you're Gregory Kozka,' the man said, almost to himself. 'You're bigger than I expected.'

Gregory stood quietly for a moment as both men took the measure of each other. Then, indicating a chair, said conversationally, 'Do you mind if I sit down?'

'Of course, of course,' Kowalski responded quickly, waving superciliously towards the chair. Gregory settled himself, crossed his legs, and waited.

Kowalski sat silently studying a typed sheet in front of him, ignoring Gregory. After a few seconds of silence he looked up and sat back suddenly in his chair.

'Well,' he said, his voice full of condescension, 'so you want to go to Poland.'

The man's mannerisms, so carefully calculated to assert his domination of the situation, were the same childish, wearying ones Gregory had seen so often before leaving Poland. He did not let it show.

'Yes,' he said simply. 'I do. As soon as possible.'

'H'mm.' Kowalski made a show of studying the paper again. 'It's your father, eh? A stroke. He seems to be very sick, from the medical reports.'

'I know. He's dying. That's why it's important I go quickly.'

The man made a clucking sound. 'So impatient, Mr Kozka.' He pronounced the word Mister with leaden emphasis. 'According to your dossier you were once just as impatient to leave.'

Gregory banished the anger that began to rise in him. He leant towards the man. 'Mr Kowalski, I repeat to you, my father is dying. He could die while we sit here arguing. Please, say what you have to say, ask me anything you have to ask me, but please don't waste time.'

Kowalski bridled angrily, stung by Gregory's directness. 'Waste time, Mr Kozka?' he said, flushing angrily. 'How much of our time has already been wasted on you?'

Gregory frowned. 'I don't understand you. What do you mean?'

Without speaking, the man opened a drawer and pulled out a small rectangular object. He threw it onto the desk. 'These, for instance,' he said, bitterly.

Gregory looked at the object and shrugged. 'Ah,' he muttered, 'the cassettes.'

'Yes,' Kowalski shouted, 'your damned cassettes!' His voice was choking with scarcely contained rage.

Gregory held up a hand. 'Mr Kowalski, how can I help it? You know how it is with Poland.' His eyes seared into the other man's face. 'I cannot help being Polish.'

Kowalski crashed a fist onto the desk and sprang to his feet. For the first time Gregory saw real hatred in the man's eyes.

'Polish?' he shouted. 'You call yourself Polish! You're all the same. You think of yourselves as patriots when all you have done is run away, to carp and criticize, and undermine the efforts of those who are trying to build something. Your very existence is a plague.' He was stalking the room, jabbing angrily at the air as he spoke. 'You encourage them. The Church, the priests, the saboteurs!'

Gregory was on his feet. 'Stop it!' His voice was resonant in the sparsely furnished room. It halted Kowalski in his tracks. 'Speak as you like of me, Mr Kowalski. But I will not hear you speak of the Church in that way. Nor of the priests.

The two men's eyes locked. 'Damn you,' Kowalski said, at length, his voice full of quiet venom. 'Damn all of your kind. You should all be made to pay for the trouble you bring.'

Gregory was silent for a moment. 'Some of us already have,' he said, simply.

The room became very still. The reference to the brutal killing of Father Popieluszko was clear. Kowalski looked strangely at Gregory, the way he might have looked at a tame bear that had suddenly opened his cheek with its claws. Gradually he felt the anger subside in him. He had been sent to do a job, as a trusted aide of the Minister. He must not let his own feelings interfere.

'Sit down,' he said brusquely, returning to his own chair.

Gregory watched him as he took his place, then sat down himself.

'As you will have supposed, Mr Kozka, your request caused a great deal of, shall I say, consternation in Warsaw. At the highest level,' he added, clumsily. 'There are many influential people who think it a mistake to allow you to return. A provocation.' Gregory's shoulders rose and fell imperceptibly. 'However, there were also those, those of us,' he added, promoting himself, 'who felt that humanitarian considerations outweighed the purely political ones. Your father, after all, had a distinguished war record. His resistance work was...'

'I know my father's record. Are you going to give me a visa?' Gregory interjected.

'His work was very valuable. Many of us felt that we, his compatriots, owed it to him to allow his son to be at his side.' Gregory moved impatiently. 'Fortunately we were able to overcome the very vocal opposition to our viewpoint.' He smiled indulgently. 'We were able to persuade them that a visa should be granted to you.'

Gregory opened his mouth to speak. Kowalski restrained him.

'Of course, there have to be certain conditions.' His

75

smile was tighter now.

'What conditions?'

Kowalski reached into a drawer and withdrew three typed sheets. The text was in Polish. He slid them across the desk towards Gregory.

'Read this, Mr Kozka. Very carefully.'

While Gregory read, Kowalski got up and walked across to the window. He stood gazing past the high wrought-iron fence surrounding the house to the street beyond. Dilapidated trunks and crippled hulks of ageing Buicks and Fords lurched over the broken asphalt. Occasionally a gleaming Oldsmobile or even a Cadillac passed. Most of those were driven by chauffeurs. He was watching one pick a fastidious path among the ruts and potholes when he heard Gregory exclaim. Languidly, he turned from the window, strolled back to the desk and sat down.

'Is something the matter?' he asked off-handedly.

'You know there is. I can't agree to these terms.'

'Oh,' Kowalski answered, negligently. 'Why not?'

Gregory threw the documents onto the desk. 'This amounts to virtual house arrest. No contact with anybody connected with the Church. No movement outside the village. No statements or contact with journalists, not even a telephone. And yet you want me to issue here a statement condemning the situation in Nicaragua, condoning the Contras, and their American backers.' He pushed the papers further from him. 'No, Mr Kowalski,' he said, 'I'm sorry.'

Kowalski scowled. 'What did you expect? I've already told you. A lot of powerful people don't want to see your face back in Poland ever. This offer is a concession, Mr Kozka, a generous concession.'

'I don't want your concessions, Mr Kowalski, I want my rights, as a Pole, not as a prisoner. If I come, it will be as a free man, not as a lackey of your people.'

'Understand one thing.' The voice was thick with sarcasm. 'You have no rights. Not in Poland. You want to be with your father. Those are the terms on which you may

76

do so.' He tapped an index finger on the sheets which lay between them. Then he sat back and looked at Gregory, resting his elbows on the arms of his chair and making a steeple of his fingers.

The two of them sat quite still for several seconds. Then, without a word, Gregory got to his feet. 'Goodbye, Mr Kowalski. God bless you.' He turned and strode towards the door.

Kowalski, startled, dropped his hands to the desk. 'But where are you going? What...?' The door closed behind Gregory.

For an instant Kowalski sat stunned, looking blankly at the door. It had just slammed on his career. Recovering himself, he bounded to his feet, knocking over his chair in his haste, and rushed to the door. He caught up with Gregory just as he finished saying goodbye to Mrs Bujak and the Consul.

'Mister, er, Father Kozka. I think you may have misunderstood me.' He smiled ingratiatingly, including Mrs Bujak and the Consul in a conspiratorial expression, and placed an arm over his shoulder. 'Please step back into the office. I'm sure we can come to an understanding.' Gregory shrugged off the man's arm and returned silently to the inner office. He waited until Kowalski had righted his chair and sat down before he spoke.

'Before you say any more, Mr Kowalski, let me tell you again, I will not agree to your terms.'

'But surely you can make a public statement on Nicaragua.' Kowalski sounded sulky. 'You've done so many times.'

'And will do again. But not at your behest. I speak out where I feel I must, Mr Kowalski. You have badly miscalculated if you think me at the beck and call of governments. Especially your own.'

Kowalski nodded. 'And the other points. Surely you must understand that we must have certain undertakings from you, given your possible influence?'

Gregory nodded. 'Of course. There are some things I

can promise. I am not anxious to go to Poland to stir up trouble. I want to do whatever I can to help my father die happy, Mr Kowalski. That is my only goal.'

Kowalski nodded and drew a large notepad laboriously from a drawer. 'Let us discuss it, in detail,' he said wearily, unscrewing the cap from a gold fountain pen.

It was over an hour before Kowalski put down his pen. He looked over his notes, reading them out as he went. He looked beneath his brows at Gregory.

'Is that a fair summary of what we have agreed?'

Gregory smiled. 'Yes, it is.'

Kowalski nodded and picked up the telephone. He pressed a button set above the dial. 'Mrs Bujak. Would you come in please?'

When she entered he handed her the notepad. 'Would you type these, please? We need an original and two copies. Quickly, please.' She smiled, two-thirds to Gregory, one-third at Kowalski, and left the room.

'Now that is all settled, how soon can I leave?' Gregory asked.

'On Monday. We have reserved a flight for you, at the government's expense.'

'That's not necessary. I have funds to pay my own way.'

Kowalski shook his head. 'Please. You are a guest of the government. A distinguished one,' he added with a renewed flavour of bitterness in his voice.

Gregory inclined his head. 'Thank you. What time is the flight?'

'Two o'clock. The Consul's car will take you to the airport. It will call for you at 11.30. Mrs Bujak has the address where you can be found?'

'I'll give it to her.'

For another twenty minutes they made desultory conversation, until Mrs Bujak returned with the newly typed pages.

Kowalski read each page quickly, signed and passed it to

Gregory, who also read it through before signing in his turn.

Finally Kowalski separated one set of copies and handed it to Gregory. 'You had better have this. Leave your passport with Mrs Bujak. The chauffeur will bring it, with the visa, on Monday.'

Gregory stood up. 'Goodbye, Mr Kowalski. Thank you. And God bless you again.' He turned and left the room.


# II


'Taxi.'

The driver swerved to a halt. He watched without curiosity as Mason clambered awkwardly into the rear of the cab impeded by the plastic bags of fruit he carried in addition to his small travelling bag.

'Heathrow.'

The cab pulled away smoothly. Normally he took his own car to the airport. Today he had decided to leave it at home. If he was gone for twenty years the parking charges would be terrible.

As the taxi cut through the West London streets he found himself avidly taking in the commonplace Sunday morning scene. People in search of newspapers strode quickly, muffled against the biting east wind that had driven away the recent cloud, leaving a perfect washed blue sky. A father, laughing, bundled two small children, clutching tiny ice skates, into the back of his car.

Mason was suddenly aware that his heart was pounding. This was a routine journey, one he had done a thousand times. Only now did it come home to him that he might never do it again. With the thought came the first fluttering of fear. On a sudden whim he turned and studied the sparse traffic behind them. There was nothing unusual. A half-dozen non-descript cars, a blue transit van, a motorcyclist, goggled and masked against the icy wind. With a shake of his head he turned back to face the front. He laughed at himself. Paranoid before he even got to the airport.

The plane was full. A sudden scent of tangerines reminded him why. Poles from among the millions settled in Britain were converging on Poland for their Christmas visits, bringing the gifts of chocolate, fruit, coffee and a hundred other items that would make so much difference to their relatives.

Mason sat back and unfolded a copy of the *Sunday Times*. Gregory Kozka's return to Poland on a private visit was a second-page feature. The article was accompanied by a portrait taken at the time of his Nobel Peace Prize. The face was intelligent and fierce. He scanned the article. It added nothing to what he already knew.

He was about to turn the page when he became aware of the bulky woman next to him craning closer. With a smile he surrendered the paper and took up another section. The woman drew back, flushing crimson, but allowed the paper to be pressed upon her. She began avidly and laboriously reading the article. A few minutes later she tapped Mason's elbow. He smiled and held out a hand for the paper. Blushing again she made a scissoring motion with two fingers and looked appealingly into his face. He laughed and nodded. Very carefully, she tore the picture of Gregory from the page and slipped it into her bag.

After the depressingly meagre lunch Mason slept. He awoke suddenly, alerted by the change in the engine note. They were descending. In a few more minutes they would be landing in Warsaw.

The arrivals building was bitterly cold, a result of the government's draconian energy conservation programme. Mason was the only one perspiring. The queue edged forward.

The passport officer stared hard at Mason as he opened his passport. He laid it down out of sight and appeared to study a list. Mason could feel sweat collecting in one eyebrow. He did not dare flick it away. The officer looked up again, fixing him with an unemotional stare. He stared back, unblinking.

The officer handed back the passport and Mason stepped through the pivoting barrier and into the customs hall. He stood still for a moment, fighting to subdue a violent twitching in his thigh muscles.

After a few seconds, he walked to the money exchange desk, queued briefly to change £200 and turned towards the customs control. He selected the queue which looked least like a group of evicted squatters, and took his place in the line.

The customs officer was a well groomed young woman. Mason handed over his passport and currency declaration. He watched her face intently, trying to detect any alteration in her smile. She kept her eyes on his currency declaration as she asked him the routine questions. She noted his heavy sheepskin coat on the declaration. As she wrote he reached into one of his plastic bags and palmed an orange. He slipped it from the bag and held it towards her, discreetly cupped in his palm. She did not appear to notice. He waggled his hand, claiming her attention. Brusquely, she pushed his hand aside, returned his passport and waved him away.

He snatched his bags and pushed his way dry-mouthed towards the door leading to the airport concourse. It was almost a ritual. Everyone gave them fruit. Several people before him had done so. His glance flickered around the crowded hall, studying the mêlée, looking for something unusual. A passenger in no hurry to get to the customs, a cleaner sweeping the same area twice. All he saw was the crush of passengers, porters and officials, all intent on their own business. He pushed his way through the heavy door and out onto the teeming concourse. The door swung shut behind him with a crash. Like the door of a cell.

Ignoring the freelance taxi drivers promoting themselves with jangling car keys and the black marketeers muttering polyglot offers to change money, he made his way through the dense crowd. Despite his racing thoughts he noticed that several people, including one of the black marketeers, wore lapel badges with a tiny portrait of Kozka staring out from them.

Barbara stood, as usual, by the door, aloof from the crowd. She wore a dark blue woollen coat with a silver-fox collar drawn close around her throat. Her shiny dark hair was completely hidden by a matching fox-fur hat. She wore knee-length black boots and no make-up at all.

The sight of her produced a tightening in Mason's chest that was almost choking. Letting his bags fall to the filthy floor he folded her in his arms. Their kiss lasted a long time. When at last he drew back his head to look into her face, both of them looked a little shocked.

'My God,' she muttered hoarsely, 'Let's get away from here.'

He drew a deep breath and nodded. Snatching his bags from the floor, he walked quickly from the building and across the windswept open space separating it from the car park. Barbara trotted awkwardly half a step behind, hardly able to match his pace.

They piled into her tiny car. Barbara was panting. 'Peter, what's up? What...?' Her next words were muffled as he pressed his lips against hers once again, holding her head between his hands. She was still panting when he released her.

'Let's go, Barbara. Quickly, please.'

She looked quickly at him, pondering a question. Then she turned the key and shoved the car into gear. Thirty seconds later they were on the road to Warsaw.

Barbara drove as though she were in a fairground, rarely changing out of third gear. Usually it amused him to watch her, her rapt expression and the unrelenting grasp of the gearstick, as though at some time in the past it had flown off and she were determined it would never happen again. Now his attention was on the rear window. He watched steadily as they drew away from the airport. Not until they were passing the grim squat buildings of the army barracks, a kilometre from the airport, without a car appearing did he relax and settle in his seat.

It took him a while before he realized what was amiss. 'Barbara,' he said, 'what's wrong? How come there's so little traffic? A football match?' A televised game could empty the streets anywhere in Eastern Europe.

She did not take her eyes off the road. 'Petrol.'

'Eh?'

'Petrol rationing.'

He laughed. 'Come on, Barbara. There's been rationing for years. It's never made much difference before. This is Poland. Everyone's got his friendly pump attendant.'

'We still have,' she said. A note of bitterness made him look sharply at her. 'Only they can't help. They've put militiamen on every petrol station. You can get it only with your coupons.'

'Wasn't it always supposed to be that way?'

'Sure. Except for the militiamen. But now they tell us it's a real crisis. Before, you could always count on a friend having some official coupons. A doctor. Someone. Now they're issued at work. Your name and identity card number is on them.'

Mason gave a low whistle. 'They *are* serious. Is it only petrol?'

She took her eyes off the road long enough to give him a look tinged with pity. 'Of course not! It's everything. Now the power cuts have started again. On Tuesday and Friday we were working in coats and gloves. Can you imagine, a telephonist in gloves?' She laughed. 'I didn't put a call through right all day.'

He smiled. 'How are people reacting?'

Her face became grave. 'They're angry, Peter. The promises have gone on for so long.'

'Has there been any trouble?'

'In the north, I hear. Up around Gdansk.'

He grimaced. It was where trouble usually began. In 1970. And again in 1980.

'The same old story,' he murmured.

'Isn't it?' She gave him a look he had never seen before. It held anger and frustration, and a hint of panic. 'Peter, I'm so sick of it.' The last words were spoken with so much pent-up emotion they came out almost as a hiss.

He reached forward and covered her hand with his. 'Has it got that bad?'

'It's unbearable. You can see it in people's faces.' She tightened her grip on the wheel. 'Oh, Peter, everyone's so tired of them. Of their lives. For years it was bad harvests, then it was the Western banks' fault for daring to ask us to repay our loans. Now they're coming on television blaming the power cuts on the weather. In Poland! They're surprised by winter!' She laughed abruptly.

Mason stared at the road ahead. She had used the word 'they' the way Poles had used it for centuries, sometimes speaking of Germans, sometimes of Russians, always of oppressors. Now it meant an amalgam of something that was Polish and yet not truly of Poland, and something that was wholly Russian. An axis of power that lay like an iron yoke between Warsaw and Moscow. She was speaking again.

'Is there any hope, Peter? Do you think it will ever change? We were so hopeful only a few years ago.'

'So was I,' he answered without looking at her. 'In the Gierek years, before it all went bad.'

She gave another short laugh. 'The Gierek years!' she echoed contemptuously. 'That was all an illusion. Where do you think all these people, Jaruzelski and the rest, were during the Gierek years?' She knew that he knew. She told him, anyway, to get it out of her system. 'Working for Gierek! Running ministries! Devising the policies they are now telling us they are just the people to correct!' This time her laugh was rich and unstrained. 'The absurd part is, they probably believe it. After all, in the world they live in there's no shortage of toilet paper, no need to be on the street an hour after they start work looking for cigarettes.

They haven't bought petrol for years. They ride around in chauffeured cars.'

He laughed, as she drew the car to a stop outside the hotel. Leaving his bags in the car he strode the few steps across the wide pavement and into the reception. The spacious hall was almost deserted. He walked quickly across the marble expanse towards the desk. He scrutinized the desk clerk's greeting, looking for nuances. He was relieved to find it the same as ever, full of insincere cordiality as she handed over his room key. Mason slid it back over the desk and turned to rejoin Barbara. The system demanded only that you be registered in the right place. It did not matter where you slept.

Fifteen minutes later Barbara closed the door of the flat behind them. She turned from the door and in the same instant was folded close in Mason's arms. They kissed eagerly, without preliminary, biting deep into each other's mouths as though seeking some deep and secret flavour that they could not live another moment without. Her hat fell to the floor.

With his mouth still locked on Barbara's, the kiss making his senses spin, Mason reached with fumbling authority for the buttons of her coat. The heavy garment slid with a sound like a sigh to the floor around her feet. Barbara's hands clawed at his spine and neck.

Made clumsy by the awesome force of his need, he could not find the hook fastening of the simple woollen dress. Hardly knowing what he was doing, he took the neck of the dress in his hand and ripped the cloth downwards. Barbara arched her body, allowing the garment to fall over her hips and gather at her ankles.

Mason lowered his head and in a tender frenzy began biting and kissing the skin above her breasts. Her response was to thrust her hips closer against him and knead her fingers harder at the back of his neck and into his hair. One of her legs twined around his, giving her leverage to thrust against him.

Barbara, her face turned upwards as she clung to him,

85

was uttering panting groans, incredulous and pleading. Flexing his knees, he bent lower until his mouth closed over the soft cloth of her brassière. His teeth and tongue probed and flickered over the taut cloth. Freeing a hand from behind her he unclipped the hook of the brassière and drew the strap from her left shoulder, uncovering one breast. He thrust forward, forcing as much as possible of the yielding flesh into his mouth. He hurled the brassière away from him across the room.

Clutching her close to him, his hands gripping tightly beneath the tops of her thighs, he carried her towards the bed. Barbara tore at his shirt, baring his chest. Almost stumbling in his haste, he laid her on the low, hard sofa-bed. He pulled off her boots and quickly threw off his own clothes. Barbara lay shaking her head and moaning, urging him to hurry.

Naked, he knelt on the floor beside her, bent low and began to blanket her body with kisses. At the same time, with a kind of careful brutality he pulled her last remaining garment, a pair of simple white cotton panties, over her buttocks and slid them over her pale legs.

He began licking the skin that stretched from her navel to the glossy chestnut sheen of her pubic hair.

'No,' she called hoarsely. 'Quickly.' And snatching at his hair she pulled him onto her.

Later Mason lay on one elbow and looked down at Barbara, laughing and shaking his head in disbelief. Their lovemaking had always been good. Today it had been utterly awesome. He bowed his head and kissed her, very softly, on the lips. He had no words.

Through the rest of the day they made love often. With less fire now but with a newly discovered need and tenderness that made them both laugh in sheer wonder. It was as though some last invisible barrier had fallen.

They ate dinner sitting on the floor and watching television. They drank vodka and laughed at the news, laughter being the only defence against the solemn catalogue of distortions. After dinner they carried the

86

vodka back to the dishevelled bed.

Many times that night as they lay entwined, murmuring softly, he wanted to ask her about the photographs, about her plan to leave. Above all, he wanted to know what she planned to do when she left. Each time he held back. It had to be her choice.

Surprisingly, she spoke frequently of the visit of Gregory Kozka. Nobody knew exactly when he was due: the official media had given the visit almost no attention. The rumour, however, was strong that his arrival was imminent.

Although, like most Poles, Barbara had been brought up a Catholic, he knew she had never attached importance to the Church. Yet now her excitement was palpable. It was plain that, religious or not, Barbara saw this man as a focus of hope. Someone who represented something essentially, purely Polish.

Each time he visited the cramped bathroom he looked at the photographs pinned behind the door of the flat. The dark hair grew low on the wide forehead. Thick black brows shadowed eyes which, even in the photograph, were an astonishingly piercing blue. The rugged, broken crest of the big nose towered over a wide, faintly cruel mouth.

Even from the picture it was easy to see the charisma that had brought congregations to their feet all over the world.

It was nearly noon when they awoke. Barbara called her office to report a phantom indisposition, managing to repel Mason's efforts to make her giggle into the telephone. They breakfasted on the remains of the previous night's dinner. At two o'clock Barbara dressed and left the flat in search of food. While she was out Mason tore a clean sheet of paper from a notepad in his case. Seating himself at the kitchen table he began writing.

## 12

'Breakfast, Father?'

Gregory awoke with a start and was immediately aware of a sharp pain in his neck. In sleep his head had slumped from the headrest and hung awkwardly on his left shoulder. Massaging his neck, he asked, 'When do we land?'

The chief cabin attendant, the only person who had been permitted to attend to Gregory, looked at his watch. 'In about two hours, sir.' The insolence of the slight pause before that last word was unmistakable. They had chosen the crew carefully.

Gregory hauled himself upright in his seat, and accepted breakfast. He drank off the canned orange juice, grimacing at the acid taste, and placed the empty glass on the seat next to him. He had plenty of room. Only two other passengers shared the compartment. They were both athletic young men, clean-shaven and well dressed, who sat on either side of the gangway where the heavy curtain separated first class from the tourist cabin. On the one occasion a passenger had tried to come through from the other cabin, ostensibly to use the toilets but probably for a closer look at Gregory, one of the men had sprung nimbly to his feet and blocked the woman's path, using the quietly authoritative manner no Pole could mistake. Gregory had understood and made no effort to penetrate the rear of the aircraft.

His efforts to engage the men in conversation had been met with monosyllables and he had abandoned the attempt shortly after take-off. For the last ten or twelve hours his only conversation had been with the surly steward.

Unknown to Gregory, the flight deck crew had all been back to look at him while he slept. The silent intervention of Gregory's two fellow passengers had ensured that they ventured no more than a quick glance at their celebrated passenger.

By the time the steward came to clear away the breakfast tray the faint popping in Gregory's ears told him they had begun their descent. He moved to the window seat, eager for a first view of Poland, but nothing was visible except the featureless grey of the heavy cloud. Then, quite abruptly, the cloud parted to reveal a landscape of fields interspersed with dark green stands of pines. Grey-white remnants of snow lay in the folds of the terrain.

Gregory's rib-cage tightened and he craned towards the scratched perspex of the window, avidly taking in the details of the landscape beneath him, watching as the shabby farmhouses grew more distinct, following with his eye the sinuous traces of the country roads. He pressed his face still closer to the window, cupping his hand around his eyes to minimize the reflection. His heart pounded. In the six years since his last brief visit his reaction had not been tempered.

They dropped fast now. He could see the figures of drivers at the wheels of their trucks. Cars were parked along both sides of the streets, far more cars than he remembered from his previous visit. They passed over another stretch of pines, and then they were on the ground, speeding along the concrete.

The aircraft drew to a halt far from the low airport building. Even before the motors had died, two black limousines and a shoal of uniformed men on motorcycles sped up to the plane and drew to a halt.

Behind him Gregory heard the clamour of the passengers in the tourist section preparing to disembark. A sudden announcement from the intercom stilled the noise. It instructed everybody to remain in their seats until told to disembark. A few loud protests were soon staunched.

Gregory shivered in a sudden rush of air as the door swung open. Two soldiers and two men in civilian clothes strode through the narrow entrance and stopped in front of him.

'Father Gregory Kozka?' The speaker, one of the men in

civilian clothes, spoke the words like an accusation.

'Yes,' Gregory said courteously.

'May I see your documents?'

He handed his passport, together with a letter, to the man. The official opened the passport and glowered at it. He looked several times from the document to Gregory. Then he read the letter which bore the letterhead of the Consulate. Satisfied that he was not dealing with an imposter, he handed back the documents and took a short step back.

'This way, please,' he said abruptly.

Gregory gathered his belongings and walked past the officials to the door.

Standing in the doorway, he did not feel the bitter wind that snatched at his thin, unsuitable clothes. For several moments he did not even take in the uniformed men that waited, looking blankly up at him, around the black cars. He was aware only that he was once again in Poland, his mind full of rushing images of the past.

A hand placed firmly in his back brought him back to the present.

'Quickly, please. We must go.'

Still gazing around at the flat, grey landscape Gregory slowly descended the steps.

A uniformed militiaman held open the rear door of the second of the two cars. Another took his bag. Gregory put a hand on top of the open door and prepared to get into the car. Pausing, he looked hard at the uniformed men, the motorcycles, the cars with their opaque windows. Without a word he walked quickly across to the first car. He threw open the front passenger door and stooped to look inside. Four men sat there, their faces turned dumbly towards him. In the far rear corner of the dark interior he recognized the sullen features of Kowalski.

He turned and walked back to his own car. With an acid smile at the men who still stood holding the door open, he got in. He was at their mercy. Only now would he find out what the government's promises were worth. He leaned back in his seat as the procession began speeding away from the aircraft. Through the dark glass which made late evening of the already dull day, he watched a bus draw up to the plane and the first passengers spill eagerly onto the steps, where they stood watching the disappearing convoy.

# 13

It was still dark when Mason awoke on the Tuesday morning. He groped for his watch. It showed 6.30. Taking care not to wake Barbara he slipped from bed and padded soundlessly to the bathroom. He examined his face in the chipped mirror. It showed no enthusiasm for the start of what might be the most crucial day of his life.

He was standing by the bed pulling on his coat by the time Barbara woke. He watched her reach out for him, encounter only space in the bed and sit up with a start. He sat down on the edge of the bed as she blinked at him, struggling to focus in the diffuse half-light. 'You're leaving?' she asked in a fogged voice. He nodded. 'But it's early,' she protested in a stronger tone, arching to see the clock.

He bent and kissed her very gently on the forehead. 'I know. I've got a big day ahead.' He settled closer and took her hand in his. 'Look, Barbara,' he said, pulling an envelope from an inside pocket, 'there's something I have to do today.' He paused, searching for words that would not alarm her. 'It might get me into some trouble.'

Despite the lightness of his tone, Barbara tensed and leant closer, studying his face. 'What are you talking about?' she demanded, hoarsely. 'What is it?' She gripped his arm. 'Tell me, please. What is it you're doing?'

He shook his head. 'I can't. It's just something I've

agreed to do. A business arrangement.' He stood up abruptly, thrusting the envelope at her. 'Here. Take this. If you don't hear from me in four days, read it. Memorize what's in it and then destroy it.'

The muscles of her face worked as though she were going to laugh. He spoke again. 'I'm sorry, Barbara, I mean it. You must do as I say. You must.' Bending suddenly, he kissed her hard on the mouth. Then he turned, picked up his bag and strode to the door.

He walked the distance to the hotel, glad of the air and the exercise after the last two days. In the crowded streets he noticed a fair sprinkling of people wearing lapel badges from which Kozka's portrait stared out.

In the hotel lobby he was surprised to hear a few of the people in Western clothes speaking Polish. Surprised until he noticed that one or two of them also wore these lapel badges. Private visit or not, it looked as though some people had come to Warsaw to savour the occasion.

The young man at the reception desk, the one he knew as Janusz, pulled Mason's room key from its cubby hole together with a cheap envelope, and handed them over.

Once in his room he opened the envelope quickly. A message was scrawled in blurred blue pencil on a single half-sheet of paper. It was simply the names of two streets which intersected a few blocks from the hotel and beneath them a time, 10.30, and a date, December 5. Today.

It was 8.15. He called room service and ordered coffee for three and ham and eggs for one.

At twenty-past ten Mason stood by a shuttered ice-cream stand watching his breath condense in front of him. The deep collar of his coat was turned up around his ears and his hands were pushed deep into his pockets. His feet were already cold. He stamped and moved his weight from foot to foot. He had been standing for twenty minutes before he heard a quiet voice behind him.

'Mr Mason?' He began to turn towards the speaker. 'No, Mr Mason, don't turn around, please. In a few seconds I shall fold my newspaper and walk away from here. Wait until I cross the road. Wait for the next pedestrian light and follow me. Don't get too close. I won't let you lose me.' The voice fell silent. Mason continued to stamp gently, his shoulders hunched.

He heard the rustle of a newspaper behind him and a man in a tightly belted blue nylon parka and a checked woollen cap stepped past him and walked to the nearby traffic light. He crossed the road as the light turned and entered a clothing store. Mason waited for the next opportunity to cross. As the light changed again he set off after the man. As he did so his contact emerged from the clothing store and turned away down a side-street, walking briskly but without hurry. Mason followed, keeping a twenty-yard distance. After two or three turns down further grim side streets he saw the man turn between two buildings and disappear. Mason arrived at the gap and turned. Concrete bollards blocked the gap to traffic. Beyond the buildings lay a cul-de-sac, the exit from which headed away from the street he had just left. Anyone following him in a car would have had to make a long detour.

The man in the parka was waving to Mason from the seat of a filthy pick-up truck with a small crane mounted on the back. Mason walked quickly over to the pick-up and slid in beside him. The driver let the clutch in sharply and the truck catapulted out of the cul-de-sac into the nearby deserted street. The man he had followed, who now sat sandwiched between the driver and Mason, half turned to face him and held out a hand. Mason shook it.

'Hello, Mr Mason, welcome. I'm sorry,' he added, glancing around the cab, 'about the transport. Frankly at the moment a private car would be a little conspicuous.' He spread a hand, indicating the road ahead, empty but for a cruising car bearing the familiar MILITIA sign on its roof.

'Don't apologize for the truck,' Mason answered amiably. 'Just tell me who you are and what you've got for me.' He turned to glance uneasily through the rear window. 'I don't want to stay in this thing any longer than I have to.'

'My name is Marek, Mr Mason, I'm a friend of Mr Brooke.' He indicated the driver, a huge man with immense hands, grey hair cut short above the eroded gristle of tiny ears, and two thick creases in the back of his thick neck. 'And this is Stan.' He driver turned to grin briefly at Mason, revealing a black gap between chipped teeth.

The names corresponded to Brooke's information. 'And what does Stan do for a living?' It was a password he had been given. He felt slightly foolish putting the question.

Stan replied. His voice was hoarse and high-pitched. 'I used to be an engineer on the ferries to Sweden.' Mason nodded. It was the right answer. The man looked more like a strip-club bouncer than an engineer.

'You have something for me, I believe. From Brooke.'

The other man nodded, lighting a cigarette. He offered one to Mason, who refused. He inhaled deeply before reaching laboriously beneath his parka and pulling a manilla envelope, half an inch thick, from an interior pocket. He held it out for Mason to take.

The envelope was surprisingly heavy. Mason hefted it in his left hand.

'Open it,' the man called Marek urged him. Only the eyes showed urgency in his placid face.

He split the end of the envelope with a forefinger and plunged a hand inside. He pulled out a small package, wrapped in cheap tissue-paper, and two sheets of paper. One, in Polish, was a letter, addressed to Professor Kodec. He scanned it quickly. It was a letter of introduction. The other sheet had on it an address, a telephone number and some instructions. Mason dropped the papers into his lap and begun unwrapping the other package. It contained a small camera and several small rolls of film. He turned the camera over in his palm, nodded and jammed it, together with the film, into the pocket of his coat. He placed the papers in his jacket and turned to find the eager eyes of Marek still on him.

'Okay,' said Mason softly. 'That's all I was expecting.' He switched his gaze to the driver. 'Stop here, I'll get out.'

Without acknowledging Mason's words the driver checked his rearview mirror, indicated, and carefully pulled the truck into the kerb, attracting no attention.

Mason shook hands with Marek and reached across to offer his hand to the driver. The big man kept both hands on the wheel and only turned to give him another quick, stained grin. Mason shrugged and got out of the truck. He watched it slot between two big delivery trucks and disappear around a wide curve. His hands in his pockets, one of them around the camera, he turned and began walking back to the hotel.

The crowd thickened as he approached the town centre. He passed in front of the three main department stores. The banners in their windows vaunting the achievements of the Party were mocked by the absence of merchandise. As he walked, he became aware that there were more uniforms on the street than usual. Militiamen stood in groups of two or three, talking quietly and stamping their heavily booted feet in a reflex attempt to ward off the cold. He noticed two cars, each with four militiamen, parked unobtrusively in a row of vans and lorries in front of the stores. Another car idled past in the slow lane. None of the policemen gave him a second glance.

In his room, he threw his coat onto the bed, which had been undisturbed since his arrival in the country, and sat down at the dressing table with the camera and the papers.

He examined the camera, and felt an urge to laugh. It was a Minox: the classic cloak and dagger spy camera. He wondered if he should start to feel mysterious. So far he only felt a little ridiculous. He opened the camera and inserted one of the tiny rolls of film. Holding the camera in front of him, he squinted through the viewfinder and took a shot of his own reflection. Satisfied that the thing worked, he put it aside.

Next, he scanned the letter. It was handwritten and he had some difficulty deciphering the Polish. Addressed simply to 'Dear Wiescek', it explained only that Mason had been sent to collect anything that he wanted to give him, that he could be trusted and that he would ensure that anything handed over would be transmitted to the West. It was signed 'Tadeusz'. Mason wondered if Tadeusz was one of the people he had met. It made no difference to his job. He laid the letter next to the camera.

The next item, the sheet of instructions and the address, he studied with more interest. The address was a place Mason had never heard of. Only when he read the instructions did he discover it was a village in the Tatra mountains in the south of Poland, a few kilometres from the ski resort of Zakopane. He was advised to fly to Zakopane and then to rent a car, the only alternative transport to the village being a daily bus. Exact details of how to get to the Professor's house were included. On the back of the sheet a pencil sketchmap showed the layout of the village. The last words on the sheet advised him to arrive in the evening.

He walked to the window of the overheated room and stared out over the bare expanse of the square in front of him. A detachment of soldiers goose-stepped across it, from the squat barracks which formed one side of the square, to the monument to the Unknown Warrior with its eternal flame which stood on the opposite side. He ran his fingernails through the hair over one ear. It was the square where the Pope had addressed a crowd of nearly half a million people a couple of years previously. He flicked a scrap of dandruff from his lapel. It was the square where trouble inevitably started.

He turned from the window. It was time to contact Professor Kodec. He replaced the camera and papers in his pocket, gave his collar a final dusting, and left the room. At the cashier's desk he changed a hundred-zlotych note for coins.

Ignoring the shouts of the taxi drivers lounging against

their cars, he walked away from the hotel to a tram stop. He boarded the first tram and rode it for a few stops until it came to a square that looked large and busy enough for his purpose. He stepped down from the tram and began looking for a telephone box.

The second box he tried, a hundred and fifty yards from the tram stop, appeared to be working. He pulled the door closed and spilled the coins he had collected from the hotel cashier on the chipped, black laminate of the shelf in front of him. He spread the sheet of paper, looked once at the number, his lips moving as he repeated it to himself, and dialled. Listening to it ring he noticed his palm was damp with sweat. He wiped it on the soft fleece of his lapel.

'Hello.' It was a woman's voice.

'Professor Kodec, please.'

'Professor Kodec can't come to the telephone. Who's speaking, please?' The voice was polite but carried unmistakable authority.

'I'm a friend of Professor Kodec. Could I speak to him, please? Just for a moment,' he added, persuasively.

'No, you can't speak to him. He is unable to come to the telephone.' There was steel in the voice now. 'Can I give Professor Kodec any message?'

There was a pause while Mason considered his next move. He held the receiver away from him and looked hard at the mouthpiece, as though he could see the woman. Deciding there was nothing to be gained by further fencing, he put the receiver back to his mouth and spoke again.

'Yes, you can. Would you please tell the Professor that Mr Mason called. Peter Mason. Is there a convenient –?'

The woman's voice cut him short.

'Mr Mason? We've been expecting your call. Would you hold on for just a moment, please. I just have to put the telephone down.'

'Uh-huh. Go ahead. I'll hold on.' He leaned back against the wall of the cabin. Through the grimy glass made half-opaque by a sudden burst of sunlight on the dirt, he watched the street. Most of the passers-by were women and children. Such men as there were were mostly elderly. Almost all carried shopping bags. After about twenty seconds he heard a clattering sound and then the voice again in the earpiece.

'I'm sorry to keep you, Mr Mason. I'm afraid my father is unwell and unable to speak to you. However, you may speak freely to me. I'm the Professor's daughter.'

'Oh, I see. Good morning.' He cleared his throat. 'Miss Kodecka,' he began, using the feminine form of the family name, 'I'm calling from Warsaw. I would like to come down to see you to – er – talk to the Professor.' He paused.

'When would you like to come? Today?'

Slightly surprised, he glanced at his watch. It was nearly one o'clock. 'I could try. It depends whether I can get a seat on a flight. If there is a flight.'

'There is,' she said firmly. 'At 5.30.'

'How about a hotel? Is there one close to you?'

'Zakopane. Book into a hotel there and hire a car. Don't leave it too late. It gets very cold up here at night and the roads can become very difficult.'

'Fine. Goodbye, Miss Kodecka, I'll see you this evening, I hope.'

He strode the short distance back to the square. Two taxis stood empty at a rank. Mason slid into the rear seat of the first.

'The Victoria Hotel.'

The cab driver responded with a surly nod and started the car. Mason tried not to catch the eye of the driver, who was sizing him up in his rearview mirror. Mason knew the routine. The cabbie had scented a Westerner. He would open the proceedings with a comment on the hardness of the times. As though not to disappoint Mason he spoke, half over his shoulder, commenting on the petrol shortage.

'You don't seem to be having any trouble,' Mason replied.

The cab driver did a double-take. 'You speak Polish?'

He concurred and they rapidly established that he was

98

anxious neither to change money nor buy caviare. The formalities over, Mason put a few questions to the driver. He was told what everyone in Poland knew, that the shortages were entirely due to the Russians taking food from Poland to compensate for their own shortfalls. The driver was planning to share a few other views he held of everything Russian when they were stopped behind a row of cars and trucks held up by a militiaman. The driver sat hammering the wheel and grumbling softly. Mason looked around. They were close to the department stores again. At the roadside stood a line of militiamen, all holding batons.

The people crowding the pavements looked only mildly curious, indifferent to a show of force that had become all too familiar.

Suddenly, Mason was aware of the braying rhythm of an approaching siren. Twisting in the seat to look through the rear window he caught sight of a flashing blue light, gaining rapidly in intensity as it approached. As he watched, two cars, surrounded on all sides by motorcycle outriders, sped into view along the deserted left hand side of the wide road, all their headlights blazing.

Mason cursed softly at the delay. 'Who's that?' he asked aloud. 'The First Secretary on his way to lunch?'

There was no response from the driver. Following the progress of the approaching cars, Mason turned until he was facing the front. The sight that met him brought him bolt upright in his seat.

From the cars drawn up around them several people had got out and were now kneeling on the wet, greasy tarmac, crossing themselves. As the speeding motorcade advanced Mason watched in astonishment as people in the crowd, at first a few, then in swelling numbers, dropped to their knees. It was as though an invisible force tracked the procession like a wind, pushing people to the ground.

The militiamen and a few lone individuals remained standing, isolated rocks uncovered by a receding tide. Some of the militiamen shifted uneasily.

Watching the scene from the edge of his seat Mason's

astonishment gradually gave way to realization. 'Well, I'm damned,' he said softly, in English, 'Kozka!'

As the convoy receded into the distance the crowd began slowly rising to its feet. The militiaman, glad to be once again immersed in a situation he could control, officiously waved the traffic back into movement. His peevish gestures brought the taxi driver back from his own reverie. Mutely, he slipped the car into gear and continued towards the hotel.

At the hotel Mason had the taxi driver wait. He shared the lift up to his room with a short, swarthy man with his shirt open to the fourth button, displaying a lot of gold and the upper reaches of a paunch. On each arm he had more gold and a simpering blonde. The girls tried to catch Mason's eye. They seemed to be inviting him to a party. It was the wrong time, the wrong place, and the wrong people. Especially the wrong people. He gave them a wry smile and walked quickly to his room, leaving the Arab looking complacent and the frolicking girls a shade disappointed.

Seating himself at the combined writing desk and dressing table, he took out from a drawer the last piece of hotel notepaper. On it, in block capitals he wrote a single-line message. He added the telex number he had memorized while still in London and added his name and room number. Taking the paper in one hand and his bag in the other, he returned to the lobby.

He walked round the reception desk to the alcove where the telex operator sat examining an incoming telex and a chipped fingernail with impartial absorption. He called her over and handed her the message. In the same hand he held two dollars, folded small, but still clearly visible to her highly trained eye.

'It's to go immediately,' he said, half question, half instruction.

She cocked her head and cursorily checked the message. 'Certainly, Mr Mason, right now.'

He eased the hold on the two dollars. With negligent

expertise she plucked them from his palm and tucked them out of sight beneath the counter.

Within fifteen minutes the message would be with Brooke. Within twenty-four hours the message from Frisch would arrive confirming that the second payment and the negatives had been handed over.

He returned to the taxi where the driver dozed at the wheel. He started awake as Mason opened the door. 'Where to now, sir?'

'The airport,' he answered to the eyes that looked at him in the rear view mirror, domestic.'

# 14

Night was falling as the high-winged Antonov began its shuddering descent towards the tiny airport serving Zakopane. The weather had turned as they flew south and for the last twenty minutes they had been tossed and buffeted in dense grey stormclouds which obscured both sky and earth. At the front of the aircraft somebody was being noisily sick.

Mason sat with his eyes closed, keeping his breathing deep and even, trying to fight back his own nausea, until he felt the aircraft bounce heavily onto the runway. Only then did he open his eyes and let the tension flow from his body. The chill of the air as the door was opened reminded him that his face was damp with perspiration. If he succeeded in what he had come for there would be no more such flights. He collected his bag from the rack and followed the handful of other passengers down the steps and out into a stinging sleet. Hunched against the bitter wind he strode through the deserted airport building, to where two dilapidated taxis waited.

He drove to the newest hotel in town, a two storey motel-type structure, built only a couple of years before but deteriorating fast. The receptionists were also agents for the Polish State car rental company.

He approached the dark girl who stood behind the desk. At that season he did not expect her to be short of cars. Nevertheless, he wore a winning smile as he told her what he wanted. After a quick flip through a file she picked up a key on a plastic tag and laid it on the desk. She drew out a form and started to fill it in.

'Do you have a room for me, for two, maybe three nights?'

Still writing she pushed out her lower lip and shook her head slowly. 'Sorry.'

'No? You're kidding. Here?' He gestured, taking in the whole building. 'You must have a room.'

Still shaking her head, she looked up. When she caught his gaze she nodded very gently at a place beside her, a spot Mason could not see.

Craning gingerly forward, as though he were expecting some kind of a practical joke, he peered behind the desk. There, in a leatherette frame, about four inches by three inches, stood a picture of Father Gregory. He rocked back on his heels and stood looking at the girl, surprise filling his face.

'He's staying here?' He looked incredulously at the tacky furniture of the lobby.

She laughed. 'No, of course not. But many people have come here, hoping to see him.'

'See him? Here?' Again his eyes swept the seedy lobby. The woman pouted, offended. He regretted his tone.

'He's in Poland on a visit.'

'I know. I saw him this afternoon, in Warsaw.'

She reached excitedly across the counter and grasped his sleeve. 'You saw him? You actually saw him?' Her eyes shone. He liked the feel of her hand on his arm. Blushing slightly, she removed it.

'Well no, not really, I saw the motorcade he was in.' He

thought for a moment of the reverence of the kneeling crowd.

The girl looked at him, a little lost, waiting for an explanation. When he finished telling her about the afternoon's incident she was gazing at him with eyes aglow. Mason was taken a little aback by her readiness to be impressed. Feeling like a groupie, he spoke again. 'But what *is* he doing around here? Why would the hotel be full?'

'He's from near here. This is a private visit. He first became a priest in a village very near to Zakopane. That's why we're fully booked. People have travelled from all over Poland, from abroad even, to be near and to see him.' She was suddenly serious. 'He means a great deal to us, you know. You can't really know how important it is for us, what,' she hesitated, seeking a word, 'what courage his coming here gives us.'

'Perhaps I can,' he answered softly. He picked up the keys of the car, breaking the serious mood. 'Do you want to show it to me?'

The paper he had been given in Warsaw lay on the seat beside him, next to an unfolded road map. He had intended trying to memorize the directions on the plane. He had even begun doing it, until queasiness got the upper hand. Now he was forced to leave the interior light on a lot of the time.

Driving with the light on in the filthy weather was hard going. The road was narrow and twisting. It wound through steep wooded mountains, past an occasional isolated house. He did not pass through anything he would have called a village until he had been driving forty minutes. Not a person stirred on the street. Who could blame them? The sleet had turned now to driving snow, laying a fresh covering on the already snow-clad hillsides. It was the kind of night when even werewolves would stay home and watch television. Even Polish television.

After nearly an hour without seeing another car he came

to a crossroads. To his left stood an abandoned barn. Apart from its darkened windows the dilapidated building did not really look much different to some of the houses he had seen on the way. He stopped the car and leant over to look at the paper. The crossroads and barn were mentioned. Following the instructions, he now turned left. The track was invisible under the new snow. He kept on it by following the electricity cable looped on poles along the roadside, aiming from one post to the next, not looking beyond. The snow fell quickly now, hungrily filling the tracks of his tyres as he passed. He began to feel like the last man on the planet.

He had gone about a kilometre along the track when he saw lights ahead of him. He stopped the car again and took up the sheet of paper. This was the village. He read carefully through the last of the directions. He wanted to arrive as unobtrusively as possible. Satisfied that this, at least, he had memorized, he dropped the sheet of paper onto the seat and drove on.

The outlying houses were scruffy, ramshackle places, set in roughly fenced gardens. The rotting carcase of a van lay on its side in one of the gardens, snow tumbling in through the empty window spaces. As he drove on, the houses were closer together until finally there was a row of shops. The shops had an empty, abandoned look, as though they were up for sale. In fact, he guessed, they were the only shops for ten kilometres around.

Beyond the shops, the street widened into a small square in which stood three or four cars, snow piled high on and around them. They had not moved for days. The right side of the square was a substantial dark brick building, the local party headquarters. A banner two feet deep and fifteen feet long sagged across the gap between the two first floor windows. He read it. It said everything was getting better.

He turned right past the building. A hundred yards further the road ran out and he was bouncing and slithering along a track that seemed to have been designed to remove sumps. He eased along in second gear past a pair of cottages. Fifty yards further, he was in front of a larger house surrounded by a high, dense hedge, and around the hedge a white fence, in good repair. The wide gates stood open. He turned in and stopped the car. He had not seen a soul since he left Zakopane.

Two wooden steps led up to the front door of the two-storey clapboard house. On each side of the door were windows, their curtains drawn. As Mason climbed laboriously from the car, stiff from his drive, the front door opened, spilling light across the snowy ground. The figure of a woman stood in the doorway.

'Good evening, Mr Mason.' Without waiting for his answer she continued with the traditional Polish greeting. '*Witam*. Welcome.'

'Good evening,' Mason replied, advancing over the fresh snow. 'Miss Kodecka?'

She held out her hand, her face still in shadow. 'Yes, Mr Mason. I am Helena, the Professor's daughter. Come in, please.'

As she spoke they shook hands. She stepped back from the threshold into the lighted hallway, inviting Mason to pass her. He followed her into the house. The warmth of the interior enveloped him like the glow from a shot of brandy. A faint odour of medication hung in the air, bringing a childhood memory of his father's long illness flooding Mason's mind.

'Can I take your coat, Mr Mason?' she asked, rather formally.

He shucked off the heavy sheepskin and handed it to the woman, who hung the coat in the cupboard among several other winter overcoats. He gazed with unconcealed interest around the hall. Everything was of honey-coloured pine: floor, ceiling, walls, even the four-lamp chandelier. At picture rail height along one wall, and up the broad staircase, were fixed a rank of antlers, each trophy mounted on a small wooden shield and bearing a plastic plaque showing a place and a date. The dates were distant.

Somebody in the family had been a hunter. He doubted if it were Helena. She looked like a librarian. He studied her.

Although he knew her to be in her mid-thirties, she could have been 40. Her severely cropped black hair was tinged with grey, and she was slender, almost gaunt. Behind round tortoiseshell glasses, deep crowsfeet were etched around her eyes. Her clothes were simple but stylish, a heavy dark green wool skirt and brown polo-neck sweater in a soft-looking wool. The only jewellery she wore was a silver neckchain with a small pendant of silver and amber. Her shoes were flat-heeled with a chestnut sheen.

Still formal, she showed him into a sitting room. The room was comfortably furnished with a big sofa, two armchairs, unmatched, and some splendid antiques. A fine writing desk caught his eye. One of the things he was pleased to have inherited from Penny was a taste for good furniture. Helena caught the direction of his gaze.

'It's nice, isn't it? My father is a keen collector. Or used to be,' she added.

Mason caught the sudden note of bitterness in her voice. He looked at her, frowning slightly. 'Used to be?'

'Before he – before he was sent away. In the fifties you could find marvellous things in Poland. Many people were leaving and were selling what they had. Many things were smuggled out, of course.' She sighed. 'So much that is good has left the country. Good things, good people. Sometimes I think even good feelings.'

Her despondency troubled him. He fumbled for the letter he carried in his pocket. 'Here, Miss Kodecka.'

'Helena,' she broke in.

'Helena. Here is a letter you ought to read.' He shrugged apologetically and gave her a quick grin. 'It confirms who I am. And why I'm here.'

She took it and put it onto a table beside her, hardly glancing at it. 'I know who you are. I know why you're here.' She spoke with surprising emphasis, not looking at him. Mason felt the grin fade from his face in slow stages. She spoke again, abruptly changing the subject.

'Would you like a drink? Some tea? Alcohol? I can offer you whisky, vodka, brandy. No coffee, I'm afraid. The local shop sold out. Three weeks ago.' She gave Mason a taut smile. He read the tension in it. The woman was at the end of her tether.

'A vodka would be fine. With mineral water, if you have it.'

She looked back at him, silent, her eyebrows raised, as if she felt vaguely sorry for him. He got the implication.

'Plain tap water will do fine.'

She nodded and left the room. Mason stood up and examined the contents of the sitting room. He began with the writing desk. It was a fine piece, he guessed late eighteenth-century. The walnut surfaces were unmarked. He looked at a framed photograph standing on the desk. It pictured a powerful tall man with a high forehead and a pipe in his mouth and one arm around the shoulders of a much shorter, dark woman dressed in a short-sleeved spotted dress. The man held a little girl of about five in the crook of his other arm. The adults smiled at the camera, the little girl looked up at her father, laughing. In the cheekbones and eyes of the woman Mason could see the resemblance to the adult Helena. He toured the room quickly, admiring several fine pieces. Everywhere in the room lay books. They were in Polish, German and English. Two or three were in Russian. Several were obviously being read at once.

He liked the room. It was comfortable and welcoming. A room that invited you to relax with a book and a drink. Helena's home was strangely at odds with the bitterness that was apparent in her.

He picked up a novel that lay open on a stool by one of the deep armchairs. It was a fairly recently published book by an American living in England. Mason had read it, but he never expected that anyone else had. He still held the book in his hand as Helena re-entered the room. She carried a tray holding two drinks, a jug of water and a large plate of tiny open sandwiches.

Helena handed him his drink. He took it from her and splashed water into it. She set the tray down on the stool from which Mason had taken the book and motioned him to sit down. He sat, still holding the book. He waved it.

'Are you reading this?' She nodded, sipping her drink. 'Enjoying it?' he added.

'Mm-hmm.' She nodded again. 'It's not bad. Interesting. Not entertaining, but interesting. Have you read it?' She looked ready to be surprised.

'Last week, as a matter of fact.' He paused. 'We're probably the only two people that have read it, apart from the man's family. How did you come by it?'

'I have a friend in England. A Pole. She left here many years ago but we keep in touch. She sends me books.'

'Like this? What's she trying to do, depress you?'

She smiled. 'No. She knows my tastes, though. Maybe it's something to do with being Slav, that we share a taste for the dark and depressing.'

'M'mm, still. This.' He let the book fall onto a table. 'I would have thought anyone living here could do without this. It makes Kafka seem positively frothy.'

'Don't worry,' she said, the note of bitterness returning, 'I'll learn nothing from it that makes things worse. For people in our position each day of our lives brings lessons enough.'

'I know it does,' he answered quickly, 'I have a lot of friends here. I've been watching what has been happening for a long time. I think I understand a lot of how people feel, as much as it's possible to without living here, anyway.'

'Really?' He was unsettled by a mocking note in her voice now. 'You understand us? You think you know how we feel?' She seemed to be deliberately making him uncomfortable.

'Not you, Helena, not individually. I mean how people in Poland feel, in general, about what's going on.'

'Ha! Yes. You know how we feel, in general.' She put heavy emphasis on the last two words. It seemed to Mason as though she were trying for a note of contempt, trying, even, to dislike him. It was puzzling. He hardly knew how to respond. At one moment she seemed on the brink of friendliness, the next instant she was spiky and distant. He decided to bring the conversation back to the main business of his visit. 'Helena, when can I meet your father?' The mention of this seemed to calm her. 'Is he here?'

She took a long gulp of her drink before she replied. 'Yes, he's here. He's always here. He's a very sick man, you know, unable to leave the house, or even to leave his room very much. You can meet him tomorrow. But only for a short while. He and I have agreed he will talk to you each day, in the morning, just until he begins to get tired. He tires very easily, you know. I have to watch him very carefully, to ensure he doesn't overdo things. I hope I can count on you to cooperate in that respect. You will remember, won't you? He is really very ill. He mustn't be excited. It could kill him.' Her voice broke as she ended.

Mason wanted to reach out and put a hand on her shoulders but held back, fearing another violent change of mood. Instead, he simply said, 'I'll remember.'

They sat in silence for a moment. When he thought she looked composed, he spoke again, his voice conversational.

'What do I do about sleeping? It seems late to be returning to Zakopane. As a matter of fact, the hotel was full already.'

She answered animatedly, suddenly aware of her role as hostess. 'We have prepared a room for you. You'll stay here, tonight. Any longer than that would mean we would have to register you with the police in the village. In the circumstances, we'd rather not do that.'

'It would seem a little, er, inappropriate, bearing in mind why I'm here,' he responded wryly. 'Although you wouldn't have to go to the police. Officially I'm still staying at the hotel in Warsaw. I haven't checked out.'

'But your business here could take several days. Surely

they'll notice you aren't actually sleeping there?'

'Well, no.' He looked slightly embarrassed. 'That is, yes they might, but I, er, I do it all the time. Not use the room, I mean.' He saw the pitying look behind her glasses.

'I see,' she said grimly. He knew what she saw. A rich foreigner arriving with a suitcase full of the latest fashions and a wallet full of dollars. He wanted to explain that Barbara was different, that he was different. He tried out on himself several ways of saying it. He decided any one of them would only get him into more trouble. He shrugged.

Helena continued, still tight-lipped. 'In that case I suppose the best solution is for you to stay here. You'll be our guest, for a few days. I hope you'll be able to stand the lonely nights,' she added with angry irony. 'Our hospitality has its limits.'

# 15

Mason sat up abruptly, spooked by the silence. He stared blankly around the room for several seconds before settling back with a sigh, realizing where he was. Light filtered dimly through the drawn curtains. He rolled over and looked at his watch where it lay on the floor beside the bed. It was a quarter to eight. He ran his tongue over his teeth and grimaced. He had forgotten to open the window.

He laughed at the irony. It had been one of his perennial small disputes with Penny. She wanted the window closed at night, he wanted it open. She won. It was a very small thing, until the day you could not stand it any more.

He clambered out from the white mound of the duvet, pulled on his trousers and padded to the bathroom Helena had shown him the night before.

Twenty minutes later he made his appearance in the

kitchen. His hair, still damp from the shower, was plastered flat, a tiny piece of toilet paper stuck on his jaw, staunching the blood from a cut. Helena looked up as he entered. She was dressed as she had been the previous evening, except that today her sweater was green, matching her skirt.

'Good morning,' she said, pleasantly. 'Did you sleep well?'

'M'mm.' He rubbed a fist in one eye. 'Too well. I'd forgotten how quiet it was up here in the mountains.'

Her interest quickened. 'You've been up here before?'

'Er, yes.' His open eye scanned the table. She caught the direction of his look.

'We'll have tea in the other room, if you don't mind. My father is already waiting for you.' She began loading the tray. 'Were you up here on business?'

'No, not really. Just for a weekend a few times.'

'Do you ski?'

'No,' he answered. 'I have a friend who does, though.'

'I see,' she said. Her tone had become icily prim, causing him to look at her sharply. She kept her eyes on the tea things.

He considered trying to explain to her that she did not see at all. That she did not know Barbara.

'Let's go in and see your father,' he said at length, disappointed. She nodded and led the way, silently carrying the tray.

Professor Kodec sat in one of the armchairs. He wore a thick, grey woollen cardigan, buttoned to the throat. A blanket was cast over his knees, concealing his legs and feet. His hair was sparse and white, and both his scalp and the backs of his thick hands were speckled with brown liver spots. Despite his obviously appalling health, he sat very erect in his chair and greeted Mason in a strong voice, extending a bony hand.

'Good morning, Mr Mason. Welcome. It's very kind of you to come so far, and in such weather.'

Mason wondered if the Professor knew about the three

hundred thousand.

'It's good to be here, Professor Kodec. It's a privilege to meet you.' He looked at the old man's fine bearing as he spoke. It was true, it was a privilege. The Professor motioned him into the opposite armchair and smiled a signal to his daughter. She advanced with the tray and handed first her father, and then Mason a glass of tea in a tarnished silver holder. The unspoken tenderness between father and daughter was palpable.

At another nod from her father, Helena left the room, flashing a look of warning to Mason as she went, that he should remember their agreement of the previous evening.

'So, Mr Mason, you've been sent to get my story from me.' He spoke in almost unaccented English. His exhausted eyes lit up at Mason's evident surprise. 'You seem surprised that I should speak English. After so long in the camps, perhaps. Well, let that be the first thing you learn from me, Mr Mason. Each evening those of us who spoke any foreign language would group together for a half hour to speak it. Monday evenings were English evenings, Wednesdays German. Before I went away I hardly spoke French, now I speak it rather well. Does it strike you as strange? It shouldn't. When one is in that situation, when things are as bad and hopeless as they can be it is vital to keep your own standards.' He paused, briefly, short of breath. He recovered, a hand on his chest, and continued. 'One must remain civilized, Mr Mason, apart from them.' He emphasized the last word.

'Who was there with you, Professor? Were they Poles?'

'Some of them. Mostly Russians. Several were Moslem activists from the Asian Republics. Very strange people,' he added thoughtfully, 'very difficult to know. We had a few Czechs, and, of course, some Estonians and Latvians. Perhaps you would think of them as Russians, Mr Mason, but I can assure you they wouldn't. They were the proudest people I have ever met, prouder,' he laughed, 'even than we Poles.'

Mason laughed with him. 'They must have given the

guards a hard time, Professor.'

'They did. We all did.' He paused, his eyes became distant. 'But the guards always had the last laugh. They have the principles of dogs and the power of gods. In the end they always have their revenge.' He appeared to be falling into a reverie. Mason brought him back to the purpose of their talk.

'Professor Kodec, if it isn't asking too much, I think we should begin going over the documents you have to show me. I shouldn't stay here longer than necessary.'

'No, no. Exactly,' the Professor agreed, starting slightly. He reached laboriously down to pick up an attaché case that stood beside his chair and hauled it onto his lap. He flipped open the two spring locks, his hands shaking a little, and lifted a few handwritten sheets from the case. He held them out to Mason who stood up and took two paces across the room to take them from the Professor. He stood in front of Kodec examining the sheets. He recognized the smudged and blotchy blue imprint of cheap ballpoints. In spite of the poor-quality impression the sheets were quite readable. The handwriting was small and neat. He wondered if it was Kodec's or his daughter's. The Professor told him.

'Helena wrote it, of course. You see my hands.' He held a hand out in front of him. Mason watched it tremble. 'I can hardly write at all these days.'

'Well, as long as you have Helena, Professor,' said Mason, still scanning the sheets. 'She's a wonderful daughter.' Tapping a finger briskly on the sheaf of papers, he looked at the old man. 'How much of it is there? How many pages?' His voice was businesslike.

The Professor gestured towards the open case. 'There's this. And some more in Helena's room. I don't know. Maybe two hundred pages, in all.'

Mason whistled softly. He was certainly not going to risk taking out a couple of hundred pages concealed in underwear. He was not certain that he had enough film to photograph all of it.

'Is it all of equal importance or can we discard some of it?'

'Of course, some would be more important, some less. We would need to go through it.'

Mason stepped over to a straight-backed wooden chair by the door, set it by the Professor's elbow, and sat down.

'Let's start,' he said, with quiet purpose.

Their first session lasted nearly an hour before the Professor began to show signs of fatigue. As if on a signal, Helena came into the room. Ignoring Mason, she knelt beside her father, setting the blanket more securely around him. She lay her own slender hand over his bony one.

'You're cold, father, it's time to rest now.' She pulled the blanket up, covering his frail hands and stood up, turning to Mason. She jerked her head sideways.

'It's time to stop now, Peter. My father must not overtire himself. That will be all the disturbance he can be allowed for today.' Giving him no chance to respond, she shepherded him, papers in hand, from the room. As soon as the door had closed behind them she turned to him, her eyes flashing angrily. 'I told you not to stay too long. Couldn't you see how tired he was? Do you want to kill him?'

Mason recoiled. 'I'm sorry Helena, we were engrossed in the papers. Both of us. He wanted to go on. He is terribly anxious for the whole story to get out.'

Her anger dissipated as quickly as it had flared.

'I know, Peter. It's not your fault. He forgets how weak he is. He is such a proud man, so determined to see the thing through. But he is so sick. I worry about him so much.' She broke into sudden sobs. 'Oh, Peter, it's so difficult. We're so alone.'

He put an arm lightly across her shoulders and they walked together to the kitchen. He wanted to be consoling, to sympathize, but even as she cried, there was a rigidity, a capacity for anger with him or with herself, that kept him silent.

As before when her moods had troubled him, he turned

to concrete matters. 'Look, Helena, I know all of this is upsetting for you, but I really don't have too much time. I need to start work on photographing this.' He indicated the papers he carried. 'Is there anywhere I can work? Somewhere with good light?'

'You can use my father's study. He doesn't use it now. I'll show you.'

She led him from the kitchen to a small cluttered study, containing a desk, a swivel chair and books. Books were everywhere. Every inch of wall was lined with bookshelves and books lay in drifts, like autumn leaves, on every surface. The desk faced a tall window. The grey light filtering through the heavy overcast matched the Professor's sweater. It was depressing and inadequate for his needs. He switched on the old-fashioned metal desk lamp. With a stronger bulb it would do.

For the next two hours he sat alone in the study, carefully photographing the pages. It was tedious work which could not be hurried. In many places the writing was so faint he was obliged to trace over it with his own pen to ensure that it would show on the photographs. Anxious to finish as he was, he often found himself compelled to read passages from the extraordinary testimonial in front of him. Provided he managed to get it out, its value in the hands of Brooke's people would be immense.

He was disturbed by Helena calling him to lunch. They ate together at the kitchen table. For much of the meal she scarcely spoke. She ate without appetite, plucking nervously at the oilcloth table covering. After a few desultory attempts at conversation, he too fell into silence. He watched her brows knit, as though she were wrestling with a problem that writhed inside her.

Despite his impatience with her flakiness, he tried to understand what was going on in her head. It was natural enough that she should be worried. Her father was a very ill man. He was conspiring to send out of the country information that Mason imagined could get him sent back to the camps, desperately sick as he was. She would certainly go to prison herself. Of course, she must be worried sick about these things.

He bit into one of the unattractive apples from a small bowl. Munching nonchalantly on the apple he spoke, his voice muffled. 'Can I see your father again after lunch?'

She started at the sound of his voice. 'I'll have to see how he feels but I think so, yes. If he agrees.'

Mason glanced at his watch. It was close to two o'clock.

'Say at 3.00? Would that be all right? I need most of another hour to finish off the stuff I already have.'

She nodded, still distracted. 'Yes, I'll have to check that he feels up to it. You made him very tired this morning,' she added, waspishly.

'Look,' he told her wearily, 'I'm sorry. We both got carried away this morning. I promise I won't do it again. Why don't you come and sit with us if you're that worried? Then you can throw me out as soon as you think your father's had enough.' He was becoming impatient and could hear the note of sarcasm in his own voice. 'How would that be?' he went on, more gently. He smiled. 'Maybe you could throw a cloth over me, like a parrot.'

She answered him with a wan smile. He did not mind, it had been a wan joke. At least it was better than the agonized frowns he had been growing used to.

She stood up. 'Okay. You get back to work, Peter, and I'll go and talk to my father.'

For another hour he worked on the documents. Many of the sheets were on cheap, thin paper and he was obliged to place blank paper, taken from the Professor's desk, beneath them in order to get the contrast the camera needed. He heard a tap on the door, followed by Helena's voice calling him softly. Together, they went to join her father, who sat in the same chair as in the morning, with the same proud, erect posture. A small foil sheet containing several tiny round pills lay on the small table beside him, together with a glass of water.

Professor Kodec opened the attaché case on his lap and

withdrew a sheaf of papers a half inch thick and they recommenced their interview of the morning. Helena's presence acted as a warning both to Mason and to her father, and Mason's questioning was more gentle than it had been during the morning session. It was well over an hour and a half before the Professor's breath began to shorten and, by mutual consent, they adjourned for the day.

In the study the late afternoon light had faded too far to be of any use. He scoured the house with Helena, looking for further lamps to reinforce the single desk lamp. Taking the reading lamp from her own room and another from her father's bedroom and equipping them all with sixty-watt bulbs, he judged he had enough light. Provided the shades did not melt in the heat of the more powerful bulbs.

At 6.20 he lay down the camera and rubbed his eyes. Since he began that morning he had photographed over a hundred pages. He stacked the sheets neatly, rapping the edges against the desk to tidy the stack, and put them to one side. Yawning, he switched off the collection of lamps and left the study. He found Helena alone in the sitting room, seated in the chair her father had been in earlier. A log fire burned in the grate, casting the only light in the room. She gazed sightlessly into the fire, oblivious to Mason's entry. He watched, his hands in his pockets, as the firelight played on her face. It made her look younger, less severe. On the floor next to her chair lay an afghan coat and a fur hat. She looked up, sensing his presence.

'Oh, Peter.' He was surprised by a strange lassitude in her voice, a resignation he had not heard before. 'I was hoping you would come out. Sit down, please, I must talk to you.'

His hands still in his pockets, he sat down on the sofa, his legs splayed towards the fire. He wondered what this very strange and disturbing woman was about to impart. He hoped it would not depress him as much as it seemed to be depressing her. Turning his elbows out, his hands still hooked in his trouser pockets, he gave her a ready-for-anything shrug.

117

'Here I am.'

'I'm going out. You'll find some food in the kitchen.' So far, the news was less impressive than her tone had led him to expect. 'I expect to be back in about an hour, maybe a bit less.' She paused, apparently struggling for words. He felt his irritation rising to the surface again. Swallowing, she went on. 'The thing you have to know, Peter, is I won't be alone.' She paused again. Mason felt something he had previously only read about; his spine actually felt cold. He stared hard at her.

'What do you mean, Helena? Who are you bringing here?' His tone was harsh and urgent. He leant forward in his seat, fighting the fear that rose in him.

She was speaking in an urgent rush now. 'Peter, you know my father is very sick. He has very few friends. Many people he used to know are afraid of coming here, afraid of being associated with someone so dangerous. He is terribly lonely and depressed so much of the time. He has one friend, from near here, from before he was taken away, who has never forgotten him, who contacted him as soon as he came back from Russia. He's coming to see my father tonight. I'm going out to get him. Peter, the name of my father's friend is Gregory. The man you know as Father Gregory Kozka.'

# 16

There was absolute silence for several moments. Relief and incredulity mingled in Mason's face. His thoughts raced.

'Shit, Helena,' he said finally, in English, in a very low voice. 'Are you kidding me?' She shook her head. 'You can't be serious. Kozka coming here?' He gestured at the room. Her eyes rested steadily on his. 'But you are serious,' he said flatly letting his hand drop to his side.

'Yes, Peter, of course I am. Gregory and my father were very close, despite their age differences. Gregory had no brothers or sisters. My father was like an older brother to him. They used to ski together whenever they got the chance.' She glanced at the photograph on the desk. 'You can't see it now, but my father was a fine athlete, a wonderful skier. Gregory, too.'

Mason followed her glance to the picture. He looked again at the big, erect man standing proudly with his family. 'I can believe it,' he answered simply. Then, more brusquely, 'But look, Helena, I have to leave if Kozka is coming. I can't possibly stay. He must be surrounded by minders. There'll be police crawling all over the place.'

The irony of his situation almost made him laugh aloud. He had been chosen for the job precisely because he was able to move around the country without being conspicuous. And now he found himself helping to host a visit from a man who was currently the principal preoccupation not only of the Polish security services but of a large part of the outside world. He stood up.

'Sorry, Helena, I have to go.'

'No, no you don't,' she said standing and placing a restraining hand anxiously on his arm. 'You can stay here. You must realize, Peter, that there are certain understandings, on both sides, surrounding Gregory's visit. He has agreed not to show himself in public, not to address meetings, not to attract attention. In return they agreed to certain of his demands. One of them was to be allowed to visit us. Alone, without policemen at his heels.'

'They're ready to let him visit your father? A man who detests them so much?'

She laughed grimly. 'My father is too sick to worry them any more. Of course, Gregory has to be totally discreet. But as you saw for yourself yesterday, in this area, after dark, in winter, there are very few people around... Very few prying eyes. Except theirs, of course!' She almost spat the last words. 'No doubt they will want to know where he is. But they have agreed not to interfere. Even those people usually keep a bargain. In the long run it suits them to appear trustworthy.'

Mason sat down, shaking his head. He rubbed both hands over his face in a futile attempt to steady the racing thoughts. 'All right, Helena,' he said with a heave of his shoulders. 'What should I do? Stay out of sight, in my room?'

'No. Why? Perhaps when I return with Gregory my father and he would like a little time alone together. Until then why don't you stay here? My father will be down in a few minutes. He would be glad of your company. He's probably more nervous than you are.' Trying for a light note, she ended with a brief falsetto laugh with a sharp edge.

'Or you!' Mason thought, as he watched her jerkily gather her coat and hat from the floor. Aloud, he said, 'For Christ's sake, Helena, why don't I just stay upstairs out of sight? I can't just stroll down here and say hello to Gregory Kozka, as though we were old friends. Remember why I'm here, Helena, please. Your father and I are virtual strangers. You and I are not exactly –' he hesitated – 'pals, are we?'

Her face clouded at his words and she busied herself with adjusting her hat. 'No,' she murmured, 'it doesn't seem as if we are, exactly.' With an effort she brightened. 'But you'll like Gregory. He's a very old friend, and a very nice man.' She walked quickly to the door.

'He may be a very nice old chum to you,' he muttered to her retreating back, 'but to two hundred million South Americans, he's practically God!'

The door closed behind her.

Alone, he paced the room. Incongruously, he found himself wondering what he should wear. He even wondered what Gregory would wear. He laughed. Vestments would add a touch of colour to the proceedings. He decided to eat. It would not seem appropriate to be chewing on a sandwich when being introduced to his first Nobel Prizewinner.

Seated at the kitchen table he examined the situation. It was improbable, but entirely possible. From the photographs of Gregory he had seen, the ages would be about right. Professor Kodec looked almost old enough to be Gregory's father but ill-health and a labour camp would account for a lot of that. He had already been aware that Gregory Kozka was from somewhere in southern Poland, though until that evening he had not known from exactly where.

From all he had read about Gregory, especially in recent years since he had become a world figure, the man was reputed never to have compromised with authority. For him to insist on keeping up his friendship with a man like Kodec, who had been broken and persecuted by the State, would be entirely in keeping with the man's reputation. As to the authorities, they had nothing to lose by permitting the two men to meet. Professor Kodec was close to death. Even if the news were to leak out it would be easy to present it as an example of the regime's humanity.

He had finished eating when he heard the shuffling step of the Professor in the corridor. Mason rinsed his plate, and cutlery under the wheezy hot tap and made his way into the living room to join him.

The Professor sat in his usual posture. The shabby grey cardigan had been exchanged for a thickly ribbed, dark blue roll-neck sweater. It imparted a faintly nautical air, and somehow made him look less sickly. The effect of better health was enhanced by the spots of pink under each cheekbone and the livelier sparkle in his eyes. His sparse hair was brushed. It was easier now to see in the figure in the chair the powerful, vigorous man in the photograph. Kodec smiled and raised a hand in greeting. The smile, too, had more life in it.

'Good evening, Professor,' Mason said, cheerfully. 'Can I get you anything? Some tea?'

'No, thank you, Mr Mason. But please help yourself. The drinks are over there.'

Mason smiled and nodded. 'Perhaps I will, yes. It might help settle my nerves. I feel like an actor on opening night.' He walked across the room and poured himself an anaesthetic slug of vodka. 'Cheers, Professor.'

'Cheers,' the Professor said, smiling. 'There's nothing to be nervous about, you know. The person you will be meeting won't be Father Kozka, Nobel Prizewinning scourge of authoritarian governments. It will be Gregory, a very g od friend of mine. The best and oldest friend I have. I will introduce you and he to each other simply as friends of mine. There's no need to feel intimidated.'

Mason laughed. 'I know that, Professor. I'm intimidated anyway. To start with, what do I call him? Father? Monseigneur? I doubt if I could do it. Already in Sunday school I was looked on as a subversive! Should I genuflect?'

Kodec laughed. It was the first time Mason had seen him laugh.

'I'm serious,' Mason continued. 'How do I address a man who's more at ease in front of the United Nations than I am in front of my bank manager?'

'Don't say anything, then,' Kodec answered. 'Let Gregory talk. He will. He's a very gregarious man. He'll be very interested to talk to you.'

'That's what I'm worried about. Every priest I've ever met has always ended up, sooner or later, trying to put in a word for God. About all I can recall from the Bible is about four out of ten of the commandments and the story of the loaves and the fishes, which, incidentally, always seemed suspect, even from a very early age.'

Kodec chuckled. 'Don't worry. I don't believe in it myself, but Gregory and I are still excellent friends.' He suddenly became serious. 'What *do* you believe in, Peter?' He asked the question as though he wanted an answer. Mason took a long swallow of vodka and waited while the heat of the slightly viscous fluid spread through him. It was a reasonable enough question. He wondered again if Kodec knew about the money. Or about Barbara. Since his

122

arrival the Professor had made no inquiry about him at all. He seemed to assume he was there out of idealism.

'I don't know,' he answered hesitantly, lowering his glass. 'Not hurting people? Not misusing people? Not letting others misuse them?'

The other man nodded. 'Hmmm.' His eyes were focused in a different place, a different time. 'You find it difficult to talk about. I don't. Twenty years in prison gives you that, at least. Time enough free from the distractions of the world to decide what's really important to you.'

The Professor's words startled him. Was he talking of his own past or Mason's future? He was still pondering whether to ask when the sound of a car drawing into the courtyard brought the Professor's mind abruptly back to the present. His eyes shone with a fierce anticipation. His hands shook slightly.

'Peter,' he said in a voice gone hoarse, 'may I ask you to leave us alone for a short while? I'm sorry. It's just that it's been a very long time.'

Mason smiled and put down his glass. 'Don't, Professor, please. There's nothing to explain.' He made for the door as the firelight glittered on the beginnings of tears in the sick man's eyes. 'I'll be upstairs,' he muttered. As he closed the door on the dimly lit room he felt a knotting sensation in his own throat. He went quickly to his room, surprised at himself.

It was over an hour later when he heard Helena's quick footfall on the polished pine floor outside his door. He was on his feet and crossing the room even before her knock.

'Peter.'

He was grinning as he opened the door. The grin faded the moment he caught sight of Helena. In the last few hours she seemed to have aged several years. Her face was more drawn, the lines around her eyes deeper than before. Her movements were clumsy and nervous. Unexpectedly, she took him by the elbow as they walked the few steps to the other room. He wondered if she were supporting him or herself.

The light in the sitting room was still dim, mostly firelight, with only two shaded table lamps casting a weak glow into the farther parts of the room. From the threshold, Mason's gaze took in the Professor, his face animated and almost aglow in the soft light. Very close to Kodec, perched awkwardly on a low leather pouffe, his back to the door, sat a big figure, hunched towards the other man. Becoming aware of Mason's presence, the visitor's head jerked around.

Mason stood transfixed as the man, dressed in woollen slacks and sweater, bounded to his feet and strode vigorously towards him, a big hand outstretched. He stared at the tall figure, the face with its thick dark brush of hair above those amazing eyes, so familiar from so many photographs. He took the outstretched hand in his own. Dark hair spilled from beneath the sleeve of the thick sweater and over the back of the hand. The handshake was pleasingly firm.

Gregory spoke up first. 'It's a pleasure to meet you, Mr Mason. Wiescek here has been telling me about you.'

Mason glanced doubtfully at the Professor, who sat beaming at them from his deep chair. He hoped it was not against the older man's principles to lie to a priest.

'I understand you're in Poland on business, Mr Mason.'

Mason nodded. 'That's right. I sell machinery. For the furniture industry.'

'Really?' Gregory's interest seemed unfeigned. 'Do you sell much?'

'Not lately,' he answered with morose candour.

'I'm not surprised. In a country where they don't have the resources to buy food.'

Mason held up a hand in laughing protest. 'Please, er, Father. I know it's indefensible. I *know* that by cooperating with the system I'm helping to sustain it. I've sat through long nights of debate on the subject. Philosophically, I'm on the side of the angels. I never buy a South African orange.' He shrugged. 'I know there's no moral difference, but I have to eat,' he ended lamely.

'And perhaps you'd like a drink, too.' Professor Kodec broke in, smiling. 'Gregory, why don't you give Peter a drink instead of starting to preach at him?'

The transformation was disconcerting as Gregory's face melted in infectious laughter. He strode towards the table where the drinks stood, carrying his own empty glass. 'I'm sorry, Mr Mason. Wiescek is right, it's a terrible habit I have. As if I were always on the lookout for someone to practise a sermon on. Is vodka all right?'

Mason nodded. Everybody in the room was smiling broadly, except Helena. She stood behind her father's chair, one hand gripping his shoulder. The hollows in her drawn face, thrown into deeper shadow by the leaping firelight, made her look close to her father's age and almost as sick. A corner of Mason's mind was irritated with her, even as he smiled at the two men. He could not shake off the feeling that her moodiness and distress were somehow connected to him, so that he was constantly examining everything he did or said to see how it might have offended her.

Gregory held out a glass to him. Mason's eyebrows flicked upwards as he took the wide water glass. Over an inch of vodka lapped in the bottom.

'Helena?' Gregory asked, holding the bottle poised over another glass. She shook her head with unexpected violence, apparently too tense to speak. He gave her a puzzled smile, then poured himself a drink as deep as Mason's. He turned to face the room and raised his glass. 'To your health Wiescek, Helena, Mr Mason.' He nodded at each of them in turn, then tilted back his head and tossed off the drink in a single draught. Drawing a deep breath Mason followed suit. This was a Polish priest, with a vengeance.

He stood with his head thrown back, letting the oily, unchilled spirit spread its warmth through his body and lay its clinging film around his gums and teeth.

He was still in the same posture when he was startled by a loud crash from the hallway, followed by the quick clatter of running footsteps.

## 17

'Good evening, Mr Mason. How are you?' Carroll's tone was silky.

Mason stared at the big square face, the damaged nose, and made no reply. Kodec and Kozka looked dumbly from the man to Mason.

'Surprised to see me here?' Carroll paused. Still Mason did not speak. 'Well,' he continued, 'we just thought we'd check on how our money was being spent. Our accountants are very particular, you know.'

Mason's glance flicked over the armed soldiers who stood on each side of Carroll. Their caps bore the single red star of the Soviet army. 'What the hell's going on?'

'Yes,' broke in Kodec, leaning forward agitatedly in his seat. 'What is going on? What are you people doing here?'

'Who are you?' It was Gregory now. His extraordinary eyes blazed and his dark face had become awesome in its anger. Carroll's own gaze flinched under the assault of those eyes. He glanced at Helena, who still stood by her father's chair, transfixed.

'Ask her.'

At his words all their eyes turned to the woman. Her eyes were fixed on a spot in front of her feet and her left hand was clenched in a tight white fist held to her mouth.

Leaning back in his chair to look up at her, her father spoke. 'Helenka, my darling,' he said softly, using the childish diminutive, 'what is it? What is happening? Do you know something about this?' He gestured with his head towards the room.

Unable to answer, she hunched her shoulders, as though seeking protection from a sudden storm. She shook her head violently. Mason watched her, wondering at her vehemence. It was much more than an answer to the question, as though she were denying her entire existence.

Carroll spoke again, his voice harsh and peremptory.

'Leave the inquest for later.' He jerked his head at Mason. 'Stand over there by the chair, with them.' To Gregory he said, in a voice that was almost a snarl, 'You, Father, Your Holiness, whatever you like to be called. Move over! Here!' He gestured to the priest to move a few feet from where he stood at Kodec's side. Gregory took two steps sideways.

'There's a message for you, by the way,' Carroll said, negligently, 'from the hospital.'

Gregory looked sharply at the man. 'What is it?'

'Your father,' the man answered casually, 'he died this evening.'

Gregory cried out as though he had been struck. Helena was shaken by a spasm and reached out a hand towards Gregory.

Carroll ignored their grief. While the two young soldiers held their guns trained on the group, he coolly pulled on a pair of thin gloves and then reached into a pocket and withdrew a small grey revolver.

Mason stiffened. He stared at the gun, knowing with utter certainty that it was the weapon they had so casually offered him in London. For the first time since the men had arrived he felt fear crawl in his stomach. Afraid of being afraid, he turned the fear to anger.

'Fuck you, Carroll, and all the oppressive bastards you work for.' The words were for himself as much as Carroll, gaining time while he grappled with the realization of what was about to happen. Carroll merely grinned, the empty, cruel grin that Mason had been seeing all his life on the faces of the brutal and the vengeful.

Breathing deeply to calm himself, he measured the distance from himself to Carroll, from Carroll to the two impassive soldiers. He would not let himself be killed in cold blood. If he died it would be in a fight. He would not die at another man's pleasure. He spoke, not because there was anything left to be said, but to buy time as he shifted his weight and gathered himself for the effort he had to make.

'If you kill me you'll never see the money again. I made sure of that.' To his own ears his voice sounded high, his words so irrelevant he almost laughed.

'Kill you?' Carroll answered, still grinning. 'Why would we kill you? We need you. You are our culprit, my friend. The capitalist dog. The unscrupulous hired killer who takes money from notorious American front operations for any deed they ask of him. A killer who bought this gun –' he brandished the pistol – 'two weeks ago, in Spain. Yes, Mr Mason,' he continued ignoring Mason's protest. 'A man using your name and answering your description bought this in Barcelona. And, of course, it has your fingerprints on it.' He paused, stupid triumph in his broad face. 'So you see, Mr Mason, you are important to us. We intend to keep you alive for a very long time.'

As he finished speaking, he slowly turned to face Gregory, who stood alone, ashen-faced in the centre of the room. Only at that moment did they all understand what was about to happen.

Helena buried her head in her hands, and screamed. Mason made as though to move towards Carroll and was frozen in his tracks by the sinister click of a machine pistol being cocked.

Only Professor Kodec, his love for his friend stronger than any fear, was able to act. With sudden vigour, he thrust himself from his chair and threw himself against Gregory, shielding him from the gun. His feeble arms clung to the priest, who stood erect, holding the sick man to him and speaking soothingly.

Carroll's face blackened with anger. He signalled to one of the guards and together they strode towards Kodec and Kozka. Each roughly grabbing an arm, they easily broke the old man's weak grip. Enraged as a thwarted child, Carroll pushed the Professor violently across the room.

Helpless, Mason watched as the Professor stumbled against the fender around the hearth and fell. He looked on horrified as the old man, falling, suddenly clutched at his chest and let out a sound that set out to be a cry and was still-born in a chilling gurgle.

Kodec lay inert, his upper body spilling from the hearth onto the polished wood floor in front of it. His eyes stared sightlessly. His sparse hair, disarranged by the struggle, looked curiously indecent.

For half a second there was no sound in the room but the crackle of the fire. Then, oblivious of any threat, Mason, Gregory and Helena converged on the body. Helena was first. She threw herself onto the immobile form of her father. As great sobs wrenched at her body she lay clinging to him, smoothing the wisps of disordered hair and stroking the still cheeks. Through her sobs she talked incoherently, perhaps to her father, perhaps to Carroll, who stood above her.

Gregory, his thoughts only for his old friend, pushed Carroll roughly aside and knelt by the father and daughter. He took Helena by the shoulders and began speaking to her in a low voice. She would not be comforted and her cries did not diminish. Gradually, though, Mason was able to make some sense of her raucous words. He recoiled speechless, as she spoke, her voice deformed with grief.

'Not this.' She sobbed. 'Not this. The Englishman. You wanted the Englishman. That was our bargain. Only the Englishman. My father would be well. You would have what you wanted. Nobody was to be hurt.' Between each short sentence her breath came in a rasp. Tears ran in two continuous rivulets down her face and fell in rapid rhythm to form dark spots of damp on her father's clothes. Carroll leaned down and took her by one shoulder, attempting to pull her clear of the body.

'Come on, come away,' he said roughly. 'I'm sorry about your father. It was an accident. We would have kept our bargain.'

She clung to her father, still weeping, near to hysteria. Shrugging, Carroll let his hand fall from her shoulder. Turning to look at the two soldiers, neither of whom had moved, he nodded at the kneeling figure of Gregory. Without a word they stepped forward and each took a hold of him by an upper arm. They began trying to drag him, still in a kneeling posture, away from the Professor's body. A heavy man, he resisted, all the while praying aloud for his friend. Behind him, Carroll stepped forward purposefully, the gun raised in his gloved hand. Mason watched him. He was surprised to find he had no more need to manufacture anger. All fear had left him. In its place was an authentic, ice-cold rage. Carroll's vacant eyes were focused on a point between Gregory's shoulder blades.

As hard as he could, Mason buried his instep into the man's groin. For a fraction of a second only, he let himself be pleased to see the man jack-knife and sink to the floor.

Mason's back was to the soldiers. Half turning, he saw the one nearest to him looking at him, open-mouthed. The young man hesitated between keeping his hold on Gregory or tackling Mason. The soldier had only a fraction of a second to regret his inaction as, continuing to turn, Mason rammed his elbow into the area just below the man's ribs. The soldier stumbled over the Professor's body and fell awkwardly, his mouth opening and closing silently. Mason felt a curious detachment as he watched the man fall, as though he were watching a film in which the sound had failed.

Reality returned with the sight of the other soldier, his face contorted, raising his machine gun. Off-balance and out of range, Mason could not hope to strike a blow. Launching himself forward, he fell onto the soldier, pushing the gun barrel away from him. The two of them fell to the floor, grappling desperately. As they fought Mason was only dimly aware of Helena running, screaming from the room.

Locked together, Mason and the soldier writhed on the polished floor. Each had one hand clamped on the gun, as with their free hands they gouged and probed, seeking to force the other to loosen his grip. The soldier was slighter than Mason but fit and wiry. Nevertheless Mason could feel the man's grip begin to weaken. He wrenched at the weapon and felt the man's fingers slip slightly on the stock. With a last effort of concentrated fury, he snatched the gun free of the soldier's grasp. Pinioning the soldier with his weight. Mason rose to one knee. He was about to stand when he became aware of an oddly rasping call behind him. Without releasing his hold on the man beneath him he looked around.

Carroll sat on the floor, one leg stretched straight in front of him, the other with the knee drawn up. He leant forward, ashen-faced, on his raised knee. One hand cupped the cloth of his clothes around his testicles. The other held the hand-gun aimed at Mason.

Hatred burned in the other man's eyes. Mason knew with absolute certainty he was going to shoot him. His past life did not flash before his eyes. Surprisingly, he thought about Barbara in Warsaw. He wondered what she would become. He saw the man's eyes flicker from him to the doorway.

In a split second several expressions tried for a place on the man's face. Disbelief was jostling outrage when he died. Mason's head rang to the crash of an explosion, as in the same instant Carroll's chest turned red and he toppled over and lay flat on his back.

His ears echoing, Mason turned to the door. In the open doorway stood Helena. At waist level she held a shotgun. Tears ran down her cheeks. Holding the machine gun by the barrel, Mason apologized briefly to the young Russian soldier and then swung the metal stock of the gun crisply at the man's head. He avoided hitting him on the temple. He hated the idea of killing a man. Especially a man who probably did not even want to be there. Leaving the soldier senseless on the floor, he walked quickly over to Helena. Very gently he took the shotgun from her. She let it slip from hands that seemed almost lifeless. Laying an arm around her shoulders he led her hurriedly into the room. He could feel her trembling under his arm. She shuddered and shied as she passed the red-stained corpse of Carroll. He guided her to a sofa. 'Father,' he called. Gregory seemed oblivious, lost in a grief of his own. 'Father,' Mason called again, more sharply. Gregory looked around, slightly bemused, as though he had been roughly awakened. 'Would you come and take care of Helena? Please. I must check if there are any more of them outside.' Gregory nodded silently. He rose from his knees and came over to the sofa.

Mason left the two of them and went to look at the other soldier, the one he had hit first. The man lay groaning, his hands clasped to what seemed to be shattered ribs. He lay looking up at him with the eyes of a terrified rabbit. Mason raised the gun. The man babbled incoherently and tried to scrabble away.

'Sorry, pal,' Mason muttered, and clipped him low on the skull with the gun. The soldier's body slackened.

He went quickly to the door, examining the gun as he went. He had never used a firearm in his life. He looked at what he thought must be the safety catch. Did 'On' mean the safety mechanism was working or the firing mechanism? For hitting people it made no difference, but if he needed to shoot someone he could end up looking pretty silly. In the hallway he paused and listened for a full minute. No sound came from outside. He flicked off the light and walked silently to the front door. It stood at an angle, its top hinge torn from the frame. He stood quietly inside the door, staying in the deep darkness of the hall, and examined the front courtyard of the house. The thick snow gave plenty of reflected light. Nothing moved.

Three cars stood in the courtyard. His own, a small Fiat which he guessed was Helena's, and a black Polonez saloon. The Polonez was surely the one that had brought the visitors. Mason remained immobile in the shadow, watching the black car and letting his eyes become accustomed to the deeper black of the car's interior. He was about to step out of the house, certain nobody was there, when a rear door of the car swung suddenly open. Startled, Mason drew back deeper into the shadow. A soldier emerged from the car. From his posture he had obviously been lying on the rear seat.

The soldier took a few paces from the car, fumbled with his fly and began to relieve himself. His back was turned to the house. Mason realized his mouth was dry. He licked his lips, gulped and held the gun firmly in both hands. He was mildly surprised to find he had adopted the posture he had seen so often in films, one hand on the trigger, one clasped around the magazine. Feeling like an impostor, he stepped from the house.

He half expected the soldier to whirl at the sound of his footfall and he had prepared an intimidating phrase. There was no footfall. The fresh snow muffled the sound completely. Surprised and relieved, he walked carefully towards him. He was two feet from the man when he spun around. The face, a boy's face, worked in bewilderment for a moment and then contorted as Mason rammed the point of the gun hard into it. With a sob, the youth doubled over and brought his hands to his damaged face. Mason jabbed the metal stock fiercely at the back of the bowed head. The soldier concertinaed soundlessly into the snow. Next to the spot where he lay steam floated from the characters of the filthiest word in the Russian language which the soldier had been amusing himself by etching in urine. Mason allowed himself a quick smile. It was the first time he had seen it done in thirty years. The first time ever in Cyrillic script.

Hurriedly, he swung the gun over his shoulder by its lanyard and stooped towards the soldier. Placing a hand under each armpit and entwining his fingers across the man's chest, he dragged him quickly towards the house. He dumped the limp body onto the floor of the hall-way and headed for the sitting room.

Helena and Gregory still sat on the sofa. Gregory was leaning towards the girl, one arm around her shoulders, the other hand gently holding one of her wrists as it lay in her lap. She had stopped sobbing now. Only her restlessly moving fingers betrayed her agitation.

'Helena.' Mason spoke softly, soothingly, probing her

state of mind. 'Helena, I need your help.' She looked at him, her eyes blank. 'I need some rope or something.' She showed no sign of comprehension. He gestured to the two prostrate soldiers. 'We have to tie these two up. And there's another one out there.' He jerked a thumb at the door behind him. 'We have to get them out of our hair while we think.' The girl stared at him, leaning towards the big solid form of Gregory, as if seeking protection. Mason raised his voice, made his tone rougher.

'Helena! Do you understand? Where can I find something? Some clothesline. Flex. Anything.'

Intelligence seeped back into her eyes. 'The basement,' she murmured. 'I think there's some rope.' Mason spun angrily, irritated by her, and left the room. He tried three doors before he found the one leading to the basement.

In the dirty, yellow light of a naked bulb he searched quickly among the accumulation of stepladders and cardboard boxes and broken gardening equipment. He found the length of new clothesline Helena had mentioned. Better still, he found a coil of thin electrical flex hanging on a nail. He took them both upstairs.

He reached the soldier in the hall just as he began to stir. He stamped his heel hard down into the man's solar plexus. The man lost interest again and Mason quickly trussed his feet. Dragging the man to a radiator, he secured his hands firmly to the thick iron pipes. The knots would not have won him a badge in the scouts, but they seemed secure.

In the sitting room, under the fixed gaze of Helena, he did the same to the other two young men. Then he asked Helena for sticking-plaster. He only had to repeat the question once. She was improving. He found the roll of plaster in the kitchen drawer she had indicated.

With the sticking-plaster and the kitchen shears he walked to each of the men in turn and stuck three narrow strips of the material vertically across their mouths. He purposely left some slack so that they could open their mouths slightly. They could grunt. They could curse him if they wanted to. But they could not shout. And if they vomited, which he knew people often did when recovering from unconsciousness, they would not choke.

Finishing with the last man, he straightened, threw down the roll of plaster and the shears and walked across to where the other two sat. Seating himself in an armchair facing the sofa, he pointed to the body and spoke.

'Don't you think you ought to tell us about him?'

For a moment she continued to look uncomprehending, and then, very slowly colour began to return to her drained face. Her voice came very softly.

'He's a Russian. Major Cherneff.' She paused, waiting for Mason to speak. He stayed silent. 'He came here some time ago, maybe two months, three perhaps. With another man.'

'Dark?' Mason asked. 'Slightly hunch-backed.' She nodded. 'Uh-huh. Go on.'

'They came with an offer.' He nodded imperceptibly. He knew about their offers.

'To your father?'

'To me. My father never met them. My father was a very sick man, Mr Mason.'

'Peter.'

'Peter. He was dying. You must understand that. He needed treatment in the West. It was the only hope for him. But you know his situation. He had just been released. They would not let him travel to the West. Even here in Poland he was restricted.' She brushed a fresh tear from her cheek. 'He was not a celebrated case. He wasn't Sakharov or Tcharantsky. They could do what they liked to him. Nobody in the West cared or made any fuss.' Her voice was turning to a whine again.

He interrupted, bringing her back to her thread. 'What was their offer?'

'They offered to allow my father to go to America for treatment. They offered to pay the costs. Only I had to cooperate with them.' She looked desperately at Mason. 'You do see? They were agreeing to help my father get

135

well. After all those years he suffered in the camps, they were promising me the chance to have him for a few more years. You do understand? I couldn't refuse them!'

'Maybe not,' he responded, despondently. 'What did you have to do?'

'Cooperate. They told me I had to help them in an operation they wanted to conduct. They told me that a man, a Westerner, would come here to talk to my father, to get his story and take it out to the West. They would arrange things so that he would be caught and exposed as an agent of the Western propaganda machine. They presented it as almost a game. My father had suffered so much, and nobody was to be hurt.'

'Except me. I was to be a candidate for Siberia. Maybe I would have been in your father's old camp,' he added, with mock cheerfulness. 'He could have given me a few addresses!'

She began to sob again. 'No, it wasn't like that. It wasn't *you*. It was just somebody. Some anonymous person. And they promised that you would only be in prison a short time. They said you were sure to be exchanged after a while, for one of their's.'

Gregory spoke softly to the sobbing woman, trying to comfort her. Mason looked pensively at him. 'And Gregory?' he asked. 'What did they say about his role?'

'Oh, Peter, nothing.' She looked up quickly at Gregory, her eyes glistening. He gave her a smile that seemed to envelope her. 'When they came here first we didn't even know for sure Father Gregory was coming. Nothing had been settled. When it became clear you would be here at the same time I contacted them to ask if we should change anything. They said no. They said everything would be for the best, the world would take more notice.'

'And you believed them?' It was as much a statement as a question. Of course she had believed them. Her love for her father had left her no choice but to believe them. She nodded violently, her body racked by sobs.

He moved across and touched her shoulder lightly.

'Don't blame yourself,' he said, softly. He turned and paced the room. 'You couldn't have imagined their real purpose any more than I could.'

'Their real purpose?' Gregory asked, his arm still tight around Helena's shoulders.

Mason looked at him for a moment, unbelieving. 'Father,' he said, at length, 'have you forgotten? Don't you remember how they dealt with troublesome priests?'

Gregory's face was startled and then, abruptly, sombre. The reference to the murdered priest, Father Popieluszko, troubled him deeply. 'You mean they allowed me here, lured me back even, in order to kill me?' His voice was almost a whisper.

Mason looked into the priest's eyes and offered no reply. It was a moment before Gregory spoke again. 'But why? Why should they want to harm me? Popieluszko was here, I was in another country, another continent.'

Mason was still wondering at the man's innocence when Helena spoke up.

'Uncle Gregory, don't you understand? Don't you understand what you have come to mean here, in Poland? Don't you see? Don't you know that you are the one man the people here really look up to, the only person on earth they would follow?'

Gregory shook his head, his face grave. Caressing Helena's hair, he spoke, half to himself. 'What is it that's going on in this country? I believed things had improved, since the changes in Moscow, at least.'

Mason stepped closer, shaking his own head ruefully. 'No, Father, you've been away too long. Things may have improved in Russia since Gorbachev, but not here.'

Gregory looked down at Helena. Very gently, he lifted her chin, making her look at him. 'Is it so, Helenka? Are things really so unbearable?'

She nodded, clinging hard to the cloth of his sweater. 'It's terrible. People can hardly get enough to eat, unless they're prepared to live on potatoes and cabbage. People with babies can't even get nappies for them. Or clothes.

Every day brings power cuts, new shortages. Can't you see it? People are so desperate.' Her voice foundered on a reef of anger and grief.

Concern flooded Gregory's face. He muttered comfort to the grief-stricken woman, all the while rhythmically stroking her hair. At length, he spoke. 'It's very difficult for me, Mr Mason. I'm a Pole. I love this country. What I've seen happen here distresses me more than I can express. But I'm a man of the Church, Mr Mason. All my adult life I've tried to do Christ's work. I have never allowed myself to become mixed up in politics.'

'Damn it, Father!' Mason turned away in exasperation. 'I'm sorry, Father,' he said, turning back to face him, 'but look. A few minutes ago they tried to *shoot* you. They brought you here and they brought me here as a scapegoat. You aren't just *mixed up* in politics. Your whole existence *is* politics. They want to get rid of you but don't dare do it themselves for fear of seeing the whole country blow up in their faces.'

Gregory gave a long sigh. 'Perhaps you're right, Mr Mason. Maybe I've been naïve. As a matter of fact I try to be, if such a thing is possible. It's a dangerous thing for a priest to become sophisticated.'

'History's full of sophisticated priests,' Mason responded, smiling.

'I know,' Gregory replied, returning the smile. 'However,' he added, jerking his chin at the room, 'we have more pressing matters to discuss than the relationship of Church and State. What do you suggest we do?'

Mason followed his glance. It would have needed more naïvety than even Gregory possessed not to see that the two corpses and three injured Soviet soldiers spelt trouble. 'We try to keep you alive and prevent the country exploding.'

Gregory squinted at him. 'And how do you propose to do that?'

Mason glanced at his watch. There were several hours to dawn. They would probably have that long. He unslung the machine gun he still carried over one shoulder and laid it on a chair. He gestured at the room. 'Clear up and clear out. Quickly!'

# 18

Gently but quickly, they lifted the body of Professor Kodec and carried it into his bedroom. Helena trailed a pace behind, convulsed with bitter sobs. They laid the body on the bed.

Stooping, her breath coming in great gasps, Helena reached down and arranged his clothing. Very tenderly, she smoothed the wispy hair back into place. Finally satisfied, she drew a blanket over him, pulling it close up to his chin. Then she bent quickly and placed a single brief kiss on the lifeless forehead.

Mason began to turn towards the door. He was halted by the sight of Gregory dropping abruptly to his knees beside Helena, a small crucifix in his hand. Helena knelt beside him. Both of them bowed their heads and Gregory began intoning a prayer in Latin.

Mason felt a flash of anger. Automatically, he glanced at his watch. He had nothing against praying, if people thought it helped. Only at present he would have preferred to run first and pray later. He did not see what difference it would have made to Professor Kodec.

He loitered by the door, shifting his weight impatiently and waiting for them to finish. After what felt like an age, Gregory crossed himself and they rose to their feet. With an inclination of his head that was his only farewell to Kodec he led the way hurriedly from the room.

Downstairs, they contemplated the body of the Russian. 'What about him?' Helena asked with a tremor of disgust.

'We leave him,' Mason said.

Mason saw the doubt in Gregory's eyes. It was a hard thing for a priest to do, whoever the dead man was. 'The only thing for us to do is get away from here. Now.'

'You're right, of course,' Gregory answered gently. 'Nothing keeps me here now. Where do you propose we go?'

Helena answered. 'We could try to cross into Czechoslovakia. The frontier is less than forty kilometres from here.'

'Uh-huh. How's the road?'

'Bad,' Gregory said, flatly. 'In weather like this almost certainly impassable. It might just be possible over the mountains, on skis, but it would be very difficult and dangerous, a lot of climbing.'

Mason smiled ruefully. 'I can't ski. Anyway, Czechoslovakia would be even more dangerous than here. We three would stand out like a sore thumb. Even if we made it as far as the Austrian frontier, it's impossible to cross. Worse than East Germany.'

Gregory nodded. 'So what *do* you suggest?'

'We stay in Poland. For several reasons. Firstly we would have at least some chance of help from the people. Secondly, Poland has a coast. That would be the last resort, though. Personally, I think our best bet is to head for Warsaw. An embassy.'

'Which one?' Gregory asked. 'Don't forget we're both Polish.' He reached out and touched Helena's arm as he spoke.

Mason let his shoulders rise and fall a quarter of an inch. 'American? Italian, maybe, given your Vatican connection. It doesn't really matter. Better not the British though. They'd resent your not making an appointment.'

Gregory laughed. 'Okay. Personally I would prefer the Americans, all things considered.'

'But surely, Peter,' Helena broke in, 'if Gregory were just to go to the militia and ask for their protection they would not hurt him. Not if he –'

Mason cut her short. 'No, Helena. The people who came here tonight were Russians but they must have cooperation from somebody in Poland. The government itself. The Security Service. The militia. It's impossible to guess. Of course, most ordinary militiamen would fall at his feet, but we aren't talking about a motoring offence. If any militiaman gets wind of us the top people in Warsaw will know within minutes. And whoever organized this has no choice now but to silence us.'

'He's right, Helenka,' Gregory agreed, grimly. 'We're dealing with madmen. The kind of lunatics who killed Popieluszko are capable of anything.' He crossed himself as he spoke the dead priest's name. 'Our best chance is the Americans.'

'Right,' said Mason firmly. 'So we go to Warsaw. Helena, take anything you need that will fit into one small holdall. Wear your warmest clothes. You never know. We may have to do some walking.' He waited until she hurried from the room before saying to Gregory, 'Father, you'll need some things, too. I suggest you take some of the Professor's, unless you would find it too offensive.'

'No,' Gregory answered, 'it wouldn't offend me. Wiescek would have wanted it so.' He, too, turned and hurried away. Mason followed him from the room and went in search of his own bag.

In less than five minutes they had reassembled in the hall.

'Helena,' Mason asked, 'how much petrol do you have?'

'Not much,' she answered, with a despairing shake of her head. 'A few litres.'

'The tank on mine is almost full. Do you have any petrol cans?'

'Of course, everyone in Poland has. It's one of the few things that are plentiful. Petrol cans and plastic bags. We are used to storing things in case of crisis.'

'Where are they?'

'In the basement.'

He started for the door. 'Do you have any rubber tubing?' he asked over his shoulder.

She frowned for a moment. 'Garden hose?' she asked anxiously. 'Would that do?'

'Yeah. Fine,' he answered as he disappeared down the steep wooden stairs of the cellar. A short while later he emerged with two plastic flagons and a metal jerrycan, and led the way out to the cars.

It was snowing again, the big flakes racing almost

horizontally on a brisk wind. It was bitterly cold.

Helena had found about a metre of hose. Mason began unscrewing the petrol cap of his rented car. Gregory stood behind him.

'Wouldn't it be simpler to take this car?'

Mason glanced up at him. 'No. Look at it. It's a Ford. How many of them are there in Poland? Helena's is much less conspicuous.' He paused. 'And, God knows, Father, we are going to need to be inconspicuous.'

He began working one end of the pipe down into the petrol tank. He looked at Helena, who was trembling.

'Helena, why don't you get in the car and start warming it up? You too, Father. There's no sense in all of us freezing.'

Gregory nodded agreement and, taking Helena by the shoulders, walked with her to the small Polski car, modelled on an old Fiat design. Mason watched their backs as he grappled with the unyielding length of pipe. The calm, reassuring figure of Gregory seemed almost to dwarf the tense, stiff-backed Helena. They seemed total opposites and yet the tenderness as he shepherded her into the tiny car spoke of a closeness, a wordless understanding, that touched him. He took a long breath and turned his attention back to the task in hand.

He felt the end of the tube touch the bottom of the tank. Withdrawing it a couple of inches to avoid drawing in any sediment, he placed his mouth over the other end of the tube and started sucking. It took several attempts, and his mouth burned with the taste of petrol, before he managed to get the liquid siphoning continuously. Leaving it flowing, he ran to the black Polonez and, with a short pointed knife taken from the kitchen he stabbed at each of the tyres in turn.

The first container was filled. While the second one was filling he ran to the Polski and emptied the first into the tank. He repeated this until the tank overflowed. The petrol still flowed from his own car and he was able to fill the jerrycan and one of the plastic flagons before the flow abated. Closing them both tightly, he put them in the cramped space of Helena's car. His fingers stung from the intense cold and the taste of the petrol was making him sick.

He ran quickly back into the house. He snatched the gun he had left lying on a chair in the sitting room and a second one from where it lay on the floor. Holding the two weapons by their straps he paused for an instant by the Russian's body.

'It would have been better for both of us if you *had* been an insurance salesman,' he said softly. 'Or even a Jehovah's Witness.'

Hunched in the front passenger seat, the stench of petrol making him dizzy, Mason squinted through the streaked windscreen. The fresh snow, driven by the rising wind, had completely obliterated the track. Without Helena's intimate knowledge of the terrain it would have been impossible even to get as far as the village without putting the car into a ditch. He looked at her. She drove crouched tensely forward, the driving seat drawn close to the wheel, seeking the extra six inches of vision through the blinding storm. Her teeth glinted on her lower lip as she concentrated.

They slid and bumped over the snow, several times bottoming sickeningly on the ruts concealed beneath the bland whiteness of the surface. He hoped the car would stand the beating under the weight of the three of them. It took them nearly ten minutes to negotiate the short distance to the village. There was an audible release of breath as they all felt the final jolt which announced the beginning of the metalled road.

Through the village they were able to drive faster, although Helena still had to use extreme caution. Several times the rear of the car swayed away from her as she tried to accelerate. Not even a dog barked as they entered the deserted main street. The same few parked cars stood in the desolate little square.

'Pull over. There!' Mason spoke so abruptly Helena shied away from him, startled from her deep concentration. He pointed to a spot close to one of the parked cars. She brought the car sliding to an abrupt halt, puzzled and afraid.

'What is it, Peter?' she asked quickly, turning to look around the car. 'Is there anybody behind us?'

He shook his head. 'Helena, do you have a tool kit in the car?' Without replying, she leant down and scrabbled beneath her seat. A second later she produced a greasy plastic box, the size of a cigar box. He snatched it from her and opened the box. A few cheap looking tools lay inside, alongside a spool of black insulating tape and a length of plastic coated wire. With a small grimace of satisfaction Mason grabbed a damaged screwdriver, a small pair of long-nosed pliers and the wire.

'Keep the motor running. I'll be back.' He stepped from the car, pushing the tools into a pocket. Under the puzzled gaze of Gregory and Helena, he ran to the car nearest to them.

He smiled grimly to himself as he approached the car he had chosen. At least the lack of consumer choice in Poland was working in someone's favour. It made it easy to find one of the same model they were driving.

Stooping at the front of the tiny car, he began scooping snow away from the front bumper bar. It took him about half a minute to dig away the packed snow and expose the number plate. He examined the plate. It was attached by two rivets to the car. Taking the bottom of it in both numb hands, he dragged it sharply upwards. With only a faint metallic squeal the thin rectangle cf metal came clear of its fixings. Moving rapidly, Mason brushed snow back into place, covering the place from which the plate had come.

Carrying the number plate in one hand and sucking the stinging fingertips of the other he moved to the rear of the car and removed the rear plate in the same manner. Satisfied that the loss would only be discovered when the car was moved or the snow melted, in a few days or a few months, he carried the stolen plates over to Helena's car.

Working as quickly as the numbness of his hands would allow, he tore the plates from Helena's car and, using the wire and pliers, fixed the stolen ones in their place. When both were firmly attached and the ends of the wire securing them neatly trimmed away, he walked around the car to examine the result. From four paces away the makeshift fixings were indistinguishable. In thirty minutes they would be so caked in ice and dirt that the numbers themselves would scarcely be legible.

He dashed the layer of caked snow from his shoulders and hair and climbed quickly into the cramped car. Breathing hard into his cupped hands, he jerked his head at Helena. She slipped the car into gear, nursing the clutch to let the tyres bite on the fresh snow, and headed for the winding mountain road.

Back at the house the telephone rang insistently. Cherneff lay staring sightlessly at the ceiling. Each of the young Russians, conscious now, and still lashed tightly to the central heating, wondered if it were for him.


# 19


The dark man slammed the heavy old fashioned telephone back onto its cradle and swore. He turned abruptly from the cluttered wooden desk and walked, scowling, to the window. He pushed one hand deep into a pocket of his well cut jacket and with the other hand he scratched at the fresh dark stubble around his jaw. He stared from the window at the meagre lights of the city. The skilfully cut jacket did not quite disguise the slight hump at the top of his spine.

'Damn him,' he muttered angrily, 'he should have called us two hours ago.' He spoke Russian.

'Don't worry so much. Major Cherneff seems a competent man. He must have a good reason for not calling. Maybe the line's down. It happens often in these mountain villages. They're up there, in the middle of nowhere. The lines are often down for a couple of days before anyone outside even notices.'

The speaker sat back easily in a padded swivel chair, scarred with ancient cigarette burns. He was a short fat man whose jowls hung in loose tiers around a sharply hooked nose, giving him the look of an owl gone to seed. He wore a loose suit of synthetic material, resembling a safari suit except for its improbable light blue colour. The jacket hung open over a nylon polo-neck sweater which strained across the mound of the man's stomach. A cigarette flapped from a corner of his mouth as he spoke, projecting an inch of ash onto the stained sweater. He spoke Russian sloppily, with many mistakes. They were all deliberate.

The other man turned from the window. His dark face angry.

'It's after three. By now he should have been back in Zakopane and ready to fly to Warsaw. All the lines from Zakopane can't be down *every* time it snows.' His voice was thick with sarcasm.

No, Colonel,' the other man answered sweetly, 'not every time. But to phone you, Major Cherneff would actually have to *get* to Zakopane. The mountain roads can be very difficult at this time of year. The weather forecast was for heavy snowstorms down in the south. You're a Georgian, Colonel Toparoff,' he added, smiling blandly, 'Perhaps you are unfamiliar with our harsher climate.'

The Russian gave the man a pitying look. 'Harsh, Comrade Dominiak?' He gave a short laugh. 'You think that a night such as this is harsh? I served for three years in Central Russia. The Steppes. That is a climate you can call harsh. In summer it's too hot to go out and too humid to think. In winter it goes down to minus sixty. That's what we would call harsh.'

The Pole smiled. 'It's true, Comrade Colonel, we can't boast such extraordinary conditions here. As usual, we poor Poles cannot match your standards. But I can assure you in Poland we find that minus fifteen Celsius with a little wind can be quite cold enough to turn a mountain road into a glacier.'

The Russian turned the words over, like a housewife inspecting a melon, examining them for irony. He was not sure if he found any.

'Do you have a helicopter down there?' he asked, irritably. He was offended by this slovenly Pole with whom he had been assigned to work. The man's clothes, his chain smoking, everything about the man was offensive. Above all it was his attitude that grated. Always polite, the Pole seemed to be somehow mocking him without being openly derisive. He resented having to use the Poles at all. It would have been better to have set up the whole operation themselves.

'Not in Zakopane itself, Comrade Colonel, no. We have some in Cracow, and in Katowice. Why?'

'I want you to send one to the Kodec house. I want you to have your men check out the house and the road. Something must have happened to them. They could be stuck on the road.'

The Pole nodded. Another half-inch of ash spilled down the straining material of his sweater. He flicked at the ash mechanically with a podgy hand, only succeeding in grinding it to a pale grey streak on the cloth. 'They could be, Colonel. It's even quite likely. Look at it out there.' The Russian followed his glance at the window. In the light of the street lamp beyond, snowflakes flew like rice being poured from a sack. 'I doubt if a helicopter could even operate in that.'

'Maybe not. Then again maybe down there it's stopped.' The Russian was becoming impatient. 'Tell them to go as soon as the visibility permits. We must know what's

147

happening. We must be ready to announce the news later this morning. We cannot afford to have rumours flying. Phone now.' The last words were an order.

With a long sigh, Dominiak leaned forward and pulled the telephone toward him. He dialled the number and half reclined in the battered chair. While he held the telephone to his ear with one hand, he expertly extinguished the damp end of his cigarette, extracted another from a crumpled packet and lit it with a disposable lighter. He drew deeply on the new cigarette, just to make it comfortable, and crossed his short legs. A band of deathly white leg hove into view above a nylon sock. With the thumb of his free hand he began an absorbed investigation of the imprint in the flesh left by the tight elastic top of the sock. He had become bored with his enquiry and began snapping the elastic top repeatedly against his calf, before the phone was answered. He spoke into the receiver as the Russian looked on, tight-lipped.

After a few moments he replaced the receiver in its cradle. This time the ash fell onto the desk.

'They are ready but the weather is filthy down there. As soon as there's a let-up they'll move. They'll go at daybreak, anyway, even if the snow continues.'

The Russian nodded grimly and turned back to the window, offering his misshapen back to the Pole's expressionless gaze.

The road, which a day before had taken Mason an hour to drive, was proving painfully slow now. The driving snow threatened to overwhelm the struggling windscreen wipers, at times reducing visibility to no more than a few yards. The headlights, too, became crusted with freezing snow, obliging Helena to stop every few kilometres to enable Mason to get out and scrape them clear. Icicles hung from the bumper and great wedges of solidified slush gathered in the wheel arches. Often the road was indistinguishable from the surrounding whiteness, forcing Helena to slow almost to a halt and creep laboriously forward on the wrong side of the road, depending on the rise of the mountainside for guidance. The interior of the car was chill, the small heater scarcely able to cope with the appalling conditions.

'You okay?' Mason asked, glancing at Helena's tense profile. 'Do you want me to drive for a while?'

She shook her head once. 'No. It's better if I do. I know the road. Not that that's necessarily going to be enough to get us to Zakopane. It's getting worse by the minute.'

Mason nodded grim assent, feeling as he did so the rear of the car once again drift sideways as the tyres lost their bite on the snow. 'How far have we come?' He was finding it impossible to recognize anything from his journey up.

Gregory answered. 'About a third of the way. No more. And the steepest part is yet to come. It could get very dangerous. There's still no parapet, is there, Helenka?'

'No. Nothing at all. There's just the road and then the drop. It's a long drop,' she added, shooting a glance at Mason for emphasis.

'Great.' He turned to look at Gregory. 'If we go over we'll have time for a brief prayer before we hit the bottom.'

Gregory grinned. 'I've been rehearsing one for a quarter of an hour now!'

They were both still grinning when they heard Helena cry out. Mason spun back to face the front of the car. They were on a steep downward curve and the road veered sharply away to their left. The car glided silently straight ahead, towards the precipice. Mason watched blankly for an instant as she twisted the wheel. It moved without resistance as though no longer connected to the car. On the suddenly steeper slope all four wheels had lost traction. Helena pumped the brake in staccato bursts. It was slowing them but would not stop them.

He screamed at her. 'Leave the brake. Steer it! Just steer it!'

She snatched her foot from the brake and began trying to steer the car gently to the left hand, uphill, side of the road. Mason had a hand on the door handle, wondering if he should dive from the car, when he felt the front wheels begin to grip and saw the nose begin to edge away from the drop. In her relief Helena made another misjudgement. She tried to accelerate away. Before she knew what was happening the rear of the car was slewing out of control. Seated next to her Mason experienced the curious sensation of being passed by the rear of their own car. He put his head in his hands and swore. Still turning, the car side-swiped a big fir tree, slid backwards for another three yards and came to a stop with its rear wheels buried deep in the roadside drift. The engine stalled.

Helena hammered the steering wheel in frustration. Her eyes glistened in the light reflected from the snow.

'Shit!' he thought angrily. 'The exasperating bitch is going to start crying again.' He tapped her encouragingly on the arm. 'Try starting it,' he said, soothingly.

She turned the key. The engine came immediately to life. 'Try to ease us out. Gently.'

She put the car into gear and gingerly let the clutch pedal up. The car vibrated and sank back another centimetre into the snow. With a word to Gregory, Mason climbed from the car. Gregory followed, and they hurried to the rear of the car. At each step the bitter wind plucked spumes of snow from their feet.

The drift covered the wheel arches. Without a word, they began digging. After a couple of minutes' furious tearing at the snow, Mason's heart began to sink. As he uncovered the metal of the bodywork he discovered the wheel arch buckled and pressed hard against the tyre. Unconscious of the pain in his fingers, he dragged at the crumpled metal, struggling to free the trapped wheel. It did not move.

He called Gregory to join him and the two of them bent to take a grip on the deformed metalwork.

Together they heaved, faces contorted, at the smashed wing, each with one foot braced against the car body. At the end of a few seconds they released their grip, breathing heavily. The metal still pressed hard against the tyre.

Mason looked pensively at the spot. 'Shit,' he said angrily, kicking the wheel as he spoke. Gregory smiled at him.

'As you say, Mr Mason,' he said very softly, 'shit.'

In a corner of Cracow airport, well away from the public buildings, a grey painted helicopter stood silently in front of an anonymous windowless hangar. A man in a heavy overcoat and astrakhan hat emerged from a small door set into one of the two big double doors. He stood for a moment, scrutinizing the sky, before abruptly turning to re-enter the building, slamming the small door as he went.

Inside the hangar he walked to a small glassed-in office where a single light burned. The office furniture consisted of a plain wooden desk, an armless swivel chair, and a leatherette-covered couch. A young man in uniform lay on the couch, partly covered by a coarse grey blanket. Deeply asleep, his mouth hung slackly open, allowing saliva to gather in the light stubble on his cheek.

The man in civilian clothes went quickly to the telephone. He began dialling, his face impassive. On the seventh attempt he got his number.

'Hello. Dominiak speaking.' The voice was clogged, as though he had been awoken from a deep sleep.

'Comrade Dominiak? Captain Diament.'

'Yes, Captain, what is it?' Dominiak's voice was muffled now as he juggled to light a cigarette.

'The snow seems to have eased, sir. It's almost completely stopped, in fact. I think we could get up to the house now.'

Dominiak drew deeply on his cigarette. As he answered, thick blue smoke billowed from his mouth and nostrils, enveloping the telephone. 'Can you? Is there enough light?'

'The pilot thinks we'll have no problem, as long as it doesn't start snowing again. You can see quite clearly.'

Dominiak chewed for a moment at the inside of his lip. 'Good,' he said. His voice was pensive. 'Good,' he repeated more strongly. 'Go ahead, then. Keep me informed.' He put the telephone down, and turned slowly from the desk as Colonel Toparoff entered the room. The Russian looked at him enquiringly.

'News?'

'Yes, Comrade Colonel. That was my man in Cracow. It's stopped snowing. They're going to try to get up to Kodec's place right away.'

'Good. Excellent.' He walked to a side table where a small saucepan of water boiled on a single electric hot plate. He took a paper packet of tea and began shaking some into a glass. He looked over at Dominiak. 'Tea, Comrade?'

The Pole shook his head. 'No thanks, Comrade Colonel. It keeps me awake.'

Captain Diament replaced the receiver with a crash. The sleeping young man stirred and made a noisy chewing sound, like a man sampling the taste of a hangover. Diament called to him roughly.

'Hey. Come on. Get moving. It's time to go.'

The young man sat up suddenly. He rubbed his face and scratched vigorously at his unruly hair. He looked vacantly at Diament, who stood over him, pulling on a pair of thick fleece-lined mittens.

'Come on. Quick,' Diament said, his voice edged with contempt. 'We don't have all night for you to make your mind up.'

Without speaking, the soldier swung his feet to the floor and laboriously pulled on his heavy boots. Then he stooped to pick up his uniform cap. Running the fingers of one hand through his spiky hair he quickly jammed the cap firmly on his head with the other, before the hair had time to assert itself.

The Captain watched pityingly. 'You look beautiful,' he said sarcastically. 'Perhaps, now you're quite satisfied with your exquisite grooming, you would be kind enough to fly me.' He turned and led the way from the office. As they went, the young soldier glanced in a small mirror hanging from a nail and fastidiously tucked an errant frond of hair back into his cap.

The two men ran the short distance to the helicopter, bent almost double to reduce the impact of the savage wind. They scrambled into the machine and slammed the sliding doors closed. The metal surfaces inside the cockpit felt brittle with cold. The pilot shuddered and reached behind his seat. He pulled out a scuffed flying jacket and dragged it on over his uniform. He turned up the collar close around his neck and started the engine.

Mason's hands were scratched and blue with cold. He sucked at the fingers of each hand in turn and swore softly. He looked at Gregory, who stood with his arms folded across his big chest, one hand buried in each armpit.

'Any ideas?'

Gregory shook his head. He nodded towards the gun that lay in the road. 'We've tried the only idea I had. We need a better lever than that.' He looked around at the trees which grew dense on the mountainside above them and shrugged. The branches grew too high to be accessible. 'What we need is a fence post.' He grinned ruefully at Mason. 'The trouble is, there are no fences.'

'What's down there?' asked Mason, indicating the road as it sloped away around the hillside.

'As far as I remember, nothing. Plenty more trees, but nothing else.'

'Are you positive? Isn't there an old farm building? A shed?'

Gregory frowned, his thick, black eyebrows knitting as he thought. 'Not that I can remember.' He turned to the car and rapped on the driver's window. The misted glass lowered and Helena's face, clouded with concern, looked out at him. Gregory reached a hand through the open window and caressed her cheek. 'Do you know of anywhere down the mountain where we might find some kind of implement? Some fencing. A hunter's shelter. Anything?'

The woman thought for a moment. 'There's a place where there might be something. There were men there a while ago felling trees. They may have left things there. I don't know.'

Gregory looked up to see if Mason had overheard. Mason removed his fingers from his mouth.

'How far is it, do you think?'

'I don't know. Two kilometres. Three.'

He made a wry face. 'Damn. I'll have to go. Father, do you want to wait in the car with Helena? I'll be back as quickly as I can.' Without waiting for a response he began running down the road, his shoes squeaking on the crisp snow.

The helicopter clattered through the darkness; Captain Diament sat back in his seat scanning the countryside and irritably wishing his feet were warmer. The pilot sat silently, his eyes alert in a face still puffy with sleep. He knew the terrain well, but the deep layer of snow forced him to sit tensely forward, craning to interpret the landmarks rendered alien by the white shadowless covering.

'Don't you have any heating in this thing?' Diament had to bellow over the racket of the motor.

The pilot stayed hunched over the controls. 'Heating? Sorry, Captain. This is a military machine you know, not police.' Diament grunted and pushed his hands deeper in his pockets. He watched the countryside slide past. In the far distance he saw the lights of a solitary car and the pale glow of the few street lamps of a small village. He yawned. At a sudden sound from the pilot he was at once alert again. The pilot pointed ahead of them. Through the curved glass of the helicopter's bubble he could make out the cluster of shadows that were the houses of the village they sought. At the far edge of the group of buildings one shadow stood apart, larger than the others.

Diament craned eagerly forward. 'That's it! Take us down!'

The pilot slid the machine expertly down towards the house. He circled once, checking for cables or other obstacles, and then set the helicopter gently down on the open area behind the buildings, which he guessed to be lawn.

Before the rotors had come to rest, Diament was out of the helicopter and running, crouched, towards the house, calling for the pilot to follow him. The young pilot waited until the rotors had settled and dropped before stepping down and following the other man around the house to the front door.

He was not surprised to see the black Polonez parked in the front courtyard. Obviously, the Captain's colleagues were already here. He was not surprised, either, to notice that the door was broken from the outside. Of course.

He was surprised, though, at the sight that awaited him in the hall of the house. The Captain knelt by a man, as young as the pilot, who lay gasping, hands and feet lashed to the pipes of the central heating. The pilot stood on the threshold, astounded to see that the bound man wore a Russian uniform. He was further astonished to see that, instead of comforting the man, the Captain had grasped him by the hair and was firing questions at him in a voice choked with fury.

The pilot shuffled and cleared his throat. His face white with anger, the Captain, still kneeling by the captive Russian, turned to look at the pilot.

'Get out,' he bellowed. 'Get back to the helicopter. Wait for me there.' He dismissed the pilot with a gesture, like a man flicking crumbs from his clothing, and turned back to question the helpless man who lay in front of him, his eyes brimming with fear.

The pilot looked on for another moment before turning to return to the aircraft. His face, as he walked back through the snow, was filled with a look of purest hatred.

## 20

Dominiak took the call on the first ring. His forehead rested heavily on the heel of one hand, as though he were trying to exorcize a headache. By his elbow a glass ashtray emerged from a mound of cigarette debris, as though it had just erupted. A glass, half-full of cold tea, stood near the ashtray. In the tea floated a half slice of lemon and three cigarette ends.

'Hello.' His voice was almost inaudible.

'Hello. Can you hear me? This is Captain Diament.' Concluding from Dominiak's faint voice that the line was bad, Diament was bellowing.

Dominiak held the receiver wearily away from him, his head still cradled in his hand, looked at it for a moment and murmured, 'Prick,' very softly. Into the mouthpiece, in a normal voice, he said, 'This is Dominiak. I can hear you. What's going on? Where are you?'

'I'm at the Kodec house, sir. Major Cherneff is dead. Professor Kodec, too. Cherneff was…'

'Wait a second,' broke in Dominiak. Lifting his head from the mouthpiece, but without bothering to cover it, he bellowed in the general direction of the door, 'Colonel Toparoff!' He was drawing breath to call again when the door opened and Toparoff came hurriedly into the room. He was in shirtsleeves and wore no shoes. Dominiak noticed that his socks were dark blue and of very thin material. Until then he had only seen socks like that on wealthy Westerners. He had always thought of them as capitalist socks. He jerked his head at a second telephone on the side table where the tea-making equipment lay. 'It's Diament. He's at Professor Kodec's. You'd better listen in.' He spoke into the mouthpiece again. 'Diament? Start again, Colonel Toparoff is on the line.'

His voice fading sometimes on the bad line, Diament told his story. The two men listened, grim-faced and silent.

'What do you want me to do?' he asked when he had finished.

'Do you know how they left and when?' asked Dominiak.

'The soldiers estimate they've been gone a couple of hours. They must have taken their own car, hers or the Professor's, that is. Cherneff's car and the Englishman's are still here.'

'What kind of car is it?' It was Toparoff who spoke.

'A Polski 500.'

'What!' Toparoff was incredulous. 'They took that? In this weather!' He gestured absently towards the window. He looked across at Dominiak. 'Can you catch them Captain?' His voice was colder than the wind outside.

'Probably. If the snow holds off.'

'Even if it doesn't, Captain. Even if it doesn't. We must have them tonight. Do you understand?' His tone was not an invitation to a discussion.

'Yes, sir,' answered Diament hurriedly. 'Oh, and Comrade Dominiak – er – Colonel, what do I do about the soldiers here?'

Toparoff answered. 'Can you get them into the helicopter?'

'No, sir. Not really. If we... I mean when we find the others we'll already be overloaded.'

'Well then, Captain, you must do what you think fit.' His voice had chilled a further ten degrees. He paused before continuing. 'You understand, don't you, Captain, what would happen if anybody outside our own little, er, group were to find out about tonight?' He waited again. From across the room Dominiak regarded the Russian silently, his face empty of all expression. 'Bear that in mind, Captain. The embarrassment to your own government and, regrettably, to mine. And do whatever you think is necessary.' He put down the telephone.

Dominiak sat for some moments, the receiver still in his hand, staring blankly at the Russian. Slowly he put down the telephone and leant back in his chair, his eyes still on

Toparoff. He crossed his legs laboriously and resumed probing the ribbed indentation where his sock elastic bit into the dead white flesh of his calf.

'Good man, your Major Cherneff,' he remarked conversationally, not taking his eyes from Toparoff's face.

Toparoff looked over at him sharply. 'He did very well.'

Dominiak continued. 'After all, with only three of your crack troops for support he had to go up against an elderly cardiac case, a priest, a lady librarian and a circular-saw salesman.' He added, in a solicitous tone, 'It can't have been easy.'

Toparoff flushed, his dark face becoming congested. He stood up angrily.

'Your sarcasm will get you into a lot of trouble, Comrade. Major Cherneff was a very good man.'

'It's a good thing you didn't send somebody second-rate.' Dominiak murmured, squinting through a cloud of blue smoke. Louder, he went on, 'Your people's incompetence may get us all into a lot of trouble, Comrade Colonel. We have discussed this too many times to be worth repeating. If word of this leaks, if it's bungled, we will have a lot more than a diplomatic problem on our hands. It will be more than a matter of America and the rest of the West cutting off credit. We could have the whole population of this country on the streets, Comrade Colonel. Looking for blood. Yours and mine. I doubt if the militia or the army could control it. I doubt if they could be relied on to *want* to control it.'

'Then we would control it, Comrade, make no mistake about that.' Toparoff's voice was angry and threatening.

'No,' answered Dominiak wearily, 'I'm in no danger of making a mistake about that. But I tell you again, Colonel: don't underestimate the power of the Church in this country. And the power of nationalism.' He shook his head. Ash fell. 'But of course, you will,' he added. 'You always have and you always will.' He shrugged. 'Let's hope Diament will do better.'

In Professor Kodec's study Captain Diament replaced the receiver and sat motionless, his hand still resting lightly on the telephone. He lifted his astrakhan hat and scratched thoughtfully at a spot which did not itch. He replaced the hat, adjusted it firmly on his head, and slowly unbuttoned the top two buttons of his thick overcoat. He reached his right hand inside the coat and withdrew a heavy, dark grey hand-gun. With a deft movement, he slid the magazine from the gun, examined it briefly and rammed it back into place with the heel of his hand.

Letting out a long sigh, he pushed himself to his feet. He looked quickly around the room. Selecting a thick feather-filled cushion from an armchair, he walked from the room.

The pilot sat hunched low in his seat. His gloved hands were pushed deep into the pockets of his flying-jacket. His youthful, unformed face was pinched with cold. He wished he had a cassette player. He wished the Captain would get a move on. He wished that he had never joined the air force. He had wanted to fly fighter planes and maybe afterwards work as a commercial airliner pilot for LOT, the Polish airline. Helicopters were okay. They were fun to fly, even. But it was less fun to sit in one in the middle of a winter's night freezing his balls off waiting for some arrogant turd of a Security Police Captain to make up his mind to go home. He closed his eyes and almost managed to doze. He was roused suddenly by two muffled thuds coming from the house. A few moments later came a third sound. He was wondering if he should get out of the helicopter and investigate when the Captain came striding around the corner of the house.

Diament eased himself into his seat. The pilot started the motor and looked questioningly at Diament. Diament looked straight ahead, frowning and preoccupied.

'Where now, sir? Cracow?'

Diament started. 'Eh! Oh. No. Follow the road. We're looking for a Polski 500 with three people in it. Stay low.'

The pilot nodded and lifted the helicopter from the

garden. The whirling rotors whipped up snow in a simulation of the storm just ended. As they side-slipped away from the Kodec house and began heading towards the sprinkling of lights of the village, the pilot caught a familiar scent in the cockpit. It was unmistakable. He knew the smell of cordite, of a recently fired gun. Sideways, he glanced at Diament. The officer sat tight-lipped, scanning the road as it slid quickly past beneath them.

Mason was enjoying his run. Without the heavy coat it would have been perfect. He tasted the air, relishing it's coldness now that he was moving and warm. He ran with easy strides, just a little flat-footed on the untrustworthy surface of the snow. His eye drank in the mysterious snowscape around him. Despite the absence of stars or moon there was light everywhere, as though the snow-covered land gave off a light of its own.

He had been running about ten or eleven minutes, about a mile and a half, he judged, when his reverie was broken by the sight of a pile of logs by the roadside, coinciding with a stitch low in his ribs. He felt cheated. Fit people were not supposed to get stitches. Letting the logical consequence of that thought rest unexamined, he loped over to the heap of logs. He brushed snow from the ends of the logs. They were freshly cut.

He looked around. No path was visible on the steeply rising land above the road or the sharply falling mountainside below. He tossed a mental coin. It came down heads and he set off, scrambling straight up the slope above him. It was hard going. He stumbled often where the snow lay unexpectedly deep in hollows. Within a few minutes his breath was coming in rasps. The stitch hurt.

He stopped and looked around him, holding his side and blowing hard. A little further up the slope, just visible through the dense growth of pines he could make out the shape of another logpile. He took a deep breath and plunged on up the hillside.

The stacked logs were cut in metre lengths. The thinnest of them was at least five inches in diameter. For his purpose they were useless. He examined the ground around him. The woodcutters would have trimmed the logs, abandoning the thinner branches where they lay. The trouble was, where they lay was now under eight inches of snow.

He began patrolling the area, feeling with his feet for the unevenness that would suggest wood lying beneath the snow. There was a lot of it. A dozen or more times he reached down to pull a branch free from the snow only to find it was too flimsy or too thick to suit him. Ten minutes had probably passed before he found what he was looking for. A branch four feet long and a uniform two-inch diameter. He knocked it against a tree to get rid of the snow. Wedging one end firmly into the ground and the other end against a tree, he tested its strength by stamping hard in the middle of it. It jarred his foot. Satisfied, he grabbed the branch in one hand and half-ran, half-tobogganned his way down to the road. He paused on the road to brush snow from his clothes. The stitch had gone. He began running back to the car.

The helicopter droned on. Neither the pilot nor Diament spoke. The policeman scanned the ground thirty metres below them. Once, a movement in the trees brought them lower to investigate. A group of deer, panicked by the racket of the machine, fled at their approach. Apart from the deer, nothing in the landscape moved.

They continued, following the road as it went close against the mountain. The height of the closely packed trees obliged them to fly directly over the road in order to see the surface. This meant staying close to the slope of the mountain. In the powerful, gusting wind it made for difficult flying. The pilot was good, skilfully countering the unpredictable movements of the air to stay on a course, like a fish remaining stationary over its nest in a violent swell.

Diament hardly blinked. He stared steadily down as the road, distinguishable only as a break in the trees, slowly descended the flank of the mountain. The noise from the rotor above him was oppressive. He was depressed. Depressed by his action back at the house, by being up all night, by the weather. He pulled his coat closer around him. Suddenly, he stiffened and crouched eagerly forward in his seat. He took the sleeve of the pilot's flying jacket in one hand and pointed at the road ahead and below with the other.

'Down there,' he shouted, stabbing with his forefinger. 'On the left.'

The pilot peered down at the road, looking for the object of Diament's excitement. It was some seconds before he saw it. At first it had seemed to form part of the snowdrift. Only slowly did he realize that it was a small car, deeply embedded in the snow, at an angle at which nobody would park.

Diament leant toward the pilot and shouted close to his ear. 'If there's anyone in the car, can they see us?'

'I doubt it,' the pilot yelled back, 'not yet. Not against this muck.' He jerked a thumb at the sky.

'How about hearing us?'

'I doubt that, too. Depends how much noise there is down there. It's a pretty strong wind. Probably making a hell of a row in the trees.'

Diament nodded. He shouted at the pilot again. 'Find a place to set us down. Far enough away so that they won't hear us or see us come in. Try around that bend,' he added, indicating a point ahead of them where the road veered to the left.

The pilot swung the helicopter in a wide arc, avoiding flying too close to the car, and then brought it back close to the slope. They were shielded from the sight of anyone in the Polski by the outcrop of the hill. The pilot scanned the area below, seeking a place where the gap in the trees was wide enough to land. A hundred yards further he saw the spot he needed, a place where the trees on the slope below did not grow above the level of the road. He would be obliged to land on the very edge of the road with the rotor overhanging, but it was possible. Provided the hard shoulder was solid and did not crumble under the weight, pitching them down the precipitous slope.

Very cautiously, he allowed the craft to drop towards the chosen spot. There was no room at all for error. To one side the tall pines threatened to snap the fragile rotor blades, to the other the mountain fell abruptly away, down to a stand of trees that waited to impale them.

At thirty feet above the ground the snow started to fly. At twenty feet visibility through the curved perspex of the nose bubble was no more than a yard. The pilot strained to locate the edge of the road. Next to him Diament sat tensely, his lips pale. The storm all around them grew thicker. On all sides only the white on white of the racing snow could be seen. They inched downwards. With a sudden lurch the helicopter rocked backward and was still.

The pilot let out a long breath and looked across at Diament. His faint smile showed only a small part of the satisfaction he felt. Diament gave only the briefest nod, reluctantly acknowledging the pilot's skill. Still smiling slightly, the pilot switched off the motor. The engine fell silent as the rotors clattered to a halt. The snow subsided.

Brusquely, Diament slid his door open and stepped down into the snow, signalling the pilot to follow. Much more carefully, the pilot opened his own door and looked out. Below him the slope fell directly away towards the distant trees. The ski-shaped runner of the helicopter had settled into the snow less than a foot from the edge. Moving prudently, the pilot slid across the passenger seat and out on the side where Diament waited, gun in hand.

'Follow me,' Diament ordered, 'and tread carefully. No noise.'

The pilot looked curiously from Diament's face to the gun in his hand. Shrugging imperceptibly, he set off alongside Diament, up the road towards the spot where they had seen the car.

★

Mason paused, breathing hard. His armpits were wet with sweat, his hands blue with cold. He leant the branch against a tree and turned his back to the wind. Opening his coat, he thrust his hands inside his jacket and began rubbing them vigorously against his body. After a minute or two sensation began to return. The tips of his fingers began to itch and then to sting as circulation returned. It hurt. He kept on rubbing until he was able to flex his fingers normally. For the twentieth time that night he cursed himself for not taking some gloves from the house. He buttoned his coat again and picked up the piece of wood. Immediately, he could feel his fingers begin to freeze again in the bitter wind. He started running again, staggering awkwardly, with the branch clasped in his right hand and his left hand thrust into his coat pocket.

Two minutes later he rounded a curve in the road and almost stumbled in his surprise. Twenty metres ahead of him stood the dark silhouette of the helicopter.

Dropping the wood, he plunged full length into the deep snow at the roadside. He lay for a moment, waiting for the shout that would tell him he had been seen. Gradually, he became aware that the loudest sound he could hear was the blood pounding in his own head. He raised his head from the snow and examined the aircraft. All was still. Slowly, he pulled himself upright, wiping snow from his face and ears. His knee hurt. He must have hit something under the snow.

Limping, he warily approached the silent black shape. He stayed close to the edge of the road. His mind was made up. If real danger appeared he would go over the edge and take his chances on the steep drop. Nothing moved.

Drawing close to the helicopter, he reached out a hand and took hold of the door handle. He yanked hard at it, ready to throw himself inside. Nothing happened. He looked again at the door.

'Shit,' he muttered, 'it's a sliding door.' He drew the door back. After quickly checking that there was nobody inside, he began a quick search for weapons. There were no firearms. By the pilot's seat, held in place by worn leather straps, he discovered a fire extinguisher, a heavy, rubber-jacketed torch and a small hatchet.

His hands made clumsy by the cold and the tension, he began fumbling with the straps. It was several seconds before he freed the torch and the hatchet. The torch he stowed in a pocket. The hatchet he kept in his hand. Deciding nobody he cared about was likely to burst into flames, he left the fire extinguisher where it was.

Clutching the hatchet and feeling like a Commanche, he left the helicopter and scrambled up the slope above the road, advancing well into the cover of the trees. Almost out of sight of the road, he turned and began running parallel to it. The steepness of the terrain obliged him to run with an exaggerated limp. His injured knee was very painful. He fell often as he struggled through the trees. Moving more slowly he would have made less noise on the freezing crust of the snow. However, he hoped he could rely on the noise of the trees, which thrashed in the strong wind, to cover any sound he made.

He advanced laboriously, always keeping the road in sight. Ahead of him, through the closely packed trees, he saw a shadow move. Then another. He crouched and began manoeuvring closer to the two figures, always keeping trees between himself and the dark shapes. They were moving very slowly and staying close to the edge of the road and the shadow of the trees.

Mason closed the distance between them, one hand clutching his knee, the other holding the small axe. Incongruously, he noticed his hands were warm. The exercise was finally beginning to take effect.

He was close enough now to see the two men clearly. A civilian in a dark overcoat carried something at his side which Mason could not see but supposed was a gun. The other man, slighter in build, wore some kind of uniform. Both his hands were pushed into the pockets of his blouson, as though into a muff. It was impossible to see if he were armed.

Abruptly, the civilian placed a hand on the arm of his companion. They stopped and stood as though listening. The uniformed man took his hands from his pockets. Mason swore softly. The man carried a small revolver in his left hand. As he watched, the civilian leant close to the other man and appeared to whisper briefly in his ear. The other man nodded. They paused an instant more and then suddenly burst into a run and out of Mason's sight.

As stealthily as he was able on his worsening knee, Mason crept forward a few yards. In the next break in the trees his whole body stiffened. He drew quickly back into the shelter of a thick tree and, very carefully, peered down at the road. Almost directly below him was the car, rammed deep into the snow. The windows were frosted with loose snow blown on the wind. They were also opaque with condensation. On each side of the car, arms extended in a marksman's crouch, stood one of the two men. The civilian edged towards the car. Mason could see the man's tongue flick nervously at his lips. He probably thought he was invisible through the steamed up windows of the Polski, but he could not be sure. At that moment he was very dangerous.

Mason looked on helplessly as the man approached the car. Three feet from it he stopped. Mason watched him steady himself. The man's face worked as he swallowed, trying to moisten his dry mouth. Mason considered the man in front of him. About forty. Too young to have seen the war. In a country with very little crime he had probably never drawn a gun in earnest before. The man was scared! Mason dare not move. Any sudden sound and he might empty his gun through the car window.

Mason realized with a fleeting sense of guilt that, together with his fear for Helena and Gregory, he was also invaded by a sense of the absurdity of the man's posture. In all the films Mason had seen as a child, a person who wanted to frighten someone else with a gun just pointed it at them. It always worked. Nowadays, everyone he saw on a screen handling a gun impersonated experts. Even housewives picking up a fortuitous stray gun to fend off a burglar were transformed into dangerous Vietnam veterans.

The man's Adam's apple bobbed in a last gulp as he reached forward and snatched at the door handle. He flung it from him with the abrupt, panicked violence of a man who had become suddenly aware he held a viper by the tail. The door flew open and sagged on a broken hinge.

'Don't move!' Diament shouted. Moving very cautiously, he edged forward, his gun playing over the car's interior. Mason could see Helena's immobile face staring straight ahead at the grey opacity of the windscreen. The policeman held the gun close to her head as over her shoulder he checked the rear seat of the car. He seemed a little disconcerted to find it empty.

Stepping a pace back from the car he motioned to Helena. 'Out,' he ordered roughly. 'Kneel down here and put your hands on your head.' Slowly and silently she complied, kneeling in front of the man. His gun still trained on her, he stooped lower and spoke into the car. 'Now you. Over here.' He flicked the gun barrel at a spot beside Helena.

Mason saw the car rock as the big man inside climbed laboriously across the driving seat. He emerged slowly and sank to his knees next to Helena. As he did so, he gave her shoulder a quick squeeze. His face was perfectly calm.

Diament moved half a step closer to them. Confident again, he thrust the tip of the gun roughly into the flesh beneath Helena's chin. He jerked her head up, forcing her to look at him.

Not knowing why, Mason silently drew the heavy torch from his pocket. Below him, he heard the man speak to Helena.

'Where's the other one? The Englishman. Where is he?' She looked mutely up at him. He pushed the gun deeper into the flesh under her throat. Her lips parted but still she did not speak.

'Once more.' Diament spoke so quietly Mason could

scarcely make out his words. 'Where is he? How long ago did he leave the car?' Her face filled with contempt, she tried to look away.

Without warning, Diament drew back and raised the gun high. His eyes dilated and his lips shrank back in an angry grimace over his teeth.

With no clear idea what he was doing, Mason flipped the switch of the torch and hurled it hard towards the group. It cartwheeled through the air, its powerful beam flashing across the three people like a strobe light. At the same moment, Mason launched himself down the slope at a lop-sided run screaming with all the force of his lungs.

# 21

Diament's blow would have opened Helena's face. Instead, he checked and spun to face the direction of the scream. Perplexity chased the anger from his face as he tried to identify the pulsing light that looped towards him. Slightly dazzled by the blinding power of the beam, his attention was split between warily watching the torch and trying to locate the source of the sudden scream. In that moment, Gregory pushed himself silently to his feet, set his shoulders, and buried a big fist deep below Diament's rib cage.

Diament's mouth gaped silently and his hands flew to his stomach as though on springs. His eyes and mouth at their fullest width, he sank silently to his knees. Then he pitched face first into the snow.

Mason, coming down through the trees at full tilt, brandishing the hatchet and feeling more like a Comman-che than ever, saw the punch thrown. He was admiring the sweet economy of it when his knee collapsed under him.

He sprawled face first down the slope and slid to a halt, amid a small avalanche, five feet from where Diament lay face down. He was empty-handed and he had snow inside his shirt. He pushed himself up onto one elbow, blew snow from his mouth and nostrils, and heard a quiet voice.

'Don't move, anybody.'

Blinking snow from his eyes, he looked up slowly. Then, wearily, he let himself fall back onto the snow. Standing by the bonnet of the car, the helicopter pilot trained his revolver on them. Gregory held Helena in his arms. She clung to his broad chest, trembling violently.

The pilot spoke to Mason. 'Move over with them. Slowly.' He sounded nervous, but his hand held the gun steady. At least he held the gun normally in one hand. But then he did not get much opportunity to watch American television. Mason rose painfully to his feet, moving very deliberately. He winced. The knee would not support any weight.

'Come on.' The pilot waved the gun irritably. He seemed to be using some anger to cover his nervousness. 'Get over with them.' He bit his lip and glanced anxiously at the figure of Diament, who still lay clutching his stomach and breathing noisily into the crushed snow beneath his head. The pilot's eyes flickered uncertainly in the boyish face. He needed someone to give him an order. Mason filled the breach. 'How dare you behave this way!' His voice was loud and confident. 'Don't you see who this is? Don't you recognize Father Gregory Kozka?'

'Huh?' The man looked uneasily from Mason to Diament. Diament's muffled groans did not give him much to go on. He looked again at Mason. His eyes were narrowed as he looked for treachery on Mason's face.

Mason returned the man's gaze, his own eyes blazing with genuine anger. He gestured towards Gregory. 'This man is Father Gregory. Can't you see? He is here as a guest of your government. At the personal invitation of General Jaruzelski.'

'Yeah, well, don't worry. So am I. I'm Mr Gorbachev. I do this as part of my policy to meet the man in the street.' He sniggered at his own exceptional wit. He glanced down to see if Diament was enjoying it, too.

'It's true, my son, I am Gregory.' The deep voice was very low. For the first time Gregory turned his face from Helena and allowed his gaze to meet the pilot's.

The next four or five seconds passed in slow motion. The jeering response got lost somewhere in the pilot's throat. Under the impact of the extraordinary blue eyes the mocking expression melted, giving way in turn to surprise, disbelief, shock, awe and something like love. For a while the man seemed to try to accommodate them all at once. The arm holding the gun fell slackly to his side, as though he had suffered some kind of internal power-cut.

'You fucking imbecile!' Diament was sitting up. He sat with his legs straight out in front of him and his hands still folded over his solar plexus. Although his shoulders were still hunched forward in pain, he had obviously recovered his voice. The pilot did not appear to hear him. Diament spoke again. His voice came through gritted teeth, sibilant and breathy, like a damaged accordion. 'Cover them, you fool.'

The pilot blinked and looked slowly round at Diament. His immature, slack features tightened as his look skittered from Diament to Gregory and back again. Shaking his head, he stepped quickly across to Diament.

'Watch them,' Diament hissed. 'And hand me my gun.' He flapped a hand to the spot where his own gun had fallen. The pilot nodded silently, his eyes on Diament's face. He stooped and collected the other man's gun from the snow. He blew a few clinging flakes from it and hefted it in his hand, testing its weight. He flipped it lightly over and caught it by the barrel. Diament held out an impatient hand. The pilot drew a step nearer to him, cocked his arm, and drove the butt of the weapon against Diament's temple. The secret policeman keeled over sideways, still in a sitting position.

Helena sobbed with renewed vigour, this time with relief, against Gregory's sweater. Mason laughed, wiped a hand across his face, and sat down heavily on the road, his back against the car.

'Thank you,' he said simply, to the pilot.

'Yes, thank you, my son.'

The awe was back in the young man's face. He stared at Gregory. Mason had probably worn a similar expression himself once, the first time he saw the Taj Mahal by a full moon. Gregory looked directly back at the man, his fierce, dark face warmed now by his amazing smile.

The pilot's next act astonished Mason. Without a word he stepped forward and dropped to his knees. Crossing himself, he reached out a hand. Gregory knew instantly what the man wanted. He released Helena, whose sobs had subsided, and turned to face the kneeling youth fully. He held out a hand, palm downward. The pilot took Gregory's big-knuckled hand very gently in his own. Cradling the sinewy hand as though it had been a butterfly, he quickly dipped his head and brushed the back of it with his lips. He remained a moment, his head bowed, and then let go of Gregory's hand and stood up.

His head still bowed, he murmured, 'I'm sorry, Father, I didn't know. I had no idea who...' He struggled for words.

'It's nothing, my son.'

The pilot would not be satisfied with being absolved. He needed to explain himself. 'I did not know it was you, Father. The Captain didn't tell me who we were looking for, or why. I'm an Air Force pilot, Father. I'm not militia, or security police. I'm just a pilot.'

Gregory touched the man's arm lightly. 'I know. These people never need to explain,' he went on, looking down at Diament. 'For the time being they can do whatever they please.'

Mason broke into Gregory's musing. 'Look,' he said, addressing the pilot, 'can you get us out of here?'

'In the helicopter? Yes. We were fully fuelled up. But where to?'

Mason looked at the other two. 'Any ideas?'

Helena shook her head. 'They know who our friends are. Nowhere would be safe.' Self-pity had insinuated itself back into her voice.

He turned quickly to Gregory. 'Father?'

'They know every detail of my life here. It would be too dangerous. For us as well as for my friends.'

'I can't help,' the pilot said, without being asked. 'My family is up in the north, near Gdansk. Too far.'

Mason bit hard at his lower lip. They had to reach Warsaw, an embassy. By dawn all trains and aircraft would be watched. Abruptly, he pushed himself to his feet. 'I think I have an idea.' All of them looked expectantly at him. He was already reaching for the lever that opened the storage space under the bonnet. He handed the cans of petrol to Gregory and Helena.

'Would you take these to the helicopter? The two of us will dispose of the car.'

Gregory looked sombrely at Mason, his look taking in the prostrate figure at his feet. 'You won't harm him?'

'No, Father. We'll only move him where it will take longer for him to be found.'

With a last dubious look Gregory turned and spoke softly to Helena. The two of them began to walk down the sloping road.

'Don't get in until I come,' the pilot called. 'The whole thing could go over the edge.'

As the pilot spoke, Mason crouched by the damaged wing of the car and deflated the tyre. With a word to the pilot, he climbed quickly into the driver's seat and started the motor. With the pilot pushing hard from behind he eased the car across the road, stopping it with its nose a foot from the drop. He jumped from the car and spoke peremptorily to the pilot. Digging his heels into the snow, the man set his back against the car and heaved. The car lurched forward and pitched down the vertiginous mountainside. They watched it cartwheel several times, bringing a small avalanche in its wake, before it crashed into a grove of pines and came to rest. From where they stood it was scarcely visible.

Mason turned away and moved to where Diament lay. He stooped, pocketing the inert man's gun, when he felt the pilot's hand on his arm, restraining him.

'Leave him,' the young man said, quietly. 'You join the others. I'll deal with him.'

Mason turned to look into the pilot's eyes, surprised by something in the man's tone. The pilot looked levelly back at him, his face expressionless. Without another word Mason nodded and, straightening, began striding down the road in the tracks of the others. When he reached the bend that would take him out of sight of the pilot, he looked back.

The pilot was dragging the slack body of Diament towards the edge. The unconcious man's torso was naked. A pile of clothes lay in the road, dark against the snow. As Mason watched, the pilot reached the edge and, his face contorting with effort, sent the man spilling down the slope. The pilot watched for an instant and then turned, snatched up the pile of clothes and hurled them far out into the void. As he wheeled and began sprinting down the road, he caught sight of Mason.

Surprise flashed across the man's face. He drew alongside and the two of them hurried on towards the helicopter. They had gone a few steps in silence when the pilot grabbed at Mason's arm and jerked his head to where Gregory and Helena awaited them.

'You won't mention that, back there?'

Mason smiled and touched the man's shoulder. 'We moved him to the roadside. Out of danger.'

The pilot nodded gratefully and they hurried on to join the other two. Seconds later, the engine coughed once and clattered deafeningly to life. At the sound there was a tangible slackening of the tension in all of them. They turned to each other, grinning with relief. Helena's grin became a laugh as she caught sight of the crusted coatings of snow that whitened Gregory's thick, unruly eyebrows.

It was the first time since he had met her that Mason had seen her laugh.

The helicopter rose, scudding at a steep angle away from the mountainside. Helena and Gregory sat in the rear, their laughter not quite extinguished. Mason sat next to the pilot, bellowing instructions into the man's ear.

For thirty-five minutes they sped across the empty landscape, leaving the mountains behind them and crossing a wide tract of open farm land, dotted with dilapidated wood and thatch farmhouses. The pilot knew the terrain well and followed confidently the directions Mason gave him. Only when they left the open land and began crossing an extensive area of forest did he pull out a map and begin studying it.

Constantly comparing the ground beneath them with the map spread on his knees he took them across the forest, over a cluster of lakes, to an area where the pines below began to thin. Some way off to their left the lights of a small town gave them a bearing. Using this and the clear straight trace of a railway they found the inconspicuous forest road Mason was seeking. From above, the road was no more than a white channel between the trees. No vehicle moved on the road. They had followed the track for perhaps three miles when Mason saw what he was looking for.

Below them, shielded from the track by a stand of pines they could make out the shape of a low wooden building. The snow on the roof almost met the drift piled against the walls. Mason shouted to the pilot and pointed to an open area behind the house studded with only a few trees. They descended. They emerged into the blinding flurry of snow whipped up by the still turning rotors and hurried towards the house. The snow was thicker than it had been in the mountains. In front of the door it had drifted to above waist-height.

'Can you start digging? I'll join you in a moment.' As he spoke, Mason was already moving towards the corner of the house. Grinning agreement, Gregory began energetically scooping the snow from the door. In another moment Helena and the pilot had joined him and the snow began to fly, baring the weathered wood.

At the side of the house Mason plunged to mid-thigh in the drift beneath a window. Reaching up into the eaves, he groped for a moment and brought down an old-fashioned iron key. A few moments later he was leading them into the house.

In the pitch darkness he felt for the matches he knew lay on the low table just inside the door. He struck one and lit the petrol lamp that stood next to them. The lamp's glow revealed a long, low room with a heavily beamed ceiling and a floor of dull red tiles that gleamed softly in the lamplight. The room was furnished only with a bed, covered with a bright cloth, a couch with some coloured cushions, a pine chest of drawers and a red-painted table and chairs. A huge open fire-place dominated the far end of the room.

Ignoring their questioning looks, Mason moved quickly to the bed. He took up the phone that stood on the floor beside it and began dialling, grateful that this one concession to modernity had been allowed in the place.

Listening to the muted clicks and whirrings on the line he wondered again whom it had been necessary to bribe to get the phone connected in so remote a spot. The ringing continued for some time, the sound very distant. When it was finally answered the voice sounded startlingly close.

'Hello.' The voice was wary, as if it was expecting an obscene call.

'Barbara? It's me.'

'Uh?' He could sense her struggling to get fully conscious. 'Who's that?' She sounded slightly peevish now.

'It's me. I'm sorry to wake you. I need help, badly. You're the only one I can ask.' He spoke hurriedly.

'All right. Okay. I'm awake now. Sorry.' The note of

irritation was gone, to be replaced by concern. 'What is it? What's wrong?'

'Look, Barbara, I can't tell you like this. I don't trust your phone. Anyway it's too incredible. If I told you everything you'd think I'd gone nuts.'

'Why? What's up?' She was really worried now. 'Tell me. Are you in trouble? Are you hurt?'

'Hurt, not really. In trouble, yes. Barbara, do you have petrol?'

'No, but I can get some. You know.' He knew. From another of the men with a basement. For a price.

'Good. Will you come and get me? Now. As quickly as you can?'

'Yes, but where are you?'

'You know the place, Barbara.' There was a moment's pause.

'Just to be sure, what time is it there?'

Automatically Mason glanced at his watch, frowning. Suddenly he laughed aloud into the telephone. By the bed stood an old alarm clock. It has not worked since he had known Barbara. Each time they came they agreed it had to be repaired and each time they left they forgot it. The hands showed 7.45.

'It's a quarter to eight.'

Gregory, overhearing, shot Mason a puzzled look.

'All right,' she replied smiling. 'I'll be there as soon as I can.' Barbara turned to the dark, middle-eastern looking man beside her and briskly shook him awake. 'Sorry, darling,' she said firmly. 'Time for you to go.'

In a small, bare room at the telephone exchange a middle-aged, unhealthy looking woman in headphones yawned as a young man entered with a cassette. Her podgy hands lay on the keyboard of the typewriter in front of her, making no attempt to screen the cavernous yawn. The man looked at a calendar on the wall above her as he handed her the cassette. The girl on the calendar was not very pretty but at least her teeth were good.

The woman took the cassette and glanced carefully at a number and the time pencilled on the label. She tossed it into a wire tray on her desk to join several others.

'I don't know who they think we are,' she grumbled, not necessarily to the young man. 'There's enough work for three people lately. You'd think they'd give us some staff. Look at it,' she implored the room. 'I've got enough there already for the rest of my shift. I don't know what they think we are. Robots!' The man left the room.

'It's time they gave me an assistant, the way this work's increased,' she complained to the closing door.

As the woman spoke, Barbara, with a full tank of petrol, was leaving Warsaw and heading south.

# 22

Toparoff flinched, like an oyster hit by lemon juice as Dominiak, for the hundredth time, scratched vigorously at his head.

'This is absurd, Comrade, absurd.'

'What is?' asked Dominiak absently, examining his fingernails for trapped dandruff.

'Diament. It's over an hour since he called.'

'Oh that! I know.'

'Of course you know. Doesn't it worry you? Surely by now they must have found something?'

'I would have hoped so. Mind you, Comrade Colonel, we don't know how the weather is down there. Maybe it's snowing again and they have landed somewhere to wait it out.'

'Maybe. And maybe Diament is another of the incompetents I'm expected to work with here.'

'Sorry, Colonel, but we do our best. We can't all be

supermen, of course. Not like Major Cherneff.' He studied the toe of his shoe as he added the last remark.

'Cherneff was good,' Toparoff snapped, rising to the bait. 'We must get the situation in hand', he went on. 'The danger of leaks increases with every minute they are not in our hands.'

'I know that, Colonel, believe me,' answered Dominiak, ruminatively. Suddenly, he rose and strode to the door. With a muttered word to the Russian he left the room. Toparoff watched him go, disdain on his face as he watched the shiny back of the improbable blue suit disappear.

It was three or four minutes before Dominiak returned. He slumped untidily into his chair. In answer to Toparoff's raised eyebrows he said, 'I've arranged for all phone lines from the area to be out of order. People will think it's the snow. At least it will prevent anyone in the village, or a surrounding one, phoning the news to the outside world. That's if anybody witnessed anything. At this hour it's reasonable to hope no one did.'

Toparoff nodded approval. 'Good. Yes. Excellent. But I think we should go further. We should send men up there to close off the whole area. Nobody should be allowed in or out until we have them in our hands.'

Dominiak looked at him sourly. 'I don't want the area closed. Do you have any idea of the effects that would have? The rumours it would start? Before we knew where we were the whole country would know about it. It's been tried before. On three occasions since 1970 we've tried to close off Gdansk when they've had food riots. Less people would have known about it if we'd announced it on the eight o'clock television news!'

'So what do you suggest?'

Dominiak patted his pockets, searching for cigarettes. 'We'll wait. Until we hear from Diament. If we have no news by daybreak, my men will search the area.'

Toparoff was staring out of the window at the pale yellow of the street lamps, his hands pushed into the pockets of his expensively made trousers. 'And if they don't find anything?'

Dominiak waved a match slowly to extinction and surveyed the Russian from behind a swirl of smoke. 'I don't know, Comrade, I really don't. I don't see how I can instruct my men all over Poland to find and arrest Kozka, for God's sake. The whole country would hear about it. We should alert the Czechs, the border patrols, anyway, to watch for them in case they crossed into Czechoslovakia. But who do we tell them we're looking for? The Czechs living up there in the Tatra mountains are as Catholic as Poles. Hell, half of them *are* Poles, ethnically.'

'So you intend doing nothing?'

'That's not what I said, Colonel. We won't act precipitately until Diament has had time to report. I don't have to remind you, Colonel, that the soldiers at the Kodec house were wearing Russian uniforms. At present there are not more than a dozen Poles, outside of myself and the First Secretary, who are informed. As soon as we sound a general alert there will be thirty-five million more.' As he spoke, he drilled the little finger of his right hand into his ear. He withdrew the finger and examined the nail for a prize. Evidently disappointed, he wiped his finger absently on the cloth of his trousers. 'No, Comrade,' he concluded, 'it's in all our interests to wait.'

Despite his swarthy complexion two white spots had appeared on Toparoff's cheekbones. He spoke through clenched teeth. 'Until daybreak, Comrade. If nothing is heard by then I shall speak to my Ambassador. We have plenty of men, Dominiak. Good reliable men we can trust. Soldiers, who know their duty.'

Dominiak took his cigarette between two fingers and, with the heel of the same hand, rubbed his face hard. He was very tired.

'I know you have, Comrade,' he answered softly.

In the tiny lean-to kitchen Mason found the decorated tin that contained tea. The water supply was turned off. He went to the door and packed snow into a pan. Returning to the kitchen, he opened the valve of the gas cylinder and began preparing tea. Helena approached the kitchen. She hesitated by the door. He glanced at her and smiled. It was a measured smile. She had been a pain and he was wary. She smiled tentatively in return and took a step into the kitchen.

'Peter. I've been wanting to talk to you.' Her voice tailed off. She blinked uncertainly behind her glasses. He smiled at her again, more encouragingly. She chewed at her lip.

'I want to apologize.' She looked hard at the flagstone floor. 'For getting you into all this, I mean. It's my fault. I helped them lure you here.'

He gave a soft snort. 'Helena, they didn't need much help. I came for the money. They offered me a lot of money, a fortune, to get your father's story. I knew I was taking a chance. I didn't realize,' he said slightly ruefully, 'how much of a chance. But I was well aware there were risks.' He turned to pour hot water onto the tea. Helena reached for the pan.

'Here, let me do that.'

He lifted the pan out of her reach and gently pushed her arm away. 'Christ, another woman who can't stand to let a man do anything in a kitchen. Get away.' Grinning, he went on pouring the water. Helena retreated a step, noticeably more at ease for the matter-of-fact exchange. She spoke again.

'But I want you to know, Peter, I knew I was getting someone into trouble. It's true, I didn't know what they really planned. How could I? But the truth is I was thinking only of my father. I just didn't care about anything else. And I'm sorry.'

He handed her two glasses of tea. 'Forget it. You did what you did for love, I did it for money.' We both, he thought, got more than we bargained for. 'The question now is whether we can get ourselves out of it.' He picked up two more glasses. 'Come on.' He let her precede him into the main room.

In the tomb-like cold of the room they sipped the tea gratefully, their hands cupped around the hot glasses. Mason addressed the pilot.

'It seems to me you might be the one in the most serious trouble here. What do you intend to do?' The pilot made a clicking noise with his tongue. 'Return, I think,' he said laconically.

'Return where?'

'To the mountain. It's probable that the Captain won't have been found yet. Those roads are very difficult. I'll wreck the helicopter and wait to be rescued.'

Gregory spoke. 'What about the Captain? He'll have you shot.'

The pilot and Mason exchanged looks. The pilot moved uncomfortably inside his clothes. He left it to Mason to speak.

'It's very cold up there, Father.' Mason spoke very quietly. 'With the wind as well...' He allowed his voice to fade. He could not tell a direct lie to this man.

Gregory's eyes burned into his own. Both men were silent. Mason dropped his gaze.

The pilot set his glass down noisily on the empty hearth, slapped his hands on his thighs and stood up. He cleared his throat loudly.

'Huh. I must get back before a passing farmer reports anything.' He looked around at them all, unsure how to take leave. 'Well, goodbye, Miss, and good luck.' He shoved out an awkward hand for Helena to shake. She took it, smiling, in both hers.

'Good luck to you, too. And thank you.'

The young man flushed and offered his hand to Mason.

'Good luck.' Mason pressed the offered hand. The man turned to Gregory who stood watching, his face grave.

'Goodbye, er, – Your, – er – goodbye, Father,' the pilot shifted his feet diffidently. He began to offer his hand and then, in a sudden movement, dropped to his knees and crossed himself, his head bowed. Gregory offered the back of his hand. The man kissed it. Withdrawing his hand,

Gregory raised both hands and felt inside the neck of his thick sweater. He withdrew a thin chain and looped it over his head. A small crucifix dangled from the chain. He slipped it over the young man's head and took a step backwards.

'Good luck, and God bless you.'

Helena turned away, her eyes brimming.

The pilot, without a further word, got to his feet and left the house.

Barbara glanced fretfully at the petrol gauge. It had been showing close to zero for some time. She was only a few kilometres from the house. Normally a full tank got her there and part of the way home. On the snow she had been obliged to spend a lot of time in third gear. The few kilometres remaining were a short drive, but they would be a long walk.

For the hundredth time she wondered what sort of trouble Mason was in. It was strange. Only a few weeks before, his turning to her would have astonished her. Accepting to drive hundreds of kilometres on such a night to meet him would have surprised her more. Now, she could not imagine refusing, or even asking why. She looked again at the quivering needle of the petrol gauge. This time she was smiling.

Gregory was doing press-ups when he heard the car. Helena was asleep on the bed, a blanket thrown over her. Mason was dozing on the short sofa, one fist beneath his head, the other between his flexed knees. For years, Gregory had not needed to sleep more than four or five hours a night. He used the extra time to read or write and to study. For half an hour every single day, he exercised. Tonight, without books, he had extended his exercise programme.

He froze, his body rigid, listening hard. He looked across at Helena. Without the severe glasses she looked much younger, and vulnerable as an infant.

The sound of the car reached him again, faint but more distinct than before. As nimbly as a man twenty years younger, he got to his feet and crossed the room. He shook Mason by a shoulder. Instantly, he was wide awake.

'What is it?' He sat up, swinging his feet to the floor. He winced at the pain as his feet hit the tiles, jarring his still-sore knee.

'A car,' Gregory answered, his head still cocked to listen.

Mason listened, too. There was no sound. He shivered suddenly. Reaching for his coat where it had fallen to the floor, he pulled it on. The weight of the gun was insistent in the pocket.

'Are you sure?'

Gregory nodded. 'Positive... It's gone now. It must have stopped some distance from the house.'

Mason still stood with his head on one side, straining for any sound. He was about to speak again when he heard, quite distinctly, the creak of a single footfall on the fresh snow. Without waiting another instant he thrust a hand into the pocket of his coat and pulled out the gun. At the same time he spoke to Gregory, his voice a low hiss. 'Father, put out the lamp. Quickly! And take Helena into the kitchen.'

For a moment Gregory stood looking at the gun in Mason's hand. Then, with a swift, athletic stride, he crossed to the petrol lamp and blew it out. Mason heard his soft steps and Helena's muttered protests as he woke her and bundled her from the room. The kitchen door closed gently.

Alone in the room, he turned to face the door. He groped for the sofa and knelt down, keeping the sofa between himself and the door. He could hear no sound but the blood pounding in his temples. Then, slowly, he became aware of another sound mingling with the noise in his head. It was the sound of the latch being stealthily raised. He flicked his tongue over his cracking lips and gripped the gun more tightly.

With sudden force, the door flew wide. A single dark silhouette stood outlined against the pale light reflecting off the snow. It was the silhouette of a man.

Mason drew a sharp breath. He felt a trickle of sweat leave the area between his shoulder blades and course coldly down his spine. The light from behind the man gleamed briefly on the long barrel of a weapon.

The figure in the doorway appeared to be listening. Abruptly, he stepped into the room. At the same time a wide beam of light sprang from a torch he carried in one hand. The beam swept the room, swinging towards the spot where Mason crouched. Mason waited no longer. He pushed himself to his feet, raised the gun, gripped in both hands, and aimed at the shadow behind the light.

'Kaszik!'

The voice was familiar. It was Barbara's. Mason stood motionless, his hands still clasped tight around the gun. The torch beam fluttered and then fell on him, dazzling him. At that moment the cry came again, a scream this time.

'Kaszik!' The voice was in the room.

He heard a scuffling from near the door. The torch fell and rolled on the tiles. 'Barbara?' he called, tentatively.

'Yes, yes.' she answered, distractedly. Then, 'It's all right, Kaszik! It's all right! He's a friend!'

Recovering, Mason ran to collect the torch. He snatched it up and turned it on the dark figure. Barbara wrestled with a wiry man of around seventy who wore rough work clothes beneath a sheepskin jerkin. In one hand he carried a shotgun. With the other he tried to ward off Barbara, who had thrown both arms around him and was screaming dementedly in his ear. Mason stepped forward and jerked the gun from the man's hand. The man swore fiercely but allowed his struggling to subside. Gradually, as he quietened, Barbara released her hold.

'It's all right, Kaszik, really. It's a friend of mine. You know him. It's Peter. The Englishman.'

Mason turned the torch onto himself, smiling into the beam. 'Hello Kaszik, how are you?' He held out a hand.

The man shook it sulkily.

'You shouldn't go skulking in the dark like that. I thought you were a thief. You're lucky I didn't shoot you, lurking like that in the dark.' As he spoke, Barbara re-lit the lamp. Its yellow light fell over the room. Mason proffered Kaszik his gun.

'Sorry, Kaszik. You're right. I was stupid. I thought *you* were a prowler.' He grinned amiably at the man.

The older man gave a low growl of disgust and snatched the gun. 'Me? A prowler! I've lived in this bit of the forest all my life. Fought the Germans here. Killed a lot of them, too.' He turned to Barbara, exasperated, inviting her testimony.

She laughed. 'It's true, Peter, Kaszik fought with a resistance group around this area, throughout the war. He's an authentic hero.' Her voice held no trace of mockery. Kaszik nodded, mollified. 'Now, Kaszik, would you mind leaving us alone.' She propelled him towards the door. 'Peter and I are *very* good friends.'

At her words the old man turned and winked obscenely at Mason. 'Good night. Good night, Miss Barbara, Sleep well, both of you.' She closed the door on his cackling laugh. She turned back, smiling, to the room. Mason stood watching her, the gun still dangling slackly from one hand.

She hit him at a run. Her whole body slammed against him moulding her curves to his harder angles in a fit so perfect it was as though their bodies were responding to some inbuilt memory of the other's shape. The gun and Barbara's hat fell to the floor. They intertwined in an embrace so joyful and so intense that Mason lost all sense of where he was. Holding Barbara to him, he moved a pace backwards. Feeling the sofa catch the back of his knees, he allowed himself to sink slowly backwards onto it, still holding Barbara hard against him.

He kissed hungrily at her face and hair. Muffled laughter mingled with the kisses, laughter that came from the pure joy of seeing each other again. Barbara burst into tears.

185

'Oh, Peter, Peter.' Her head was buried at his chest, blurring her words. 'I've been frantic. What's happening? Are you all right? Are you in trouble? Why are you here? The gun. What…?' He tightened his hold around her and stroked her thick hair, murmuring reassurance. He waited until her sobs subsided before he spoke.

'It's a complicated story, Barbara. Yes, we're in trouble. Deep trouble,' he added, almost to himself.

'We?' she questioned, twisting to look at him. 'You mean both of us?' He kissed her hair again and wondered how to tell her. He rehearsed a few beginnings to himself. None of them sounded plausible. Finally, he nestled his head close to hers and said softly in her ear, 'Barbara. Gregory Kozka is here. He's in the kitchen.' He heard her watch tick. Very slowly, she released her hold and pushed herself off him until she was far enough away to focus on his eyes. He lay looking at her, a slightly embarrassed smile on his lips. He wondered if she was ready for more.

'Peter,' she said, after a moment, 'you're serious, aren't you?'

'Yes. I'm afraid he is.' The voice came from above her. She started and wrenched herself around to face the new voice. She looked blankly at the face smiling down at her, shot a panicky glance at Mason, and then again stared speechlessly into the glinting blue eyes.

Mason pushed them both into a sitting position. 'Barbara,' he said wryly, 'let me introduce Father Gregory Kozka. Barbara Wisniewska.'

Gregory made a slight bow and extended a hand. 'Delighted to meet you, Miss Wisniewska.'

Barbara looked up at him for a moment, still in mute astonishment, and then slipped from the sofa to her knees. She took Gregory's hand and kissed it. She drew back and crossed herself. Mason took her arm and pulled her back onto the sofa.

'Sit down, Barbara.' He raised his voice. 'Helena!' She emerged tentatively from the kitchen. 'I'd like you to meet Barbara Wisniewska. Barbara, this is Helena Kodecka,

186

Professor Kodec's daughter.'

They shook hands. Helena smiled affably, Barbara warily. She was ready to be jealous.

Speaking rapidly, Mason outlined for Barbara the events since he had left her flat. She listened without a word. When he had finished, she looked hard at Gregory and Helena, as though needing confirmation of what he had told her. Their set expressions gave her the confirmation she sought.

'Peter,' she said slowly, 'in other circumstances I'd say the mountain air had gone to your head. Whatever made you get involved in something like this?'

He stood up abruptly and turned away, avoiding her eyes. 'I don't know, Barbara. I...' He broke off, looking down into the wide green eyes that gazed up, filled with concern, into his. For an instant, he was on the brink of telling her, telling them all the true answer to her question. 'I just had to,' he ended, almost inaudibly. Louder, he went on, 'But look, we can't let you get mixed up in this, Barbara. I had no right even to ask you to come here. We have to get to Warsaw, into an embassy. The US embassy if we can. Time is very short. We have to leave here now. We would like to take your car. We'll arrange it to look as though we stole it, of course. We'll make some mess here, tear out the phone. Arrange it to look as though we attacked you. There would be nothing you could be reproached for.'

She stepped forward and placed a hand lightly over his mouth. 'Be quiet. If you leave here I'm coming with you. But my car's useless. The tank's absolutely dry.'

He pointed to the petrol containers that stood inside the door. 'Remember where you are,' he told her softly.

# 23

The weather had worsened. As they headed north-east the furious wind met them head-on. The windscreen wipers scraped arthritically at the ice that formed a film across the glass. Even with the heater at its maximum, only a diminished semi-circle of the screen stayed clear, forcing Barbara to hunch low in her seat in an effort to keep the road in view.

For probably the seventh time, they halted while Mason ran to the front of the car, crouched low against the wind, and scraped the headlights clear. His ears and fingers stung. He wiped his running nose with the back of his hand. Despite the cold, he enjoyed being outside the car, in the clean wind. He thought, quite suddenly, of the boat moored down at Brighton and wondered when he would next sail it. He wondered, too, if Barbara would enjoy sailing. He hoped so. Penny had always started to get seasick before they left the A23.

He returned to the car on the driver's side and opened the driver's door. 'Do you want to move over? I'll drive for a while.'

Barbara nodded and squirmed across the car into the passenger seat. She left a hand available for Mason to brush, not quite by accident, as he slid behind the wheel. Adjusting the rearview mirror he caught Gregory's eye. He raised his eyebrows.

'Everybody okay?'

Gregory smiled softly. 'We're fine.' There was something in the set of his shoulder that made Mason suspect that he might perhaps be holding Helena's hand. The way an uncle would. He let his eyebrows down slowly and drove on.

The woman stretched, removed her headphones and scratched the crown of her head with luxuriant concentration. She lifted a watch that hung from a thin chain between her unyielding breasts and studied it slowly. She sighed noisily, tilted in her chair, plucked the rucked cloth of her synthetic dress from beneath a thick thigh, and replaced the headphones. Nearly an hour left of her shift.

She lit another cigarette and crumpled the empty packet into the wastepaper basket by her chair. Inhaling noisily, to express her deep conviction that she was altogether too fine for the world, she reached for another cassette.

A quarter of an hour later she dragged the typed sheet wearily from her machine and pushed it, folded double, into a perforated manilla envelope. Copying from the cassette, she noted the time and telephone number on the envelope and pressed a bell-push set under the rim of her desk. She picked up a thermos flask and unscrewed the cap. She upended the flask over a plastic cup. No more than half an inch of coffee ran into the cup. She was still peering accusingly into the shallows, as though they had broken a promise to restore her youth, when the young man came in and collected the cassette and the manilla envelope.

Toparoff was furious. The white spots on his cheekbones contrasted with his congested face. He slammed a fist on the desk. The telephone rang faintly under the impact.

'Fuck it!'

Dominiak sat, morosely studying a half inch of ash at the end of his cigarette.

'The incompetent bunch of pricks!' Toparoff strode to the window. He was trembling with rage. He turned back to face Dominiak. 'You told me this Diament was good. Your pilot too. He was supposed to be the best you had. God protect us from your worst!' He broke off and turned away again, too angry to speak.

Dominiak spoke quietly, without looking up. 'Captain Diament was good, Comrade Colonel. The pilot, too. He has done a lot of flying for us. Conditions tonight must have been very difficult.'

'Difficult?' Toparoff spread his hands in despair. 'Of course they were difficult. Mountains are always difficult in winter. What do you expect? Pilots flying for the Polish State Security don't expect to work on the French Riviera, do they?'

Dominiak looked up at Toparoff. He spoke very coolly. 'No, Comrade, they don't. They expect rough weather. And sometimes rough treatment. It looks as though this young man may have found both. I have arranged for him to be brought here as soon as the hospital releases him. His aircraft was wrecked, you know. We don't yet know the extent of his injuries.'

'Much more important, does he know who was in the car?'

'Apparently not, Comrade. It was the first thing I had checked. Like you, I didn't want him impressing the nurses with his brush with celebrity. In any case, he is being looked after by trustworthy people.' Dominiak looked suddenly glum. 'As trustworthy as we are likely to find, where an attempt on the life of Gregory Kozka is concerned.'

Toparoff sneered. 'Bah. I'm sick of hearing that. The question is, Comrade Dominiak, where are they now? They've had hours to get away. And you seem to be be doing nothing.'

Dominiak shook his head wearily, finally dislodging the precarious ash from his cigarette. 'No, Comrade, not nothing. All the roads in the vicinity are being patrolled by my men.'

'And Czechoslovakia? They could have been across the border hours ago.'

Dominiak shook his head again. He blinked slowly. 'No, Colonel. I doubt that. All the reports coming in say that the highest roads are impassable. They can't have walked into Czechoslovakia. The fresh snow must be over a metre deep up there. From all the facts we have, we feel certain they must still be in the area.' He ruined the remaining half of his cigarette in the ashtray and buried his face in his plump hands. He was exhausted.

Toparoff's voice slid into his consciousness as though his brain were being injected with ice. 'Look, Comrade Dominiak, enough is enough. I'm tired of your half-measures.' He buttoned his jacket and shrugged it more snugly onto his misshapen shoulders, as though donning his authority. 'I'll speak to my Ambassador now. We'll see how long it takes to find them, Comrade. When we really look.' He reached for the telephone.

Centuries of ancient resentment welled in Dominiak, overwhelming his weariness. With surprising speed, he reached out a hand and clamped it over the telephone.

'No, Colonel. Not yet. No Russian troops on the streets.' The two men's eyes met. Within the fleshy folds of his dewlaps, Dominiak's jaw was set. Their hands overlapped on the telephone. The contest lasted perhaps two seconds. It was the Pole who spoke first.

'At daybreak we will have helicopters patrol the whole area. Every building will be searched. The police are already checking every household that owns a car to make sure it's where it should be. If a vehicle has been stolen anywhere in the area we will know it within the hour. We are lucky, Colonel,' he added wryly. 'The people down there are still not too affluent. There are not so many motor vehicles that we can't keep track of them. Perhaps in Moscow it would be different,' he added, his voice suddenly waspish.

The Russian turned, disgusted, and walked over to the table where a glass of tea stood half empty. He drank some of the tepid tea, and then picked the half slice of lemon from the glass and sucked at it. He picked the crescent of rind from between his lips and, very deliberately, let it drop back into the glass. All the while he held Dominiak with a hostile, unblinking stare. When he spoke his voice was scarcely audible.

'As you wish. You have until seven.' He looked at his watch. It was thin and gold on a crocodile strap. Dominiak glanced at his own. It was scratched and steel. The strap was leather, the holes enlarged through use. Both watches showed 5.35.

Although the weather had not improved, the driving had become slightly easier. Though it was well before six o'clock, lorry traffic had already started. Their deep, wide tracks were easy to follow so that just staying on the road was less of a problem. An occasional light showed in the farms and villages along their route.

Mason was tired and cramped. Throughout the drive he had been in constant expectation of the flashing lights of a militia car, or the racket of a helicopter overhead. Every few kilometres now they passed hitchhikers. Usually they were women shrouded in layers of thick clothing carrying bulging shopping bags or baskets. From their increasing number he guessed they were nearing Warsaw. His eyes flicked again to the petrol gauge. The tank was showing close to a quarter-full. In addition they still had several litres in a can in the boot. He flashed a quick grin of satisfaction at Barbara and pressed her hand where it lay on her thigh.

'How are we doing, Mr Mason?' Gregory's voice came softly from the back of the car. Mason, whose own face was haggard with tension, was actively impressed each time Gregory spoke by the man's profound calm.

'Okay.' He could also just make out the gloss of the top of Helena's hair as she slept, supported by Gregory's big, solid shoulder. 'We must be getting fairly close to Warsaw.' He cocked an eyebrow at Barbara. 'Are we?'

'I'm not sure.' She held the end of her sleeve in her hand and rubbed at the windscreen with a circular motion of her forearm. It did not help. The screen was opaque except for the lower portion. She tried the same on the steamy side window. The world outside was a pallid blank. 'There's nothing I know.' She leaned across Mason and studied the trip metre. She was still for a moment, calculating, and then her strained face cleared and she beamed around at them all.

192

'Peter, it's great. We can't be more than forty kilometres from Warsaw.'

At 5.45 a young man in jeans and a sports jacket tapped lightly on the door of Dominiak's office. He entered without waiting for a response, a manilla envelope in his hand. He walked to Dominiak's desk, treading softly, and handed over the envelope. He noticed that Dominiak looked older, his podgy face slacker than usual. The other man in the room, whom the newcomer had heard was Russian, stood immobile, staring from the window.

The young man backed away from Dominiak and withdrew. As he closed the door behind him he gave a low whistle and mimed wiping his brow. The atmosphere in the room had been chilling.

Dominiak stuck a thick finger into the envelope and slit it untidily open. He withdrew a single typed sheet and read it through.

'Damn!' He spoke through gritted teeth.

Toparoff turned only his head. Traces of a sneer had remained like a watermark on his face. Over his shoulder he asked, 'What is it now, Comrade Dominiak? More news from your crack team?'

Without replying to the man's crude sarcasm Dominiak held out the paper between his fingertips.

'What is it?' the Russian asked sharply, turning fully away from the window.

'A phone-tap report.' Dominiak's voice was hardly above a whisper. 'On a woman. A girlfriend of the Englishman. A prostitute. Not one that cooperates with us. Apart from that we've nothing against her. We've only been tapping her phone regularly since the Englishman was marked out for this job.'

'And?' Toparoff's tone was impatient, waiting for an excuse to turn into anger.

'He phoned her early this morning.'

'What? From where?'

'The south. They're not completely sure. The conversation

was very short. They weren't able to complete the trace.'

'But from the mountains?' Toparoff spoke with the vehement certainty of a man dreading contradiction. He moved a pace closer to Dominiak's desk.

Dominiak shook his head, very slowly, as though his neck had corroded.

'No.' Toparoff had to lean forward to hear him. 'I'm afraid not. He seems to have called from somewhere well away from the mountains. Somewhere north of Cracow.'

The silence in the room was absolute. Then Dominiak was aware of a low hissing sound. It rose in volume until he was aware it was the Russian's voice. The hiss condensed into words.

'Stupid, stupid bastards. Incompetent pricks. North of Cracow? What time did he call?'

Dominiak dropped his eyes to the paper.

'Two-sixteen.'

Toparoff opened his mouth. No sound came out. He closed it and tried again. 'A quarter past two!' He snatched the typed sheet and scanned it. He clapped a hand to his head and tossed the paper back at Dominiak. 'If she left to get him then...' He broke off and took three quick steps to a wooden-framed map of Poland on one wall. He studied it for a moment and then turned back to face Dominiak. His dark face had whitened. Dominiak wondered if it was anger or fear of failure.

'They could be in Warsaw by now!'

Dominiak nodded. 'They could.'

'By God!' Toparoff was almost screaming. 'It's taken nearly four hours to get a report on the phone-tap.' His brow darkened in a scowl. 'They could be in the American Embassy right now. If they are, Comrade, I'll have you shot.'

The Pole looked calmly from beneath his puffy lids into Toparoff's eyes.

'I know you will, Colonel,' he answered quietly.

Toparoff recovered control of his voice. 'Let's suppose the worst has not happened. The weather is terrible. They could still be on the road somewhere between there and Warsaw. I want roadblocks all round the city. I don't want a dog to enter or leave without being checked. And we must cordon off the Western embassies.'

Dominiak nodded. He reached for the telephone. His fingers, stained deep orange by nicotine, were on the phone when he felt the Russian's hand on his. He looked up. The other man was smiling the coldest smile he had ever seen.

'No, Comrade. Things have reached too critical a stage. I will speak to His Excellency the Ambassador now. He will contact your superiors.'

'No, Colonel. Let's use our men. The militia can handle roadblocks. We have our best army units around Warsaw. They can attend to the embassies. Don't put Russian soldiers on the streets. Colonel, I beg you.'

Toparoff was no longer looking at him. He was dialling a number, stabbing rapidly at the creaking dial with an immaculate finger tip.

Dominiak stood up. His head bowed, he moved away from his seat and gestured towards it.

'Here, Colonel,' he said, 'make yourself comfortable.' Slumped, his hands pushed deep into the patch pockets of his misshapen suit, he walked over to the window and stared out at the deserted street. He wondered what he might see there before the day was out.

# 24

The fine old aristocratic mansion where the Russian Ambassador resided lay set back from the street behind thick twelve-foot railings. Suddenly, high in the building a faint light radiated from a crack between curtains. A sentry, stamping in the snow in front of the building was surprised. He did not think he was near the end of his shift yet. For the thousandth time he wished he had a watch.

The Ambassador was a squat man with a flat face in which high cheekbones crowded close beneath his eyes, suggesting a hint of Mongol blood. He sat up cross-legged in the bed, the bedclothes thrown back. He wore no pyjamas. Greying hair, which now grew sparely on his head, swathed his shoulders and chest, descending to meet the black curls which rose almost to his navel.

He sat quite still, listening without expression to the voice on the telephone.

'A pity, Colonel. A great pity,' he said finally, without a trace of scorn in his voice. 'You may proceed. I will take the responsibility. Moscow is in agreement, as you know. I prepared them for this some time ago. I shall inform them immediately that, with the greatest regret, we are obliged to proceed.'

He listened, once again immobile, while Toparoff asked another question.

'Yes, of course, Colonel. I shall inform the Poles. I'll telephone the General myself,' he added, in a negligent tone, 'after I speak with Moscow. Our garrison commanders are informed, Colonel. You have full authority. Keep me informed.' Without waiting for any further word from Toparoff, the Ambassador put down the telephone. For a few seconds he sat, massaging his belly, his gaze dying unfocused on the opposite wall. Abruptly, he gave a single short laugh, and shook his head once in an expression of surprise that was almost pleasure. He looked down at the pillow beside him. His wife lay looking up at him in quiet enquiry. He smiled fleetingly at her, squeezed her shoulder, and swung himself off the bed.

He left the room, collecting a dark grey silk robe from an ornately uncomfortable chair as he went. The adjoining room was a study. He pulled on the robe and sat down at a desk. The desk was huge and empty, with ferocious carved feet. His thick, squat body and broad provincial face did not suit the desk.

He reached out a short arm and pulled a green telephone closer to him. The handset had no dial. He picked up the phone and waited. After a few seconds of static a voice came on the line.

'Yes?'

'Ambassador Boshkov.'

'I know. What is it, Ambassador?' The voice held a hint of condescension.

'Give me the First Secretary.' His own voice was curt.

'Comrade Gorbachev is not available, Ambassador. What is it about?'

The Ambassador grew suddenly impatient of the contest. 'World War Three, you fucking half-wit! Give me Comrade Gorbachev. Now!' The Ambassador had a tone of voice that, throughout his career, he had kept for the occasions, so frequent in the system, when petty struggles for status threatened the objective. It worked now, as always. After a few seconds further wait and the inevitable clicks and crackles, the familiar voice came on the line.

'Comrade Ambassador, good morning. I understand you have something urgent to tell me.'

The Ambassador allowed himself a small smile, and began speaking.

The traffic was heavier now. The snow on the road was rutted and grey. Mason watched the dilapidated trucks grind through the muck ahead of him, belching unburnt diesel into the beam of his headlights. The filthy fumes being sucked in through the heating system were combining with his fatigue to make him feel desperately sick. He consoled himself that the flow of traffic meant he could follow the lights ahead and forget about his mud-caked headlights.

Anxiously, he looked at his watch. It was a minute after six. Dawn would not be long. He stayed in third gear, keeping one hand on the gear lever and looking fretfully for a chance to pass the truck. None came. A procession of heavy lorries ground past going south, their headlights dazzling on his grime-caked windscreen.

Barbara tapped his arm. 'We're nearly there. That garage,' she pointed to a feebly lit filling station, 'is only a few kilometres from town.'

He grunted. 'Keep your fingers crossed. We're not there yet. Not until we're in an embassy.'

'Which one are you going to try?' Gregory asked from the darkness behind Mason.

'The American. First.' He grinned, half turning to look at Gregory. 'They'll have the best coffee.'

'No, Mr Mason,' rejoined Gregory, laughing. 'They'll have the most coffee. The Italian will have the best coffee.'

'*Touché*, Father. Anyway, not the British. They'll have Nescafé. And even that will turn out to be congealed in a lump at the bottom of the jar. They'll be very apologetic and offer us tea.'

'I like tea.'

'So do I, but not after a drive like this at 6.30 in the morning. I want coffee. Lots of it.'

'With milk,' Barbara added, smiling.

'Hot,' he said, pedantically, 'but not boiled.'

The thought warmed him. The rhythmic swinging of a torch up ahead chilled him again. The single working brakelight of the truck ahead glowed weakly under its crust of mud.

Urgently, he wound down the window and thrust his head out into the freezing air. Beyond the truck, almost obscured by the flying snow, a shadowy figure swung the torch beam rhythmically through a wide arc.

'What is it?' Gregory was leaning forward between the front seats, straining for a view of the road.

He closed the window. 'Police I think.' He could see nothing behind the powerful torch beam. The traffic edged slowly forward.

'What should we do? Run for it?' Gregory's voice was still deep and matter of fact. Mason's palms sweated on the wheel. 'No. I think we should stay in the car. If we have to make a break for it we have a better chance than on foot. Not much better,' he added, with a hint of irony, 'but better.'

The nose of the car was almost under the overhanging tail of the truck in front. Behind them a tanker lorry had closed up, hemming them in. Mason watched the truck shudder and edge forward. Taking his right hand from the wheel he wiped the palm quickly on his coat and then slid the hand into his pocket. He let his fingers close around the butt of the gun.

The lorry jerked forward again, its wheels spinning, as though the driver might have breakfasted on vodka and was having a little trouble with the clutch. Mason salivated, trying to moisten his bone-dry mouth, as he stayed close behind the wheezing lorry.

Without warning, the lorry belched a cloud of oily smoke and sped away. Mason was face to face through the windscreen with a uniformed militiaman holding up a torch. On the carriageway lay a shape, dark grey in the headlights. A darker grey stain flowed from the shape until it exhausted itself in the snow. At the roadside, with all lights full on, stood a police van and a private Volkswagen Golf. The Volkswagen had a crumpled offside wing. A very pale man stood talking animatedly to two more militiamen. Mason became only slowly aware that the policeman with the torch was signalling to him. His hand closed on the gun. Then it loosened again. He was being told to move on. The militiaman was gesturing angrily to him to get started, around the inert figure in the road.

In a flurry of wheelspin and disbelief, Mason pulled noisily away, showering the corpse with slush. Usually the sight of an accident victim, horribly common in Poland, turned the pit of his stomach to ice. This once, he gave the dead man no thought at all.

'Christ,' he said, banging the heels of both hands gleefully on the rim of the wheel, 'an accident. Just an ordinary accident.' He looked around at the other three.

Barbara was laughing and miming fanning herself, Helena was grinning and holding Gregory's arm. Even Gregory seemed to have forgotten to give a passing thought to the victim in the road. Mason drove on, closing on the single tail-light of the truck ahead of him.

'I think,' he said happily, 'we're going to make it.'

Toparoff's calls had brought each of the four Soviet barracks around Warsaw frantically to life, like disturbed ants' nests. Raw-boned young blond recruits from the Russian republics mingled with the shorter, darker, olive-skinned men from the Asian republics of the Central and Eastern areas, as they ran, still pulling on greatcoats, their weapons trailing, to assemble close to their transport. They stood in slightly ragged ranks, advancing in turn to collect an issue of live ammunition. Their faces were closed, pinched by the raw chill. The few that did show any animation examined their ammunition clips and stole curious glances at each other.

Each truck-load of men was commanded by a young officer. None of the officers was Asian. As soon as the ammunition was distributed, the officers spoke a few words to the men, who broke ranks and scrambled into the canvas-covered trucks.

The officers ran to climb into the cabs beside the drivers. Although the men and the drivers were completely mystified, the officers had received instructions for just this contingency some days before. Each of them drew a large scale map of Warsaw from a transparent plastic pouch and began giving instructions to the driver.

All around Warsaw, motorists and pedestrians, civilian and militia, watched in stupefaction as the camouflage-painted lorries roared from the camps and sped out into the still-dark city. They careered noisily through the snow-covered streets. Frequently they forced cars from the road in their headlong race, leaving astonished drivers gazing after them, the surprise in their faces turning to hatred as the realization slowly dawned that the soldiers who watched blankly from the backs of the trucks were not Polish but Russian.

The operation was timed to take no more than twenty-five minutes from the moment they left the barracks to the setting up of roadblocks on all roads into the city and the encirclement of the principal 'sensitive' spots; embassies, television and radio stations, telephone exchanges, the main hotels, even certain churches. Especially certain churches. Toparoff and the Ambassador had been fully in agreement on that. Once word leaked, demonstrations would focus on them.

Toparoff himself sat on the edge of Dominiak's dilapidated seat, leaning tensely over the desk. Since his call to the Ambassador the telephone had not been out of his hand. Immediately after speaking to the Ambassador he had called his own immediate superior in Moscow. The conversation had been short and unpleasant. Dominiak, listening as he stared motionless from the window had found a certain grim consolation in hearing the Russian's discomfort. Even if Toparoff were not the architect of the scheme, he it was who had been assigned the planning and execution of the sensitive project. Dominiak knew that from the time it began to go awry, Toparoff's career, and perhaps his life, had suddenly lost their value. He also knew that Toparoff knew it. For a while, he would be very dangerous indeed.

He turned to face the Russian. The man's carefully cut hair was in disarray, the blue-black stubble on his jaw deepening the shadows in his drawn cheeks.

'What will you do, Colonel, if you don't find them this morning? They may not have come to Warsaw at all. They could have gone anywhere.'

Toparoff stared at the desk, his hand still on the telephone. He made no reply.

Dominiak smiled a very small smile. 'I'm just curious, Colonel,' he said very quietly, 'just curious.' He turned back to the window and began another cigarette.

Toparoff spoke. His voice had taken on a gritty, hoarse

edge. 'They'll come to Warsaw. They have to. Where else could they go? They'll try to get to an embassy. I'm certain of it. In their position it's the only thing to do.'

Dominiak nodded to the deserted street. 'You're probably right, Colonel. A foreign embassy. The foreign press. They are the best defence they have. They would be fools not to go to an embassy if they can. If they make it before you find them, then by this time tomorrow, Colonel, we are going to be on the front pages of the Western press. In very large type.' He shrugged. 'I was nearing the end of my career, anyway.' He turned again to Toparoff, who still sat blanched and haggard in the same posture. 'More tea, Colonel?' Dominiak enquired evenly.

The road was easier now, a dual carriageway with a low grassy division separating the lanes. Mason was able to drive a little faster, passing the sagging and dilapidated lorries instead of being obliged to stay in line and eat their exhaust. Dispirited buildings, yellow light oozing faintly through heavily grimed windows, crowded the road. Occasionally they passed a filling station where a few dim lights asserted that it was open and not abandoned, as a casual observer might think.

'This is it, Mr Mason. This is practically Warsaw.' Gregory's voice was tinged with an almost boyish excitement. 'In another few kilometres we're in town.'

Mason caught his glinting look in the mirror and smiled. 'That's right. Personally I'm amazed. I just don't understand it. We have hardly seen a policeman since we left the house. I thought by now they would have been crawling all over us. Could it be,' he added, as an afterthought, 'you've been praying for us?'

Gregory's grin made him look somehow ferocious. 'I've been praying for you for years!'

'Well,' Mason retorted, laughing aloud, 'another night like this and I may have to start revising my opinion of the power of prayer.'

Their laughter died away abruptly. Racing towards

them, on the other side of the highway were two canvas-covered trucks. Their dated, bull-nosed look and camouflage paint identified them as military. One of the trucks drew to a halt on the far side of the wide road. The second, without warning, began a sharp U-turn fifty metres in front of the car. Mason heard Barbara draw in her breath sharply.

'Russians,' she hissed, pointing at the single red star on the door of the cab. The front wheels of the lorry were already up on the low divide between the carriageways.

'Shit!' Mason scanned the road behind him in the rearview mirror. There was nothing behind them for three hundred metres. If he turned now, in full conspicuous view, he would be advertising their presence. In the heavily loaded little car he doubted they could out-run a truck on the straight highway. He was still weighing his options when a tremendous crash came to them. Helena woke, wondering where she was.

A tanker, heading south behind the army lorry, had been unable, on the packed snow surface to swerve around the lorry as it swung across his lane. The nose of the tanker had clipped the rear end of the lorry, jerking it a metre off its path. The tanker spun and came to a stop broadside across the road.

The officer jumped down from the cab of the lorry and ran around to the back of it. Mason felt his stomach knot as he saw the gun in the officer's hand. The lorry driver climbed slowly down from his cab, dazed from the impact. He began gesticulating, apparently remonstrating with the officer. They were quite close now and saw the officer's face contort as he bellowed at the men in the truck. As they drew level they saw the soldier turn on the driver, who had approached close behind him, complaining. Without appearing to say a word, the officer swung his gun. Mason heard Helena gasp at the impact. Blood welled vividly, spreading instantly to the driver's clothes. Instinctively, Mason began braking, seized by the old, irrational desire to intervene on the losing side. It was Gregory's voice, quietly insistent, that brought him back down to reality.

'Drive on, quickly. We can be of no help here.'

Without a word, Mason swivelled his foot back to the accelerator. Carefully, to avoid skidding, he accelerated away. In his rearview mirror he watched several soldiers in full skirted greatcoats placing two heavy red and white poles in a chicane across the road behind them.

# 25

Barbara, Helena and Gregory swivelled in their seat, straining to watch the Russians through the streaked rear window. Gregory commentated for Mason. Troops had swarmed from the trucks and set up the red and white poles on both north- and southbound carriageways. Soldiers, some with Kalashnikovs and others with short machine guns began flagging down traffic. Mason was surprised to hear Gregory's familiar cataloguing of the types of arms.

'You surprise me, Father.'

'Why?' Gregory asked distractedly, still watching the scene behind them.

'You know about guns. Personally I wouldn't know a Kalashnikov from a side of bacon.'

'Didn't you do military service?'

'No. We haven't had military service in England for twenty-odd years.' He paused. His next thought seemed too incongruous. He voiced it anyway. 'Did you?'

'Of course. Like everybody.' Mason could hear the smile in the low untroubled voice. He tried to catch Gregory's eye in the mirror but got only the dark silhouette of the back of his head.

'You're serious! What did you do? Chaplain?'

'No. Paratrooper!'

Mason jerked around in his seat. 'You. A paratrooper.' He shook his head.

Gregory turned to face him, smiling broadly. Without altering his level tone, he said, 'We're about to leave the road.'

Mason swung back to face the road and yanked the wheel. Once they were back on an even keel Gregory continued. 'It's true, Mr Mason. For two years I was in a parachute regiment, stationed in Katowice. Before that I worked in the mines.'

Mason, at the wheel, visualized the big-knuckled hands behind him. It was easy to imagine them holding a drill. Easier than picturing them holding a chalice. He glanced at the amused blue eyes in the mirror. 'Stick around, Father, we may need you.'

He drove as fast as he dared through the streets. The trams were already crowded. The new snow in the city streets was already dulled and grey. In front of a still-unlit kiosk a queue had already formed. A sudden image came to him of London shops in mid-December, vibrant with light and crammed with shoppers. He felt melancholy come at him at a rush. He swallowed and pushed the feeling aside. They sped across the bridge spanning the Vistula river. The rutted asphalt drummed at the tyres. He felt as though he were driving over a cattle grid. Maybe, in a sense he was. Maybe the whole town was a trap where, once in, he would never again get out. He pressed his foot a little harder. Ice lay like broken glass in the river, cracked and random.

Ahead of them, to the left, stood a seven-storey slab of a building on which several flags hung cheerlessly. A flurry of movement in front of the building caught his eye. Uniformed men scurried around the broad steps that ran the length of the façade. Parked on the pavement, only partly hidden by three barren plane trees, stood a covered truck.

Barbara started at the sight: 'Soviets', she murmured.

Mason felt Gregory's hand touch his shoulder. The touch was light, reassuring.

Moving into the right-hand lane, he eased his foot off the accelerator, slowing to the speed of the sparse traffic. Cruising, they passed in front of the squat building. It was the Party headquarters. Between the ungainly pillars of the façade the khaki-clad figures were taking up positions. Their immature faces were blank as they stared out at the straggling knot of passers-by who had begun to gather on the wide pavement.

Mason watched the silent crowd. 'What the hell's going on?'

Helena spoke for the first time in a long while. 'Isn't it obvious?' Her tone was bitter. 'They know what's happened. They know we're in Warsaw. Or at least that we would be trying to get here. We're too late.'

Mason glanced across at Barbara. She was looking at him, trying to bite back a smile. 'It's great to have you along, Helena. You keep our spirits up tremendously!' He looked quickly at Helena over his shoulder. She looked back at him, unblinking, for an instant. Then she, too, broke into a sudden smile.

'I'm sorry, Peter. I just can't stop thinking that if it hadn't been for me none of this would be happening to you all.'

'To all of *us*. Forget it. You were used by them. We all were. The only thing that matters now is how we get out of it.' As he finished speaking he spun the wheel hard, taking them onto the broad riverside highway that led to the embassy district.

He drove as fast as he dared amid the few cars. Across the wide river he saw a blue light flash briefly. It could easily have been an ambulance. He drove for about a kilometre. All four of them were straining for a sight of any car or uniform that might have been military or militia. They saw none. At a sign from Barbara, he turned off the riverside road into a narrow street that climbed steeply away from the river, between two parks. Barbara and he had often fed the squirrels in the parks in summer. Now they looked desolate and hostile.

As they reached the top of the slope Mason became aware his mouth was parched. He salivated and rolled his shoulders in an attempt to relax. He felt Barbara's light touch on his arm again. He glanced at her. Her hair shone in the light of the old-fashioned street lamp. He gulped softly and concentrated on his driving.

'We're almost there, Peter.' Barbara's voice was a whisper.

'Yeah.' His own voice was neutral, his eyes scanned the road ahead The buildings were big houses, set well back from the road. In summer this was a leafy suburb. Now the houses stood out starkly behind rows of skeletal trees and their high, black-painted railings. They turned another corner.

Mason felt Barbara stiffen, and heard Helena's indrawn breath, as a young soldier stepped abruptly from a sentry box into the middle of the pavement ahead of them. He seemed to stare straight at them for a moment, and then suddenly he stamped his feet, wheeled, and began marching directly away from them. He was just a soldier on sentry duty outside one of the many buildings in the area used by foreign embassies, or by the Party.

The relief in the car was palpable. Mason unclenched his fingers from the wheel and splayed them, trying to relieve the cramped muscles of his hands. They drove on through the deserted street. There were no pedestrians. In this part of Warsaw nobody walked. Everyone used cars, mostly chauffeured.

Gregory asked the question Mason had not wanted to hear. 'Supposing the American embassy is already closed off. What do we do?'

'I don't know. Go somewhere else. Another embassy? Does anyone have any ideas?' Mason looked at Gregory, but addressed them all. There was a short silence. Helena spoke first.

'I don't know anybody in Warsaw. Nobody I could

trust. In any case, it would be too dangerous. All the people we knew are well known to…to them!'

Mason nodded. 'Barbara?'

'I don't know, Peter. I have nobody in Warsaw. No family. No close friends. Most of the women I know here are just, you know, like me.' She looked at her hands in her lap, embarrassed.

'Then they must be fine women.' Gregory said it very quietly.

Mason enclosed her hands in one of his and pressed them. 'Father? Any ideas?'

'A church, perhaps. There are several priests here in Warsaw whom I know we could rely on. The trouble is,' he said reflectively, 'the people who are out to get us know quite well who they are, too.'

'We may have to take a chance on that,' Mason answered. 'We don't have many options.'

Barbara spoke again, her voice trembling now with excitement. 'Peter, it's the next turning. On the right. The Embassy entrance is on the right, about three or four hundred metres along.'

He slowed the car in preparation for the bend.

They turned into the road where the embassy stood. It was empty. From the sudden rush of air Mason realized none of them had been breathing. The little car picked up speed. They could see the usual white-painted sentry box near to the heavy iron gates. It was impossible to know if anybody was in it.

For the first time Mason wondered how they would deal with a sentry. Normally they were passive enough, allowing visitors to the embassy to come and go freely. But normally he had arrived alone, at a normal visiting hour, and not before dawn, accompanied by a few friends, who happened to include Kozka, all of them on the run from the Secret Police, the militia, and the Red Army. That was the sort of thing that could make a difference.

They approached the Embassy. They were within thirty yards of the tall gates and still the street was deserted. They drew level with the sentry box. The door was closed. Through the small grimy window in the door they could not see into the darkness of the interior.

Mason braked sharply in front of the Embassy gates, defying a large No Parking sign painted on a white board. He pushed himself quickly from the car and hurried, still hobbling slightly from his sore knee, to the gates. They were locked.

Swearing softly, he turned back towards the car. As he did so, the door of the sentry box was thrown open and Mason found himself meeting the unfocused gaze of a young soldier. The soldier's tunic was open to the third button, his hair tousled and his face puffy with sleep. The grip on the short machine gun was firm, however, and the muzzle was level with Mason's stomach.

'Good morning,' Mason called, hearing the blood pound in his temples.

'What do you want?' the soldier responded sulkily. 'This is an embassy, and it's closed. Clear off.'

'I know it's the embassy,' Mason answered, his accent ostentatiously American, his smile still in place. He took a step towards the sentry. 'I'm an American. I need to get inside, to talk to someone. I had a message at the hotel. It's my mother, in New York. She's been taken to hospital.' As he spoke he moved a further two steps towards the sentry.

'You can't get in until they open,' the sentry answered, less surlily. 'That's not till ten.' He allowed the gun barrel to droop. 'Come back –' He was cut short by a harsh ringing inside the sentry box. Half-turning, he reached in and snatched the phone from its cradle on the wall.

Half-facing away from Mason, the man had allowed the gun to hang loosely at his side. Mason's eyes were on the young man's face. Another step would be enough. Casually, still smiling, he drifted a pace nearer. He gathered himself, preparing to hurl himself onto the man. Without warning, the gun barrel slashed upwards and smashed him across the face.

Mason's senses exploded in a yellow flash. When his

vision cleared he was on his knees in the snow. The sentry stood over him, menacing him with the gun and shouting to the others to get out of the car. Mason fought down a violent wave of nausea. He shook his head in pain and defeat. The call had come seconds too soon.

A car door slammed. Above him, he saw the sentry's face cloud. Following the sentry's gaze, he turned to face the car. Gregory was advancing very deliberately across the pavement, his face perfectly calm, his hands out-turned to show they were empty. The sentry's dull features worked perplexedly. Whoever had phoned had obviously not told him who would be in the car.

The gun barrel swung towards Gregory. He continued to advance towards it. The man gripped the gun harder. Very quietly, like a man addressing a dangerous dog, Gregory spoke.

'Don't shoot. We mean you no harm. We mean no harm to anyone. Put down your weapon. There is no need of it.' The quiet voice was hypnotic.

The soldier shrank back half a pace, as though seeking the protection of the cabin. The gun remained unwaveringly on Gregory. 'Stop. There,' he called, his voice rising shrilly. 'I'll shoot.' His eyes flickered from Gregory to Mason. 'I mean it. I have orders. Stop!'

Still Gregory advanced, his deep, warm voice intoning reassurance. His eyes held those of the young soldier. He was within three paces of him. The soldier's throat worked nervously. 'Stop!' he cried in a voice cracking with strain, 'I'll shoot!'

Gregory began another cautious pace forward. With a choked exclamation the sentry tightened his grip on the gun. His eyes narrowed and a sudden flood of frightened rage filled his face.

Without warning, Mason vomited. The vile stream broke with a slapping sound at the soldier's feet. The man's face contorted in a look of incredulous loathing. Reflexively, he sprang back. A heel caught the raised sill of the sentry box, causing him to stumble. Cursing, he grabbed at the doorframe for support.

Mason was only half-aware of the dark shape that swooped close in front of him. The nausea passed. His eyes regained their focus, revealing Gregory crouched by the sentry, one knee in the small of the man's back. With one hand Gregory held one of the man's arms twisted hard behind his back. His other hand reached around beneath the man's neck to clutch the cloth of his uniform collar. If the man struggled, the slightest tensing of Gregory's arm would be enough to cause his forearm to cut viciously into the soldier's throat, choking him.

Mason bent and snatched up the fallen gun. He jammed the barrel into the sentry's neck as Gregory scrambled to his feet. The sentry remained motionless, his eyes wide with terror. 'Stay there,' Mason hissed, backing away from the man. He looked up at the gates. They were of thick steel bars, over ten feet high, and topped by a set of savage, many-pointed spikes. The spikes could be cushioned with the seats from the car. With the sentry box as a platform it was possible. He had begun to turn to the car when a sudden shout made him whirl around.

Barbara stood, half out of the car, pointing to the far end of the street, panic filling her eyes. Three hundred yards away, a dun-coloured truck had drawn across the end of the street. As they looked on, half a dozen soldiers sprang from the canvas-covered rear of the vehicle and began man-handling oil drums, probably filled with concrete, into place across the roadway.

'Oh shit!' Gregory exclaimed.

Mason threw him one fast, incredulous glance and they were both sprinting for the car. By the time they reached it Barbara was gunning the motor. Gregory dived headlong for the back seat, Mason threw himself into the front beside Barbara. The car shot from the kerb. As the door slammed shut, a faint shout came to them over the whine of the labouring engine.

Barbara threw the car into a wild three-point turn. Mason watched the soldiers. One of them was pointing excitedly in their direction and gesticulating to his comrades. They gained a few seconds as the soldiers hesitated, unsure what to do. Then all but two of them began scrambling over the tailgate. The remaining pair ran to drag the oil drums aside. Smoke billowed from the exhaust and the nose of the truck swung towards them.

Mason twisted to face Gregory. 'Where now?' He was aware that he was shouting. Gregory was craning to see through the rear window. Next to him Helena sat watching him, silent and white-faced.

'I don't know. Anywhere, so long as we lose *them.*'

Barbara crouched over the wheel, her eyes fixed on the snow-covered road. 'Where, Peter?' she pleaded. 'Tell me where to go.'

He hesitated only an instant. 'Across the river! Try to get over to Praga.' She nodded and settled lower over the wheel. Praga was the working class district on the other bank of the Vistula. It had suffered less destruction during the war. Its tangle of narrow streets would offer more chance of shaking off the truck than they would ever have in the newer, wider streets of the city centre.

He screwed round in his seat again. The truck was racing along behind them, its canvas-covered hood swaying as it barrelled over the pitted tarmac beneath the surface snow. They had about three hundred and fifty yards start. On a straight run the powerful truck would outrun them in minutes. And shooting would be easy.

# 26

He scanned the road ahead of them, on the lookout for military or Police vehicles. The adrenalin charge from the immediacy of the danger had driven all the fatigue and nausea from him. Even his knee had stopped hurting. He glanced behind. Gregory sat with his face pressed close to the mud-caked glass of the rear window. Helena clung to him, her fingers biting into the cloth of his sleeve.

'How are we doing?'

Gregory answered without looking round. 'They're gaining.'

Mason turned quickly to Barbara. 'Start turning! Anywhere! Don't let them get a run at us.' He turned to the front. 'Here!' he called, indicating a narrow street to their right.

Barbara threw the car into the turn. Mason snatched a grab-handle as he felt the rear wheels slew and threaten to break away. He relaxed again as the tyres bit once more into the fresh, untrodden snow.

Incongruously, he was aware of a faint sound of laughter from the rear seat. He looked around to see Gregory and Helena disentangling themselves from the heap into which they had been thrown. He had barely taken in the sight before the truck came lurching around the bend behind them, its canvas hood swaying crazily and snow flying from its wheels as it took the turn.

'Turning left.' Barbara's voice was cracking with excitement.

Each of them grabbed for something solid as they hurtled into the turn. Pressed against the door, Mason looked at Barbara. A private smile played on her lips. Her eyes shone. 'Are they catching us?' she asked, trying to catch Gregory's eye in the mirror.

'It's hard to say. I doubt it.' His voice was amused. 'Their soldiers must be getting seasick, anyway.'

They raced along the road. They were leaving the embassy district now and the pavements were peopled with muffled figures trudging stolidly into the chill, damp wind. Heads turned to watch as they rushed past, alerted by the high drone of the labouring engine. There were even two or three other cars being gingerly eased through the snow. Mason winced as Barbara insouciantly sped past them, indifferent to the prospect of oncoming traffic.

Ahead of them, the road mounted an incline and joined the main road which led across the river to the tortuous streets of the Praga district, and to hope of a respite. They hit the main road with the finesse of falling masonry.

In the centre of the wide road, a dense crowd stood clustered on a 20-yard-long island waiting for a tram. The snow on the road had been packed to polished ice by passing traffic. All four wheels lost their grip simultaneously. Broadside, the car slid towards the crowd. Barbara grappled futilely with the unresponsive wheel. A few people in the crowd glanced up at the approaching sound of the engine. Their leaden expressions dissolved into astonishment and fear as the car glided towards them. The nimbler ones leapt away from the edge, sending those in front of them crumpling to the ground.

Mason braced himself with his right hand. With his left hand he reached over and shoved at the horn button. The sudden note shook more people into a realization of what was happening. Startled faces stared in disbelief. Some stood transfixed. Others scrambled to get out of the car's path, adding to the confusion as they, too, fell against the heap of bodies struggling on the wet ground.

Mason grunted as both the offside wheels slammed against the six inch high kerbstone separating the tram stop from the road. With that eerie sense of clarity and detachment that often accompanies catastrophe, he seemed to be observing from outside as the car turned slowly onto its side. At the same time, he was aware of a tram crashing to a cacophonous stop just in front of them. The outstanding sensation in his mind was the furious clanging of the tram's warning bell.

He fell heavily onto Barbara. He lay awkwardly, but still, for just the instant he needed to know he was unhurt. Goaded by the thought of the onrushing truck, he scrambled to his feet.

'Anybody hurt?' he called as he groped for the door above him. Through the window he could see only the dark grey of the overcast sky. Then a face, both angry and concerned, appeared at the window, looking down at him. He rose to meet it as first Barbara, then Gregory, and then Helena, muffled beneath Gregory's beefy form, grunted assurances.

The door above him was wrenched open and hands reached in to haul him out. He was almost catapulted onto the street. Barbara followed. All around them people cursed and gesticulated angrily.

Mason looked around him quickly for any sign that any of the bystanders had been hurt. Seeing that nobody appeared to be injured, he began to shout urgently over the noise of the crowd. Suddenly, he realized that his voice was coming ridiculously loud to his own ears. The crowd had fallen silent. All their eyes looked past Mason. Brushing aside the momentary feeling of foolishness, he looked behind him. Gregory's big head and shoulders protruded from the doorway of the car, as though he were emerging from a drain. His reassuring smile was as natural as if he were standing in a drawing room.

'Good morning.' He said it softly. Then, placing a hand on each side of the doorway, he swung himself athletically from the car. The crowd remained silent as he turned and helped Helena from the car. She slid to the ground and stood beside him, blushing and smoothing her skirt.

Mason half knew what was going to happen next. Nevertheless, he could not help watching in faint awe for a few precious seconds as first a hesitant few, then many more, of the crowd, began to kneel. He watched as they sank silently onto the wet asphalt as though pressed down by an unseen hand. Most of the crowd were kneeling, and Gregory appeared to be preparing to speak, before Mason recovered himself.

Grabbing Gregory and Helena each by an arm, and nudging Barbara with his chest he bundled them quickly towards the tram which had stopped a few yards away from them.

'Come on. Quickly. Move. Onto the tram.' His urgent

215

words were addressed to Gregory, who seemed reluctant to move, casting an apologetic look at the faces looking up at him. 'For Christ's sake, Father. Come on. The soldiers will be here in seconds.'

'Yes. Yes. I know,' Gregory mumbled, allowing himself to be pushed towards the dirty grey bulk of the tram, still looking down at the upturned faces.

Mason looked up at the tram driver. Through the streaked glass he could see the slow astonishment fill the man's face. Mason signalled him to open the door. The folding door concertinaed to the sharp gasp of escaping compressed air. Mason shoved the others roughly up the steps into the crowded interior. He turned back to the crowd. He felt an odd twinge of embarrassment to see all the pale, curious faces now turned on him. He grasped the lapel of a thick-set man with a wide, tough, dilapidated face and jerked him to his feet. Mason spoke very fast.

'Get everyone to crowd around the car. The Russians! Troops! They'll be here in a few seconds. They're trying to kill him! Gregory! Try to delay them.'

He turned and leapt aboard the tram. The door closed and the clumsy vehicle began to gather speed, its discordant bell clanging. Mason turned to watch the scene they had left behind. The man he had spoken to was gesticulating and shouting. Mason smiled. The man was taking his responsibilities seriously. As he watched, the kneeling people rose and gathered in a rush around the car. Many of them spilled out into the road. Several of them lay down in the road and began writhing as though injured. An open truck and a private car were brought to a halt by the confusion. Instantly several men had swarmed about the truck and begun enthusiastically hurling its load into the road. Mason smiled. He was still near enough to see the expression on the face of the truck driver as he climbed, carefully, out of his cab.

Two seconds later he stopped laughing. The Russian truck barrelled out of the side street and slewed to a halt. Its front wheels were almost touching one of the gifted actors struggling on his back on the packed snow.

Mason turned to point out the truck to the others. His jaw fell an inch at the sight confronting him. Among the crowd packed into the tram, only three were standing. Himself, Gregory, and, looming above all the passengers, who either knelt or half-knelt slumped in their moulded plastic seats, a man in the distinctive hated uniform of the militia, a gun holstered at his belt.

Gregory looked steadily at the policeman, who stared back at him. The man's face seemed strangely small between his flat peaked cap and the big collar of his winter coat. His gaze dropped. He studied the floor at his feet. Gradually the hundred or so upturned faces turned from Gregory, following his gaze. They looked silently at the uniformed man. He shifted his weight and his eyes flicked over the ranks of silent faces below him. His hands rose to his thick leather belt which carried the holster. He tugged at the belt, making an imperceptible adjustment to the position of the buckle, as though preparing for an inspection. His hands dropped to his sides. The fingers of both hands clenched two or three times. He coughed and then, as though some psychological retaining wall had broken, he swept off his cap with one hand and knelt among the crowd.

Gregory smiled at him, and began to talk to them all, his voice loud over the clattering of the tram.

Mason did not listen. Instead he crouched to look into the driver's rearview mirror. They were speeding away from what seemed to be a scene of absolute chaos. The Russian truck was still halted, partly obscured by a milling crowd.

As Mason watched, more people spilled from the pavement to join the throng. Their number increased the confusion. Drivers of halted vehicles stood by their cars or leant from their cabs gesticulating angrily. He could make out the figures of the young Russians thrusting with their rifle butts, trying to clear the crowd. He felt a faint stirring of sympathy for the overwhelmed conscripts. They were

217

caught up in something they could not understand. It would need very little to turn the crowd into a lynch mob.

He turned back to study the road. Eighty metres ahead of the rushing tram a red light shone dimly. A stream of cars traversed the lines ahead, bucking as they crossed the uneven rails. The driver was turned looking back in slack-jawed awe at Gregory.

'Look out!' Mason bellowed.

Startled, the man whirled to face the front. Alarmed, he began slowing the tram.

'No,' Mason shouted. The man looked at him in astonishment, a strand of tobacco hanging from his gaping lower lip. 'Don't stop,' Mason urged. 'Those soldiers, back there! They're after Father Gregory. Go on! Never mind the light! We must go on!'

The driver squinted shrewdly at Mason and then turned to look once again at Gregory. His eyes came back to meet Mason's. His face split in a sudden grin, showing a mouthful of ruined stumps of teeth.

Reaching quickly above his head, he grabbed a brass handle and yanked it downwards. The tram's bell began jangling insistently. They were close to the crossing. From the tram they could see the faces of motorists turning quickly towards them, full of fear and anger as they accelerated hard out of the path of the huge vehicle rushing at them.

A last car tried to cross. Mason could see the driver crouched over the wheel as though he were urging his car to greater speed. He saw the driver's hand extend, reaching for the gear lever. The car stopped dead. He had missed his gear. The car lay with its nose squarely across their track. They saw the man claw at his gear lever, his pale face clearly visible as it turned to face them set in a grimace of panic.

Mason felt a sensation like a ball of ice in his stomach. The great unstoppable mass of the tram careered towards the helpless man. They were almost upon him. Mason was bracing himself for the shock. His mouth was open to shout a warning when the car suddenly gave a single lurch and leapt three feet backwards.

The crash came anyway. A deafening sound of smashing metal brought all of them, even Gregory, instantly back to the present. Mason spun to see the damage. The car, a tiny Polski, like Barbara's, was spinning away from them on the snow, miraculously still upright. He glimpsed the driver's face through the grimy window. He was alive, and cursing them vigorously.

The tram driver was cackling gleefully. He pointed ahead of them to a crowded stop. Faces were turned expectantly towards them. He raised a questioning eyebrow.

'Shall I stop?' He sounded reluctant, as though he did not want to spoil the fun.

'No! Keep on over the bridge.' The driver nodded. He did not appear to question his authority. Mason tried not to let it go to his head. Still wearing his maniac grin the driver flexed his fingers once and took a firmer grip of the bell-lever.

Several hundred metres ahead of them stood the ungainly monumental columns that marked the beginning of the long bridge across the broad Vistula river. On their right, before the bridge, loomed the frowning bulk of the party headquarters they had passed on their way into town.

Mason could see the dull brown canvas hood of the truck still parked among a stark cluster of trees. As they raced past the astonished crowd at the tram stop, their speed undiminished, he could make out the scene on the steps of the building.

The Russian soldiers were still in place, strung at 3-metre intervals between the squat stone columns of the façade. On the broad paved space at the foot of the steps leading to the entrance a crowd had gathered. The crowd was not yet dense but from all directions people were hurrying towards the building, drawn by the sight of the crowd itself. Polish militiamen were drawn up in a thin line at the foot of the steps, between the crowd and the Russian soldiers.

The speeding tram drew abreast of the scene. Abruptly a dark object sailed out of the crowd and cartwheeled towards the building. It landed half-way up the steps and shattered. It was a bottle. Mason gave a quick laugh. In Poland a lot of people carried bottles to work.

From other points in the crowd other objects began sailing towards the building. They flew well over the heads of the militia to fall at the top of the steps or bounce off the grime-blackened columns. They were aimed at the Russians. Mason swivelled to watch as they sped past the scene. For the first time, he became aware that Gregory had finished speaking. The passengers were turned to the windows, mutely watching the scene. A few rose, craning towards the windows.

'Russians!' a voice called angrily. More people crowded to the windows.

'Bastards! What's going on?'

'What are they doing there?'

The voices rose to a furious babble.

The driver had turned to Mason. A look of outrage had replaced the grin. 'Russians!' he spluttered. 'Did you see? They were Russian soldiers, those.' He jerked a thumb over his shoulder.

Mason nodded and gave the man a quick smile, obliged for the information. 'Yes. I know. Can you drop us on the other side of the bridge?' They were racing across the Vistula. 'There,' Mason called, a few seconds later, as the tram rattled between the thick brick columns which marked the extremity of the bridge, 'at that street.' He pointed to a spot ahead of them where a narrow side-street led off the main road.

Without a word, the driver brought the huge machine lurching to a halt, its wheels screaming on the wet rails.

With a sound like a cat sneezing, the doors flew open.

'Thanks.' Mason tapped the driver on the bicep with a closed fist and stepped carefully down into the road. He

220

gave Barbara and Helena a hand as they followed him. Gregory came last, taking time to say a word to the driver, who stood staring after them.

'Let's go.' Mason herded the others ahead of him, pushing them towards the labyrinth of small streets that lay off the main thoroughfare. As they plunged into the narrow entrance Gregory turned to wave benignly to the passengers that remained on the tram. Most of them had already disembarked and were even then hurrying back over the windy bridge to join the crowd in front of Party Headquarters.


# 27


Toparoff was ashen. Throughout the conversation he had just had he had spoken scarcely three words. Now he sat staring at the silent telephone as though it were an object he had never seen before. Dominiak eased himself upright from his position, half-sitting on the radiator beneath the window, and coughed softly. He hammered himself gently on the sternum with the fore-finger and thumb of a loose fist and spoke.

'Something wrong, Colonel?' he asked negligently. He pulled a crumpled cigarette packet from his pocket and excavated its interior while he awaited a reply. None came. And there were no cigarettes. He squeezed the empty packet in his fist and lobbed it in the direction of the waste paper bin. He missed.

'A problem?' he asked again, as he moved with his odd, dainty, walk towards the door. Toparoff's eyes continued to look, unfocused, at the telephone. Slowly he raised his eyes to Dominiak's back as the Pole opened the door.

'Corporal.' Dominiak teased a worn banknote from his

pocket and passed it through the opening. 'Here. Get me some cigarettes.' He half-closed the door and then seemed to remember something. He yanked the door open again.

'Oh, Corporal.'

'Sir?'

'Have you got any on you?'

The young corporal grinned and extracted a packet from his breast pocket. He handed them to Dominiak, who instantly shook one free and bit it from the pack.

'Thanks,' he mumbled, smiling through the cigarette. He closed the door and turned to face Toparoff. He was surprised to find the other man's eyes on him.

'What is it, Comrade Colonel?'

Toparoff looked stunned and dishevelled, like a man who had just woken up in an alley after a night on the town and was still trying to remember how he got there. His tie hung loose. Dominiak noticed with satisfaction that there were two small stains on it.

'They're here.' He paused, overburdened by the information he was imparting. 'In Warsaw.'

The fleshy folds of Dominiak's face transmitted no reaction. 'How do you know?'

'They were seen.' The Russian's voice was hoarse. 'They tried to get into the American Embassy.'

Dominiak's hooded eyes narrowed further. He squinted at the man opposite.

'You had men at the American Embassy?' A faint inflection turned the statement into a question.

Toparoff nodded. 'Yes.' He ground the heel of his hand against one eye in a gesture of fatigue and despair. 'We had men there, Comrade. They prevented them entering the Embassy.'

His last words stopped Dominiak dead in the act of reaching into his pocket for a light. Dominiak weighed the implications of what he had heard. He got the worst over first.

'Gregory's not dead?' He was faintly surprised to find how much he cared about the answer. His eyes were locked onto Toparoff's face, looking for signs, trying to give none.

'No, he's not. None of them are.'

Dominiak lit his cigarette and drew on it so hard it burned down a full centimetre. He exhaled before he spoke.

'What's happened then? Where are they?'

'They got away.' His voice was almost inaudible. 'Our soldiers lost them.' His voice rose, strengthened by sudden anger. 'Because of a bunch of fucking Poles! They were mobbed. The bastards staged an accident.' He gripped the edge of the desk, his knuckles and his face both pallid in the dirty light. 'They let them get away. We lost them.'

Dominiak nodded. 'Congratulations,' he said softly. 'Have the riots started yet?'


They plunged deeper into the tangled streets and alleys of the Praga district, moving as far as possible from the highway. The increasing numbers of people on the streets obliged Gregory to continually duck and conceal his face with a hand. It could only be a matter of time before he was recognized. Mason looked around them. They needed some place to hide, to shelter while they worked out a plan. Fifty metres further up the street, on the opposite side to where they stood, a middle-aged couple emerged from a gateway surrounded by an unkempt hedge. Behind the hedge stood a crumbling villa. As the couple turned and began walking briskly away from them, Mason urged the others forward.

Walking fast, but without an appearance of urgency, they drew level with the house. Behind the gate two steps led up to the front door. The hedge shielded the door from view except for anyone standing directly opposite. Ignoring their questioning looks, Mason led the way across the road and up to the front door, signalling to Barbara to wait by the gate.

As he had hoped, there was only one bell-push. The house had escaped being divided into flats. He pushed the button and waited. He pressed again. No sound came from the house. He looked at Barbara.

'Anyone coming?' She shook her head. Without pausing, he took a single step back from the front door and slammed his foot in a flat-footed kick just below the lock. With a single sharp splintering sound the door swung open.

'You know how to do a lot of things, Mr Mason.' Gregory said dubiously, as they crowded into the cluttered hallway.

'It's my upbringing,' he answered, with a shrug. As he spoke he took a hundred-zlotych note from his pocket, folded it into a tiny pellet and held it in the doorframe as he closed the door. The door jammed shut.

He turned to face the others. 'Right,' he said, briskly, 'we need an idea quickly. What do we do now?' Helena and Barbara both looked uneasy, probably at being in someone else's house.

'There's the church of Father Popieluszko,' Gregory offered. 'It's very close to here. There are people there who would help us. The only thing is...'

Mason finished the thought Gregory left hanging. 'The only thing is they will have been joined by men in uniform. Probably Red Army uniform.' He shook his head. 'That church already had the fittest congregation in the whole of Poland. For every grieving widow there's a young man with a telephoto lens snapping visitors. Forget it.'

He was silent for a moment hoping one of the others would speak. Nobody did. 'I might know someone,' he said reluctantly.

'Oh, Peter!' Barbara said, snatching at his sleeve. 'Someone who could hide us? Somebody you could really trust?'

He shrugged. 'I think so. He's a friend.'

'A Pole?'

'Of course.'

'Have you known him long?'

'Ten, twelve years. I don't know if I can ask him to get

mixed up in something like this. He has a family.'

'Is he a Catholic?' Helena broke in.

'Probably. He's a party member, from way back.' He knew it made no difference, he was looking for an excuse, a reason to hold back.

Helena took the excuse away from him. 'So what? The older ones were Catholics long before they were Communists. You must try. We have no one else.'

He looked at her for a moment longer and then with a quick nod, he looked at his watch. 'I'll phone.'


Andrzej Zulawski shuddered as he stepped out into the morning air. He pulled his coat tighter around him and turned, smiling, to speak to his wife, who stood in the doorway. From inside the house the telephone began to ring. A flash of irritation passed over Zulawski's face. He looked at his watch and then at his wife. Then, with a shake of his head, he started down the steps towards the car. With a last tiny wave, his wife closed the door behind him.

He settled his bulk into the driving seat and turned on the radio. The motor fired at the fourth attempt. He drew slowly away from the kerb. Routinely, knowing the road was deserted, he glanced in the mirror. As he looked, he saw his wife emerge, running awkwardly in the thick snow, and signal him frantically to stop.


It was full daylight, or as near as it gets to daylight on an overcast December morning in Warsaw, before Mason, standing well back from the lace curtains saw the battered Cortina turn into the street and make its way hesitantly towards the house, as though the driver were studying the house numbers. With an exclamation he turned from the window and ran down the stairs.

The moment the car drew up in front of the house Mason opened the door and shepherded the other three out of the house. As he left, Gregory dropped a note he had

225

been writing onto a low table. It was an apology to the owners of the house.

Mason closed the door behind them, using the banknote to keep it shut. Waving cheerfully to the windows of the house for the benefit of the neighbours, he descended the cracked steps in the wake of the others, and slid into the seat beside Zulawski.

Zulawski's tough peasant face split into a broad grin. He stuck out a hand and briefly enveloped Mason's. Then without speaking, he coaxed the elderly gearbox into first and catapulted them away from the kerb. They were two blocks away from the house before Zulawski slowed to a normal speed. Mason began speaking, making brief introductions. Zulawski half turned his head to acknowledge each of the three people in the back seat in turn.

'It was very kind of you to come, Mr Zulawski.' Gregory said.

The big shoulders in front of him rose and fell. Zulawski grunted and turned to look at Mason. 'You've been stirring up trouble,' he said flatly.

'Party Headquarters? We know. What's happening now?'

Ahead of them a militia van emerged from a side-road and stopped at the kerb. With quick economy Zulawski signalled and turned sharply into a narrow turning to the right. He resumed speaking. 'A few minutes ago the place was ringed with Russians. A hell of a crowd was building up. They were throwing all sorts of junk. Militia sirens were going all over the place. It looked as if it might be getting very ugly.'

'Do you think it could become really bad?' Gregory asked, frowning deeply.

Zulawski shrugged. 'It depends. Frankly, it will depend whether people know *you're* involved.'

Gregory's thoughts went to the people hurrying from the tram back towards the scene Zulawski described. 'I'm afraid they do know,' he said despondently.

'Well, if they do,' Zulawski answered roughly, 'anything could happen. If people here think the Russians have done something to harm you...' He broke off without completing the sentence. 'By the way,' he went on after a pause, 'what *have* they done? How did you all get into this?'

Helena spoke up. Speaking quickly, in clipped sentences, she recounted the events from the arrival of Gregory at her house the previous evening. Zulawski listened impassively, his eyes flicking from the road to the mirror, constantly on the alert for police or soldiers. When she had finished Zulawski remained silent for a while. Finally, he picked up the question that lay, like the corpse of an animal nobody wanted to touch, between him and Mason.

'Peter, for Christ's sake, what were *you* doing at the Kodec's house? You never told me you knew them.'

He shifted, glancing uneasily at Helena. 'I didn't.'

Zulawski stiffened, hardly aware of Mason's answer. His eyes were fixed on the mirror. All of them looked around. Two army trucks were hurtling up from behind them on the wrong side of the road. Preceding them sped a militia car, its siren screaming. Zulawski pulled the car over to the right and slowed. Sweat trickled from his hairline. The two vehicles sped past without slowing, ignoring a red light. The occupants of the car sank back into their seats as the tension ebbed from them.

'Damn!' Zulawski muttered. 'Things are really hotting up.' As he spoke he accelerated hard, causing the rear to sway as the tyres fought for a grip. He drove well and hard, sending the car drifting into the turns in the little-used side-streets. Matter-of-fact, his concentration apparently all on the road, he spoke again to Mason. 'Well?'

Mason hesitated another instant. 'Okay, Andrzej,' he said at last, 'you deserve to know.' Very quickly, all the time braced against the car's wild turns, he outlined the story of the visit of Carroll and Brooke. The only part he omitted was that concerning Barbara. He finished the story, not liking the sound of himself. Zulawski pondered a moment and then gave a low laugh.

'What's funny?'

'Don't you see?' he glanced over his shoulder. 'The contract. That's why they cancelled it.' He shook his big head unbelievingly, at the same time slotting the car expertly into the heavy traffic of a broad tree-lined avenue.

'What contract?' Barbara asked, frowning.

Zulawski replied. 'They planned the whole thing. It's obvious now. I was set up to negotiate a business with Peter. It would have made him rich. Then, at the last moment, on the morning we were supposed to sign it, in fact,' he caught Mason's eye and shrugged, 'I was told not to proceed. No import licence,' he added, raising his hands off the wheel in a small gesture of defeat.

'Wasn't that unusual? Didn't you think it was strange?' Helena asked. Her curiosity sounded aggressive.

Zulawski smiled. 'Look, my dear. I don't know where you have been living for the last twenty or thirty years. Me, I've been in Poland. I've been told import licences were cancelled before now *after* I've signed a binding contract. We've been taken to court all over the Western world. My name is known to judges all over Britain and the United States.' He shrugged again. 'What do you want me to be? A hero?'

'Don't look now,' Mason murmured, 'but maybe this morning you've just become one.'

Zulawski squirmed. 'Bah,' he said gripping the wheel tighter.

'But what was the point of it?' Helena was insistent, leaning forward to address Zulawski. 'Why did they involve you?'

This time Mason answered. 'As Andrzej said, they wanted me to feel I was going to get rich. So that they could disappoint me. They hoped that while I was still feeling sorry for myself I would be more open to a proposition that would put everything back in shape. A calculation,' he said, brightening suddenly, 'in which they proved to be eminently correct.' He grinned vivaciously at his companions. 'So, from being modestly well off, bored and temporarily downcast, I'm now reasonably wealthy, scared stiff and pursued by troops and police of half the Warsaw pact. Funnily enough,' he added, smiling at Barbara, 'I've never been happier.'

'That's because you're nuts,' she answered, reasonably.

Zulawski grunted, apparently in agreement, and stopped the car in front of a narrow three-storey house set in a row of similar houses. Bare trees lined the street, which in spring and summer would be leafy and pleasant. Now it looked dingy and bare, the broken surface of the street apparent even under its coating of snow.

Zulawski's hand went to the door latch. 'Do you have something to conceal your face?' he asked, twisting towards Gregory. Gregory brandished his handkerchief, smiling. 'Great. Come on then, let's get inside. Quickly.'

The grey light reached grudgingly into the room, dulling the yellow light of the overhead neon strip, without having the strength to make it redundant. Dominiak's eyes were sore and gritty. An eighth of an inch of grey stubble clothed the folds beneath his jaw. He scratched at it affectionately, as though it were a bed of delicate plants he was tending. A young man entered with a tray holding a white porcelain jug of coffee and fresh cups. Dominiak watched in silence as the man placed the tray on the side table, took up the old tray with its stains and abandoned, half-empty glasses in which half-slices of lemon lay like wrecks. He waited until the man closed the door behind him.

'If you'll forgive me putting it so crudely, Colonel,' he said carefully, 'it looks as though we've fucked up.' He watched Toparoff's face. Saliva clung in a white film at the corners of the Russian's mouth. He still sat in Dominiak's exhausted-looking chair. One thumbnail picked with a soft clicking sound at the edge of the desk, as though he thought that by peeling away the desk top he could peel back the events of the last few hours.

'Yes, Colonel, we fucked up. Thoroughly,' Dominiak replied, taking a step closer to the desk, his eyes still fixed on Toparoff's motionless face. Slowly the Russian's eyes focused on his.

'Eh?'

'We screwed it up. We're finished. You've heard the news.'

'The news?' Toparoff's face went blank again for an instant. 'Oh. The business over at the Party building. Of course. That's nothing. It's under control.' His voice sounded hollow, as though he were speaking in an abandoned warehouse. 'Our men can take care of that. It's just a disturbance.' He flapped a hand. 'We've dealt with plenty of situations like this before. It's always the same, here. It was the same in Czechoslovakia in 1968. The outcome is always the same. When we show our strength these people have no stomach for a confrontation.'

Dominiak's eyes glinted. He advanced another step. 'We're not dealing with Czechs,' he said very distinctly. 'We're dealing with Poles.'

'Ah, stop it Dominiak. You're all the same. You think you are different. Your famous national pride. It's not worth that.' He snapped his fingers. As he did so the young man who had brought in the coffee burst into the room. He held a piece of paper with a few lines of type on it. Choking back the answer he was about to give, Dominiak took the paper from his hand. He scanned it. His brow furrowed and then cleared again. He nodded to the man, dismissing him, and turned to Toparoff. His anger was back under control. He gave the Russian a wide smile, pulling his top lip off his teeth in parody.

'So it's all under control.' He let a note of sarcasm sidle into his voice. He shook the piece of paper. 'It's under control in Warsaw, where there's a riot going on and your soldiers are likely to start shooting people at any moment. And it's under control in Gdansk, where –' he glanced down at the message on the paper – 'several thousand people are already gathered around the monument to the dead shipyard workers. And it's under control in the Ursus factory where the whole day shift has just downed tools and walked out, demanding that we produce Kozka.'

Toparoff rose tentatively to his feet. 'That's impossible,' he said, in a low rasp. 'Word can't have spread so quickly. Surely...'

'Of course it has. What do you think happened after the phoney accident? Do you suppose they all evaporated? For Christ's sake, Colonel, dozens of people must have seen them. He's the best known face in Poland.'

'But in the street, in ordinary clothes, would people recognize him?' Toparoff asked desperately.

Dominiak made as though to slap himself on the forehead in exasperation. Then he let his arm fall to his side. 'Colonel,' he said, scarcely audible, 'half the people in that tram queue were wearing the man's photograph. On their lapels, for fuck's sake.'

The Russian stared sightlessly down at the desk as though he had not heard Dominiak's last words.

'But how can the word have spread? Aren't all telephone lines out of Warsaw blocked? And telex, too?' He sounded almost as though he no longer cared.

'Public ones, certainly. They are all down, to the provinces and abroad. Official lines, our own for example, the militia's, the military, are of course still working.'

'Well, then,' Toparoff asked, a little more animated, 'how could word have got to Gdansk, and to Ursus if nobody can get a message out of Warsaw?' He looked pleased with his own reasoning.

'Colonel,' answered Dominiak with a weary patience, 'have you still not understood? We're talking about Kozka. Father Gregory Kozka. Can't you understand what's happening? The soldiers, the militia, even my own men, for Christ's sake, anyone with access to a telephone who knows anything, even a hint of a rumour, is talking about nothing else. And another thing you had better try to get into your head, Colonel, is that half of them, if they had to choose, would be on his side and not ours.'

He stood looking at Toparoff, his dewlaps quivering as he tried to keep a grip on his anger. There was a short silence. Then, with a suddenness that made Dominiak recoil a step, Toparoff straightened and glared at the Pole. His lips were white. He stabbed a finger in the air.

'Then we must catch them.' Dominiak's eyebrows lifted slightly at the renewed authority in Toparoff's voice. He was like a dying serpent that had collected its strength for a last strike. 'That's the only thing that matters now. We have to hunt them down, wherever they are.' Dominiak waited impassively for him to finish.

'What if Gregory just turns up? In the street I mean. If he just emerges in front of a crowd somewhere. The people would tear anyone to pieces who tried to touch him.'

'I will give the order now to my men and you will give the same one to yours.' His voice had regained all its coldblooded confidence. 'Whenever and wherever he is found, he must be stopped. Shot if need be. Like a dog.'

## 28

'They'll shoot you like a dog,' Mason said with calm conviction. The faces around the comfortable, overheated living room were grave.

'Do you think they would dare, Peter?' Helena's face was pale, emphasizing the darkened crescents beneath her eyes. 'Would they dare to touch him openly, in front of people?'

'It's not a matter of daring any more, Helena. They can't let Gregory live to tell what happened. Nor any of the rest of us,' he added with a grim gaiety. 'Look at it through their eyes. Almost anything is preferable to the truth. If Gregory were to be shot now they could tell any story. He's away from the place he agreed to stay. If he's seen in public he draws a crowd instantly. They would accuse him of sedition, of trying to stir up a revolt. Christ,' he added as an afterthought, 'he *would* be provoking revolt. His very presence does that.'

'But surely nobody would believe them.' Helena's voice was plaintive. Mason felt a twinge of pity. He had seen so often how hard it seemed to the people living closest to it to allow themselves to understand the corruption of the system.

'Of course nobody would believe them,' he answered gently. 'They don't need anybody to believe them. They just need something that's plausible in their own terms. Don't you see that, Helena? All they want is something to cloud the issue long enough until it dies.'

'He's right.' Zulawski looked up from the act of pouring brandy into the coffees his wife had placed on a low table beside his chair. 'When Father Popieluszko was killed, do you think anyone believes it was done by a single maverick secret police captain acting on his own?' He looked around the room. 'Of course not. Everyone here knows absolutely that the orders came from the top.' He began giving out the coffee. 'Popieluszko was a danger, they had him eliminated. You are a much bigger danger, they are much more determined to get rid of you. The only difference is that with you the international implications are wider. Which is why they tried to pin the blame on Peter.' He smiled at Mason who bowed slightly in mock appreciation.

Gregory nodded slowly. 'You think it's as bad as that?'

'Of course it is, Father,' Zulawski replied with a hint of impatience. 'Walesa was lucky. They managed to defuse the danger of Solidarity before it became necessary to take the most drastic step. But don't you think it was discussed? Don't you imagine it still is?'

Mason sipped gratefully at the hot coffee. It tasted lousy but the brandy improved it. He closed his eyes and let it warm him before he spoke.

'All right, Andrzej. We all seem to understand the situation fairly clearly. They want to kill us.' He looked cheerfully around the room. 'So,' he sipped coffee again,

233

'what do we do next? Plainly we can't stay here. We've already involved you and Elisabeth more than we had any right to do.' Zulawski's wife, Elisabeth, a thick-set, homely woman, smiled shyly at him from the kitchen doorway. She shook her head to indicate her disagreement, still too shy of Gregory's presence to speak. Mason watched his friend's face. Zulawski seemed to be pondering a matter of great importance. He sighed and spoke.

'You have to contact Solidarity. Their underground network. They have channels. Maybe they could get you out of the country. I don't see any other way.'

'Thanks for the advice.' Mason's voice was tinged with irony. 'How shall we contact them? An ad in the paper. 'Fugitive priest and henchmen seek passage to the West'. A box number?'

Zulawski did not smile. He looked at his wife. She nodded almost imperceptibly.

Zulawski swallowed once and then said, in a voice that was almost a whisper, 'We're in contact with them. Elisabeth is. A cousin of hers...' He broke off, unwilling to say more.

They sat stunned, their eyes on Elisabeth's plump face, shiny and unmade-up. She blushed and batted a loose lock of hair off her forehead.

A grin spread over Mason's face. Rising from his chair he crossed the room and threw both arms around Elisabeth.

'Elisabeth! You!' Mason drew back and looked into her face. 'That's wonderful.' He closed his arms around Elisabeth's matronly bulk again. She giggled.

Mason stepped back, keeping one arm around Elisabeth's shoulders. 'How soon can we contact them?' he asked, suddenly businesslike.

Elisabeth disengaged herself from Mason and with a practised gesture slipped her flowered cotton pinafore over her head and cast it onto a chair. With a small wave and a shy, slightly grim, smile she left the room.

Mason watched her affectionately. He had known her since he had first met Andrzej. She had been more slender then, but had from the beginning shown an almost motherly affection for him. An affection that had grown and been reciprocated over more than a decade. Throughout that time her calm good sense had been the perfect foil to her husband's robust and extravagant habits. Now he found himself looking at her with new wonder as he watched her go, shyly and without exhibition, into what could be acute danger. Any contact with the underground Solidarity organization must be dangerous. Every few weeks the police prised another leader from hiding. Even casual collaborators were given heavy gaol sentences.

Hearing the front door close softly, he sat down, chewing pensively at a fingernail. The room was silent. The silence was broken by Zulawski. He cleared his throat loudly and took up the brandy bottle. Grabbing the coffee jug in the other hand, he pushed himself noisily to his feet and with nervous bonhomie began dispensing coffee and brandy into their cups, in about equal measures. Nobody refused.

It was less than twenty minutes before they heard the key turn in the front door. Mason and Zulawski were on their feet simultaneously, looking expectantly towards the door. Mason was smiling, still chewing a fingernail. Zulawski frowned and automatically fed himself the last slug of coffee and brandy.

She came in, her shiny face radiant from cold and satisfaction. Drawn to her husband as though by some special shared gravity she nestled close under the protective shelter of his encircling arm.

'They're coming,' she whispered.

Mason looked exultantly at Barbara. 'When?' he asked.

'I don't know. Today, anyway. We are to wait here. They'll contact us.'

'Great.' Mason's face clouded abruptly. 'I mean, is that okay? Elisabeth, Andrzej, may we stay?'

'Yes,' broke in Gregory in his beautiful, measured voice.

'Please tell us if you would prefer us to leave. We have no right to ask you to run such risks for us. Please do...'

Zulawski cut him off, gruffly. 'Nonsense, Father.' He looked around at them all. His arm tightened around his wife's shoulders. She blushed again.

'Of course you can stay here. You must. There's no alternative. There's no danger to us, as long as we are all sensible, and careful.'

Mason tried to interrupt. The danger was there, he knew, and the responsibility for involving his friends was all his. Zulawski read his thoughts and over-rode his effort to speak.

'Now, you must all be exhausted. Why don't you all get some sleep? Even if it's only an hour or two it will help. You may be in for some hectic times.'

Mason woke abruptly in the total darkness. For an instant he felt something akin to panic, a feeling that he was at the bottom of a well. Turning onto his back, his mind struggling to organize his thoughts, he felt the warmth of another body. He drew back sharply, as if the other body had been red-hot. His mind grappled futilely with the parts of a mental jig-saw, unable to piece them together. With a suddenness that made him grunt in surprise, blinding light filled the room. His head jerked back and a hand flew to his eyes as though acid had been dashed in his face. Very slowly, he parted two fingers and squinted guardedly through the slit. Light flooded in at the window, next to which stood Zulawski, a broad smile on his face and one eyebrow cocked in a beginning of lasciviousness. One hand still clutched a bunched fistful of curtain.

Relief and comprehension flooded over Mason. He tried to say several things at once, ran into a verbal traffic jam and settled for an inarticulate groan. He flopped extravagantly back onto the pillow.

'Sleep well?' Zulawski asked, still grinning and holding the curtain.

'Eh? Oh. Christ. Mmm. Andrzej.' As he spoke he

reached for his watch. Not finding it, he floundered back onto the deep pillow. 'What time is it?'

Zulawski left the curtain and took two steps towards the bed. He crouched and picked up Mason's watch from where Mason in his fatigue had dropped it, a yard from the bed. He glanced at it as he handed it over.

'Twelve-thirty.'

Mason studied the watch himself for a moment. 'What day?' he asked morosely, after a pause, still gazing studiously at the watch.

Zulawski laughed and gave Mason's shoulder an affectionate shove. 'Same day. You've been asleep three and a half hours or so.'

Mason wiped a hand across his clogged eyes and blinked. He felt oddly light-headed. It was a feeling he remembered. The feeling he used to get the day after parties, when he had gone to bed at dawn. A New Year's day feeling.

'You'd better get up.' Zulawski said, pushing himself athletically up from his crouching posture. 'They're downstairs.'

'Who are?'

'The people who might get you out of this.' He made for the door. 'The coffee's waiting, too,' he said over his shoulder as he left the room, 'and there's a razor in the bathroom.'

Mason watched the door close. He rubbed the gritty deposits from the corners of his eyes. He felt a headache beginning. He shook his head, trying to lose both the headache and the slightly unreal feeling that his lack of sleep was inducing. Momentarily giving up, he slid back down beneath the billowing duvet and moulded his body to the warm outline of Barbara. He nuzzled his face in the luxuriant brown hair that spilled over the pillow.

'Hey.' She made no movement. 'Hey,' he repeated a little louder. She shifted her weight. He slid an arm around her body and cupped his hand over her breast. He squeezed it gently. 'It's time to wake up,' he said softly.

He felt her stir and heard a faint murmur. She settled closer to him. He knew she was awake now. His hands brushed softly over her stomach and thigh, coming to rest on her hip. Barbara stirred again, pressing herself more insistently against him. His grip tightened and he burrowed his lips into her hair, kissing her neck.

'We should go down,' she muttered.

'M'mm,' he agreed, his voice muffled by the kisses he continued to give.

'They're waiting for us.' She turned her head towards him as she spoke.

'I know,' he said, and began kissing her mouth. 'I'll save time by not cleaning my teeth.' Barbara turned, laughing, into his embrace.

When Mason finally rose from the bed his head had cleared and the incipient headache had dissolved. He smiled. He had always had suspicions about the idea that virtue was its own reward. Looking around him he realized for the first time that they must be in Andrzej and Elisabeth's own bedroom. A pang of guilt intruded into his thoughts, mostly related to the state of the sheets. He fended it off by recalling the many occasions, mostly at trade fairs in Poznan, when Zulawski had appeared on his stand with a mumbled request for the loan of his hotel-room key while a big-breasted blonde, barely out of her teens, hovered in the middle distance smiling shyly. They were not always pretty but invariably young, blonde and buxom.

As he dressed Mason wondered whether he was susceptible to any particular type of woman himself. He watched Barbara as she pulled a sweater over her head. She was big-breasted, broad-hipped. Completely different to Penny, who had been slim, blondish and bony-faced. He came to the conclusion he just liked women.

In the bathroom he found the razor lying ready on a fresh towel. The bathroom was steamy and damp. Somebody had been in shortly before him. He supposed

Gregory or Helena. Whoever it was, he soon discovered they had used the last of the hot water. He slipped off his clothes. Then he washed quickly and shaved very gingerly. The razor was an old-fashioned, double-edge safety razor of the type his father used to assemble and strip down with such deliberate precision in some of his earliest childhood memories. His nostalgic affection for it did not survive the bloodletting. By the time Barbara entered the bathroom he was naked except for several thumbnail sized pieces of the rough brown toilet paper with which he was trying to staunch the flow of blood from the cuts around his jaw.

Barbara walked past him and, with an easier intimacy than he had been aware of before, she hoisted up her skirt and sat down on the toilet.

'Tell me, Barbara, seriously, do you think Solidarity can really help us?' He peered appraisingly into his underpants and, with a faint grimace, pulled them on.

'Yes. I hope so. If anybody can, it's them. Why, don't you think so?'

'I don't know. I thought they were finished. Even if most of them are out of gaol. From all I've been able to hear Walesa or Bujak, or the rest of the prominent ones, can't fart without the Secret Police getting it on tape.'

She giggled. 'You're probably right. Most of the original leaders are gone. But don't forget, Peter, there were eleven million members only a few years ago. Even if they lock the big names away remember there were the regional organizations, the factory branches. These low-level people move up to replace the leaders. They are people nobody's heard of, but they are there.'

'I know, but are they organized? We don't need a few leaflets photocopied, Barbara, we need somebody to get us out of the country.' She shrugged. 'I can't say. All I know is that millions of people are still loyal to the ideas of Solidarity. And a lot of people would probably be ready to help. Don't do that, you filthy creature,' she interjected suddenly. He looked sheepish.

239

'Surely I'm allowed a sniff of my own shirt. I'm going to meet people.'

'What difference will sniffing your armpits make?' she asked incredulously.

'Well,' he answered defensively, 'I'll know if I have to keep a distance.'

She tossed her head and made an exasperated clucking noise. 'Anyway, all I know is what I hear. People say they have a network, that they can do many things. The rumour is that Jurzak and Klapecki –' she named two of the few leaders who remained at large – 'move in and out of the country, to the West, quite often.'

Mason had finished dressing. His clothes felt stale and limp on him. Carefully, he peeled the scraps of paper from his chin. In the mirror his eyes fixed on Barbara's. 'A lot of people here would like to be in their position, Barbara,' he said pointedly.

She stopped dead in the middle of adjusting her skirt and stood immobile, frowning at his reflection. After a moment she made a tiny grimace and crossed the room. She thrust a hip at him, pushing him from the sink. 'Move aside,' she muttered, without further comment.

He watched as she took up a comb and ran it quickly through her glossy hair. He loved the solid look of it as it fell heavily back onto her shoulders.

Together they left the bathroom and descended the polished pine staircase.

From behind the door of the living room they could hear low voices. Mason pushed open the door to allow Barbara to precede him into the room.

## 29

Silence fell on the room as they entered. One man, a newcomer, who had obviously been speaking, was looking

warily towards the door. Mason noticed one hand stayed in
the pocket of the quilted coat the man still wore despite the
heat of the room. Another stranger stood by the window,
sharing his attention between the street and the arrival of
Mason and Barbara.

Zulawski sprang to his feet and urged them into the
centre of the room. The two men relaxed perceptibly.

'Peter, Barbara, come in. Are you feeling refreshed?'
Mason thought he caught a faint irony in his friend's look.
'This is Chris.' He gestured towards the man in the coat.
'And this is Edward.' The slight emphasis with which he
spoke the names instantly convinced Mason they were
false. He began to offer a hand to the man named Chris.
Seeing that the man made no move to respond, he let his
hand fall back to his side.

A handsome man Mason estimated to be in his middle
thirties, Chris resumed talking. His flowing cavalry-officer
moustache, redder than his hair, bobbed as he spoke. His
voice was distinct but very low, making them all strain to
catch his words. Mason was wondering if it were a
theatrical ruse to increase his command when he noticed
that the telephone handset was buried beneath a thick pile
of cushions and clothes and that the thick curtains, except
for the narrow gap through which Edward kept his watch,
were drawn.

'We must act very quickly,' Chris was saying, 'before
the Russians clamp down on the whole country. Already
they're all over Warsaw.'

'We know. What's going on over on Jerezolimskie?'
Mason asked naming the street where the Party Headquarters stood.

'They broke up the crowd with water cannon. The
people have moved down into the old town. There's a
running battle going on now. We're also mobilizing our
people in Gdansk and Radom. Katowice, too, the mines.'

Gregory's face was pained. 'Because of me? Is there
nothing I can do to stop it, before there's bloodshed?'

Chris shook his head sharply and held up a hand. 'No,

Father,' he said fiercely. 'The time has come for this. We all have to see it through now. You were the symbol, that's all, the catalyst. The anger has been there for a long time. We have been ready.'

'But if I went to them? If I gave myself up to them?'

'They would shoot you,' Chris answered, flatly.

Gregory looked at him as though he had been struck. He was about to protest when Zulawski broke in. 'He's right, Father. Don't imagine they wouldn't. Father, you are a dangerous symbol. Like Allende or Castro for the Americans. In South America, the Americans do it, in Afghanistan, or South Yemen, or here, the Russians. What's the difference? Nobody's going to *war* over a dead priest.'

Gregory looked bleakly around the room. Chris spoke again, gentler than before. 'You must let us get you out. Alive, you will always represent hope for people here.' He added, almost in a whisper. 'We have enough martyrs in Poland already.'

Gregory started at the reference. 'Yes,' he said, almost to himself, his eyes cast down to the floor, 'you're probably right. Everything I have ever stood for in my life has been opposed to violence. I don't...'

'There is a time, Father,' Chris broke in, 'when resistance is the only way.'

Gregory raised his head and looked at him. 'How do you propose to get us out?'

As the morning had worn on Toparoff had been swinging from depression to outbursts of almost uncontrollable anger. He was screaming into the telephone. Two uniformed Russian officers sat across the desk, Dominiak's desk, from him. Both of them sat with their jaws clenched so tight the tendons jerked under the skin below their ears.

'Well, stop them! Disperse them! What?' He listened for a moment, a deep vertical furrow above the bridge of his nose. 'I don't give a shit about that. Do it yourself, you've enough men.' He slammed the phone down and sat breathing heavily. 'The fool,' he muttered. He looked up at the two impassive faces across the desk from him as though suddenly aware of their presence. 'It's the shipyards,' he said bitterly. 'Gdansk. They're refusing to go back to work after their break. Our people say the militia are dragging their feet. The workers are demanding that Walesa be allowed to speak to them.'

'And will he, Comrade?' asked the older of the two soldiers, evenly.

'No. No!' Toparoff shook his head violently as though the question were a swarm of bees. 'That was one of the first things we did, to get him out of the way. He's being brought to Warsaw. For an interview.'

In the neighbouring office, among the busy young men preparing telexes and a cacophony of voices speaking into telephones, Dominiak sprawled with half his rump and one thick thigh hitched onto a desk. He smoked calmly. He appeared absorbed in using an index finger to push into a pattern a collection of paper clips which lay on the desk. Through the open door he heard Toparoff's voice subside from the shrill shout and heard the crash of the phone being replaced. He grimaced wryly at the man seated at the desk who responded with a silent laugh and a minute shrug.

Dominiak heaved himself off the desk and put his cigarette, still burning, into an ashtray by the typewriter. Automatically the seated man reached out and pushed it further from him.

Dominiak moved towards the door. As he entered the inner office, he saw the older Russian's eye focus on his waist. Looking down expectantly, he found a shirt-tail had escaped from his straining belt and protruded beneath his tunic. With a grunt, he began stuffing it laboriously back into his trousers as he advanced across the room. The Russian dropped his eyes fastidiously.

'More news, Comrade?' he asked jauntily.

Toparoff scowled. 'The Gdansk shipyards. And now my people tell me the militia are reluctant to intervene. They

243

even want my people to withdraw their men.' He had begun fuming again.

Dominiak walked around behind the desk to Toparoff's left. With a muttered apology he leant across the Russian and opened the top right-hand drawer. He withdrew a can of peanuts. Straightening, he ripped the ring-pull seal off the can and grabbed a handful. Cupping them in his palm, he clapped his hand to his open mouth. He lapped at the nuts until he had cleaned his palm. Chewing contentedly, he proffered the open can to the two uniformed men.

'Nuts?' he offered genially. A crumb of peanut arched from his mouth to land on the chipped desk. Nobody accepted. Dominiak shrugged. 'Will they withdraw?'

'Of course not.'

'Why not? The militia have handled it before. Especially in Gdansk.' He laughed. Nobody else did. 'They've had a lot of practice up there.'

'Well, this time it seems to be different,' Toparoff replied with angry sarcasm. 'And you know it. You said so yourself. Half the militia are on the other side, not on ours.'

Dominiak nodded. He swiped another fistful of peanuts into his mouth. 'Do you want me to do anything?' he asked, his voice muffled. 'Arrest anybody?' he added, matter of factly.

The older Russian spoke again. 'Thank you, Comrade Dominiak. It won't be necessary. Our people have instructions. We have full authority.'

Dominiak squinted at the Russian. The grey hair of the man's eyebrows was longer than the close stubble that ventured below his hat at the back of his neck. Around the man's ears the skin was shaven so close it shone. The face had a rugged, ageless look, like a football manager in uniform. It could easily have been a kind face. It's immobility made it harsh.

'Authority, General? For Soviet soldiers to arrest our militia officers? Whose authority are we talking of?'

The officer looked directly at Dominiak, his face closed.

'The highest, Comrade.'

Dominiak whirled to face Toparoff. Some nuts spilled from the can. 'What's he talking about? What is this authority he's talking about?'

Ambassador Boshkov had exchanged the silk dressing gown for a dark grey suit and a maroon tie. They did nothing to disguise the chunky outline of his squat figure. Although he had taken the time to dress, he had not moved from the room where the green telephone stood on the vast empty desk. The telephone trilled softly.

'Boshkov,' he said curtly.

'Ambassador? Good.'

Boshkov tensed as he recognized the slightly rasping voice. He tugged at the knot of his tie. 'Yes, Comrade First Secretary. What can I do for you?'

'You can bring me up to date.'

Boshkov sought for a cue in the icily matter of fact tone, a clue to how his own performance was being judged. He found none. 'Yes, Comrade First Secretary, certainly.' In the old days they had used first names with each other. 'We have the situation under control. There has been some trouble, mostly here in Warsaw, Katowice and Gdansk. And of course at the Ursus factory.'

'Of course, at the Ursus factory,' the First Secretary mimicked sarcastically.

It disconcerted Boshkov. He ran a finger round his collar, yanked his tie loose and unbuttoned the collar that bit into his thick neck. 'Yes, First Secretary. They are always in the forefront of trouble. Whenever there's a chance to idle.' He laughed nervously. 'The miners, too, have been troublesome. Some of them are refusing to come off shift. We've put men, ours, around the mines. So far the situation is reasonably calm.'

Again the rasping voice broke in, a suggestion of exasperation in it. 'Tell me, Comrade Ambassador, these miners, they know about the situation. Even though they spent all night down a *coal mine*?' His last words were thick with sarcasm.

'Er – yes – it seems so.' The Ambassador's composure was shaken. He rubbed nervously at the back of his neck. 'Comrade Toparoff assured me telephone and telex lines were blocked. I don't know how it happened. It's the same thing in Gdansk, in the north. I don't...'

'Ambassador,' the voice broke in wearily, 'does it occur to you that if people digging coal half a kilometre underground know what's happening, then everybody knows? The whole country must be aware of it.'

'Er – yes – I... I do realize it.' The ambassador was angry at the sound of himself stammering. He breathed deeply. 'It's probable that rumours are all over the country by now. There have been a few attempts at demonstrations this morning, mostly in the places I've just mentioned.'

'And what was the outcome?'

'We broke them up,' the Ambassador responded shortly.

'M'mm.' There was a short pause. 'And how about the Poles? How are they reacting?'

'So far, very well. I have been in constant contact. Ah, they seem to, ah, accept our position. They have reservations, of course.'

'What kind of reservations?'

'About the use of our troops.'

'Whose troops do they want us to use?' The tone was sour. 'Their own would be useless. They would stand and watch. How about the situation in Gdansk? I hear their militia are balking at our men moving in around the shipyards.'

Boshkov was startled. 'You know about that?' he said, hurriedly. 'Yes. It was a problem. We had to show them we were serious. It's under control now.' He wondered where the First Secretary had got the information. He wondered who was reporting to Moscow on his own activities. Probably the rat-faced little bastard they had sent him as a butler. Our local commanders have instructions,' he went on, 'to use all force necessary to quell any trouble. I have instructed, through our Polish friends, of course, that their militia should be kept on a tight rein with no more than a token uniformed presence on the streets.'

'How did they take that? After all, they're their streets. At present,' he added.

Boshkov could not make out if the last comment was a joke. He insured himself with a half laugh. 'Ha. Yes, Comrade First Secretary. Quite so. They took it quite badly, as a matter of fact. I was obliged to explain some – er – painful truths to the General and a few of his people in order to get them to see my point of view.'

'He should understand. He fought alongside the Red Army in the war. He is a practical man.'

'Yes,' Boshkov agreed, 'I think he does understand. We talked about our Army. We talked about it a lot,' he added with grim humour. 'He – how can I put it? – grasps the realities. Also,' he added briskly. 'he knows there are plenty of people sympathetic to us who could easily take his place.'

'Don't underestimate him, Ambassador.' The tone was suave. 'Whatever else he may be, he's a patriot. Keep close to him, try to win him over. We have discussed it here. It would be a pity to lose him.'

'No, First Secretary, I won't. I'm keeping him informed and – er – discussing, every move with him.'

'Good. We rely on you. Toparoff and his people have blundered. The situation could become very grave, very quickly. You must keep it bottled up. Do you understand? You must. Whatever is necessary you will do. You can get me at any time of the day or night. I have given the instruction that you are to be put through immediately.'

'Thank you, First Secretary, you can count on me.'

'I know I can, Dmitri.' The Ambassador's acute antennae quivered at the sound of his first name, like a stag scenting a hunter. 'Remember how Hungary transformed poor late comrade Andropov's career during the '56 uprising.' Boshkov listened intently to the suddenly

247

amiable tone, waiting for the barb. 'Put yourself in Andropov's situation, Dmitri, and imagine for a moment what would have become of him had he failed.' The Ambassador was silent for a few seconds, weighing the other man's words. 'Yes.' Deliberately omitting to use any title, Boshkov continued. 'I'll bear it in mind.'

'Good. Goodbye, Dmitri.' The First Secretary paused. 'Catch them.'

There was a click and then the soft droning of a dead line. For fully thirty seconds Boshkov sat immobile. His wide flat face was like a carving. Suddenly his eyes focused on the telephone in his hand. He looked faintly surprised, and replaced it abruptly on its rest. Pushing himself to his feet, he strode to a mirror in an elaborate gilt frame and stared at himself. He inhaled slowly through his nose, swelling the massive chest beneath his buttoned jacket. He tightened his tie emphatically, exhaled noisily, and wheeled away from the mirror.

Picking up a different telephone, he jabbed a short finger at the dial.

'General Jaruszelski,' he snapped into the phone. 'Boshkov.' He examined his fingernails. They were heavily ribbed, like deer-horn. 'General. Boshkov again. You've heard the latest reports?' He did not wait for a reply. 'We have to react, General. We must keep the upper hand. The First Secretary and I have just been speaking,' he paused to let his words sink in, 'and I have to ask your cooperation in one more thing, General. I would be grateful if you would arrange for radio and television announcements to be made immediately, and repeated every hour. There will be a curfew. Beginning tonight at six.'

# 30

Mason stood at the window, rocking gently on his heels and trying to contain his impatience. It was almost three hours since Chris and Edward had left the house. The street outside was unusually animated. He watched in silence as people, mostly elderly, hurried past clutching shopping bags. They had no doubt heard the news of the six-o'clock curfew on the radio and were now rushing to stock up before they were confined indoors.

He sighed softly and turned from the window. Gregory and Andrzej sat intent on a deadlocked chess game. Helena sat in a wooden kitchen chair at Gregory's elbow, in solemn and silent encouragement.

Barbara entered noisily from the kitchen carrying a tray loaded with glasses of tea.

'Tea-time,' she crooned breezily. Her entry dispelled the church-like atmosphere.

Zulawski looked up and grinned at her winningly. Mason knew the look.

'She's mine,' he said, laughing.

Zulawski shrugged. 'It's instinctive,' he said helplessly.

'I know,' Mason answered. 'You randy old bastard,' he added in English.

Barbara handed the tea around.

'Where's Elisabeth?' asked Mason pointedly.

'Gone shopping. Like everybody else.' Zulawski looked ruefully at Mason, as though he had been caught in a minor way of cheating at cards.

'What's randy?' Gregory said conversationally.

'Eh?' Mason choked on his tea.

'Randy. What does it mean? I don't think I've come across it before.'

Mason swallowed. Everybody wanted to improve their English these days.

'No. I doubt if you have, Father. It's – er – slang. You

249

wouldn't have needed it, really.' Gregory still watched him politely. 'It's used for men who – er – like women.' He knew he was floundering.

'Oh! Not homosexuals, you mean?'

'Well, er, definitely. No, definitely not homosexual. The opposite.'

'Heterosexual? For example, could you describe yourself as 'randy'?' He paused reflectively. 'Am I 'randy'?'

Mason felt he was somehow on the brink of an abyss.

The doorbell rang. Their heads jerked towards the window. Between the narrow gap in the curtains they could see a vehicle drawn up at the kerb in front of the house. Mason was first to the window. Without touching the curtains he squinted through the narrow gap. His eyebrows twitched in surprise. Through the close packed shrubs of the front garden he could see the high sides and the frosted windows of an ambulance. The doorbell sounded again, a longer, more insistent ring. Feeling Zulawski at his shoulder, Mason leant aside to give the other man a clearer view.

'It's an ambulance,' he said doubtfully, as Zulawski leaned forward to look.

'Civilian?' Helena inquired, her voice anxious.

'Looks like it.'

'Shall I answer the door?' Helena was already moving briskly across the room.

Zulawski and Mason exchanged a look.

'No, Helena, you stay here. Andrzej and I will get it.' He looked at Zulawski for approval. Zulawski nodded assent as the bell rang for a third time. Mason touched him on the elbow. 'Come on.'

They left the room under the silent gaze of Gregory and the three women.

A shadow slid across the frosted glass panel of the front door. Mason started. The outline of a uniform cap was clear against the glass. Without a word, he drew a knobbed walking stick from a bentwood stand holding a variety of umbrellas and walking sticks and stepped into position behind the door. He nodded to his friend. Holding the latch at arms length, Zulawski unfastened the door. It flew open and a grey, uniformed figure almost threw itself into the hallway, bundling Zulawski backwards in its haste. As Zulawski, caught off balance, staggered backwards, Mason took a pace forward, looped an arm around the man's neck and yanked him hard backwards, the stick upraised in his other hand.

He found himself looking down into the face of a much younger man whose frightened eyes were fixed on the heavy stick poised above his head. The man struggled to speak, tugging feebly at the arm locked around his throat.

'Let him speak, Peter,' said Zulawski quickly, concern and surprise in his voice. 'He looks like an ambulance man.'

Mason would not have recognized the uniform. He eased his grip on the man's Adam's apple. The man, still bent over Mason's hip, attempted a nervous grin.

'Chris sent me,' he managed to say, still eyeing the stick. 'Chris and Edward. I'm Tomek.'

Mason bit his lower lip and exhaled hard through his nose. As he did so, he lowered the stick and helped the pinioned man upright.

'I'm sorry,' he said simply. 'I thought you were police.' He threw an arm over the young man's shoulders with exaggerated bonhomie. 'We're very nervous, as you can see.' He dropped the stick onto a low table. 'We weren't expecting a uniform.'

The young man was reassured. 'I've got some instructions for you.' he whispered. To make it official he stooped and recovered the peaked cap which had fallen off in the brief struggle. A blue plastic holdall he had also been carrying had fallen to the floor in the mêlée. Mason gathered it up and handed it to the young man. One handle was broken. He could not remember seeing a bag like that that did not have a handle broken. Maybe they were manufactured that way.

'We know.'

'What?' the ambulance man asked stupidly.

'The instructions. The plan for getting out of here. Chris told us to expect you.'

'Oh. But, I've got to explain the details to you.'

Mason and Zulawski looked at him expectantly. The man remained silent.

'Well?' Mason said, coaxingly.

The man was beginning to look sullen. 'I thought,' he began, 'well, that is, I was told that I would be speaking with Father Gregory.' He hesitated. 'Personally,' he added, with a hint of a pout.

'Ah,' said Zulawski 'Of course. Let's go in.'

The three faces were turned expectantly as they entered the room.

'This is Tomek,' Mason said cheerfully, drawing the young man into the room. 'Tomek, this is Father Gregory Kozka, this is Helena, and this is Barbara.' He might as well have been speaking to the sideboard. Tomek stood rigid just inside the room. After a moment's debate with himself as to which hand was available, he snatched off the cap and stood as though Gregory were going to inspect him. After a while he realized he would not, and felt bold enough to advance a couple of steps. Gregory beamed at him.

'So you're the young man who's going to extricate us from our trouble,' Gregory said warmly. 'It's very kind of you to come.' He extended a hand, inviting Tomek to come forward. The man stammered and advanced another step. Suddenly, like a boxer taking too much punishment, his legs gave way. He tottered and sank to his knees, crossing himself with his crushed cap as he went.

While they went through the now-customary hand-kissing routine Mason looked studiously at his watch. Barbara looked as though she might cry, Helena watched Gregory, and Zulawski chewed the inside of his lip, concentrating hard on finding a morsel to his taste.

Tomek stood up. No longer sullen, he looked flushed and excited.

'I don't want to get in the way of anything,' said Mason blandly, 'but it's almost 3.00.' He glanced pointedly at his watch again. 'The curfew starts in three hours.'

Tomek looked at Gregory, as though for confirmation. Gregory nodded.

'Yes, my son. Tell us what we must do.'

Fumbling in his excitement, Tomek dragged open the zipper of the holdall and began removing clothing from it. He tossed the garments in a heap on the table. Satisfied there was nothing left in the bag he began sorting the clothes into two heaps. He pushed one heap towards Mason.

'Try and put these on.'

'What are they?' asked Mason, approaching the table.

'It's a uniform like mine. You're going to be an ambulance driver. An assistant. I'll be the driver,' he added assertively. Mason picked up the tunic. He fingered the cloth non-committally and began stripping off his jacket.

Tomek pushed the other pile of clothes away from him, vaguely towards Helena. He gestured, taking in both the women. 'This is a nurse's uniform. There's only one. I'm sorry.' He looked down, embarrassed. 'It was all I could get,' he mumbled. 'There were supposed to be two. I could only get one.' He looked desolate.

'That'll be okay,' said Helena, gently. 'One of us can be the worried wife.' She caught Gregory's eye and laughed. 'Sister?' she asked, raising an eyebrow.

Barbara was holding the nurse's uniform blouse against her bosom. She looked from her own swelling sweater to Helena's gentler slopes. 'I'm afraid that's going to be me.' They giggled.

Dominiak felt like a stranger in his own office. Toparoff and the two taciturn officers presided over a noisy mêlée of angry telephone conversations and hurrying messengers carrying telexes and scribbled notes. In the outer office the telephone rang incessantly. All the news was bad. Reports were flooding in from all over the country of angry demonstrations and lightning strikes. In several places the local Party offices had been invaded and ransacked by demonstrators. Reports were coming in of local party officials being attacked in their offices. Militia stations had been stoned.

Along with the party officials' panic stricken cries for help there was another element which Dominiak had never witnessed in previous trouble. They were asking for explanations.

'What did you expect?' Dominiak asked, his jowls trembling with anger. 'The scheme was crazy from the first. This was always on the cards if it went wrong!'

'We don't need that kind of advice, Comrade,' answered the younger Russian officer, icily.

'Well you need some kind of advice, Colonel,' Dominiak retorted hotly, 'Because at the moment you're heading for a general insurrection!'

'Really,' the officer sneered. 'And you don't think we could handle it?' He looked contemptuously at the Pole.

'I'm sure you can, Colonel.' Dominiak was quivering. 'The way your people handled the thing up there in the mountains. Badly.' He fumbled for a cigarette and thrust it with a trembling hand into his mouth.

'Comrade Dominiak,' the young officer said, urbanely. Dominiak looked at him sharply. 'Your cigarette's the wrong way round.'

Reddening, Dominiak snatched the cigarette from his mouth and replaced it with the filter tip between his lips. He lit it and drew deeply and deliberately. He despised himself for letting them see his anger.

'And your people, Comrade, they're doing splendidly, I suppose?' It was the older officer. His sarcasm was veiled but unmistakable. 'All of your informers, all of your men, what help have they been?'

Dominiak answered in a low voice, without removing the cigarette from his mouth. 'So far, none. We need some time. Remember we only discovered they were in Warsaw a matter of hours ago. When your soldiers failed to catch them,' he added pointedly. The officers stiffened. Toparoff looked too drained to react. 'We'll have news soon. I'm confident of that. There's not a group in the country where we don't have our people,' he said in a sudden burst of professional pride. 'Not one. They'll have to make contact with someone if they want to get out of Poland. Probably with Solidarity, or the Church. Either way, I'll be informed of it.'

'H'mm,' the Russian answered sceptically. 'Perhaps so, Comrade. And perhaps not.' He paused. 'Frankly, I hope so. By catching them quickly you would be doing your country a great service.' As the man spoke, a new note in his voice caused Dominiak to look with sudden concentration into his acute blue eyes. He met Dominiak's gaze without any change of expression. For a very brief moment a silence lay between them. Absently, Dominiak inserted the orange-tipped finger of his right hand between the buttons of his shirt. He turned away from the Russian's gaze, scratching reflectively at his chest.

# 31

Zulawski waved from behind the curtains, knowing nobody in the ambulance could see him.

'Good luck,' he muttered, and threw back the inch of cognac in the wide tumbler.

At the wheel of the ambulance as it sped away from the house, the young driver gripped the wheel so hard his knuckles shone white in the surrounding gloom. Mason could see the pulse thumping in the man's neck.

'Relax,' he said affably. 'You look as if you ought to be the one back there.' He jerked his head towards the rear.

The driver swivelled his head quickly towards Mason and just as quickly back to the road. He attempted a smile. 'I feel like that. I'm scared,' he added frankly.

Mason touched his arm. 'So am I,' he said softly. 'We're all pissing ourselves. All the more reason to try to relax and drive carefully. The last thing we need is to be buried in the side of a truck right now.'

The man nodded. 'I know,' he agreed, and gripped the wheel tighter. Mason smiled despite himself. In the space of a few hours the man had seen his world upended. He had begun his day, like any other, a simple ambulance driver. Now, at four in the afternoon he was in danger of his life. Even if he had volunteered, it was plain from his nervousness that he was in no doubt about the extent of the danger. The man was terrified. And yet he was doing it. He had none of the obvious attributes of a hero, he did not appear especially brave, or clever, or positive. Nevertheless he was ready to risk his life. For his country? For Kozka? For revenge on the Russians? For reasons as mixed, probably, as his own. He slid back the frosted glass screen that divided the cab from the rear.

'How's the patient?' he enquired cheerfully.

Gregory raised his big dark head from the white wedge of the pillow. 'He's in great danger. Having attendants like these is giving him a temperature.'

'I know what you mean. Nurses' uniforms have always had that effect on me too.' It was true. Helena flushed. 'Is everything ready,' Mason continued, 'in case of trouble?'

Helena held up a transparent plastic bottle holding a liquid. A tube ran from the bottle to Gregory's naked forearm where it was held in place by a wide band of sticking plaster.

'How's that?' she asked. 'Convincing?'

'Very. What's in the bottle?'

Helena shrugged. 'Ask the driver.'

The driver, overhearing, sniggered. Mason looked at him suspiciously.

'It's vodka.' Tomek spluttered at the humour of it. 'It's

mine. I keep it in a plasma bottle.'

Mason leaned his head closer to the opening. 'Father,' he announced slowly, 'you're living every self-respecting Pole's dream. An intravenous vodka transfusion!' He spoke to the driver again. 'Doesn't anybody ever complain?' he asked, still disbelieving. 'About the smell, at least.'

'Smell? Ambulances smell of alcohol all the time, like hospitals.'

Feeling himself the centre of attention had relaxed the driver, and he slackened his merciless grip on the wheel. Abruptly, his whole body stiffened again. 'Militia,' he hissed, his eyes riveted on the rearview mirror. Mason twisted hard in his seat. Through the clear upper part of the rear window he could see a motorcyclist in the familiar hated uniform swinging into the road behind them. As Mason watched, the headlight of the motorcycle cut suddenly through the afternoon gloom and the driver crouched lower as he accelerated towards them.

Mason spun back to face the front. Two hundred yards ahead of them four men, soldiers, lounged by a truck. From the colour of the uniforms, they were Russians. He leant forward for a view in the wing mirror. The motorcyclist was no more than forty yards behind them.

'What do I do?' the driver's face was moist.

'Nothing.' Mason turned to the trio behind him. 'Trouble,' he said, laconically. He slid the screen closed. 'Drive normally. Stop if he tells you to.'

In the rear of the ambulance Helena fixed a mask connected by a rubber tube to an oxygen cylinder over Gregory's face. Only his eyes were visible. He winked at Helena as she clamped the plastic container into place above him, simulating a drip feed. Barbara sat hunched on the bench across from the stretcher on which Gregory lay. She was trying on expressions like hats. Finding one she liked she kept it, hoping it was suitable for a grieving sister.

Mason looked again in the mirror. He was just in time to

see the rider lean and sweep out of his sight as he began to overtake. A moment later he flashed past the driver's window. He waved them down with three short downward jabs of his hand. The driver looked anxiously at Mason. Sweat dripped from his eyebrows, making dark spots on the cloth of his tunic.

'What shall I do?' he asked, hardly daring to move his lips. Fifty yards away the group of Russian soldiers had turned to watch them, their interest roused by the sight of the motorcyclist. The militiaman jerked his bike onto its stand and dismounted. He strode back to the ambulance, his hands resting lightly on the white-webbing belt holding his holster. The man's eyes were invisible behind smoked goggles.

The driver sat like a frightened rabbit. His hands shook.

'Open the window, for Christ's sake,' Mason's words emerged in an urgent murmur through the fixed smile which he wore for the approaching policeman. 'And wipe your brow. You look as though you just got out of the shower.'

Without speaking or removing his mesmerized gaze from the militiaman, the driver wiped the sweat from his glistening brow and ground the damp palm of his hand against the cloth of his uniform trousers. With the other hand he lowered the window. The militiaman saluted perfunctorily.

'In a hurry?' he asked. His voice was neutral, his eyes still invisible behind the goggles.

'Er – yes. Yes, we are,' the driver stammered. He jerked a thumb towards the rear of the ambulance. 'An emergency.'

The militiaman nodded. 'Where are you heading for?'

The driver swallowed noisily. He paused before saying softly, 'Plock.' Mason saw the militiaman's lips purse in surprise. 'Plock? This way? You're off the track. This isn't the road for Plock.'

'No. I wanted to avoid the town centre. I hear it's blocked solid. Demonstrations,' he added, forlornly.

The policeman nodded sharply. 'It is,' he said briskly. 'You're right.' Abruptly, he turned away from the window. 'Follow me,' he called over his shoulder, walking quickly back to his machine. He straddled the bike and jerked it forward from its rest. He stamped on the old-fashioned kick-start and the engine roared. He set his blue warning light blinking luridly in the afternoon gloom and wheeled in a wide arc, signalling them to follow.

Mason squeezed the driver's forearm as the man sat erect, blowing hard with relief. 'Great!' Mason told him enthusiastically. 'You were terrific.'

The driver grunted sourly as he swung the ambulance behind the motorcycle.

'Cheer up,' Mason encouraged. 'We've got a police escort. What more do you want? It'll cut an hour off our journey.'

The driver looked resentfully at him. 'Maybe. Or fifty years off my life.'

Mason turned to look at the driver more squarely. He studied the sullen profile. 'How's that?' he asked. 'He's going to take us through town. He'll get us all the way to the edge of town, if we're lucky. Who's going to suspect us if we arrive at a checkpoint with him for an escort?' Mason's voice carried a hint of irritation.

For a moment the driver offered no reply. Instead he concentrated on following the policeman who was setting a hot pace through the light traffic. 'That's not the point,' he said finally in a peevish voice.

'What do you mean?' Mason asked sharply. He was becoming increasingly exasperated. 'Of course it's the point. With luck he'll get us through the checkpoint.'

The driver shook his head violently. He looked depressed. 'It's the wrong checkpoint.'

'Yes, Excellency, that's what I said. Singing.' Toparoff's voice was hollow with the strain of the last hours. 'There must be ten thousand of them, at least. And they're apparently just standing there, singing. Nothing else, just

259

singing that damned song, over and over.'

The Ambassador paced the spacious room, dragging the telephone with him. A secretary scuttled a pace behind him, ready to take notes. Boshkov was in a cold rage. 'Stop them.' He heard himself beginning to shout. He paused and in a more modulated voice went on. 'Break it up. Get them off the square. Do you need anything? Are you getting all the cooperation you need?' Boshkov paused, staring from the big window down at the snowy street beneath him. There were six sentries now, instead of the usual two. 'From our own people, I mean, not from the Poles. I can imagine,' he went on contemptuously, 'what help you're getting from them.'

'No, Excellency, we don't need anything. Nothing at all. We, that is the General and I,' Toparoff glanced at the older officer who still sat poker-faced across the desk from him, 'are getting first class cooperation. First class! We –'

Boshkov interrupted, speaking with deliberate sarcasm. 'Then why are they still on the square, Comrade? Why are you permitting them to defy us?'

Toparoff's assurance crumbled further in the face of the Ambassador's frigid sarcasm. 'We'll see to it, Comrade Ambassador.' He kneaded the telephone flex between the fingers of his free hand. 'I shall authorize firmer action right away.'

'Do that, Comrade Toparoff. Please. I want them cleared away by curfew. Do you understand that, Comrade? Get rid of them, by any means necessary.' Without waiting for any further response, the Ambassador clamped the telephone back onto the rest which he held hooked in the fingers of his left hand. Without a word he handed the telephone to the secretary, a handsome, sturdily built woman, with short blonde hair and a faint auburn moustache. As she replaced the telephone on the desk, the ambassador strode to the door and turned the key in the lock. He turned back to face the woman, his face expressionless. He began peeling off his jacket.

'Come,' he said, smiling slowly, 'there is just time before curfew.'

Toparoff blinked, momentarily nonplussed by the Ambassador's peremptory dismissal of him. As he sat under the eyes of the General, he became aware of a soft whistling from close by the window. It was three or four seconds before he realized what the tune was. Toparoff sprang to his feet, beside himself.

'Stop it!' His voice broke in a scream. He trembled.

Dominiak turned slowly from his place at the window. 'Stop what?' he asked affably. His eyes might have been mocking under their puffy eaves of flesh.

'That tune!' Toparoff shouted, leaning forward over the desk, supporting himself on bunched fists. 'You're doing it deliberately.'

Dominiak raised his eyebrows and looked in appeal at each of the two officers in turn. He gently placed an accusing finger on his own breastbone. 'Me?' he asked, disbelievingly. 'Doing what?'

'Whistling.' Toparoff almost choked on his words. 'That tune!'

'Oh, *that*,' Dominiak answered with an air of relieved enlightenment. 'You were just talking about it on the phone. It reminded me. It's very popular with the people here. Can't remember who wrote it. It was first sung at the song festival up in Sopot a few years ago. It's become a kind of anthem here, since then.'

Toparoff, as he listened to Dominiak's benign explanation, was becoming apoplectic. 'I know all about it, Comrade,' he spluttered. 'I'm well aware of its significance, Solidarity and all that nonsense. I'm not stupid.' Dominiak made no answer, leaving the Russian with the last proposition on his hands.

White-lipped, Toparoff sat down. 'The Ambassador wants Victory Square cleared,' he said, staring down at the desk in front of him. 'He insists on it. He wants it cleared by curfew.' As though on cue, the eyes of all four men in

261

the room flicked to their wristwatches. 'Can you provide enough men to do it, General?'

The General nodded impassively. 'Yes. I have three hundred men I have been holding out at the airport. They can be in the town centre in a matter of minutes.'

'Do they have everything they need?'

The General looked hard at Toparoff, as though he had not fully understood. 'They are soldiers, Comrade Toparoff,' he said, almost in a whisper. 'The only thing they need are their orders.'

Toparoff returned the look. The deep shadows beneath his eyes and pallid, grey-tinged face were in stark contrast to the rugged healthiness of the officer and his look had a glittering, feverish quality.

'Well, give them, General,' he said, speaking as softly as the other man, 'give them.'

# 32

The eyes of the two men locked for a moment before the General, with an almost imperceptible shrug, reached for the telephone.

Dominiak watched the exchange in silence. Beneath the slackness of his jowls, the muscles of his face set firmer. He began to speak. His dewlaps trembled with the effort to control his anger.

'General.' The officer looked up sharply, arrested by the new note in Dominiak's voice. 'There are ten thousand innocent citizens out there. There are women and children. Babies. They aren't doing anything. They're just *singing*, for Christ's sake.' He could hear his own voice sounding loud in the utter silence around him. His eyes flicked across the three faces that watched him. None of them offered him anything. Dominiak plunged on, his

262

voice echoing in his own head, 'At least wait until curfew. Give them a chance to disperse. If you send troops against them now, in their present mood, anything could happen. People will be killed. Children, maybe. Why not wait, for a while at least? Things are bad enough already. Why not..?' He broke off abruptly, aware of the futility of what he was trying to do.

The silence that followed was broken by the soft whirring as the General began dialling.

'Perhaps,' drawled the younger officer, 'Comrade Dominiak ought to get some rest. He seems to be overwrought. He's become a trifle – er – sensitive.' He cocked an eyebrow insolently at Dominiak. 'M'mm Comrade?'

Dominiak swallowed twice. His tongue flicked at his lips, as though he were about to retort. Then he spun abruptly, and walked from the room, slamming the door.

Several of the young officers looked up sharply as the crash of the door rang out over the jangle of telephones and the hubbub of a dozen conversations. Some looked quietly away, others looked on, allowing their curiosity to show as Dominiak leant heavily against the door. Slowly, he recovered his calm. He wiped a hand across his mouth. Becoming aware of their eyes on him, he spread his hands and gave a quick, slightly embarrassed laugh.

'We're having a little disagreement,' he said grimly.

Some of the men who had looked away turned back to him as he spoke.

'What about?' asked the man sitting nearest to Dominiak, ignoring the insistent ring of one of the phones on his desk.

'Tactics!' Dominiak's voice brimmed with contempt. 'They're sending their troops to Victory Square. They'll be going in with everything. Tear gas, water cannon. Guns, if necessary. They'll have orders to break it up quickly and they'll do whatever it takes.'

'But they can't!' The speaker was a slightly older, owlish looking man who was trying to distract attention from his

263

baldness by the cultivation of luxuriant sideburns. 'They should let them be. If they move now with people in the mood they are –' he glanced at a typed report on his desk – 'it could explode. It's – it's a powderkeg! Can't you do anything?'

Dominiak pushed himself away from the door, smiling affectionately at the speaker. 'Your turn of phrase might not be original, Stefan, but you're right. People are going to get killed tonight.'

'I hope it's going to be Russians,' somebody muttered.

Dominiak turned sharply, intending to reprimand the speaker, when another man called to him.

'Comrade Dominiak, it's for you!' The man held the telephone towards his chief.

'Who is it?' Dominiak mouthed, taking a reluctant step away from the proffered phone.

The man cupped a hand over the mouthpiece. 'He calls himself Witek the tailor,' the man said with a dubious grimace. 'He says he must talk only to you.'

At the sound of the name Dominiak stiffened. He started towards his own office and then, remembering, scowled at the closed door. He hesitated for a moment and then said, 'Put it through to the phone outside.' Moving with anxious speed, he padded to the outer door of the office. Beyond the door was an ante-room where three men lounged, half-heartedly reading newspapers.

'Out,' Dominiak barked, alleviating his brusqueness with a smile. 'I need to be alone.' He shooed the grumbling men out of the office, made sure both doors were shut, and took up the phone as it rang. He grunted his thanks and waited for the change in quality of the line that told him the young man next door had replaced his own phone.

'Dominiak speaking.' He waited.

'Colonel Dominiak. It's you?' The voice was low and frightened, and the words came very fast.

'Yes, this is Dominiak. Who's this?'

'Colonel, this is Witek. Witek the tailor.' The voice

paused, waiting for the grunt of recognition, which Dominiak gave. As he listened Dominiak tugged a dilapidated notebook and a propelling pencil from the inside pocket of his jacket. 'I've got some information for you. It's very important.'

'Good. Go ahead.' Dominiak sat hunched over his notebook, his face eager despite the measured tone of his voice.

'Colonel,' the man began, his agitation manifestly growing, 'I must be very quick. I just learned that contact was made early today with one of our cells. I...'

'What time today?'

'I don't know exactly, Colonel. Earlier. This morning, I think. Anyway, I know arrangements have been made to move four people from Warsaw.'

'Where to?'

'I couldn't find out, Colonel. I couldn't ask. Honestly, my situation is so dangerous...'

'I know. Go on. What *do* you know? When are they moving? How? Where will they leave Warsaw?'

'Well, I think they may be on the move already. They were supposed to be picked up a short while ago. Anyway they are moving out of Warsaw by the roadblock in Rozlucka Street.'

'Where's that?'

'Ursynow district. It's in the development of new flats out there. That's why you haven't heard of it, Colonel,' the voice added ingratiatingly. 'Apparently there are no Russians there. The militia on the checkpoint seem to be sympathizers. You'll have to act quickly, Colonel. They plan to go through the control at 5.30. It seems their men come on at 5.00.'

Dominiak rolled his forearm and glanced at his watch. 'Anything else?'

'Only one thing Colonel.'

'Huh?'

'Well', the voice continued in a wheedling tone, 'Colonel, I know it's only a rumour, but they're saying that one of the four, Colonel, is Gregory Kozka. I just wondered, if it's true, if my help would be – er – borne in mind.'

'Bollocks!' said Dominiak distinctly, putting down the phone. He grimaced. A lifetime of dealing with informers had not tempered his disdain for them.

Rising and stuffing the notebook into his inner pocket, he began striding quickly towards the inner door, towards the offices where Toparoff and the two officers now ruled. His hand was on the door handle when he heard Toparoff's voice rise above the murmur of voices on the other side. He paused, listening.

After a further second's pause his hand fell back to his side. He turned and opened the far door. In the corridor outside the three men sprawled on wooden chairs were engaged in a desultory debate. They sat up expectantly as the door opened, anxious for Dominiak to abdicate and let them reoccupy the office. It was warmer than the corridor.

He jerked his chin at one of the men. 'Come on, Stan. Let's go.'

The man he addressed shrugged and stood up laboriously, pushing his newspaper into an outer pocket of his grey anorak. He was a bulky man, much taller than Dominiak, with a big belly suspended in front of a deep broad chest, like a wrestler gone to seed. His battered face split in a wide grin as he followed in Dominiak's wake.

A fresh fall of snow had just begun to fleck the windscreen of the ambulance as Helena and Barbara crouched by the open screen anxiously watching the road. Ahead of them the motorcyclist barrelled through the traffic.

'It's funny,' said Barbara at Mason's shoulder, 'all the traffic seems to be heading the same way.'

Mason nodded. 'And the people. Look.' He indicated the broad pavement where people hurried in the same direction as themselves. Hunched against the snow and the easterly wind which accompanied it, most of them looked sombre as they bustled along, hardly speaking.

'It's strange.' Helena spoke now. 'So near to curfew, I would have expected people to be getting off the streets by now.'

'If they intend to keep the curfew, my dear.' Gregory had appeared behind the two women.

Mason glanced at him. 'Do you think they won't? There'll be a hell of a mess if they don't.'

'I know,' Gregory replied, soberly. 'But I've seen this before, back in the fifties, when I was a young priest. I know that look, and that walk. I've seen this kind of defiance before.'

'What happened then?' asked Mason, his eyes on the rushing crowd.

'People died. Mind you, they were bad times. Stalin was only just dead. Attitudes were different then.' The note of hope in his last words was tentative.

For a few seconds they were all silent. The quiet was broken by the driver.

'What's going on?' he asked peevishly, speaking almost to himself.

Mason turned his attention from the pedestrians to the road ahead. A short way in front of them, a knot of cars had drawn to a halt. Beyond the cars were two parked trucks. Among the stopped cars drivers stood with their door open, gesticulating angrily. On the pavements pedestrians had also halted, forming small crowds which grew as they watched.

'Patient, back to bed,' said Mason grimly.

The faces of Gregory and the women disappeared from the opening. Ahead of them, the militiaman was looking back over his shoulder and signalling.

'What's he want?' the driver muttered sullenly.

'To follow him. Stay close,' Mason answered. As he spoke, the motorcycle swung through a gap in the central reservation and began picking up speed on the deserted left hand carriageway. The driver followed, almost losing control as he swung the ambulance through the tight opening on a road made greasy by the new snow. Close behind the motorcycle they sped towards the hold-up.

'The siren,' Mason said urgently. The driver tense and pale, did not appear to hear him. 'The siren!' Mason almost shouted in the man's ear. 'Put it on!'

Tomek started, then reached forward and flipped a switch on the dashboard. Instantly, the strident swooping scream of the siren blared from the roof above their heads. Mason winced. He was grateful he was not a patient.

Fifty yards ahead of them two Russian soldiers stepped into the road, each holding a light machine gun levelled at the approaching ambulance and escort.

It was useless. No matter how hard he tried, Dominiak could not get comfortable on the back seat of a Polonez. It felt as though he were sitting on a shelf. He murmured a soft obscenity. Seventy years of western motoring technology to steal from and they could not even get the back seat right. He preferred not to think about the rest.

'Ursynow,' he growled bearishly. 'Rozlucka Street.'

'Never heard of it,' replied Stan cheerfully from the driving seat, where his bulk seemed to flow into every available inch of the cramped space, his belly almost engulfing the wheel.

'Neither had I until ten minutes ago. It's new. Use your map.'

'I haven't got a map of Ursynow. Warsaw, but not Ursynow.'

'Stan,' said Dominiak, pleadingly, 'you must have. We're the police, for fuck's sake. The Secret Police, at that.'

'Maybe we're *too* secret. Anyway we haven't got a map of Ursynow. It's not ready yet. It's too new.'

'For Christ's sake, most of it's been up for two years now,' Dominiak responded, exasperated.

'That's what I said,' Stan rejoined, spluttering with delight. 'It's too new!'

They both laughed.

'Well,' said Dominiak resignedly, 'I suppose we can

always ask someone when we get there.'

'Yes,' Stan agreed, looking at his superior in the mirror. 'We can ask a policeman!'

Dominiak waited for the big man's shoulders to stop heaving. 'Oh, and Stan,' he said quietly. 'take us by way of Victory Square, will you?'

In less than five minutes the black car drew to a halt in a side-street leading to the square. Ahead of them a Red Army truck stood broadside across the road. A half-dozen soldiers stood strung across the road. Their raw adolescent faces stared sightlessly over the heads of a knot of people that stood in front of them, craning to see past the truck for a view of the scene in the square.

Stan shouldered his way ahead of Dominiak, pushing through the group of onlookers who, as they moved aside, muttered and threw resentful looks at the two men. They stopped in front of one of the soldiers. Dominiak showed him his identity card. The young man was unmoved. In Russian which was perfect and unaccented, in contrast to the pretence he had always made to Toparoff, Dominiak cursed the soldier. The man blinked and looked stung.

'Where's your officer?' Dominiak snapped.

The man gulped uncertainly and indicated the back of the truck. 'In there.'

With a contemptuous look at the soldier Dominiak strode to the rear of the vehicle. With quick agility he hauled himself up over the tailboard. In the canvas enclosed truck an officer, no older than the soldiers, sat half-sprawled on a wooden bench. He turned in surprise towards Dominiak, a walkie-talkie held against one ear.

'Who are you?' he cried, making to get to his feet.

Dominiak flashed the plastic covered identity card. 'We're sent by General Tarpov,' he said sharply. 'Tell your men to let us through.'

Surprised by the firm tone, the man reacted the way Dominiak would have predicted in a man trained all his life to fear authority. He dropped the walkie-talkie and scrambled to his feet. Without even a glance at the identification he rushed to the tailboard and leaned out.

'Let these men through,' he barked, as though it were his own idea.

Dominiak scrambled down and he and Stan walked quickly towards the square. Stan noticed the sound first. He stopped and placed a hand on Dominiak's arm.

'Listen,' he said, 'hear it?'

Dominiak listened for a moment. He too heard the low sound of massed voices. He looked up into Stan's big face. The tall man was smiling languidly, airing derelict teeth as he listened. Dominiak shook his head.

'Not you, too,' he said, with a wry affection. 'Come on.'

Already they had an oblique view of the crowd. Men and women and a sprinkling of children stood close packed and motionless beneath the falling snow. Just as they were about to reach the corner giving them a full view of the square, a series of reports sounded in a ragged volley. They both stood frozen, hearing the echo rattle off the buildings opposite them, and then, without a word, they broke into a run.

The huge square was packed solid with people. On the far side the graceless rear of the Opera House looked like a beached liner. On two sides stood hotels and a row of frowning three-storey buildings with pretentious pillared façades and under-sized windows. On the fourth side they could see the monumental arch sheltering the eternal flame behind which stretched the stark trees of a small park. Around the arch several puffs of smoke still hung in the air.

As they watched they were aware of a sudden stirring in the crowd close to the arch. In several spots, grey smoke wafted from among the people and hung sluggishly before being whipped away by a gust of wind.

'Tear gas!' Stan almost spat the words. As he did so another volley sounded, followed a split second later by more puffs of smoke. The movement in the crowd intensified as those within range tried to escape the falling gas grenades.

Dominiak gave a soft whistle and pointed towards the park. From between the bare trees surged a line of vehicles, several of them surmounted by water cannon. As they came close to the edge of the crowd the water cannon abruptly began spewing their hugely powerful jets of foaming water into the helpless throng. The heavy vehicles moved irresistibly into the crowd. The sea of heads swirled and parted as people stampeded out of the path of the oncoming machines. In one instant when the crowd parted Dominiak caught a momentary glimpse of soldiers advancing between the moving vehicles, flailing at the retreating people with batons.

Screams filled the air, mingling with the sound of singing from the people on the near side of the square, who still stood stoically, refusing to be moved.

Dominiak and Stan watched in appalled silence as the water cannon ploughed through the seething crowd. Suddenly Stan grabbed Dominiak's arm and pointed. Dominiak looked up just in time to see an object loop through the air to fall close by one of the machines. It trailed a thin arc of black smoke. As they stood looking another, and then a third object were launched from the heart of the crowd. The third one struck a water cannon. Dominiak drew breath sharply as a sheet of orange flame flashed across the front of the vehicle and blazed fiercely, the flame surprisingly bright in the evening darkness. The sound of a cheer carried to them over the screams and the singing.

'Molotov cocktails!' Stan said, in a low voice that seemed to carry an undertone of admiration.

Dominiak nodded, looking sharply at the other man. 'Yes,' he said neutrally. 'I saw it too.' He turned away. 'Let's go. There's nothing we can do.'

As they made to leave, their attention was drawn to a sudden swirl of activity in the crowd, more violent than before. Without a word they both turned back to watch. Craning to see the cause of the new disturbance, they caught sight of batons being brandished as the soldiers using them beat a path through the crowd towards the spot where they stood.

With the suddenness of a stone hitting a lake, the fringe of the crowd parted and a young man burst, running, onto the empty street. His face twisted with effort and fear, he sprinted towards the street corner where Dominiak and Stan stood motionless. The moment he entered the street he caught sight of the truck and the line of armed soldiers. He baulked and came to a halt, almost losing his footing on the slushy surface. Panic-stricken, he looked to right and left. High walls on both sides offered no escape. They could hear the man's whooping breath and could see the rise and fall of his chest as he stared around him. The neck of a bottle with a ragged fragment of cloth sticking from it protruded from the man's pocket.

As Dominiak and Stan watched the youth's terrified indecision, two soldiers broke from the crowd. One of them called a sharp command in Russian. The young man shied at the call. With a frantic glance over his shoulder at his pursuers he bent low and began running towards the truck. The soldier who had called unslung his weapon from his shoulder and dropped to one knee. As he ran, the man pulled the bottle from his pocket and, slackening his pace for only an instant, he lit the cloth wick with a lighter he held in the other hand. While the soldier tried to aim the weapon the man continued in a jinking run closer to the truck. Fifteen yards from the lorry he straightened and hurled the petrol bomb spinning towards the vehicle. The whoosh of the bomb exploding against the cab of the truck and the crack of the rifle were almost simultaneous.

The young man's back arched forward, his head snapped back and he plunged, spread-eagled, into the fresh whiteness of the road surface and lay quite still.

Dominiak and Stan ran to the spot where the body lay, holding out their identification at arm's length before them, wary of the edgy soldiers who eyed their approach with aggressive mistrust. They looked down at the man. His eyes were still wide-open, staring sightlessly into the gutter. Stooping, Dominiak brushed a hand lightly over the man's eyelids, closing the eyes. He was no more than nineteen.

Straightening, he looked from one soldier to the other. The officer from the truck was firing questions at them as their expressions flickered from unease to guilt, to indignation and even to a brief look of satisfaction. Dominiak stared at each in turn, his eyes narrowed and his jaw clamped. He started to speak and then, spinning on his heel, he began walking quickly back to their car.

As he preceded Stan to the car, his head bowed in deep thought, Dominiak did not notice the scream of the siren or the insistent flash of the blue warning-light of the ambulance that sped past the end of the street.

# 33

Mason's estimation of the militiaman had risen. The man had handled the Russian roadblock perfectly. Just the right mixture of authority and disdain had cowed the troops, a couple of half-witted conscripts, into allowing them to pass with nothing more inconvenient than a sullen look.

'I hope he handles the next one as well. It might not be so easy, though,' he added, 'getting out of town as getting in.'

The driver grunted agreement. 'Not this way,' he said disconsolately. 'The other way would have been a piece of cake.' The whine was back in his voice.

'Well,' said Mason, allowing his irritation to show, 'we'll have to worry about that when we get there, won't we? Anyway,' he added with cheerful pomposity, 'adversity tempers the soul.' Mason thought that was probably a proverb. The driver who stared morosely through the windscreen, offered no opinion.

The speedometer flickered around the 90-kilometre mark as they sped through the empty streets. The snow was heavier now, obscuring the few tyre tracks on the road. On every second or third corner stood dirty brown trucks. White streamers trailed from their exhausts as the drivers and officers lolled in the heated cabs while rows of pinch-faced conscripts sat huddled on benches in the backs. Occasionally they passed groups on foot, stamping and slapping their arms around their chests as they tried to ward off the bitter wind.

The groups of soldiers grew more frequent as they approached the heart of the town. Although many turned to watch their conspicuous progress nobody attempted to stop them. As they drove nearer to the main square Mason noticed that instead of merely waiting around, the troops had blocked off entire roads, using their vehicles as barriers.

Led by the motorcyclist, they raced behind one of the hotels that fronted onto the square. On the pavement stood a dozen military trucks, each with a red star on the cab door, negligently parked. They were guarded by a handful of conscripts who huddled disconsolately in the shelter of their trucks.

They sped past a narrow street that led to the square. As they passed Mason heard a sharp crack ring out. At the same moment he saw the outline of the truck which stood across the road limned with a sudden flame.

'What was that?' he asked.

The driver shrugged. 'What?'

'That noise. And that truck. It looked as though it just exploded or something.'

'That noise was a rifle.' The voice was Gregory's.

Mason turned to look through the partition. Gregory's face was deeply troubled.

'A rifle? Are you sure?'

Gregory nodded. 'Certain. As I told you I was a soldier

myself once. Also I've heard the sound before, right here in the streets. It's not a sound you easily forget, Mr Mason.'

'I can believe you.' Mason answered soberly. 'But surely they aren't shooting?'

Gregory shrugged. 'Somebody is. Maybe it was just a warning. But you saw what happened to the truck?'

'The explosion?'

'Yes. Flames but no sound. If you ask me, that was a Molotov cocktail.'

Mason lifted an eyebrow. 'You've seen those before, too?'

Gregory nodded gravely. 'Hm-hmm. The first time was in Katowice. In the days before the ... liberation.' He had hesitated before pronouncing the last word. 'The people rose up against the Germans. They had no weapons. We had to use what we had.'

'We?'

Gregory looked him in the eye. 'Yes. I helped. I was a boy, still in my teens. Boys my age had been killed fighting in the resistance.'

'Yes, I know. It's just that I'm well ... I didn't think somehow that *you* would have been involved.'

'Because I'm a priest? I wasn't one then. At that age the resistance seemed almost like a game.'

'It doesn't seem like one now,' Mason rejoined softly.

The ambulance rushed on through the flying snow, away from the centre of the city. Far from emptying as the hour of curfew approached, there seemed to be a growing number of people on the street. No longer streaming towards the centre, they gathered in swelling crowds at major crossroads. Everywhere the crowds gathered Soviet trucks laden with troops hovered close by. Several times the ambulance was forced by the denseness of the crowd to slow while their escort cleared a way for them through the mass of people.

They rode mostly in silence, Gregory and the two women crowded behind Mason, their faces pressed together at the small aperture. They watched grimly as they sped past several minor confrontations between the crowd and the Soviet soldiers. They were no more than arguments in which the crowd shouted and gestured at the impassive troops. Until about the fourth or fifth scene.

Their convoy had emerged into a bleak open square where two broad roads intersected. A dense crowd filled the square, obliging them to slow almost to a walk and giving them plenty of time to take in the scene around them. Above the heads of the crowd several banners, supported on sticks, carried the familiar logo of Solidarity. Most of them were held by people safely protected at the centre of the crowd.

Suddenly, quite close to the ambulance, another banner rose and unfurled. It was close to the fringe of the crowd, provocatively close to where a platoon of soldiers stood in a close rank evidently under the command of a youthful officer in a flat peaked cap, who stood slightly to one side of the group. As the ambulance approached, Mason tensed. He could see the faces of the crowd as they taunted the Russians. The hatred in their faces was as unmistakable as the anger in the faces of the soldiers.

Small missiles, coins or keys, began to fly towards the Russians. Mason saw one wince as something caught him beneath the eye. Mason lowered his window. With the rush of icy air came the sound of the taunts and with it now came a background of chanting. The slogan of Solidarity.

Close by the soldiers, three members of the militia stood in a silent group, observing the scene without making any effort to intervene.

Quite suddenly, the face of one of the soldiers twisted with rage and he broke from his colleagues and plunged into the crowd. Abandoning himself completely to his anger, he began belabouring a middle-aged man with the stock of his rifle. As the man staggered, his arms raised protectively in front of him, the three militiamen acted. Breaking into a run they tore into the crowd and tried to interpose themselves between the unfortunate man and the infuriated soldier.

They were about level with his window when Mason saw the soldier raise his weapon and, with deliberate force, drive the wooden stock against the head of one of the militiamen. The man buckled and fell into the crowd. Mason had just time to see the rest of the Russian soldiers break rank and start into the crowd before they were past the spot and drawing away.

He closed his window. He felt sick. He turned to speak to the others. Only the faces of Helena and Barbara were visible at the window behind him. Barbara's look of enquiry turned to concern.

'What is it, Peter, what happened? You're quite white!'

He smiled a wan acknowledgement, but instead of replying he twisted violently to peer into the rear of the ambulance.

'Where's Gregory?' Mason asked urgently. As he spoke he saw Kozka's broad back as he made his way towards the rear doors. 'What are you doing?' Mason called sharply.

Gregory did not turn. 'I'm going back there,' he called. 'To see if I can help. I have to try to stop them. Stop the ambulance,' he added, louder to the driver.

The driver looked anxiously at Mason. His foot eased off the throttle as he hesitated.

'Keep going,' Mason almost snarled. Startled at his ferocity, the driver rammed his foot to the floor. They were clear of the crowd now and the distance between them and the violent scene widened rapidly. Gregory was fumbling with the door latch.

'Stop it!' Mason was roaring. Even Gregory responded. He looked around.

'You can't go back there. How many more times do you have to be told? They'll kill you. They have instructions. They'll simply shoot you.'

'But they're killing people back there. My people. I must try to help.'

'I'll come with you.' Helena said softly. She had made her way to Gregory's side. She laid a hand on his forearm.

277

Mason groaned. 'Go on,' he said wearily. 'Go! Both of you. They'll shoot you first,' he looked into Gregory's troubled eyes, 'then Helena. After that the crowd will attack them and they'll start shooting the crowd.'

Still looking at Mason, Gregory covered Helena's hand with his own. He looked back through the window at the receding fight and then at Helena. Slowly, Gregory nodded and turned reluctantly from the door. As he crouched there, dressed only in slacks and a white T-shirt, his face gentle and perplexed, he looked so vulnerable Mason felt his own chest tighten.

He turned back to face the front. 'Oh, shit,' he said, sighing. The driver was looking at him, questioning.

'Keep going,' he told him, dully. 'Follow the policeman!'

As they approached the edge of town street lights grew sparser. Identical blocks of flats lined the roads, many with the strangely unfinished look so familiar to Mason. As though the builders had left for another site with a promise to return that they had never kept. The driver's tongue flicked at his lips. In the light reflecting from the fresh snow cover Mason could see the silhouette of the man's Adam's apple as it bobbed above the neck of his tunic.

'Nervous?' He knew it was a silly question. He just wanted the man to speak; to loosen up. As tense as he was he could be worse than useless when trouble came.

The man tried to reply, missed his pitch and gave out a dry croak. He cleared his throat and tried again.

'Yes. I am. I'm shit-scared. Aren't you?'

'Uh-huh. Sure.' Mason was not sure if it was true. To his own surprise he felt his senses tingling not with fear, but a kind of excitement. He went on lying to the driver, though. 'I'm crapping myself. How long before we reach the checkpoint, do you think?'

The driver shrugged. 'Don't know. It can't be far. I don't really know this part of Warsaw but we must be very near the edge of town now. Five minutes, maybe.'

Automatically, Mason glanced at his watch. Ten to six. 'Have you got your papers?'

'Yes, of course I've got mine.' He put a sulky emphasis on the last word. 'How about yours? And theirs?' He tossed his head petulantly towards the trio of faces behind him.

'Well, theirs would be a great help in maintaining the subterfuge,' Mason said cheerfully. 'Especially Gregory's.' He looked at the driver's disconsolate expression. In a suddenly serious voice he continued. 'If they need to see papers they can see yours. If it comes to having to show theirs, or mine, we make a run for it. Or,' he added looking intently at the driver, 'we stay and fight it out.'

The driver's Adam's apple leapt. Mason settled back in his seat. If it came to a fight the man would be useless.

He let a half minute pass, watching the lights come on in the prematurely dilapidated flats.

'If we do have to make a run for it,' he asked the silent driver conversationally, 'where is it we're heading?'

'I'm not supposed to tell you.'

'Perhaps not, but I think you'd better.' He paused. 'In case you get killed.'

The driver looked at Mason as though he had invited him to imbibe rat poison. 'Killed?' The idea seemed to strike him for the first time as a serious possibility.

'You might. We all might. Or we might all get waved through the control and wished good night. It's just that if you do get hurt and one of us had to drive it would be nice to know where we're supposed to be going.'

The driver ruminated silently, chewing vindictively at his lower lip.

'Please. You may as well tell us. You can't be endangering anybody now. We're all in this together, whether we like it or not.' Gregory's voice, coming softly from the darkness behind him seemed to put some force into the man. He straightened his shoulders.

'Konstanczyn,' he said. 'It's about fifteen kilometres from Warsaw. Maybe a bit less from here.'

'I know it,' Mason said. He caught the faint surprise in the driver's side-long look. 'There's a nice restaurant there. Or used to be, when they could get meat. Who, or what, is waiting for us at Konstanczyn?'

'Chris and Edward. And some other people.'

'It'll be nice to see them. I've been missing them since this afternoon.' His tone dropped from flippancy to sudden earnestness. 'How do they plan to get us out?'

The driver shrugged. Mason shrugged. He looked at the three pale faces just visible behind him and wondered if they were shrugging, too. He smiled at Barbara and got a quick, tense smile in return.

On the road ahead of them a red light swung in a warning arc. In the dull orange light of a street lamp, amplified by the snow, a small knot of soldiers watched alertly as they approached. The customary truck stood broadside across the road, leaving room for only one car to pass with care.

# 34

'Quickly, get back there,' Mason hissed. The three faces disappeared. He turned to see how the driver was shaping up. Badly. The man was trembling and sweat once again glistened on his upper lip and his brow.

'For Christ's sake,' Mason muttered very distinctly, his eyes straight ahead. 'Shape up. Pull yourself together. You'll get us all killed.' The man made a low whimpering sound. Mason turned to the aperture behind him.

'Barbara,' he said peremptorily, 'give me that damned vodka.'

Behind him Barbara caught the urgency in his tone. She ripped the bottle from its fixing, removed the cap and tube and handed it through the gap into Mason's waiting hand.

'Here!' With a rough gesture he pushed the bottle at the driver. The man's eyes flicked to the bottle. Like a drowning man clutching at a floating spar, he clamped a hand around it and wedged it with a practised gesture to his lips. Mason watched him take three or four big swallows before snatching it away and thrusting it back into Barbara's waiting hand. The driver gasped noisily and drew his sleeve across his lips.

'Feel better?' Mason asked.

The driver pushed his spine against the back of the seat and set his shoulders. He smiled a manful smile and nodded.

'Good.' Mason slapped his arm encouragingly. 'Remember who it is you're carrying back there. All of Poland will be grateful to you.'

The thought of Poland's gratitude did not prevent the man sweating. Beads of perspiration, squeezed from him by fear and alcohol, gathered and skidded down his face. His collar showed a dark band beneath his chin. Mason was getting edgy himself. Systematically, he began deliberately relaxing each muscle group in turn by alternately tensing and relaxing them. He continued even as the motorcycle drew to a halt close to the soldiers. The ambulance drew up behind it. He kept his breathing even, drawing long, slow breaths through his nose and exhaling through his mouth. Beside him he sensed the driver sitting like a rabbit awaiting an interview with a stoat.

The militiaman spoke to the soldiers and gesticulated towards the ambulance. Mason saw one of the soldiers, apparently in charge, shake his head. He pointed to the ambulance and appeared to speak to his men. Two of the men broke away and began to approach the ambulance. They held short machine guns loosely across their chests. They were ready for trouble, but not altogether expecting any.

They came close to the driver's side. The driver sat immobile, his arms stretching rigid to the wheel, his hands clutching the ridged plastic wheel so that the tendons in his wrist stood out. One of the soldiers rapped sharply on the window with a gloved fist. The driver started and spun his head to look into the face looking at him. He made no other move. Impatiently the soldier made a gesture and mouthed something.

'Open the window,' Mason urged. 'Quickly.'

The man looked sharply from the window to Mason, a look of utter misery on his pale face.

'God damn you,' Mason fumed. 'Open the window.'

Speechlessly, the young man turned away and began fumbling futilely with the door. The face at the window was becoming angry. Abruptly the door swung open.

'Your papers.' The soldier's podgy face leaned into the cab. He recoiled as he caught the brunt of the driver's breath. 'Your papers,' he repeated with stupid insistence.

Quivering, the driver pulled down the visor above his head and slid a torn plastic wallet from where it was held by a frayed rubber band. In his discomposure he dropped the wallet to the floor between his feet where snow had melted to form a muddy scum. He picked it up, brushed some of the damp grit which clung to it onto his trousers and passed it, still streaked with filth, to the soldier.

The trooper took it from him with a peevish look, and began a laborious examination of its contents. His companion leaned past him and spoke to Mason.

'Documents,' he said brusquely.

Mason spread his hands and grinned foolishly. He jerked a thumb at the rear of the vehicle.

'In the back.' He sat motionless, the imbecile grin still on his face.

'Come,' the soldier said. With a jerk of his head he indicated to Mason to join him and disappeared towards the rear.

Without letting his half-witted expression slip, Mason hauled his sheepskin coat from where it was stowed in the narrow space behind his seat. He descended slowly from the cab and shivered as the bitter wind flailed at his clothes. Shuddering, he pulled on the coat and began walking slowly to the rear of the ambulance, his hands deep in his pockets. The snow had stopped.

The Russian stood impatiently by the double doors, irritably trampling the fresh snow with his thick boots. As Mason reached for the door handle he saw the Russian's eyes alight on his coat. For the first time Mason felt a pang of real fear as he saw the glint of suspicion enter the soldier's eye.

Catching the man's eye, he gave him another grin, full of stupid cunning. With one finger and thumb he held one edge of the coat, near a buttonhole, and turned it out, showing the man the glossy fleece of the lining.

'Nice, huh? Not Polish. A grateful patient. American,' he said, speaking a pidgin version of Polish that he had sometimes heard Poles use to Russians, usually as a refined form of humiliation.

He watched the man's eyes and was relieved to see the suspicion give way to envy. The soldier removed a glove and reached out and tentatively fingered the coat. He brushed the backs of his fingers over the softness of the lining. For an instant Mason thought he saw something like sadness replace the envy in the man's eyes. Then, reverting to his earlier abruptness, he signalled Mason to open the doors.

Helena whirled around, a look of fury on her face.

'Get out of here,' she cried angrily, as the soldier climbed through the open door, 'what do you mean by delaying us? This man is sick, can't you see?'

The soldier flinched under Helena's blazing gaze. He lowered his eyes. Like many people he was slightly in awe of nurses. Nevertheless he continued advancing into the ambulance, mumbling a clumsy excuse in Russian. Helena went on tongue-lashing him, as Barbara sat with her face buried in her hands. She had no need to simulate the deep concern that showed in the eyes that looked out at the intruding soldier.

Gregory lay still. His eyes were closed and he breathed

with resonant regularity into a mask that Helena held clamped to his mouth. His powerful arms lay limply on the grey blanket that covered him. The scene struck Mason as altogether convincing. The soldier, too, had no doubts about the authenticity of what he was seeing. Mason fought to keep any trace of irony from his expression as he saw the soldier glance at the opaque plastic bottle suspended above Gregory and the tube lashed to the thick hairy forearm. He saw the soldier falter and shift uncomfortably. Helena, too, had caught the hesitancy and stepped up her abuse. Without warning, Barbara, overwhelmed by the tension and her fear, burst into tears. The soldier gulped and blushed. Turning, he started to leave the ambulance, throwing Mason a man-to-man look that was meant to express the vast exasperating sweep of his eighteen-year-old experience of women. He put a foot on the step as though to leave the vehicle and then with a violent, abrupt shake of his head and shoulders, like a cow shaking off a pest, he turned and made his way back towards where Gregory lay. Helena cursed him louder, while Barbara shook as tears rolled between her extended fingers and ran in quick rivulets down the backs of her hands.

The soldier stood over Gregory, gathering resolve to defy Helena's scolding. He gestured to Helena, wanting her to remove the mask from Gregory's face. Keeping a hand on the mask she shook her head and pointed with her free hand to the oxygen cylinder propped in the corner of the ambulance, close by Gregory's head.

'I can't,' she said, her voice quivering with an emotion she contrived to convert into indignation. 'He must have the oxygen. He's very ill. He may die.' Her voice was growing desperate.

With an impatient shake of his head, the Russian reached a hand towards the mask. With a small sound Helena tried to brush his arm away.

Behind the soldier, Mason slid a hand into the pocket of his coat. His hand closed around the pistol which had lain there since the previous night. Very slowly he began withdrawing the gun. The weapon was not yet out of his pocket when Gregory, feeling a hand clasp roughly at his mask, opened his eyes. Before the stooping soldier had the slightest chance to realize what was happening, Gregory had passed his right arm around the back of the man's neck. Grasping his own left arm just above the elbow, he slid his left forearm beneath the man's chin. Instantly he brought his forearms together, crushing the man's neck. The soldier's eyes bulged and both his hands flew up to claw ineffectually at the arm choking him. Like everyone caught in a strangle-hold he could think only of fighting for breath, forgetting to fight for his life.

Mason wanted to applaud. He knew the hold himself but had never seen it applied anywhere but on a judo mat. It was unbreakable. Gradually the soldier's gasps abated and his flailing limbs became still. Carefully releasing his hold, Gregory allowed the inert man to slump to the floor. Swinging his legs from the bed, he leaned over the man and laid two fingers on the side of the man's neck.

Mason let the gun slide back into his pocket. 'Very nice,' he said softly. 'How is he?'

Gregory caught Mason's look and smiled. His smile was slightly embarrassed. 'Just unconscious. He'll soon come around.'

'Now what?' Helena asked.

Mason looked around at the three faces. Nearest to him Barbara crouched on the edge of the low bunk. She was trembling. He reached out a hand and gripped her shoulder. Helena, too, was fighting fear. Her face worked with the effort to stay in control. Gregory, squatting easily by the soldier, radiated an utter calm.

'We have to make a break for it.' Mason seemed to hear his own voice as though it were a stranger's. He felt no fear now, only a bitter anger mixed with a grim determination to bring them through. He turned towards the door. 'Keep quiet,' he hissed, 'and hold onto something.'

He stepped soundlessly down onto the fresh snow. Very

cautiously he made his way back towards the cab, staying very close to the side of the ambulance. He paused before reaching the door, drew a deep breath, and slipped with studied casualness into his seat. He slammed the door behind him, grinning good-humouredly at the Russian who still stood by the driver's open door. The Russian looked at Mason and frowned. His eyes flickered to the window behind the driver and back to Mason. He was worried. Grinning suggestively, Mason jerked a thumb over his shoulder and made an obscene gesture. Intrigued, the soldier climbed onto the step of the cab, leaned across the driver and peered through the aperture towards the rear.

Without removing the gun from his pocket, Mason shot him.

'Come on,' he snarled at the driver, 'let's get out of here. Go!'

The driver sat stupefied, his arms pinioned under the sprawling corpse of the soldier. He looked dumbly at Mason, his jaw hanging slackly.

'Drive, you fucking half-wit!' Mason bawled. He grabbed the collar of the soldier's uniform and heaved. The slack body slid like a seal off an ice floe across the driver's lap and onto the snow.

A few yards ahead of the ambulance the officer in charge froze in the act of lighting one of the militiaman's cigarettes. He stared uncomprehendingly as a dark stain oozed from the fallen soldier into the snow around the body. Suddenly, flinging the match from him, he began scrabbling to unfasten the heavy brown leather holster at his belt.

'Go!' Mason's mouth was an inch from the driver's ear. 'Run him down, you prick. Go on!'

Mason's desperation or a sudden realization of the immediate danger seemed finally to trigger a reaction in the driver. Sobbing in his throat, he slammed the long gear-lever into first. The wheels spun for a tantalizing moment and then the ambulance bucked forward as the tyres bit into the soft snow. Mason saw the next second or two in slow motion. He saw the militiaman dive spectacularly clear as the roaring ambulance crushed his motorbike. The Russian stayed his ground as he grappled with the swivel catch of his holster. Mason saw him look up at the windscreen, his face distorted with rage as he drew the big black gun from his belt. He was aware of a violent yellow flash at the instant that the nose of the ambulance smashed into the man, breaking him against the truck.

'Reverse. Reverse,' Mason bellowed at the driver. 'Drive around the truck. Come on. Let's go.' Above the din of his own voice and the roar of the motor he was aware of another, higher sound. Glassy-eyed the driver reversed the ambulance. As its crumpled nose drew away from the truck's side the Soviet officer concertinaed stiffly to the ground.

The driver crashed the gear-lever back into first and gunned the ambulance towards the narrow gap between the truck and the high kerb. Metal screamed as the wheel rims bit into the granite of the kerbstones. On the other side the bumper of the truck gouged a deep channel in the metal of their vehicle as they squeezed past.

They were past the truck but the high-pitched screaming sound continued. Puzzled by the sound, Mason turned to the driver in time to see the man slump forward over the wheel and then abruptly pitch sideways through the still unlatched door of the cab and onto the road. Mason stared for a fraction of a second at the suddenly empty seat before reaching down and jerking hard on the handbrake. The ambulance slewed to a stop at an angle across the empty road. He scrambled across to the driver's side and leapt down into the road. A few yards behind him the driver lay in the road, writhing weakly, the scream now no more than a continuous low keening. The whole of one sleeve was clinging wetly to the arm inside it. The fist below the sleeve clenched and unclenched feebly.

Mason began running back to the man. After only three

paces he was arrested by the sight of several soldiers emerging, dishevelled and hatless from the interior of the lorry. They had evidently been asleep inside.

One of the soldiers turned to face Mason. For an instant they faced each other, incredulous. Then, with an exclamation the soldier began to unsling his gun. Mason looked once at the driver. Then, with an imperceptible lift of his shoulders, he wheeled around, took two strides and leapt for the cab. He threw himself into the driving seat and started the stalled motor. As he let up the clutch he heard the staccato cough of a machine gun and saw a neat row of four holes open in the windscreen in front of him. Leaning away from the window, he fought to get some speed on the ambulance without losing the back on the treacherous surface. As the vehicle straightened he glanced at the scene in his wing mirror. There were now three soldiers preparing to fire. As he watched, his muscles tensed in expectation of a striking bullet, he was astonished to see the three men dive for the shelter of the truck. A yard in front of them, snow spouted in a series of almost simultaneous eruptions. He watched, puzzled, in the mirror as the men cowered. As he accelerated away, still keeping his eyes riveted on the mirror, he saw the truck give a sharp lurch and settle at an angle. The off-side tyres had burst, sending the soldiers scrambling for cover.

Suddenly, Mason began laughing. The tension of the last moments flooded out of him as the distance between the ambulance and the roadblock grew. He roared with laughter, slapping the heel of one hand on the rim of the wheel as he realized what had happened. In the mirror, silhouetted against the snow behind them, he saw the figure of Gregory. He stood, legs splayed firmly, in the open doorway at the back of the ambulance. Looking almost like a toy in his big hands, he held the machine gun belonging to the soldier who lay unconscious by his feet. He turned to look at Mason. His big face was blank. Slowly, beginning with a narrowing of the extraordinary eyes, Gregory too broke into a huge laugh. He looked apologetically at the gun in his hands and threw it away from him, onto the bunk.

Still laughing, he stooped and took the Russian soldier by the shoulders. With a single heave he slid the man over the sill. The man rolled over once in the virgin snow and lay still. Gregory slammed the doors to and turned to face the others. 'Helena,' he said quietly, his eyes sparkling, 'I think a transfusion would do us all good.'

She nodded vigorously and fumbled for the bottle holding the vodka. Gregory uncapped it and offered it first to Helena, who sipped, and then to Barbara who tipped it purposefully to her lips. Gregory took a long swig, sighed loudly and passed it through the opening to Mason.

Mason swallowed deeply, and handed the bottle back to Gregory. 'Keep the machine gun handy,' he said, 'in case anyone tries to breathalyse me on the way to Konstanczyn.'

He looked into his wing mirror. Nobody pursued them. The truck was useless, thanks to Gregory. It would surely take them a certain amount of time to call in help. The weather was filthy. The wind-whipped snow would fill their tracks within minutes. It also made it hard for a helicopter search to find them.

His eyes strained to see in the uniform white expanse in front of him. The snow lay deep across the flat fields and the road, making it impossible to see where the road ended and the fields began. Leaning tensely forward he kept his eye on the telegraph wires that accompanied the road. A hurried glance at his watch told him it was just after 6.00. Even at the speed he was forced to keep they could expect to be in Konstanczyn in under half an hour. If they were not in a field.

## 35

Dominiak stared sightlessly at the road, oblivious to the monotonous throb and squeak of the windscreen wiper. In his mind's eye he saw over and over the scene he had just witnessed. He could not erase from his mind the sound of the young man's hoarse breathing, nor the eyes, staring blindly upward at the falling snow. The boy had looked so utterly ordinary. Not heroic. Not elegant. A detail that remained curiously insistent in Dominiak's mind was the soles of the man's shoes as he had lain lifeless there in the road. They were holed. It was such a private thing. He was somehow ashamed for the man that the assembled Russian soldiers would know it.

He was roused by Stan shifting his big bulk laboriously behind the wheel and grunting. He started and looked at him in an unfocused way, like a man suddenly wakened from a vivid dream.

'What?'

'They're late, if they're coming. It's after a quarter to six.' Stan held up his wrist so that Dominiak could see his watch.

Dominiak squinted at it, Automatically, he checked his own watch. 'You're right. It is. Still, look at the weather. They could have been delayed somehow in town with all the trouble.'

'Unless they're walking.'

'I pity them if they are. It's filthy out there.' They both gazed morosely out at the driving snow.

'Maybe they've been caught!' Stan said suddenly.

Dominiak jerked his head around to stare at him. The idea resonated strangely in his head. He frowned. 'Turn up the radio. We'll soon find out.'

As Stan leaned awkwardly forward to adjust the volume of the two way radio, Dominiak arched his back to ease the discomfort of the hard seat. He tugged at his belt-buckle with a thumb. Sitting too long in a car always gave him stomach cramps and made him want to fart. The radio burst, hissing, to life. A clamour of distorted voices filled the car.

Without a word they listened to the oddly surreal, one-sided conversations. Their practised ears had no difficulty in recognizing many of the voices despite the foolish quacking quality imparted to them all by the radio receiver. None of them spoke of Gregory. But all of them spoke of trouble. From the calls they heard, the reports of new trouble, the pleas for help, it was obvious that it had spread all over town; that there was an increasing number of incidents between the Polish militiamen and the Soviet troops.

Several minutes passed. On the street outside nothing moved. The militia on the roadblock eighty yards from them stamped around in the snow, flapping their arms to generate some warmth in their muscles. Dominiak noticed that two of the men seemed to look more often at their watches than the others, as though they too were expecting something.

Abruptly, their attention was seized by a burst of excited talk from the radio. At once Stan reached and turned the volume higher. Utterly quiet, they both leaned eagerly towards the metallic voice, listening intently. Gradually the meaning of what they were hearing became clear. Stan slowly twisted in his seat until he was looking Dominiak full in the face. Somewhere deep in the man's eyes, he thought he saw a flicker of something that might have been satisfaction.

'So they're out,' Stan said in a voice that carried that same almost imperceptible suggestion of pleasure. 'Now what do we do?'

'Find a phone.' Dominiak replied, softly. 'Quick.'

The door of the office stood open. The men outside sat in awed silence as Toparoff's voice climbed to a crescendo of rage.

'You let them go!' he screamed. 'Your men. Your best people, and you let them slip through your fingers. Boy Scouts could have performed better.' Saliva clung at the corners of his mouth.

Inside the office the two officers sat impassive before Toparoff's onslaught. Outside, one of the young Poles sniggered. He stopped abruptly with an embarrassed gulp as Toparoff's enraged face appeared at the open door.

'Dominiak!' Toparoff was still screaming. 'Dominiak! Where is he?' he snarled, looking around the closed faces in the room. Angrily he slammed a bunched fist against the door frame. 'Where is he? You!' He stepped close to the man nearest him and pointed threateningly. 'Tell me, quick. Where's your boss?'

The man swallowed and blinked. Toparoff grabbed a handful of the man's shirtfront and pulled him forward across his desk. The man rose half off his seat, his chest thrust awkwardly across the desk. 'Well?'

'I d...don't know.' His glasses fell to the desk. He groped and replaced them, fumbling nervously. 'He got a call. About half an hour ago. He went out. He...'

'Where did he go?' Toparoff broke in. 'Who called?'

'We don't know, Comrade Toparoff.' It was the older, owlish man who spoke. 'None of us know where Colonel Dominiak went, or who called.' The man's voice was icily calm.

Toparoff looked dumbly at him, as though at an animal that had suddenly spoken with a human voice. Slowly he released his grip on the shirtfront of the first man, who sank back to his seat, still adjusting his glasses.

In a voice suddenly calm, Toparoff asked, 'Can we contact him? Quickly. I must speak to him. It's important.'

'He left with Stan,' the man responded. 'They have the radio in the car. We could try that.'

'I'll try it myself.' Toparoff turned and disappeared into the inner office. A few seconds later he strode from the room, hurriedly but fastidiously adjusting the collar of a dark blue topcoat. He swept through the outer room without a word, his eyes staring straight ahead, his purplish lips tightly set.

The drivers lounging on the hard wooden chairs of the bare ante-room sprang upright as the door flew open and Toparoff burst in, the door swinging wildly. The pages of a newspaper slid with a swish to the floor. The three men stood immobile, each of them determined to make no move, no expression, that would draw the Russian's malevolent attention. He jabbed an index finger at one of them, whose gaze rested resolutely on the far wall of the room.

'You!' The man looked at Toparoff, hoping desperately he was mistaken.

'Me?' he mouthed.

Toparoff was already on his way out of the room. With a grimace at his colleagues the man followed him. Too impatient to wait for the trundling lift, Toparoff hurried down the bare concrete stairs with the driver almost running at his heels. They passed through the guarded steel door into the cavernous underground car park without even a nod to the surprised sentry.

The driver broke into a run and opened the door of one of the row of several black cars. Toparoff threw himself onto the seat without a glance at the driver. He chewed his lower lip mercilessly. The driver jumped in, tugged once at his rear view mirror and gunned the engine. He sought Toparoff's eyes in the mirror, his own brow creased in enquiry.

Speaking in a low voice the Russian intoned their destination. It was the roadblock which the ambulance had left no more than five minutes earlier. Responding to the urgency in Toparoff's voice, the driver threw the car into gear and raced in a scream of tyres towards the exit. The sentries at the gate took an involuntary step back as it catapulted across the pavement and onto the deserted street.

The driver was skilful and took delighted advantage of

the empty streets, throwing the car into blistering four-wheel drifts on bends and sending arcs of snow showering the silent pavements.

'Get Dominiak,' Toparoff told him, when they had been driving for a minute or so.

Without slowing, the driver plucked the microphone from the radio and began calling.

On the northern edge of the city Stan cruised the bleak spaces between the peeling slabs of the apartment buildings. Two telephones had not worked. He spied a third, nestling next to one of the desolate prefabricated supermarkets that served the area. With a grunt, half-aimed at Dominiak, he accelerated towards it.

Dominiak slid quickly from the car and picked his way through the snow, trampled and dirty here from the feet of the evening shoppers. He slipped a coin into the box and let out a slow sigh as he heard the whir of the dialling tone.

A woman's voice answered. It sounded peevish.

'Witek, please.'

The voice became guarded, but stayed shrewish. 'Who can I say is calling?'

'Dominiak.'

There was a short pause. The telephone box stank of urine. He pushed the door open three inches and inhaled gratefully at the blast of icy air.

'Hello, Mr Dominiak?' The familiar whine irritated Dominiak as soon as he heard it.

'Witek? Yes, it's me. They didn't show.'

'What?'

'They didn't arrive at the checkpoint. Nobody came.'

'What? It's not possible.' The whining tone rose. 'There was no mistake. They were to leave that way. It was all agreed. You know, me, Mr Dominiak. All the information I give you…'

Dominiak cut short the rising tide of self-justification. 'I know. It's all right. They just didn't show, that's all. They were expected, that was obvious. Something must have

294

gone wrong.'

'But I was sure. They were to leave this evening.'

'Shut up! I'm not blaming you. They left all right, only not by the way they were supposed to, for some reason. Now, then,' he paused an instant, 'Where did they go?'

It was the man Witek's turn to pause now. The silence lay between them like the surface of a lake. Dominiak was first to disturb it. 'Tell me, Witek,' he said softly. He could almost hear the man recoil at the threat in his voice. 'You know and you're going to tell me.' The silence fell again. It lasted perhaps three seconds.

'But, Mr Dominiak, they'll *know*. I'm the only one who knows who won't be there. I have a family, Mr Dominiak, children. If I tell you, if they find out it was me, I'm dead.' The thin voice rose in protest.

Dominiak's slack lips scarcely moved as he replied in a voice hardly audible. 'And what, Witek, do you suppose will happen to you if you refuse?'

While Dominiak telephoned, Stan watched the empty street and listened to the metallic babble from the radio. His head cocked abruptly as his ear filtered a familiar sound from the cackling stream. He slid the volume control higher. He recognized the voice of the other driver. Involuntarily, he reached for the microphone to reply. Then he checked and settled back in his seat. Let Dominiak decide.

The car rocked as Dominiak almost fell into the back seat. He was breathless. Stan nodded at the radio. 'They want you.' He said, neutrally. 'Comrade Toparoff would like to talk to you.'

For a moment their eyes met in the mirror. Quite suddenly they both laughed and Stan, reaching laboriously in front of him, flipped the receiver off.

Five seconds later the Polonez was hurtling through the snow towards the potholed, two-lane road that led out of Warsaw, there to join the road to Konstanczyn. Dominiak checked his watch again. It was ten past six.

*

Toparoff sat impassively as the driver fought the car through corners one-handed, while repeating for the thirtieth time the call for Dominiak into the microphone held in his right fist. He let the microphone drop in exasperation.

'Sorry, sir,' he told the silent figure behind him. 'I can't get them. They must have left the car.'

Toparoff broke from a bitter reverie. 'Keep trying,' he barked. 'Who told you to stop?'

The driver flinched and snatched up the instrument which hung swaying on its grubby spiral cord. In a leaden monotone, he resumed his attempts to contact Dominiak, intoning the words into the microphone. Each time he paused to allow Dominiak to speak they heard only the sibilant crackle of the empty air. They turned left, without pausing for the red traffic light, and began speeding along the wide deserted road which led them to the edge of the city. On the straight, the driver flicked a glance at the man slumped in the seat behind him. Accustomed in recent days to the immaculate grooming and the confident, domineering manner of the Russian, the sight shocked him. Toparoff's hands were pushed deep into the pockets of his open coat. His tie hung loose at the unbuttoned throat of his shirt, one collar point stuck up awkwardly from his jacket. His hair, normally slicked perfectly back in a widow's peak now protruded in ragged clumps across his crown. Beneath the dark hair the face, drawn and hollowed with fatigue and shadowed by beard, showed only a hunted cruelty. The muscles beneath one eye twitched.

The driver turned back to the road, settling his shoulders more solidly against the back of his seat. Toparoff's eyes had chilled him. There was something in them that made the driver feel vulnerable. They were the eyes of someone on the brink of madness.

Twice they were stopped by patrols enforcing the curfew. Both times the aggressive young conscripts were reduced to cringing apologies by the scalding force of

Toparoff's outbursts. They were nearing the fringe of the city. They turned off the main axis, cutting through a development of flats. Lights shone in all the apartments. Not a soul moved on the streets.

'How long now?' Toparoff's voice had a rough, accusing edge.

The driver kept his eyes on the road. 'Four or five minutes, I think.'

'Well, hurry, damn you, hurry!'

The driver nodded and increased the pressure on the accelerator. His face set resentfully at the contemptuous tone of the Russian's voice.

Three minutes later they saw the blue pulse of light from the roof of an ambulance. Behind the ambulance stood the canvas-topped lorry. Several men hurried around the vehicles.

Before the big car had come fully to a halt, Toparoff had jumped clear. He stumbled to one knee, collected himself and, without pausing to brush the snow from his clothes, ran towards the knot of soldiers. Two of the men, on seeing the car halt, had spun to face it and now held guns trained on the approaching Toparoff. He shouted to them in Russian. Reluctantly, they lowered their weapons as a sergeant stepped between them. He saluted Toparoff.

'Where are they?' Toparoff began abruptly, flashing a perspex-fronted leather wallet at the sergeant. The sergeant glanced at the wallet and perceptibly straightened.

'I don't know, sir. They went through there.' He pointed past the truck and down the empty road.

'How did it happen? Tell me. Quickly.' His nostrils flared angrily. The man blinked, glanced again, nervously, at the wallet in Toparoff's hand, and began speaking rapidly. He stood rigidly to attention as he spoke.

Toparoff listened silently, the muscles beneath his eye twitching constantly, until the man finished the brief story. Then he asked simply, 'Where's the driver?'

'He's in there, sir,' he answered, indicating the

dun-coloured military vehicle with the red cross painted on the side and the blue light on the roof. 'He's very badly injured,' he called to Toparoff's already retreating back. 'He's been shot, sir.'

Toparoff was climbing into the ambulance.

The injured driver groaned continuously. Two uniformed men crouched over him, working feverishly at the vivid red wound close to the man's collarbone. They hardly looked up as Toparoff stepped heavily between them.

'Can you talk?' he said roughly, addressing the wounded man. The man's eyes rolled to look dazedly at the face above him. One of the two men attending him looked up sharply at the sound of Toparoff's question.

'Who are you?' he asked sharply, scowling at the intruder. 'Can't you see this man's wounded? Get out.'

Negligently, Toparoff withdrew his identification from his pocket and coolly allowed it to hang in front of the speaker's eyes. The man began examining it angrily. Then the anger drained from his face. He paled and tapped the forearm of his companion. The other man looked round irritably, still swabbing the wound. He followed the eye of his colleague and he too took in the proffered card. He swallowed and then got slowly to his feet.

'Colonel?'

'Can he talk?' Toparoff jabbed his chin at the prostrate man.

'A little, I think. But he must not, Colonel. He's very badly hurt.'

In a sudden movement Toparoff pushed the man aside. The man staggered, his feet trapped against the bunk at ankle level. By the time he recovered himself Toparoff was kneeling by the wounded driver. He snatched a handful of the man's hair and leant his face close to his.

'Colonel,' began the ambulance man who still crouched next to him, 'stop it. Leave him alone. He may be dying. He's...'

'Shut up,' Toparoff hissed. 'Both of you. Get out and

298

leave us alone.'

The two men hesitated. 'Get out,' he screamed. 'Now.'
The two men looked at him for an uncomprehending
moment. Then, very slowly, they began to move towards
the door. 'Close it,' Toparoff snapped, his breath coming
rapidly, as the second man descended from the ambulance.

Five minutes later Toparoff jumped down from the back
of the ambulance. Without a word to the watching soldiers
he ran to the car where his driver still waited.

'Konstanczyn!' he snapped. 'Quickly.'

As the driver eased the big car through the narrow gap
between the immobilized truck and the kerb the two
ambulancemen ran to their vehicle and disappeared inside.
Seconds later, as the black car sped away, one of them
reappeared at the door of the ambulance. Ashen-faced, he
vomited onto the snow.

# 36

Mason stopped the ambulance. The snow had overwhelmed the cranky windscreen wiper and a thin opaque
layer of ice covered the glass, completely obscuring the
view of the road ahead. He cursed and began a fierce but
methodical search of the cluttered shelf beneath the
dashboard for a sharp instrument. He found a few lengths
of flex, a small torch, some odd gloves and a collection of
broken tools, but nothing that answered his purpose.

Three faces watched anxiously from the opening behind
him. He hammered the steering wheel in frustration. Then
his face brightened.

'Of course,' he exclaimed. He turned to the opening.
'Quick, Barbara. The vodka.'

With a fleeting expression of surprise she disappeared into the darkness behind her. A second or two later, she thrust the opaque plastic bottle into his waiting hand. With a grunt of acknowledgement he opened the cab door and sprang to the ground. Pulling his coat around him, he clambered onto the dilapidated bumper bar and sprinkled vodka onto the windscreen. Immediately, the strong spirit began soaking its way through the icy film, turning it to mush. Satisfied, he jumped down. Moving quickly he prised open the bonnet, ripped the cap from the windscreen-washer reservoir and upended the bottle into it. Vodka spilled over the hot engine, giving off fumes that brought tears to his eyes.

Tossing the bottle aside, he ran back to the cab and scrambled behind the wheel. Three sweeps of the wipers cleared the slush. He threw the ambulance into gear and set off again, accelerating as hard as he could without losing the rear on the treacherous surface. Despite his excursion into the cruel cold outside his shirt was sticking to his sweat-soaked back.

He looked at his watch. It was 6.20.

'Barbara,' he asked glancing at her. 'Do you have any idea how much further it is?'

She shrugged and pushed back a thick lock of brown hair from her face. It fell back immediately.

'Not much.'

'Not much idea, or not much further?' Gregory asked.

She smiled. 'Both. I think. I would guess we ought to be there in ten minutes or so.'

'I hope you're right,' Mason said grimly. He looked quickly at his mirror and ran his tongue over his lips. 'They must be after us by now. We can't have more than a few minutes' start on them.'

Involuntarily, his three passengers looked around and squinted through the rear window. The flying snow reduced their visibility to no more than 80 yards. Mason looked again in his mirror. The white blanket merged with the falling snow into a featureless monochrome blur. Had there been a Russian tank 100 yards behind him he would not have seen it. He increased the pressure on the throttle and hoped one was not.

Toparoff spat curses at the driver, urging him to greater speed. The driver muttered a resentful oath in response and hunched closer over the wheel. He peered through narrowed eyes into the featureless tunnel of white revealed by the headlights. They had seen no other vehicle since leaving the crippled truck behind them.

Behind the driver, Toparoff sat crouched on the edge of the seat. One hand gripped the back of the front passenger seat, the other fidgeted at his mouth as he chewed the manicured nails ragged. His breathing was fast and irregular.

They passed a road junction where the road they were on was joined by one from the right. It was discernible only from the line of the fence which edged the road and by a wooden signpost which leaned at a reckless angle, the result of some earlier collision. The information on the boards of the signpost was totally concealed by the clinging accumulation of snow.

'What's that?' Toparoff asked the driver gruffly. 'Do you know where we are?'

The driver replied without taking his eyes from the road. 'Uh-huh. About 20 kilometres from Konstanczyn. I can't remember exactly. Do you want me to check?' he added, easing the pressure on the accelerator pedal.

'No, no.' Toparoff answered curtly. 'Push on, quickly. Catch them.'

The driver shrugged and settled over the wheel again. The effort of staring into the blackness, the swirl of the rushing snowflakes and the rythmic slapping of the windscreen wipers was beginning to hypnotize him.

A couple of minutes later the flat trace of the road curved through a thick copse of trees. In the shelter of the trees, protected from the ferocity of the wind, the snow gave an impression of easing. It drifted gently downwards instead of being lashed into a headlong horizontal rush.

Toparoff gave a sudden cry in his throat, startling the driver from his trance-like concentration. He pointed agitatedly to the road a few metres ahead of them.

'Look!' he called.

The driver blinked and tried to focus, slowing the car. He scanned the snow in the area to which Toparoff pointed.

'Stop,' his voice broke hoarsely. The driver stamped on the brake, bringing the car sliding to a halt almost broadside across the road. Before it had come to rest, the Russian had sprung from the car and raced to a spot just ahead of them. He crouched, pointing exultantly to something in the snow. The driver left the car and ran to join Toparoff. He looked down at the object of the Russian's interest. Embedded in the soft snow, but covered only with a light sprinkling of snow, lay a wide-mouthed bottle made of translucent plastic. The driver gave a low whistle. Turning, he scanned the surrounding snow. Forgetting himself, he clutched the Russian roughly by the shoulder. 'Look!' he cried, pointing.

A few feet from them, clearly visible, shallow ruts not yet filled by the snow led away from where they stood. Toparoff bounded to his feet.

'It's them,' he said, almost inaudibly. 'Those are their tracks. They can only be ahead of us by minutes. Come on. Quickly.' He turned and ran for the car.

Almost at the moment that Toparoff's car roared from the shelter of the copse in pursuit of its quarry, another car, the black Polonez driven by Stan, emerged onto the main road at the point where the signpost leaned its obliterated pointers at the ground. Stan swung the wheel and slewed expertly onto the blanketed highway. Even before he had straightened the car, he gave a roar of triumph. He jerked his massive jaw at the road ahead.

'Tracks!' he said, by way of explanation to Dominiak,

who sat crouched tensely, close to the big man's shoulder.

Dominiak followed his gaze. Despite the driving snow the indentations of a car's tracks, although rapidly blurring under fresh snow, were still clearly visible. 'Come on. Faster, can you? We've almost got them.'

Stan nodded and allowed his foot to ease a little more pressure onto the accelerator. With the faint tracks to help guide him he could afford a little more speed. Dominiak remained crouched at the edge of his seat, his head thrust forward, straining for a better view of the road ahead. All the while he frowned deeply and plucked repeatedly at his slack lower lip, pinching it reflectively between forefinger and thumb.

'Hurry it up, Stan. And watch for tail-lights. If you see any, for Christ's sake douse our lights and don't come too close. Let's try and see what they're up to.'

Mason swore under his breath, a steady, unbroken stream of every curse he could call to mind, repeated like a mantra. The screen was icing up again. The spirit in the washers was helping but the worn rubber of the blades was too ineffectual for the conditions. His field of vision had shrunk to a short arc a couple of inches wide close to the bottom of the screen. Their speed had dropped to no more than a running pace. Swearing aloud, he lowered the window and stuck his head into the icy slipstream.

With his eyes narrowed, almost closed, against the snow and wind he was able to see just enough to keep the ambulance on the road. Steering with one hand and shielding his eyes with the other he increased speed a little. Every few seconds he twisted to look behind, straining every nerve for a sight or sound emerging from the murk.

Within a minute ice began forming on his eyebrows and hair. His exposed hand and face were stinging with the cold. He sucked at his fingers in an effort to restore some life to them, wondering how long it took to get frostbite.

His fingers were still in his mouth when, out of the swirling snow ahead loomed the chipped sign, partly obscured by snow which announced KONSTANCZYN.

With a shout of triumph that was whipped away on the wind, he drew his head back into the cab. Gregory's face beamed at him from the aperture. Helena's face was buried in his shoulder and her shoulders heaved as she sobbed with relief. Barbara smiled, and then looked suddenly serious.

'What now, Peter. Where do we go now? What do we do?'

He shrugged. Still sucking at his numbed fingers, he answered in a muffled voice. 'I don't know, Barbara. All the driver had been told was to get us here. Or, at least, that's all he told us. I hope they'll find us.'

He had only just finished speaking when a uniformed figure stepped into the headlights and signalled them to stop.

His chest pounded as he stopped the ambulance. Through the semi-opaque windscreen Mason watched as the figure ran to the passenger side. The face appeared at the window, topped by a militia cap.

Mason drew his breath with a sharp hiss and reached into his pocket. His hand closed over the gun as the policeman yanked the door violently open.

'Mr Mason?'

He nodded dumbly. Turning his attention to Gregory, the man crossed himself briskly.

'Where's Tomek?'

Mason frowned.

'The driver,' the other man said, with a hint of irritation.

'He got shot,' Mason said softly. 'He may have been killed.'

The militiaman's face turned suddenly melancholy. He shook himself. Then he slid into the passenger seat. 'Drive on,' he said, pointing ahead of him. 'Hurry. I'll tell you when to stop.'

They drove for a kilometre or so through the deserted main street to the far side of the village. All the while the

militiaman did not speak a word. Suddenly he laid a hand
on Mason's arm. 'Here,' he said, brusquely. 'Pull over and
stop.' Before the vehicle had come to a stop the man had
one foot on the running board. 'Come on,' he said sharply,
'Leave the ambulance and follow me. The others are
waiting for you.' He began hurrying between two
buildings.

Mason jumped from the cab and ran around to the rear.
He opened the door and handed the two women down.
They stood ankle-deep in the fresh snow. Gregory
appeared at the door. He sprang nimbly down to the road.
In his right hand he held the stubby barrel of the machine
pistol.

His eyes met Mason's for a moment. Then, transferring
his weight slightly onto his right leg, Gregory swivelled
and hurled the weapon from him. The gun swung in a long
arc over a low building by the roadside. They both
watched it disappear.

'Good,' Gregory said with a quick smile. 'I feel better
now.' He turned and began walking quickly after Helena
and Barbara.

For a moment Mason stood watching as Gregory strode
away from him. He touched the metal of the gun in his
own pocket. Then, with a quick movement of his head he
began running after the group.


# 37


They followed the militiaman at a trot. The track led
between a series of dilapidated wooden buildings like the
out-buildings of a bankrupt farm. He herded them along,
all the time glancing nervously behind him. Ahead of them
a huge building loomed. The walls were roughly pointed

breeze block under a curved roof of corrugated iron.

They ran along the side of the building, following a path already trodden in the snow by other feet. As they rounded the corner Mason, bringing up the rear, halted in astonishment. In front of him, just visible in the struggling light of three lamps along the front of the building, stood a single white-painted pole. Standing stiffly out from the pole, snapping in the fierce wind, was a windsock. The building was a hangar. An aircraft hangar. And 80 yards away, at the very edge of his vision, stood a tiny yellow and black aircraft.

His face awash with surprise and excitement, he turned to speak to the others. He was alone. They had disappeared through the immense double doors into the interior of the building. He ran to join them.

Chris and Edward stood in the middle of a small knot of people making hurried introductions.

'This is Roman,' Chris said, indicating a squat, balding man with dissipated grey shadows beneath his eyes. 'He'll be flying you out.'

'Where to?' Mason asked. 'Just out of curiosity.'

'Denmark,' the pilot replied simply.

His eyes lifted a fraction. 'In that?' He jerked a thumb towards the open door.

'It's been done,' the pilot said very quietly. 'More than once.'

Mason smiled ruefully.

'It really has been done,' Chris intervened. 'Not to the Danish mainland. To Bornholm. Do you know it? It's only a hundred kilometres or so off the coast.'

'I know. Only first we have to reach the coast! In this.' He looked upwards, beyond the open door to where the snow slanted through the pale lamplight.

'Mr Mason,' said the pilot with grim insistence, 'I'm telling you it's been done. And in weather just like this. In fact, the filthier the weather, the better our chances. Nobody's going to find us once we're aloft.'

Mason smiled, and glanced around at the group. 'What

are we waiting for?' he asked with a shrug.

'Nothing,' the pilot answered laconically. 'Let's go.' He gave a short, hard handshake to each of the three men who were remaining behind, turned and strode out into the snow. Barbara stepped forward and kissed each of the three men on both cheeks. Her eyes glistening.

'Thank you,' she whispered.

Helena and Mason shook hands with them all. Mason looked expectantly at Gregory.

'Go on to the aircraft,' he said in response to Mason's inquiry. 'I'll join you in a moment.'

Mason nodded and followed the women quickly out of the building. Turning for a last glance as he left the hangar, Mason saw all four men standing with their heads bowed, their hands clasped in front of them. Gregory was speaking softly.

At a trot, they followed the pilot towards the aircraft. He swung himself with an easy acrobatic movement onto the wing. Helped by his hand and with Mason lifting, Helena and Barbara scrambled up and into the cramped cabin. Mason sprang neatly onto the wing and wedged himself into the narrow remaining space next to them. The pilot slid into his seat and began checking his controls. The door stood open, waiting for Gregory to fill the empty seat next to him.

Toparoff crouched forward, his pale, blue-jowled face almost alongside the driver's in his anxiety to see through the darkness ahead.

'There!' he rasped. With a hand that trembled he pointed through the windscreen to the dark shape at the roadside. 'Stop!' He almost screamed the word at the driver. Without a word the man stamped on the brakes, at the same time flipping the switch that killed the car's lights.

Toparoff was out of the car first and running at a low crouch towards the stationary ambulance. A pistol appeared in his right hand as he ran. The driver came up to him as he warily approached the vehicle. A sudden gust of wind pushed the rear door abruptly open. Both men started, swinging their guns onto the empty doorway.

Toparoff swore. Abandoning stealth, he ran to the ambulance and looked quickly inside.

'Come on,' he urged, running to the front of the vehicle. 'There must still be tracks.'

From the trampled spot by the cab door several sets of footprints merged into a single well defined path leading away from the road. Some distance away Toparoff could see the orange glow of electric lamps. With a gesture to the driver to be silent and follow, he set off at a run along the well trodden furrow in the snow.

The pilot had started the motor and now sat drumming impatiently on the moulded grips of the joystick. 'Come on,' he muttered, 'what's he doing back there?'

'Praying,' Mason told him, without irony.

The pilot's face showed a flash of irritation. He was about to reply when Mason spoke again.

'Here he comes, look.'

The tall figure of Gregory emerged into the pool of light in front of the building, followed closely by the three slighter figures of the other men. With what seemed to Mason like agonizing slowness, each of the men stooped and kissed Gregory's offered hand. Then he shook hands warmly with each of them, clasping their hands in both of his. At last, with a wave of acknowledgement towards the waiting aircraft, he began loping across the intervening snow.

Mason watched him run, admiring the easy, athletic stride. Gregory had covered perhaps a third of the distance to the plane when there was a yellow flash, followed immediately by a second one from the darkness next to the hangar. An instant later, Mason saw Gregory glance anxiously back over his shoulder.

Two men had emerged from the shadows. One had stopped by the group of men and appeared to be training a weapon on them. The other sprinted with a strange lop-sided stride in pursuit of Gregory.

Gregory looked back again. For a moment his stride faltered, as though he would turn back. Then he dropped his shoulders and began running hard towards the aircraft.

His pursuer loosed off two shots as he ran. Gregory kept going without looking back. He was within twenty yards of where they sat. In the cramped cabin the pilot silently readied himself to take off. Mason and the women screamed encouragement.

Suddenly, Gregory's hunter dropped to one knee. Holding his gun in both hands, his arms stiffly held out in front of him, they watched as he deliberately tracked the running man ahead of him. Mason's mouth was parched.

They saw the flash and this time they heard the sound of the shot over the noise of the engine. He heard Helena catch her breath in a sound that was a gasp and a sob. Gregory stumbled. Mason watched as though mesmerized as Gregory, on all fours, raised his head and looked towards them. With an immense effort, as though he were utterly exhausted, he clambered once more to his feet and tottered a few more steps before sinking to his knees. Raising his head he threw out an arm, the back of his hand turned towards them in an unmistakable gesture to them to leave him behind.

The pilot, his face set and emotionless amid Helena's screams and Barbara's choking sobs, began easing the plane away from the fallen man. Mason watched the gunman climb to his feet and slowly begin to approach the helpless priest. The pilot lined up the plane for the take-off that would take them to safety. With a sudden roar, Mason threw open the door and hurled himself out on to the wing of the moving plane and to the ground. He stumbled, recovering his footing, and began sprinting towards the prostrate figure of Gregory. As he covered the short distance he dragged the gun from his pocket and fired.

His aim was wild but the shot startled the man, who seemed to notice him for the first time. The man shied and swung his gun in Mason's direction. Mason squeezed the trigger again.

With an expression that was more annoyance than anything else, the man threw himself full-length to the ground. For a delirious instant Mason thought he had killed him. Then he saw the man lazily arranging himself in a marksman's posture, his elbows digging deep in the snow as he settled.

Mason reached Gregory's side. Stooping, he dragged at the hurt man's shoulders, pulling him to his feet. He slung Gregory's arm over his shoulders and began half-walking and half-dragging him towards the now stationary plane. He half-turned and fired in the direction of the prone man. Again his aim was wild.

He tried to cajole Gregory into a run. It was useless. Gregory's right leg trailed and buckled with every step. Hopelessly, Mason tried to jink as he went, impeded by the weight of the other man dragging at his shoulders. A shot sounded.

The noise and the impact exploded simultaneously in his head. Slowly Mason became aware of snow filling his mouth and nostrils. Choking, he rolled over. He could feel no pain. He was aware of Gregory struggling in the snow beside him.

He noticed, with a strange sense of complacency, a red stain on the snow between his side and his arm. He looked up at the figure sauntering slowly towards him.

'Hello, Brooke,' he choked. 'You look awful. And you've got snow all over you.'

Mechanically, Toparoff flicked at the snow which caked the front of his blue topcoat. His face broke into a sneer as he looked down at him. 'Still flippant as ever, Mr Mason.' He made a clicking sound of disapproval. 'Not for much longer, I'm afraid.'

Mason tried to shrug. A pain, beginning somewhere in his ribs, seared through his brain, and he swore through clenched teeth. He looked up at Toparoff and, very deliberately, spat. He was too feeble to pull the gesture off. Spittle ran down his chin.

Toparoff gave a quick whinnying laugh. He shook his

head in admonishment, stepped forward, and jabbed a heel into Mason's injured ribs. Mason screamed.

'You bastard,' he muttered.

Toparoff ignored him. He stepped over him and looked down at Gregory. The Russian's nostrils flared and beneath one eye the skin jerked in small, convulsive clusters of movement.

Mason lay powerless, able only to watch as the Russian stood over the priest. The hand holding the gun directed at Gregory's chest was rock steady, despite the fact that the Russian was trembling violently. Toparoff tried to speak but the words would not come clearly through the paralysing hatred that gripped him. Gregory crossed himself and his lips were moving.

The shot when it came was shockingly loud and close. Mason flinched reflexively, sending the pain once again burning through his consciousness. He closed his eyes until the pain had peaked. When he reopened them the Russian had gone from his sight. He raised his head gingerly and looked around. Toparoff lay sprawled beside Gregory, face-down and motionless in the snow. The deformity at the top of his spine was emphasized by his awkward sprawling posture.

A group of people ran towards them, led by a slack-jowled soft-stepping man holding a gun. Mason stared up at them as they clustered around. He recognized the group he had left at the hangar. He looked hard at the other two. He gave a violent start, causing another shock of pain which knocked him flat on his back again.

'You,' he blurted. 'Marek! And Stan!' He frowned, recognizing the man who had handed him the camera and instructions and the unforgettable face of Stan, the huge driver.

Dominiak shrugged. 'Uh-huh.' He knelt by Toparoff and felt the vein in his neck. He stood up again, deep in thought. Abruptly, he pushed his gun into his pocket and turned away, walking a few steps into the snow. Stan watched him in silence for a moment and then walked slowly over to join his chief. They stood side by side, ignoring the bitter wind. Neither of them spoke. Each of them was aware of the scale of the decision they had just taken.

Behind the two men, several pairs of hands worked feverishly, cutting away the cloth from the wounds of Gregory and Mason. Edward brought a box of equipment from the ambulance. The militiaman and the pilot were soon in command, both of them seeming to have experience of treating wounds. They put both Gregory and Mason through quite a lot of pain before they pronounced. Gregory had received a bullet in the calf muscle. It seemed to have passed clean through the muscle, leaving a painful but clean wound. Mason's damage was less clearcut. The bullet had struck a rib, smashing it. The two men working on it could find no exit hole, but they could find no entry hole either. It looked likely that the bullet had glanced off the rib, breaking it and tearing flesh but without entering the rib cavity and endangering his lungs. Neither of them was going to die.

Despite their pain, they grinned at each other when they heard the news.

With reasonable expertise their wounds were cleaned and bandaged. Mason's arm was bandaged fast across his chest. They sat him up. Barbara pulled his coat over his naked shoulders. When he winced at the effort she kissed him quickly on the forehead.

The two of them were helped to their feet. Grimacing, Mason looked across to where Stan and the man he knew as Marek stood talking gravely, their voices very low.

'Marek,' he called softly. The man made no sign of having heard. Mason called again, louder. 'Marek!'

Dominiak started and wheeled to face him. His puffy eyes scanned the curious faces of the group clustered around the body of the Russian. With a wry smile to his companion he walked over to join the group.

Mason extended his free hand. Dominiak took it and gave it a single quick shake. He turned to Gregory, who stood supported by Chris and the militiaman, and shook his hand too. For an instant a silence fell over the group. Gregory was the first to speak.

'Who are you?' he asked, simply.

Dominiak chewed at his lower lip for a moment. Then, looking levelly around at the faces in front of him, he withdrew from his pocket the plastic folder holding his identification. Flipping it open, he held it out to them.

The only sound was the wind whining around the hangar. The knot of figures stood dumbfounded, their eyes riveted on the dog-eared document. A few paces away, Stan stood with his feet planted wide apart, his hands tucked into his armpits. With slow force, a grin peeled the flesh back from his ruined teeth.

Overcoming their incredulity, Mason and Gregory both began speaking at once.

'But why..?' They looked at each other. Mason nodded to Gregory.

'But, if you are who this says you are –' Gregory indicated the identity card – 'why did you do this?' He shifted his gaze to the fallen Russian. 'You stopped him.' He looked back at Dominiak. 'Are you going to arrest us?'

Dominiak looked hard at the priest. With a sudden sniff, he looked down at his feet and then again at the group in front of him.

'No, Father. I'm not going to arrest you. Not any of you.' He looked down at Toparoff. His face became angry and melancholy at once. 'They're killing Poles. His people.' He jabbed a toe into the ribs of the prone man. 'Here in Warsaw, in Gdansk, all over Poland. The bastards,' he added, turning away suddenly. Gregory reached out and laid a hand on Dominiak's shoulder.

'Is it worse than before?' he asked softly. 'It's happened before, remember?'

Dominiak nodded. 'I remember. Yes it has happened before, but not like this. It's all over the country tonight.' He shook his head so violently his loose jowls flapped. 'Damn it, this isn't like before. Before it was always our

313

own people keeping order. With Russian support, maybe, but still our own people. What we're seeing now is war!'

Gregory frowned. His hand dropped from Dominiak's arm. 'How can I help?' he asked simply.

Dominiak pushed the plastic wallet back into his jacket. He pressed the heel of his left hand against his left eye. He kneaded at the dark skin beneath his eye, hooking his fingers into his dishevelled hair.

Inhaling deeply, he turned to look squarely at Gregory.

'You could stay,' he said in a voice that was scarcely audible. 'You could stay here and lead us. All that's happening here is for you. The people would follow you.'

Gregory could hear himself breathing. He searched Dominiak's slack features for some clue, some hint of irony, that would defuse the suggestion. He found none. The heavy eyes returned his look, steady and expressionless.

'I can't,' he said hoarsely. 'It's impossible. I have to leave. To return to the village. My work. I...I...' He shook his head sharply, regathering his composure. 'No,' he said in a firmer voice. 'I'm sorry. We must leave.'

Dominiak shrugged, still holding Gregory's eyes. 'I understand.' He jerked his chin towards the waiting aircraft. 'Goodbye, Father.' He held out his hand. Gregory grasped it quickly, muttered a blessing and turned awkwardly, leaning on his supporters.

Mason stepped forward. 'Thanks, again,' he said softly.

Dominiak shook his hand and gave him a wry grin. He did not speak.

Mason took Barbara by the arm, and began hurrying after Gregory.

They watched as Gregory was lifted bodily onto the wing of the small plane. They watched as, using his powerful arms, he dragged himself through the restricted doorway of the cockpit. Beyond the dark outline of Gregory's head and shoulders, Mason could make out the pale form of Helena, sitting quite still in her seat. He brushed off a stirring of annoyance that she had not

314

bothered to join the rest of them in trying to help Gregory and himself.

He braced himself against the pilot's shoulder, preparing to push himself up into the cabin, when a choking roar, like the cry of a beast, broke from inside the cabin. Alarmed, Mason pressed himself against the open doorway.

In the cramped interior he saw Gregory crouched close to Helena. He was cradling her head in his arms and alternately moaning and bellowing with pain or rage. A neat black hole showed high on her right cheekbone. She was dead.

Stunned, Mason began to reach out a hand to Gregory. Then, cursing, he turned abruptly away and folded Barbara in his good arm. He swore repeatedly as despair, anger, futility and grief crowded his mind. Guilt, too, for the elation he had felt at each bullet that had missed him, not knowing that one of them had found Helena. He inhaled deeply, trying to marshall his emotions. They had to leave. He turned back to the aircraft. Barbara and the pilot helped him into the cabin.

Tenderly, he laid a hand on the distraught man's shoulder. Gregory, wrapped in his grief, was unaware of Mason's presence.

He shook Gregory's shoulder, quite roughly now, and leaned close to him. 'Father,' he said distinctly, 'we have to go away from here. There is nothing we can do.'

Gregory turned his head very slowly and stared blankly at him, as though he had spoken in a strange incomprehensible language.

'We must go now,' Mason repeated softly. 'It's too dangerous. We cannot delay.' Gregory continued to stare at him, his eyes vacant. 'She's dead, Father. Helena's dead.' He tightened his grip on Gregory's shoulder, trying to penetrate the grief. 'We must leave. Now, Father, quickly.'

Understanding percolated slowly back into Gregory's face. At the sound of a single, sharp obscenity they both

315

turned to face the door. Dominiak had pushed his way through the knot of people standing in the snow and crouched now on the wing, staring into the dark interior. His small shrouded eyes looked with muted expectancy at Gregory's changing expression.

All three of them were silent. Gregory stroked the hair of the woman cradled in his arm. Very gradually, his face set, the muscles of his jaw tightening perceptibly. With infinite care he withdrew his arm from behind Helena's head, allowing it to rest against the scarred cloth of the seat.

He reached an arm towards the hunched, impassive figure of Dominiak.

'Help me out,' he said softly.

The aircraft vibrated alarmingly as it gathered speed. The noise rose in the cabin making futile any attempt at speech. The pilot eased the joystick towards him. Abruptly, the vibration was stilled and the noise dropped away to a drone that seemed almost soothing after the racket of the take-off.

Wincing, Mason slid an arm laboriously around Barbara's shoulders. Smiling through the pain which pumped from the wound in his side, he leaned towards her and without a word placed his lips on hers. They kissed until the pain made him break off with a gasp.

The aircraft tipped onto one wing as the pilot swung around to face northwards to the Baltic. The snow had stopped at last. Looking down Mason and Barbara could see the group making its way slowly towards the dark shape of the hangar. They could make out clearly the two men from Solidarity and the militiaman carrying between them the long shape that was the body of Helena. A few yards ahead of that group the limping figure of Gregory was supported by Dominiak and the bigger bulk of Stan. Close to the hangar entrance a figure lay spread-eagled in the snow. It was the driver who had brought Toparoff, still lying where a blow from Stan had earlier left him.

As they passed overhead the leading group stopped and craned upwards. First Gregory and then the others raised a clenched fist in a salute. The pilot rocked the wings in acknowledgement.

'*Sto lat*,' Mason muttered. 'A hundred years.' He continued looking back long after the tiny figures had faded into the darkness.

At length he broke off from his reverie and turned from the window. Barbara was pawing ineffectually at the ribbons of tears that coursed down her cheeks. Very tenderly, he leant and placed an arm around her shoulders. With his other hand he lifted her chin so that her brimming eyes were looking into his.

'Well, Barbara, this is finally it,' he said gently, his voice almost drowned by the noise of the engine. 'You won't be needing the lady in Berlin.'

Barbara jerked upright, and something akin to panic flitted across her face. 'You knew?' she gasped, her voice a rasping whisper. 'But why...?'

Mason's mouth closed over hers, choking off any further words. 'Later, my darling,' he murmured, 'just now there's something more important I want you to know.' His arm closed around her, pulling her to him. For an instant more her eyes stayed on his. Then, with a sigh that seemed to release all the tension of the last twenty-four hours, she surrendered to his embrace.

# Hammond Innes

'The master storyteller' *Daily Express*

**Air Bridge**
'Hammond Innes achieves a mastery sense of urgency as
the story rises to the climax.' *Daily Telegraph*

**Campbell's Kingdom**
'A fast and expertly-managed story . . . The Rockies, the
squalid "ghost towns", the oil-boring – these are memor-
ably presented.' *Sunday Times*

**Golden Soak**
Embittered and disillusioned with his life, Alec Falls fakes
his own death and starts for Australia – and the Golden
Soak mine. But he is not the only person interested in the
derelict mine. The shadows of the past and the blistering
hell of the Australian bush combine in a deadly maze which
Falls must unravel if he is to survive at all . . .
 'Pace, atmosphere, tension. Evokes Australia as few
other books have done.' *Listener*

**The Black Tide**
The details of maritime fraud, international piracy and the
working of Lloyd's insurance are presented with an
authority that give *The Black Tide* an uncanny credibility.
 'Exciting . . . credible . . . a polished novel.' *Sunday
Express*

FONTANA PAPERBACKS

# Gerald Seymour

writes internationally best-selling thrillers

'Not since Le Carré has the emergence of an international suspense writer been as stunning as that of Gerald Seymour.' *Los Angeles Times*

HARRY'S GAME
KINGFISHER
RED FOX
THE CONTRACT
ARCHANGEL
IN HONOUR BOUND
FIELD OF BLOOD
THE GLORY BOYS
A SONG IN THE MORNING

FONTANA PAPERBACKS

# Fontana Paperbacks
# Fiction

Fontana is a leading paperback publisher of both non-fiction, popular and academic, and fiction. Below are some recent fiction titles.

- ☐ FIRST LADY Erin Pizzey £3.95
- ☐ A WOMAN INVOLVED John Gordon Davis £3.95
- ☐ COLD NEW DAWN Ian St James £3.95
- ☐ A CLASS APART Susan Lewis £3.95
- ☐ WEEP NO MORE, MY LADY Mary Higgins Clark £2.95
- ☐ COP OUT R.W. Jones £2.95
- ☐ WOLF'S HEAD J.K. Mayo £2.95
- ☐ GARDEN OF SHADOWS Virginia Andrews £3.50
- ☐ WINGS OF THE WIND Ronald Hardy £3.50
- ☐ SWEET SONGBIRD Teresa Crane £3.95
- ☐ EMMERDALE FARM BOOK 23 James Ferguson £2.95
- ☐ ARMADA Charles Gidley £3.95

You can buy Fontana paperbacks at your local bookshop or newsagent. Or you can order them from Fontana Paperbacks, Cash Sales Department, Box 29, Douglas, Isle of Man. Please send a cheque, postal or money order (not currency) worth the purchase price plus 22p per book for postage (maximum postage required is £3.00 for orders within the UK).

NAME (Block letters) _____

ADDRESS _____

_____

_____